The
PALACE OF
IMPOSSIBLE
DREAMS

The
PALACE OF
IMPOSSIBLE
DREAMS

The Tide Lords:
Book Three

JENNIFER FALLON

A Tom Doherty Associates Book
New York

THE PALACE OF IMPOSSIBLE DREAMS

Copyright © 2008 by Jennifer Fallon

First published in Australia by Voyager, an imprint of HarperCollins*Publishers*

Maps by Russell Kirkpatrick

A Tor Book
Published by Tom Doherty Associates, LLC
175 Fifth Avenue
New York, NY 10010

www.tor-forge.com

Tor® is a registered trademark of Tom Doherty Associates, LLC.

ISBN 978-0-7653-1684-4

First U.S. Edition: June 2010

Printed in the United States of America

0 9 8 7 6 5 4 3 2 1

For Fliss . . .
welcome to the family

OCEAN
STERILA.

FYRENNA
Fyr Mamsest.
Fyr Firdha.
Byrmeze
Fyr Dykhoben.
Fyr Gunda.
Fyr Elutjud.
Byrm Ice
Desert.
ANDELIA.
Fyr Camptor.
Vyn.
Hepatic Pt.
PALINOVIA.
Perzyn.
Rhodkyl.
Maynx.
Abyzinan.
Cape Cloan
Mogy.
Denthmask I.
Symeze.
Koryt.
Entrade.
Cycadia Coast.
Serane.
Planse.
Hanford.
Gambond.
Luscelle.
Valley of the
Tides
Lebex.
Herno.
Fiorna.
Darra.
Baleen Bay.
CAELUM
Oran.
Tirene.
Port
Whalebone.
Desert of
Caelum.
Ryrie
Pandelle.
THE PERI
SHEVRON MTS.
Cabo Bord
Byrne.
Rigantha.
Whitewater.
Balkor.
Dry
Cooper.
Sorbay.
Galan Tesne.
Pas Enhedra.
Sanorna
Sea.
Solmain.
Noellens.
GLAEBA.
Armada
Gulf.
Great
Ramana.
Cabo Forlorn.
WESTLANDS.
Cabo Fairweather.
Denrah.
Northwaite.
Ramanabela.
Eastmost
Head.
OCEAN
TEMPURA.
Dewdrop Is.
Petra.
Sallarh.
CHELAE
ISLANDS.
Relese.
Baranbutol.
Sunthwaite.
Bryenze.
Tenseris.
The Dark Shore.
Butla.
Tosca.
Kurlah.
Irigiray
Bell Hook.
TORLENIA.
Skileff.
Twiene Highlands.
Gidass.
Elvere.
Ramanta
Bight.
Abbey of the Way of the Tides.
Ramahn.
GREAT INLAND
DESERT.
Bhukase.
OCEAN
DOCILAE.
Stormway Head.
Junction
The Burning Waste.
Demon's Breath.
Tavaryan
Oasis.
Pholdaar.
Isp.
Essandaar.
COMMONWEALTH OF
ELENOVIA.
Lanfall.
Contanya.
Meli Sdar.
Fiumtuk.
Y Brave
Espec Museh.
Ansari.
Kanevdun.
Bohin.
CYLENIA.
Panopoly.
VETORIA.
Narmen.
Kelgyn.
Ramushta.
Dome.
Udeyshire.
Rees.
Pypsis.
Cape Narmen.
ERICANIA.
Irile.
Empty
Bay.
Suaescape.
Elishass.
(abandoned)
OCEAN
FOMENTIA.
Shiptrap
Peninsula.
Bitter
Sea.
Bitter Peaks.
Kentaryon's Prison.
Ice Fields of Jelidia.
JELIDIA.

The
PALACE OF
IMPOSSIBLE
DREAMS

PROLOGUE

One thousand years ago . . .

Tryan studied the sorry line of prisoners standing on the edge of the cliff, wondering idly how much wind he would have to call up to blow them off, one by one, and onto the rocks that pockmarked the valley far below.

None of this would be necessary, of course, if they would just tell him what he wanted to know. Life was easier for everyone on Amyrantha when people did what Tryan wanted.

He turned and motioned Elyssa forward, noticing the slight hesitation before she did as he bid. Her interest in this little adventure was fading, he suspected; had been for a while—ever since the last time they'd met up with Cayal.

For now, though, she was still his sister and willing to play her part, even if it was less than enthusiastically.

"Which one should we kill first?" he asked, in a voice loud enough to be heard by the prisoners. A few whimpers of fear were all they dared, but he could tell his threats were having the desired effect. The twenty or so prisoners were chained together, after all, which meant he really only had to toss a few of their number off the cliff for all to be in peril.

"*We?*" Elyssa asked in a voice meant only for him. "Don't you mean which one *you* should kill? This is your idea, not mine. I want no part of this, Tryan."

"One of them has the Chaos Crystal."

"If one of these sorry mortals had the Chaos Crystal, you'd know it by now, I'm quite certain." Elyssa cast her disinterested gaze along the line of naked men, women and children shivering in their chains on the edge of the precipice. "Tides, it's not as if one of them is hiding it in their pocket, now, is it?"

Tryan frowned and cast his eyes over the pile of personal belongings he had stripped from this small group of refugees. Other than their clothing, a few tools and weapons, and a set of tattered, but clearly beloved Tarot cards in a singed leather case, there was nothing to be found. No maps. No instructions . . .

Which meant one, or perhaps all of these Cabal members, had memorised the location of the Crystal. Tryan was quite prepared to murder every man, woman and child, until one of them confessed who it was.

"One of you has something I want," he announced to the group, studying their faces as he spoke, searching for some flicker of comprehension or a whisper of deceit; anything that would indicate one of these wretched humans knew what he was seeking. Trouble was, they all looked universally terrified, so it was a little hard to tell. "If you tell me what I want to know, I will let you live. If you don't . . ."

He let the sentence hang. They were standing with their backs to a cliff, after all. Terrified as they were, he didn't think he needed to belabour the obvious.

His prisoners remained stubbornly silent.

Tryan was losing patience with them. And he didn't have a lot to start with.

"One of you . . . perhaps all of you miserable creatures . . . knows the location of the Chaos Crystal. Tell me now, or . . ." He scanned the line of prisoners, his eyes fixing on a lad of about fourteen on the right. Thin, pale and shivering, the boy held his cupped hands in front of his shrivelled manhood, in a vain attempt at modesty. He was second from the end of the line, tied next to a plump and equally terrified fair-haired woman in her mid-thirties, who—given the protective way she was trying to shield him—was probably his mother. ". . . or *she* dies first," he finished, pointing at the woman, while keeping his eyes fixed on the lad.

Tryan waited. The boy said nothing.

"Have it your way then."

Tryan flicked his wrist, sending a violent gust of wind toward the line of prisoners. The woman screamed, staggering under the onslaught, loose stones under her feet tumbling from the cliff's edge as she scrabbled to maintain her balance. Several of the other prisoners screamed too, as their chains tugged them backwards.

Not the lad, however. He remained stony faced and unmoved by the threat of impending death, even with his mother barely holding her balance beside him.

Tryan stepped forward, annoyed at the lad's determination.

"I *will* kill you," he said.

The boy slowly raised his head to meet Tryan's eye. What the immortal saw there disturbed him greatly. The boy was frightened witless, but an edge of defiance lurked beneath the surface of his fear that no amount of threats or intimidation was going to pierce.

"You can't kill all of us," the boy replied.

"Shows how little *you* know," Elyssa muttered behind Tryan.

The immortal ignored the snide remark from his sister and took a step closer to the boy, convinced now that this defiant child held the key to the information he sought.

"You know, don't you?"

The boy shivered and trembled in the crisp mountain air, but his resolve didn't waver.

"There is nowhere you can run, boy," Tryan warned, leaning so close he could feel the boy's warm breath on his face. "No place you can hide. No place I can't eventually find you."

"There's one place you can't follow me," the boy said in a trembling voice, his courage all the more impressive for it.

Tryan smiled coldly. "Is that what you think?"

The lad nodded.

"And where is this remarkable place I can't follow you?"

The child smiled at him then, his fear falling away, almost as if he had resolved some internal torment and was content with his decision. He squared his shoulders, glanced down the line at his fellow prisoners, looked the other way at his terrified mother, and then back at Tryan.

"You can't follow us into death," the boy said.

Before Tryan could stop him, the boy stepped backwards off the precipice, taking the line of prisoners with him. His weight alone should not have been sufficient to drag the others with him. He was just a boy, after all. But they'd fallen, nonetheless. Or jumped. Allowing themselves to be pulled off the cliff like that amounted to the same thing. Nobody resisted. Nobody fought to stay upright or tried to cling to the edge. The wind he'd conjured to terrify them into compliance whipped away their screams on the way down.

Tryan was too stunned to react in time. He never thought to break their fall or had time to cushion it with air. Seconds later, the bodies landed some four hundred feet below him with a series of soft "thuds," leaving the immortal standing on the cliff staring after them.

"Well, *that* plan worked a treat," Elyssa said coming up beside him. She looked down at the pile of broken bodies for a moment and then at Tryan.

"Scared them into killing themselves before they could tell you anything, eh? There's an interrogation technique I've not seen before."

Tryan turned from the cliff's edge. "Shut up, Elyssa."

"Didn't exactly go the way you planned, then?" she taunted.

He glared at her angrily. "I told you to shut up."

She shrugged and turned to look at the ruins of the refugee camp. "And I told you that if you want to find the Chaos Crystal, why not play nice and go ask Maralyce where it is?"

"Maralyce would have it by now if she knew where it was."

"She's got a better idea than you, I suspect."

Tryan stared at her. "What are you talking about?"

"She's not tunnelling through the Shevron Mountains for her health, you know."

"Then we must find the Crystal first—before she finds it and gives it to Lukys."

"Why?"

"Because he who controls the Chaos Crystal," Tryan said, kicking a small box tiled in nacre over the edge of the cliff to join its foolish owner, "controls the Tide."

He looked down at the pile of possessions he'd taken from the Cabal refugees, frowning, annoyed by how futile this whole exercise had been. They'd spent a useless hour searching their effects as he stripped them, to no avail. In a fury, he kicked at the pile, sending many of them drifting down after their owners.

"Oh, well, now that was mature."

In a burst of frustration, directed mostly at his sister whom he couldn't harm because she was immortal, Tryan cried out, drawing on the Tide. His angry outburst caused the edge of the cliff to shatter and crumble, tumbling after the pitiful belongings in a fall of rocks that sealed the graves of these pitiful mortals along with every trace of them.

Elyssa jumped back with a squeal as she almost lost her footing, and then she turned on her brother. "Feel better now?"

"Don't look at me like I'm a fool, Lyssa," Tryan said. "Because he who controls the Tide . . . controls the universe."

PART I

The tide keeps its course.
—James Howell (1594–1666)

Chapter 1

The heaving motion of the ship was making Arkady queasy. Although she'd sailed often enough on the Great Lakes of Glaeba, it was nothing like the rolling gait of an oceangoing slaver. It didn't help much that she was crammed into a low, crowded cabin with five other women in a space that could, if one was being generous, be considered room enough for two.

"Elbow me again like that, ya stupid bitch, an' I'll knock y'unconscious," someone threatened sleepily. The comment wasn't meant for Arkady. Although she couldn't see much in the dark, unlit cabin, Arkady was lying on the floor, straight and rigid, between Saxtyn on her left and the youngest of their group, Alkasa, on her right. Both women were sound asleep.

Arkady couldn't sleep; she'd barely slept since leaving Elvere. Even if the pain of her newly branded breast hadn't been keeping her awake, her status as slave, and endless agonising over what her future might hold, were more than enough to fuel her insomnia.

It was one thing to grow up in a society where slavery was commonplace, quite another to discover she was now the slave rather than the master. It wasn't the cramped, smelly quarters below decks, where the only sanitation was a rarely emptied bucket; it wasn't the porridge-like gruel they served the prisoners once a day or the stale, rancid water that did little to hydrate the slaves because it had given most of them diarrhoea; it wasn't even being branded like a prize mare that made a part of her want to curl up and die inside.

No, for Arkady Desean, the worst part was the intolerable realisation she was now somebody's possession—that she was of no value to anybody but her faceless, distant owner.

The other slaves had informed her that their owner now was one Filimar Medura, a Senestran slaver of considerable means who owned not only Arkady, but all the other slaves aboard, not to mention the ship itself. He ran a fleet of slavers, according to her cellmates. In fact, the entire family's wealth, for more generations than anybody cared to remember, was based on the trade in living flesh, both human and Crasii.

The ship lurched again. Arkady shifted uncomfortably on the hard deck, unable to turn because of the press of Alkasa's dead weight beside her, and unable to breathe because of the stifling heat. A noise distracted her, coming from above. There was a porthole in the cabin, left open to afford some small hint of fresh air. Not that it did much to relieve either the smell or the feeling she was slowly being asphyxiated.

There was a moment or two when she thought there might be somebody on the ship even worse off than she was. At night, when the only sounds in her cramped prison were the not-so-soft snores of her fellow slaves, the creaking of timber and slosh of the waves against the hull, Arkady sometimes heard voices speaking a language she didn't understand on the deck above. Often they laughed, apparently taunting one of their crewmen.

Occasionally, listening at the porthole, she learned something useful. Or rather, one of her cellmates did. Arkady didn't speak Senestran well; she couldn't understand very much of what they said.

She'd learned something useful earlier this evening, however, which was the main reason she still couldn't sleep. Saxtyn had overheard the sailors talking. They could all overhear the crew talking, but only the debtor slave understood their language well enough to translate it for the others. The captain, according to ship's scuttlebutt, had told the sailors they could have the batch-bought slaves for entertainment in their off-duty hours, once the ship was clear of Torlenian waters.

Arkady's value as a slave, she knew, was defined by her gender. Male slaves in Senestra were generally more valuable, deemed more useful as workers. Females were required for such mundane roles as seamstresses, weavers and nursemaids and the like, but only a rare few were lucky to be chosen for that fate. Generally, human female slaves were kept to entertain the male workers, be they slave or freeborn, in the many mining camps, farms and floating estates belonging to the Senestran nobility. To entertain and to breed the next generation of slaves was their function. It was, according to Alkasa, the only thing women were good for in Senestra, and Arkady had better get used to it if she planned to survive.

There was a double standard at work here, which peeved Arkady no end. Senestran men would never dream of treating their *free* women so rudely. Quite the opposite. Senestran men, particularly high-born Senestran men, treated their women with a level of respect bordering on idolatry. That, conversely, was the reason for their fondness for human female slaves.

Wives are for heirs, slaves are for fun, was a Senestran saying Arkady was only just beginning to appreciate.

So now, in addition to the pain from being branded with a hot iron and facing a lifetime in slavery as a whore, there was the problem of how she was going to avoid being handed around the crew; hence the reason Arkady was lying here, wide awake, trying to figure out a way to escape.

She had no intention of becoming a whore. Worse than a whore. Whores, at least, were paid for their efforts. Being pack-raped on a daily basis by the crew of a Senestran slaver for an indeterminate length of time before being on-sold to a mining camp for the same purpose was not a future Arkady was willing to contemplate.

She would rather die. And she had pretty much determined that suicide was the only course of action left open to her.

Escape was impossible. She couldn't fit through the cabin porthole. And even if she was willing to take her chances in the open water, there were the five other women chained to her to consider. The shackles they'd worn in Elvere had been replaced by a much more simple, yet equally effective set of chains that kept the women close together, whether they liked it or not.

Rescue was unlikely. Cayal, the only living soul on Amyrantha who might have the means and the will to rescue her, had no idea where she was. If Tiji had been able to prevent Arkady being shipped out of Elvere as a slave, she'd have done it. Her husband, Stellan, was probably dead by now, hanged by the immortal Jaxyn for his own nefarious purposes; and Declan Hawkes, the King of Glaeba's Spymaster and her childhood friend—perhaps the only other person she knew who might risk everything to save her—didn't even know she was in danger.

And even if he did, what could he do from Glaeba? She was half a world away, on the open sea, sailing toward Senestra.

She tried not to dwell on the fact that it was probably Cayal's fault she was here, sold into slavery and lost to everything she had ever known or loved. In his blind enthusiasm for death, he'd thought only of his own desires when he'd so willing left Arkady with his enemy, the Tide Lord Brynden, as a hostage. *What was he thinking?* Surely it must have occurred to him that the Lord of Reckoning would go for the more immediate revenge, by harming Cayal's lover—Brynden would have assumed, knowing Cayal, that Arkady could be nothing else—rather than wait for the possible chance to see an end to him, a dubious prospect given they were both immortal.

What was I *thinking*, Arkady berated herself silently, *to go along with such an idiotic plan in the first place?*

But there was little to be gained by agonising over how she got here. She'd be much better employed finding a way to escape.

Arkady was neither innocent nor blind. She knew what lay ahead of her, and it wasn't the wild imaginings of a duchess suddenly confronted with cruel reality. Arkady had been in this place before.

Thoughts of suicide were not uncommon among slaves, particularly new ones. As a result, the Senestrans wisely ensured their valuable possessions lacked the means to act upon them. Arkady allowed herself a small, sour smile, thinking she and Cayal finally had something in common. *We both want to die, and for wildly different reasons, we're both unable to act upon it.*

At least she *could* die, she supposed, which was something to be grateful for. Confronted with every deadly weapon known to man, Cayal was still unable to end his torment. *Her* biggest problem, Arkady knew, would be finding a method that was quick enough to ensure death. She was never left alone, so even if she'd been able to tear her shift into strips to make a noose and then find somewhere in the low, cramped cabin to hang herself— unlikely, given she couldn't even stand upright—the others would stop her before she had a chance to tie the first few knots.

No, Arkady needed a method that was quick and irreversible. She would only get one chance at this and did not intend to survive it. The punishment for a slave caught attempting to escape through death would make being handed to the crew of the *Trius* seem mild by comparison.

Arkady needed a weapon, although she couldn't imagine any circumstance that would involve a sailor willingly surrendering such a dangerous implement to a mere slave—and the sailors were the only ones who had what she needed: a knife or a marlin spike preferably . . .

Or a scalpel, she thought, as the vaguest hint of a plan began to form in her sleep-starved mind. Arkady pulled down the shoulder of her shift to examine the scabbed-over burn of her slave brand. The interlinked chain symbol was hard to make out in the gloom, but she could tell, just from the dull throbbing pain, that the burn was probably healing cleanly.

Pity. If it was infected, she could ask to see the ship's doctor and have some hope of being treated. Live slaves were the Senestrans' lifeblood, not dead ones. They would treat a slave with an infected wound—and the treatment would be lancing the wound to drain the pus.

To do that, the ship's doctor would need a scalpel.

Arkady pondered the idea for a time. If the doctor came to lance an infected wound, and she was quick enough, she could grab the scalpel from his hand and slice through her own carotid artery before anybody had time to react. It was quick, clean, relatively painless, and unstoppable. Once her artery started pumping blood across the cabin, no doctor, no matter how skilled, would be able to stop it. It was a better than even wager that any doctor stuck on a Senestran slaver wasn't the best practitioner, anyway . . .

There was one fatal flaw in her plan, of course.

The salve they'd applied in Elvere after she was branded had done its job. The wound was clean and healing nicely.

But maybe, she thought, warming to the idea of a quick and painless death, *if the wound* looked *infected* . . .

Arkady wished her mind was clearer; that she was less driven by hunger, pain and fear. Plans formed in such a hasty manner were inevitably filled with holes and pitfalls, and she couldn't afford to mess this up.

If the wound looked infected . . . she repeated silently, wondering how to effect such a deceit. She could make it genuinely infected, readily enough. There was a bucket in the corner of the cabin—she could smell it from here—filled with plenty of material for infecting an open wound. The trouble was, a genuine infection would take a few days to manifest. She needed an infection serious enough to warrant the attention of the ship's doctor by sunrise.

Tomorrow morning they would leave Torlenian waters.

By tomorrow morning, Arkady needed her wound to be angry and red and swollen.

Still trying to solve the problem, Arkady was distracted again by a noise from the deck above—a thumping sound, followed by taunting voices and cruel laughter. She didn't know what they were saying, but she'd heard them before, and their tone, if not their words, was easy enough to understand.

They're probably tormenting some poor cabin boy. Killing time until they can start raping the female slaves, once we're on the open sea . . .

She wished they'd stop. Their harsh laughter was a brutal reminder of the fate that awaited her, one she could well have done without.

By breakfast tomorrow, I need to be oozing pus.

Breakfast—when they brought the slaves their one meal of the day. That hideous porridge-like gruel that looked like . . . pus.

Arkady smiled in the darkness.

She had the means, after all, to end her life.

All she needed was a bowl of gruel and an inattentive ship's surgeon.

Arkady closed her eyes, and found, surprisingly, that she was sleepy after all. She wiggled a little to turn on her side, elbowing Alkasa's shoulder out of the way, and mentally shut out the tormenting laughter from above. She finally drifted off to sleep just as the sun crept over the horizon, content that later in the morning she would be dead and the nightmare, for her at least, would be over.

Chapter 2

Tiji had travelled by ship before, but never on one so small, so crowded, nor so fast. The little sloop sliced through the waves like it had wings, carrying her further and further from the life she had known toward a future she had always dreamed about, but was too frightened to believe could ever be real.

The little boat was crewed entirely by chameleon Crasii. No amphibians dragged this craft through the waves. The *Liberator* travelled at the whim of the wind and the current, and seemed to dance across the wave tops with the joy of her freedom. Now she had her sea legs, Tiji was in a position to appreciate the little craft a lot more than when they'd first left Elvere in Torlenia several days ago.

That had been a dark time of seasickness and guilt. Fortunately, the seasickness had faded.

Now only the guilt remained.

"You're looking very forlorn."

Tiji turned from her perch in the bow to find Azquil, the chameleon who'd help kidnap her off the streets of Elvere (just as she was on the brink of saving Arkady Desean from being shipped off to the Tides-alone-knew-where as a slave), making his way forward.

The chameleon Crasii who'd kidnapped her proved to be a highly organised group of reptilian Crasii. Known among their own kind as the Retrievers, that's precisely what they did. They hunted down and retrieved the Lost Ones—children stolen from their hidden settlements, deep in the humid wetlands of Senestra, by hunters seeking the special skills of the chameleon Crasii. The more successful raiders stole the smallest children, they told Tiji, and then sold them to circuses and freak shows as curiosities.

And sometimes to spymasters like Declan Hawkes because of their camouflage abilities.

The Retrievers had sympathised with her when she'd told them about her life in Glaeba, appalled she had been used so foully, first by the circus where Declan had found her, and then by Declan Hawkes himself, whom they likened to an evil tyrant, bent on destroying her spirit with his overbearing control over her. At first she couldn't understand why. She'd thought her life quite good. Yes, she was a slave, but she'd had a master for whom she would have cheerfully died, an interesting job, was cared for, fed, sheltered and never wanted for anything.

Azquil and his friends didn't think that was anything to get excited about.

Despite her protests, the Retrievers were convinced she'd been held against her will. She couldn't explain to them, especially Azquil, that her loyalty to Declan was motivated by affection not fear.

In fact, when she mentioned she loved Declan, even though she'd meant it in the most platonic sense of the word, the young reptile had looked at her with great concern and whispered, "Among our kind, such a relationship would be considered, well, more than a little unnatural. Perhaps it would be wise not to mention, to others, your . . . attraction . . . to this male of another species."

"I'm not attracted to him."

"You claim to love him."

"I love seafood too, but that doesn't mean I want to settle down with a lobster."

Azquil had laughed then and hugged her. "You are such a delight, Tiji. Most of the Lost Ones we retrieve are such tragically damaged souls. I've never met one with a sense of humour before."

Tiji had smiled too, and felt her skin tones flickering, which was the chameleon equivalent of a blush. It wasn't his compliment that had made her feel that way, however; it was the fact that he hugged her.

Tiji was quite taken with the notion of being hugged by Azquil.

It wouldn't do to let him know that, however. She had no idea of the customs among her own people about that sort of thing. For all she knew, Azquil had a wife and a dozen younglings hidden away in the swamps and he was just being nice to another "tragically damaged soul" he'd rescued.

"I was just thinking," she said, as Azquil settled in beside her, looking over the railing to the water below.

"You seem to do that a lot."

"Are we not a thoughtful species?" Tiji found it strange that she had to ask that, but she knew nothing of her own people; not their traits, their likes and dislikes, their fears . . .

"Thoughtful, perhaps," Azquil said. "But maybe not as lost in it as you seem to be. Is something troubling you?"

She nodded, seeing no point in lying. "I've abandoned my friends."

"You talk of the humans who enslaved you, Tiji. They were never your friends."

"I wasn't mistreated, Azquil."

"The Trinity says that if you cage a bird and shower it with the best food and endless affection, it won't alter the fact that the bird cannot fly free."

"I wasn't caged," she said, not sure who the Trinity was, and not particularly interested in their homespun wisdom. "I had diplomatic papers, for pity's sake!"

Azquil smiled at her tolerantly. "Tiji, please, I am not trying to demonise your former slave-masters, who, by the sound of it, were better than average. It's just, well, freedom can take some getting used to. The Trinity says finding the courage to move on is the only thing that stops us looking back."

"When I look back, all I can think of is seeing Lady Desean in that slave wagon, heading for the docks, on her way to the Tide-alone-knows-where. My job was to keep her safe, and I let her be sold into slavery."

"You didn't *let* her do anything. This human woman you fret about so, is not your responsibility." He leaned forward and took her hand. "Can you not see that, Tiji? Can you not see how conditioned you are to believe their self-serving lies? This woman was your master, and yet, when an ill befalls her, you somehow believe it was your fault."

"I should have done something!" she insisted, pulling her hand away. This guilt wasn't going anywhere soon and she needed to explain—even to someone who patently didn't care about the fate of the Duchess of Lebec—why she felt responsible.

"What could you have done?"

"I . . . don't know." And that was the rub. There was probably *nothing* she could have done to prevent Brynden taking his revenge on Cayal by selling the one person on Amyrantha the Immortal Prince seemed to care about into slavery.

"Tell me what happened."

"Why?"

"Because this is bothering you so much you're barely eating. Perhaps, if I understand better . . ."

Tiji smiled, feeling her skin flicker in a multi-coloured blush. "Actually, me not eating has more to do with your cooking, Azquil, than my despair."

"Even so," he said, smiling, "it's eating you up. You will never be truly free until you have put this behind you."

He was probably right, so Tiji took a deep breath and gave Azquil an edited version of what had happened since she'd left Glaeba. She told him of the death of the King and Queen of Glaeba; about how Arkady had been disinherited because her husband was implicated in their deaths. She told him of Arkady's friend, Chintara, the Imperator's Consort, who'd arranged to hide Arkady in the Torlenian desert at the Abbey of the Way of the Tide, without actually mentioning that Chintara was the immortal Kinta. Or that Kinta's lover, Brynden, the Lord of Reckoning, was holed up in the abbey, awaiting his chance to take Torlenia as his own, once the Tide returned.

She told them of running into Cayal, the Immortal Prince, although she didn't refer to him as that. She called him Kyle Lakesh, the name he'd been using when he was a condemned prisoner in Glaeba. She told Azquil how Kyle had saved them from a sandstorm and then escorted them to the abbey, where he was heading anyway to ask a favour of an old enemy.

And then she told him of the deal between Kyle and the monk at the abbey (neglecting to mention the monk was actually the immortal Brynden), resulting in Arkady being left with him as a hostage, while Kyle went to fetch another . . . friend . . .

And then she explained how she was supposed to meet up with Arkady in Elvere, only to discover the monk had betrayed Kyle and sold Arkady into slavery.

When she finished her tale, Azquil searched her face with concern. "And you somehow think this is your fault?"

"I should have followed Arkady. I know I probably couldn't have stopped Bryn . . . the monk, selling her into slavery, but I could have bought her out of it again. I had diplomatic papers on me and she's a member of one of Glaeba's most prominent families."

"Then don't you think someone else will go looking for her?"

"Anybody else looking for Arkady at the moment is likely to want her arrested or dead," Tiji predicted grimly.

"Then your duchess is probably safer where she is."

"What do you mean, *safer*? She's a slave, Azquil! Who knows *what* they're doing to her."

Azquil wasn't moved. He shook his head. "You claim you were well looked after as a slave. In fact, you almost resent having been granted your freedom, you're so adamant on that point. Why, then, do you assume this human woman's slavery will be any more onerous than you insist yours

was? Perhaps, like you, she will find a good master and gain the very protection she went into the deserts of Torlenia to seek."

Tiji couldn't really answer that, and in the end she didn't have to, because at that moment a school of dolphins surfaced beside the *Liberator*'s
bow and began racing the little sloop across the waves. At the shout of delight from the Crasii at the helm, which alerted them to the dolphins'
presence, everyone on board hurried to the side to watch them leaping out
of the water, laughing delightedly at this good omen.

Despite herself, Tiji couldn't help but be enchanted by the smiling creatures leaping so joyfully across their bow. She was soon laughing so hard
she could pretend, for a time at least, that Arkady's fate wasn't going to be
as bad as she feared.

Chapter 3

Declan Hawkes woke to the sound of rain on the shingles. He lay there for a time, in the darkness, listening to the downpour, the sound comforting and ordinary. It was just before dawn; his ability to sense such things now magnified beyond belief since surviving the fire that had made him immortal.

A few feet away, on the other pallet they'd crammed into the lean-to beside Maralyce's cabin to cater for this influx of unexpected visitors, Stellan Desean's deep even breathing indicated the former Duke of Lebec was still sound asleep. Declan guessed the others in the cabin would still be asleep too. Shalimar would be snoring softly on the pallet in front of the fire, while Nyah, the little princess Declan had rescued from Caelum, would be curled up in a ball beside Maralyce, still not used to having to share a bed with anybody.

It wasn't long, however, before other things intruded on Declan's peaceful contemplation. He could feel things now that he'd never felt before; knew things—like exactly what time it was—without knowing how. He could, if he concentrated, feel every single raindrop, sense the tension that held its shape, and its pain as it splattered on the ground. It was as if, along with immortality, he had acquired another sense; one that let him touch things on a hidden level not accessible to mortal men. The ability both fascinated and frightened him because he knew what it was.

He was touching the Tide.

Maralyce had tried to explain it to him, sensing his gift even before he knew about it, although she hedged around acknowledging his ability in so many words. She knew a lot—this immortal who'd turned out to be his great-grandmother—that she wasn't sharing with anybody. She knew things about Declan; things about his mother and things about his grandfather that Shalimar didn't know about himself, and she dribbled the information out like tidbits fed to a puppy one was patiently training to be a loyal and well-behaved companion.

She also knew—Declan was quite certain—the identity of his father, a mystery that had, until now, never bothered him overly much. His grandfather, Shalimar, was a foundling raised in a Lebec brothel, after all. His long dead grandmother was a whore and his mother was born there too. She had grown up in the house and inevitably worked there until she died of consumption when Declan was still a small child. Given his mother's profession, the number of men who might have fathered him ran into the thousands and Declan had never really felt the need to sift through such a sordid list of names—had such a list existed—to find the culprit.

Until now.

Until the list had shrunk from hundreds of faceless strangers to a handful of immortals he could actually name.

It was, he had decided, the only explanation for his immortality. He had survived the fire in the prison tower because he wasn't *just* half-immortal like his grandfather, who was dying from the effects of being mortal and having the same ability to touch the Tide so recently awakened in Declan. No, he'd survived because in addition to the immortal blood he'd inherited from Shalimar through his mother, he'd inherited even more from his unknown father. That tiny fraction more—that difference between being half-immortal or five-eighths—meant he might have lived and eventually died in ignorance . . . or been exposed to the elemental forces that awakened his potential.

Fire. The essence of the Tide Star itself.

Worse, he could wield the Tide, could touch it on a level he was certain concerned even Maralyce. Assuming he'd inherited *that* ability from his father too, then his father was probably one of the Tide Lords. *That* narrowed down the candidates to just seven men: Tryan, Lukys, Kentravyon, Pellys, Brynden, Jaxyn and Cayal, the Immortal Prince.

Maralyce had told him some of this over the past few weeks. Most of it he'd worked out for himself, because she didn't seem all that inclined to help. There was no sense of family or comradeship among the immortals. You sank or swam on the Tide as you could. You found your own way, just as the others had.

It was common for pupils to turn on their masters, apparently. As far as Declan could tell, no immortal was going to teach another, potentially more powerful immortal, a single thing more than they absolutely had to.

Which left this new immortal with one burning question . . .

What was he going to do with the rest of his life? His endless, *endless* life . . .

Declan sat up abruptly, not yet ready to contemplate the future stretching before him. He would live for today, for now . . .

And let the future take care of itself.

A shadow moving across the yard caught his eye. He tossed the blanket from his pallet over Desean, who needed protection from the cold far more than Declan did, and rose to his feet. He didn't need to wonder who owned the shadow. Now he was immortal, he could sense any other being in the vicinity linked to the Tide.

"Can't sleep?" he called after Maralyce, his breath frosting in the cold rain, as she headed toward the entrance of the mine. She was carrying a bag of tools and a pick, so he guessed she was planning to be gone for a while.

"Sick of all these visitors, more like it." She stopped, turning to face him, squinting at him in the pre-dawn light as he crossed the yard to stand before her, unconcerned by the drizzle. Rain no longer bothered him, nor the cold. His body adjusted itself now, preserving his natural body heat the same way it had made the scratches on his face disappear. That was the truth of immortality—perpetual healing.

"What about Shalimar?"

"What about him?"

"You said he needed your help. He's been getting worse for days now."

She shrugged. "Can't be helped."

"He's your *son*, Maralyce. You're not just going to abandon him to a horrible death, are you, just because you're annoyed at having to put up with a few houseguests?"

Maralyce looked away. Had it been anybody else, Declan might have thought it was guilt making her unable to meet his eyes. But she was immortal and he doubted guilt was an emotion that bothered any of them overly much, after a while.

"What do I need to do then?" he asked with a sigh, when he realised appealing to her better nature wasn't likely to work.

"Keep him well supplied with mead," Maralyce said. "That should ease his pain until he dies."

His great-grandmother's callous instructions were designed purely to aggravate him, Declan suspected. "And how long will that be? A day? A week? A month?"

Her eyes narrowed as she squinted at him in the gloom. "You can feel the Tide now, Declan. You tell me."

That was the first time she had acknowledged it openly. He wondered why she'd waited until now—when she was planning to abandon them—to mention his ability to touch the Tide.

"So you're telling me he'll die when the Tide peaks?"

She shook her. "He'll die when he's good and ready; when his body's had enough of being pulled every which way by the undercurrents. There's nothing more I can do for him."

Her statement was so confident, so *final*, Declan knew there was no further point to arguing about it. "So you're leaving then."

She nodded and jerked her head in the direction of the cabin. "Don't let them eat me out of house and home while I'm gone, eh? It's getting too late in the year to make the trek down the mountain for more supplies."

"When will you be back?"

"When I feel like it." She shouldered her pack a little higher and then frowned. "You gonna be all right?"

Declan shrugged. "Do I have a choice?"

"Nothing worse than a self-pitying immortal, Declan. Get over it."

"That's your favourite piece of advice, isn't it? *Get over it*."

"That's because it's *good* advice."

He sighed again, wondering if there was anything more futile than trying to get a straight answer out of Maralyce. "Anything in particular you want me to do while you're gone?"

She glanced around the small clearing, her eyes resting on the towering pile of chopped logs stacked outside the cabin. "You could chop some more firewood."

Declan glanced at the woodpile. "I meant anything *other* than contributing to your campaign to single-handedly cause the complete deforestation of the Shevron Mountains."

Maralyce was not amused. "You'd do well to watch that tongue of yours, lad. I can stay pissed at someone for a very long time, you know."

Declan didn't doubt that for a moment. "What did you want me to tell the others about your sudden departure?"

"Anything you like," she said, turning back toward the mine entrance. "I ain't here to mind their tender sensibilities. That's your job." She turned, raised a hand in farewell, and then hesitated and turned back to face him, her face creased with concern.

"Changed your mind already?"

"There'll come a time," she said, ignoring his question, "that you'll want to know more. I ain't the one to teach you what you want to know, Declan, despite what you think."

"Then who is?"

"Lukys, probably, although I'm reluctant to recommend his kind of aid to anyone. But before you seek him out, be damned sure you want to know what he has to offer. You can be immortal, lad, and not be a Tide Lord. You can be like some of the others who've made peace with their immortality, like Arryl and Medwen . . . Live your life as unobtrusively as possible . . ." She searched his face for a moment and then shook her head. "But you won't. You're young and curious and no matter how well intentioned, the lure of the power you have access to now, will prove too much. Just remember, eternity is a long time to be watching over your shoulder for your enemies to find you."

Before he could respond, she turned back to the mine, and a moment later was swallowed by the dark maw of the entrance.

Declan stood in the yard for a time, the rain dripping down on him, wondering what had really prompted Maralyce to up and leave. And her dire warning. He knew she wasn't happy with this unexpected influx of houseguests—Maralyce hadn't been shy about letting them know of her irritation—but that didn't explain her leaving now. If anything, she seemed more the type to stay, determined to keep her eye on these annoying interlopers to make sure they didn't steal anything.

Still, Declan wasn't really surprised she'd gone. There had been an air about Maralyce recently, almost as if she was mentally tapping her foot with impatience, waiting for everyone to leave her alone so she could get on with her work. He wondered what she did down there in her mine that was so damned important. Declan was fairly certain it wasn't simple greed. He'd never met another soul who cared less about the trappings of material wealth.

And what had she meant by telling him he didn't *have* to be a Tide Lord? Did that mean he *could* be one? That he commanded the same sort of power as the Immortal Prince?

He didn't have a chance to wonder on it for long, however. As the first rays of the dawn touched the mountaintops, a scream split the air. High-pitched, distressed, young and female, it came from inside the miner's cabin across the yard. Declan ran for the cabin, almost colliding at the door with Stellan Desean who'd been woken by Nyah's screams. They burst into the cabin together to find it lit by a single candle on the table. Still dressed in her borrowed nightgown, Nyah was leaning over Shalimar, who was lying in front of the fire.

"What's wrong?" Desean asked, a step ahead of Declan, looking around for the danger that had prompted Nyah's panic.

Nyah looked up, her face streaked with tears. As she let go of Shalimar his shoulder rolled to the side to reveal his eyes, open and staring and lifeless.

"He's dead," Declan said in a flat, unemotional voice.

Stellan Desean bent down, gently pulling Nyah away from the old man's body. "Come on, lass, it'll be all right . . ."

Declan stared down at Shalimar's corpse, at his paper-thin skin and his now peaceful features, wondering if he felt nothing because he'd been expecting this or because now he was immortal, he was no longer capable of normal human emotion.

Holding Nyah as she sobbed against his chest, patting her back with a fatherly hand, Stellan glanced up at Declan. "We'll have to find Maralyce and tell her."

"She knows," Declan replied with absolute certainty.

The former duke looked at him curiously for a moment and then turned to Nyah. "Why don't you go outside for a breath of air, your highness?" he suggested. "Splash some water on your face. You'll feel better."

"But . . . Shalimar . . . he's . . ."

"I know. Don't you worry about it. Declan and I will look after him."

Sniffling loudly, Nyah, with some reluctance, did as he asked, pushing past Declan on her way outside.

"You're very good with children," Declan remarked as he closed the door behind her.

The duke smiled thinly. "Arkady used to tell me what a good father I'd make." Stellan squatted down to examine the corpse. "He's stone cold; must have been dead for hours. I'm so sorry, Declan."

"He's out of pain now."

Desean looked up at him. "Did the Tide kill him, do you think?"

Declan nodded. *The Tide . . . or Maralyce holding a pillow over his face to end his torment.* He wasn't sure what made him think that, but the idea seemed plausible. Death was such a gift to an immortal; something to be bestowed with love, not dealt out as punishment. He wouldn't be surprised to learn she had hastened Shalimar's end because she could no longer ease his suffering . . .

Tides, when did I start sympathising with an immortal?

"Declan?"

He blinked, and realised Stellan Desean was speaking to him.

"Sorry . . . did you say something?"

"I said, do you want to move him outside? To the forge, perhaps? Until this rain stops and we can bury him?"

Declan nodded, and moved to pick up Shalimar's feet and together with the former Duke of Lebec, he helped carry his last remaining mortal relative outside.

Chapter 4

Arkady woke up groaning when Alkasa poked her in the back to tell her breakfast had arrived. Mindful of her plans for suicide by faking illness, Arkady moved slowly and painfully and hoped it was enough for the others to notice. For once the stifling heat of the cabin was useful, making her clammy skin look flushed and unhealthy. It might have been better if she'd refused her food too, but she needed the gruel to make her wound look filled with pus, so she couldn't afford to turn it away.

Once she had her meal, she retreated to the back of the cabin near the bucket and sank down to the floor, glancing around at the others. Foul as it was, this gruel was their only sustenance and all the women were intent on their own meals. The sailor who'd delivered it had eyed each one of them speculatively as he'd spooned the slop into their bowls, his eyes settling on Alkasa for a moment, before moving on.

The young woman smiled at him, took her meal and pushed her way between two of the other women, and then bent her head close to the bowl as she fingered the slops into her mouth. Cutlery, besides being a potential weapon, was not considered necessary for slaves.

Trying not to be too obvious, Arkady scooped up the slops with her fingers and smeared the porridge around the burn on her breast, gritting her teeth against the pain. When she had what she thought looked like a pus-filled scab over the clean scab underneath, she pulled her shift closed and ate the rest of the tasteless porridge. Then, while the others were still distracted, she suppressed a shudder and dipped a finger into the foul-smelling bucket on the floor beside her. Trying very hard not to think about it too closely, she wiped her damp finger around the edges of the scab, taking care to ensure she didn't touch the wound itself, which struck Arkady as being rather silly. She was doing this to gain the means to end her own life, after all. She wasn't planning to be alive long enough for her wound to become genuinely infected.

After that, it was just a case of waiting for the sailor to come back to collect their bowls. She leaned against the wall with her eyes closed, trying to look ill—not a hard task when one was sitting on the moving floor of a cramped, airless cabin beside a half-full ablution bucket. She groaned occasionally for effect, until even Sharee, the oldest of the female slaves, asked her what was wrong.

"I feel sick," Arkady said.

"We all do, you stupid bitch," the woman replied unsympathetically. "So do it quietly."

"Not seasick," she groaned. "I think my burn is infected."

The woman, who like Arkady was sitting on the floor with her back to the bulkhead, opened her eyes and studied her Glaeban companion curiously. "Show me."

Arkady pulled aside her shift, hoping that in the gloom of the cabin, her gruel-encrusted scab would pass casual inspection.

"Tides," remarked Alkasa, who was sitting beside her. "It smells like shit."

Quite literally, Arkady agreed silently, pulling a face she hoped gave the impression she was in intense pain.

"You'd better tell 'em," Saxtyn advised. "They tend to get mighty pissed when a slave goes down for something simple like that. And they'll blame the rest of us if you die of blood poisoning."

Arkady nodded and closed her eyes, leaning her head back, silently thanking her husband's aggravating, snobbish high-born friends for all their instruction on the proper care of slaves. *One didn't have to care about them*, Lady Jimison used to say, *or even like them, but one was wasting money if one let them die unnecessarily.*

She wondered how long it would be before the sailor came back; how long after that before the ship's surgeon appeared.

And how long after that, she would be dead.

"Get up!"

Arkady knew enough Senestran to understand the order. She scrambled to her feet at the sailor's command, stunned to realise he was fumbling with the keys on his belt to release her from the chains that bound her to the other slaves. She'd expected the doctor to visit her, not the other way around.

A few moments later, Arkady found herself standing in the hall, as the sailor locked the slave cabin behind her. He shoved her forward, indicating she should precede him up a narrow companionway to the deck above. From there he led her past several closed doors, until he finally stopped at one carved with intertwined ivy leaves, the Senestran symbol, she supposed, for a medical practitioner. The sailor knocked and then opened the door and shoved her inside without waiting for a response.

He said something in Senestran to the doctor—presumably along the lines of *I'll be back when you're done with her*—and slammed the door behind him.

Arkady struggled to regain her balance on the moving floor and looked around. The cabin was larger than the hole she and the other slaves occupied, and much cleaner. There was a bunk under the porthole, a desk beside it, a small table laid out with a series of achingly familiar instruments Arkady remembered from her father's surgery and an examination bed (which she supposed doubled as an operating table) against the other wall.

In the middle of it all stood an effeminate-looking young man no older than Arkady, with long dark hair, an immaculate waistcoat and white silk shirt, and the most impressive black eye and bruised jaw Arkady had ever seen—even after watching her father patch up countless street ruffians in the slums of Lebec.

Perhaps, she thought, *the noises we've been hearing at night weren't some hapless cabin boy, but the ship's doctor being tormented and beaten.*

Of all the things she'd been expecting about the ship's doctor, to find that he looked even more damaged than her was not among them. It beggared belief, and for a moment she forgot herself.

"I'll bet *that* hurts," she muttered in Glaeban, wincing in sympathy for the beating this young man must have endured.

The young man looked up sharply. "You're Glaeban."

"You *speak* Glaeban," she replied, equally surprised and unable to think of anything more intelligent to say. Her plan had been to look ill and on the verge of collapse, but she'd been expecting a drunkard with no hope of a future or much care for his patients. For all that the ship's doctor looked as if he'd just been chewed up and spat out by a Jelidian snow bear, Arkady doubted her gruel-covered wound would pass even the most distracted glance by this sharp young man.

Time for my back-up plan, she thought.

Pity there is no back-up plan.

"I studied in Glaeba for a time," the doctor said.

"Ah . . . that would explain it . . ."

"I would not have expected to find a Glaeban noblewoman in the holds of one of my father's slavers," he said, studying her with interest. "What happened? Debtor slave?"

"I suppose you could say that," she said. It wasn't really a lie. She'd been sold into slavery, after all, to settle the debt between two immortals. "What makes you think I'm a Glaeban noblewoman?"

"You speak too well to be a poor man's wife. Do you have a name?"

"Kady."

"Is that your real name?"

"It's near enough."

"And what can I do for you, Kady Near Enough? You appear healthy, given your circumstances. Yet you'd not have been sent to me unless they feared you were mortally ill."

"I . . . my brand . . . the burn . . ." she said. "I think it's infected."

He indicated she should take a seat on the examination table. "Where is the brand?"

Arkady sat on the table and then hesitated, certain now that her ruse, far from giving her an opportunity to end her life painlessly, was about to plunge her into far deeper trouble. Gingerly, she pulled the loose shift aside, exposing her breast.

In a business-like fashion the young man leaned forward to examine the wound. He studied it for an inordinately long time, touching her breast with hesitant fingers, before standing up and turning to the wash bowl on the table beside the instruments, where he began to wash his hands, the water sloshing around with the motion of the ship.

"Your wound seems to be suffering from indigestion rather than infection," he remarked, speaking Glaeban so she could understand him.

"Sorry?"

He glanced over his shoulder at her. "That's porridge, not pus. And the smell? That's either deliberate or the result of poor personal hygiene."

Arkady covered her breast in annoyance. There would be no scalpel to snatch from this young man's distracted hand. No quick end. No easy death from loss of blood . . .

"I . . . I wanted to see you," she said, for want of a better reason for her deception. *I wanted to steal a scalpel and kill myself*, might not be a wise confession to make at this point.

"Why?" He turned back to her, this time with a washcloth in his hand. Arkady turned her head as he cautiously exposed her breast again and began to wash away the muck.

"It got me out of the slave cabin," she said.

Arkady risked a closer look. The young man was concentrating on his work. As she suspected, in the better light of the doctor's cabin it was obvious that her burn was clean and healing well. But the doctor was blushing crimson as he worked, making Arkady wonder how many naked breasts this young man had actually handled before.

Not many, she decided, as he stepped away from the table to rinse out the washcloth. There was a noticeable swelling in the front of his trousers that she was fairly certain wasn't the result of anything other than good old-fashioned lust.

"Tides," she said, pulling her shift up. "How long have *you* been at sea?"

He glanced down and managed to blush an even deeper shade of vermillion, if that were possible. "I'm . . . I'm so sorry . . . I didn't mean to . . ."

Arkady stared at him in shock. "Why are *you* apologising? I'm the slave here."

"I'm not . . ." He stopped and then shrugged helplessly. "I'm not very good at dealing with women, I'm afraid. Slave or freeborn." He tossed the washcloth into the bowl and turned to look at her. "Actually, I'm not very good at dealing with my own gender, either, as evidenced by my many impressive cuts and bruises."

"Why did they beat you up?" she asked, partly out of curiosity and partly out of the need to stall her return to the slave cabin for as long as possible. On that beautifully neat tray just out of arm's reach lay the means for her escape. If feigning interest in this young doctor's woes meant a chance at getting her hands on a scalpel, Arkady was prepared to sit here and listen sympathetically while he poured out his entire life story.

"I think they're under orders to toughen me up."

"Are you serious?"

He nodded. "My name is Cydne Medura."

She waited, assuming there was more to the statement, but apparently not. "I'm sorry, is that supposed to mean something to me?"

He smiled. "If you were Senestran you would have heard of me. My family is very important."

Medura. She remembered where she'd heard it before and nodded in comprehension. "So when you said you were surprised to find a Glaeban noblewoman on your father's slaver you meant . . . what's-his-name . . . Filimon Medura?"

"Fili*mar*," he corrected.

"I would have thought being the owner's son would have protected you from the crew's excesses," she said. "Not made you a target."

"One would think," Cydne agreed, wiping his hands. "But I suspect my shipmates are acting on orders from the captain."

When Arkady didn't react to that, he added, "I'm on this cruise because my father believes a few months at sea will make a man of me, you see. He's a very efficient sort of fellow, so if I'm here and the aim is to *toughen* me up, he'll have taken steps to make damn certain that's the inevitable outcome of my journey."

She studied his bloodied eye and bruised jaw for a moment. "Not enjoying the process much, I'd say."

"Not much, no."

"I'm sorry."

That made Cydne smile even wider, which had the unfortunate effect of making him seem younger than he was. Given his profession, and that he had studied in both Senestra and Glaeba, it was likely he was closer to thirty than twenty, but he didn't look it, which would have done little, Arkady guessed, to help his cause.

"Pity from a slave," he sighed. "Now I am truly depressed."

"I'd be happier dead than in *my* current predicament," Arkady said. "So any time you want to swap places, doctor . . ."

"You should be getting back," he said, looking away uncomfortably. "Is there anything else you need?"

Rescuing, she replied silently, but there didn't seem much point. Arkady slipped off the edge of the examination table, which had the unfortunate effect of placing Cydne between her and the tray of instruments. Her chance—if it had ever really been a chance—was gone. There wouldn't be a second trip back to the doctor's cabin for her infected burn—or for any other reason.

He stepped past her, put his hand on the latch, ready to open it and call back her guard . . .

"Wait!"

"Was there something else?"

"Take me," she blurted out, unable to frame a more delicate suggestion in the split second she had to turn this around. She would never, *ever*, get another opportunity like this.

"I *beg* your pardon?"

"You're being picked on by the crew because your shipmates think you're . . . you're . . ." She fished around for the right word, not sure how to frame it, gambling her life on the fact that she had only a moment to convince this man to help her. "Because they think you're not a real man . . ."

Cydne was blushing crimson again.

"The captain has ordered the female slaves may be used by the crew as soon as we clear Torlenian waters," she added in a rush. "That's about an hour from now, isn't it?"

"I suppose . . ."

"Well, you don't want to keep getting beaten up and I don't fancy being repeatedly raped. Please, doctor. Tell the captain *you* want me for your bed; that you want me to stay here with you."

Cydne looked horrified by her suggestion. "Why, in the name of the Tides, would I do something like that?"

"Because if you have a woman of your own, the crew will be satisfied, your father will think you're a real man and I won't have to find another way to kill myself."

The blood drained from the young doctor's face. "Is *that* why you came here? Why you pretended your wound was septic? Were you hoping I would give you something for the pain? Enough to kill yourself?"

Arkady shook her head. "Actually, I was planning to steal a scalpel and open my carotid with it."

"How do you even know where your carotid artery is?" he asked with a bewildered frown.

"My father was a physician."

Cydne looked too confused, too dazed to make a decision about anything, let alone make the unheard of leap of faith required to help this strange Glaeban slave he'd known for all of five minutes.

Significantly, though, he hadn't yet opened the door or called for the guard.

"You know nothing about me," the young man said, after a moment. "For all you know, *I* might be your worst nightmare."

"My worst nightmare is spending the next few weeks being handed around the crew for their entertainment," she said. "I doubt, even at your most perverse, you could do worse than that."

"Do you also assume I'm not interested in women?" he asked, more than a little defensively. "Is that why you're throwing yourself on my mercy? Because you think I have no lustful interest in you?"

Arkady wanted to scream at him. Instead, she took a deep breath and hoped she sounded rational, not desperate. "I've seen the evidence of your 'lustful interest,' doctor. It scares me a whole lot less than being pack raped."

"But I know nothing about you . . ."

"And the only thing I know about *you* is that you know I faked an injury to get here and you haven't reported me yet. I'm taking it on trust that your silence means you're a decent human being. You're going to have to take it on trust that I'm one too."

He stared at her indecisively for a moment and then pointed to the instrument tray. "There. That long piece with the grip in the middle and the flattened hooks at the end, next to the scalpels. What is it?"

"A bone lever," she said with reasonable confidence. "It's used for levering broken bones back into place; sometimes for extracting teeth that have rotted and broken off in the gum."

"And the thing next to it? With the flat head?"

"It's a cautery. It's used to seal wounds; sometimes for destroying skin tumours and warts."

"And the hooks next to that? What are they used for?"

"The blunt one is for raising blood-vessels; the sharp ones are for seizing and raising small pieces of tissue for excision and for holding the edges of wounds open. Please, doctor, I'm not lying. I can help you. I just need you to help me."

He didn't respond immediately, but when he did, Arkady's heart sank. The doctor opened the door and called for the guard before turning back to watch her suspiciously, but not without doing a quick visual check of the instrument table first, to be certain that all the scalpels were still there.

The sailor appeared in the doorway a few tense moments later and said something to the doctor. The young man squared his shoulders and rattled off something else that made no sense to Arkady. Once he was finished speaking the sailor glared at Arkady for a moment, and then slapped the doctor on the shoulder and burst out laughing. He said something else Arkady didn't understand and left, laughing all the way down the corridor.

"What did you say to him?" *Did you report my fake wound? My attempt to escape my fate by throwing myself at you? The fact that I was planning suicide?*

Any one of those explanations might have evoked the laughter of the sailor the doctor had sent away without her. Even now, the guard could be on his way to report her crimes to the captain . . .

"I told him I wasn't sending you back," Cydne replied, turning to face her. Arkady almost fainted with relief as he added, "I told him I'd heard the captain has made the female slaves available for the use of the crew and I wanted this one for myself."

Arkady could have cried with relief. "Thank you."

He shook his head sadly. "You are thanking me for nothing, Kady. I am still one of the crew. And you are still mine to do with as I want."

But you're going to have to sleep sometime, Arkady thought, sniffing back unexpected tears and quite deliberately not looking in the direction of the tray of instruments where the scalpels lay.

Turns out I have an alternate plan, after all.

Chapter 5

Cayal's journey across the desert to Elvere was relatively fast, although it was uncomfortable. For one, he was on foot, and he stopped for nothing—not to eat, drink or rest—in the two days it took him to reach the city. This was one of those occasions when his immortality was a blessing rather than a curse. He didn't hunger or thirst or tire the way a mortal man would, or a mortal beast of burden, for that matter, which is why he chose to cross the desert on foot. Riding a camel may have been more comfortable, but it would have been much much slower.

It proved easy enough for Cayal to track Arkady down once he reached Elvere. There was really only one slave concern of note in the city and they pretty much controlled the movement of all slaves in and out of the port. Posing as a buyer, Cayal had hardly any trouble gaining an audience with the slave trader Brynden had sent Arkady to.

He described Arkady quite specifically and asked the man how much he wanted for her.

The slaver had treated him to an oily, apologetic smile and informed him he didn't have the Glaeban woman Cayal described. He had, however, recently acquired a Caelish woman of similar stature and appearance that his lordship might be interested in.

Cayal was relieved beyond measure . . . Until the slaver announced he'd recently branded the slave in question, batch-sold her to the Medura Shipping Company for eventual placement in the Senestran mines, and shipped her out several days earlier.

At which point, Cayal exploded with fury.

With the Tide on the turn, Cayal's anger was a tangible thing. The freak storm that lashed the city for more than a day, unroofing houses and swamping the slums with its torrential downpour, was nothing more than a reflex. For a time, Cayal even relished the feel of the rising Tide as he channelled its still nascent power . . .

But the unseasonable hurricane that swept across Elvere was fairly pathetic, given what he would be capable of once the Tide peaked. It made him feel a little better, even if it achieved nothing else useful. Even the thrill of the Tide faded too quickly, however. Within a day, Cayal's rage was spent, and he was forcefully reminded of the reason the Tide no longer offered re-lief from his despair.

Besides, a part of him argued, he should probably let her go. Arkady Desean had a bad habit of making him forget his purpose. He was sorry for her—sorry she'd been sold into slavery—but worse had happened to him in his eight thousand years, and besides, she was a smart, tough woman. If any-body could find a way to survive such a fate, Arkady would. Cayal wanted to die, he reminded himself, and Lukys was insisting he'd found a way to make it happen.

I should listen to Lukys. Take advantage of the rising Tide and put an end to this endless existence while I have the chance.

He would be a fool to pass up an opportunity that may not come again for some ten thousand years, all for the sake of a woman who didn't want him, didn't love him, and tricked him into thinking there might be some reason to his existence, when eight thousand years of experience told him quite the opposite.

So Cayal, after three days of savage weather and countless mortal casu-alties, let the Tide go.

And yet the storm raged on . . .

Once he'd calmed down enough to take note of his surroundings, Cayal quickly discovered why the storm continued to rage, despite his attempts to calm it. He could feel the reason tingling along his arms. He could feel it resonating in his bones. He could feel the disturbance in the Tide; the ripples of another presence nearby on the surface of the magical ocean from which the Tide Lords drew their power.

There was another Tide Lord in Elvere, working mischief with the storm Cayal had set off in his rage.

The identity of the culprit was easy enough to deduce. It wasn't Brynden, Cayal was sure. The Lord of Reckoning was too careful of his mortal charges to allow such a storm to harm them. He'd be trying to end it, not feed it. Besides, he was busy trying to take over the country. Kinta was in Ramahn already, paving the way for his return. He wouldn't allow the most important port in the north to be destroyed. He wanted to rule Torlenia. He needed the commerce that passed through this port too much to allow any harm to come to it.

For similar reasons, Cayal doubted any of the other Tide Lords who could—on a good day—be considered reasonably sane, were responsible for this. Which meant it was likely to be one of them who wasn't sane, narrowing down the candidates to Kentravyon or Pellys.

Both men had been driven insane by immortality, something Cayal tried not to think about too often, for fear of having to examine his own sanity too closely. Kentravyon was living proof of what happened when you swam too deep into the Tide and couldn't find your way back again. It had ended with him believing he was God and they'd had to band together and bind him in ice, to save the world from his delusions. Until Lukys had inexplicably decided to revive him, he should have remained in Jelidia where he could hurt no one.

Pellys's madness had a much less complicated cause. During a bout of depression eight thousand years ago, he had persuaded Cayal to decapitate him, knowing that when his head grew back—as did any part of an immortal separated from their body—it would grow back unburdened by the memories of his insanely long life.

The trouble was, the decapitation, in addition to destroying the entire nation of Magreth, had destroyed all the knowledge and experience that a person brought into immortality with them. Pellys had the mind of a petulant child with no conscience. It made him curious, amusing—and dangerous beyond comprehension.

Given that Kentravyon, even if he'd been revived by now, was—hopefully—in Lukys's custody somewhere in Jelidia, and Lukys would discourage such a wanton display of power so soon after the Tide had turned, that really only left Pellys.

Once he knew who he was looking for, it didn't take long to track down the other Tide Lord. He could feel him in the Tide, even more so when he was drawing on its power. His presence drew Cayal like iron filings to a magnet.

Cayal found the Tide Lord on the sixth day of the storm sitting on a high bluff, overlooking the slaughter yards of the Elvere abattoir. As usual, Pellys had sought out creatures who were about to die so he could bask in their mortality. He was sitting cross-legged on the bluff, wearing a bloodstained leather apron that even the incessant rain had been unable to wash clean, which spoke of more than a passing fascination with the abattoir. He'd probably, Cayal guessed, been working there as a slaughterman.

"Hello, Pellys," he said, after climbing the storm-swept bluff where the Tide Lord was perched, the better to watch his handiwork wreak havoc on the city.

The older man glanced up, unsurprised to find Cayal standing there. He grinned. "I like your weather."

Cayal lowered himself to the sodden ground beside Pellys. The waters of the harbour below churned in the storm, a sinister grey soup that blended almost seamlessly with the sheeting rain. "It's time to make it stop now, Pellys."

"But I can feel the Tide. Haven't felt the Tide for a long time. It feels good."

"I know, but you need to let it go."

"I didn't start it, you know." He turned to Cayal, frowning. "It's not my fault. Why do people always think it's *my* fault?" He'd been like this ever since his head had grown back. It was more than childish petulance; it was as if his regenerated brain had lost something in the regrowth, some capacity to advance beyond infantile reasoning and deal with more adult concepts. Like consequences.

"Nobody's blaming you, Pellys."

"You started it, didn't you?"

Cayal didn't answer that. There didn't seem much point.

"I always get blamed for stuff you do."

"Then let's stop this before there is something else to blame you for."

Pellys seemed to consider that notion for a moment . . . and then abruptly, the rain stopped. Without the artificial encouragement of a Tide Lord, the weather immediately began to right itself. With unnatural speed, the clouds started to break up, allowing the sunshine through in spears of light bright enough to make Cayal squint.

"Better?"

Cayal nodded. "Much better."

"I need a woman," Pellys said. "Always do, after I've been riding the Tide."

"And with such a charming seduction technique, I'm sure you'll find them lining up for you, Pellys, my old friend."

The immortal smiled. Sarcasm was completely lost on Pellys. "Did you come to Elvere to find me?"

Cayal knew better than to tell Pellys the truth. "Of course I did."

"You haven't looked for me for ages."

"You've been hiding, haven't you?"

That gave Pellys pause. He nodded and then shrugged. "Still, would have been nice if you looked."

"I'm here now. That's what really counts."

Pellys nodded again and then turned to study Cayal, his face splitting into an enormous grin. "You're all wet."

"Yeah . . . funny about that."

His eyes lit up. "Did you want to sink some ships? I like the way the people all scurry about like ants when you sink their ships."

Cayal sighed, wondering why he was even remotely surprised that Pellys hadn't changed since the last time they'd crossed paths. Admittedly, he'd not been an intellectual giant, even back before Cayal decapitated him, but now . . .

There, but for a headsman's dead mother, go I, Cayal thought.

Pellys had no memories of his past before Cayal had put an end to his suffering by removing his head, just this infantile innocence coupled with the power of a Tide Lord. Of course, taking Pellys's memories had been the easy part; having a Tide Lord with the self-awareness of a newborn and the power to split a continent had proved the real problem. Magreth had sunk into the ocean in the process of Pellys's regeneration. *Would I have destroyed Glaeba the same way*, he wondered, *had they beheaded me instead of trying to hang me?*

Would Arkady have survived?

Given her fate now, she might have been better off had his decapitation been successful. She'd be dead, more than likely, but she might consider that a more desirable state than slavery. But there was no point in wondering what might have been. The decision to let Arkady go had just been taken out of his hands.

With the Tide on the rise, and Pellys already fantasising about mass-murder on the high seas, Cayal knew he had to get him away from here.

He needed to take him somewhere safe; somewhere he could do the minimum amount of harm. There was always enough trouble when the Tide Lords regained their power with the turn of the Tide, without someone like Pellys running around, wantonly destroying things just for the pleasure of watching them die.

Then Cayal realised it wasn't so much a "where" he should take Pellys, but a "who." Lukys had been around even longer than Pellys. He'd know what to do with him; know how to distract him.

They might even be able to use him. Lukys had said they needed the power of several Tide Lords, after all, to wield this magic he'd promised would end Cayal's life. Brynden wasn't going to help—Cayal wondered what made him think he ever would—and he'd rather spend the rest of eternity in torment than ask for Tryan's assistance with anything. The idea of tracking down Elyssa was equally frightening, because there was only one sure way to secure her cooperation—and, even for death, Cayal wanted to avoid that. Perhaps his stumbling across Pellys like this was more than fortuitous coincidence. If he took Pellys back to Lukys's place in the desert, when the older man got back from Jelidia with Kentravyon they might have enough power to do this thing, and rid Cayal of this life he was so desperate to be done with.

"I've got a better idea," he said. "Let's go pay Lukys a visit."

"Do you know where he is?"

Cayal nodded. "He has a villa not far from here. It even has goldfish."

Chapter 6

They buried Shalimar on the side of the mountain, on a frosty morning the day after he passed away. A simple wooden plank, into which Nyah had roughly carved his name, marked his final resting place.

The little Caelish princess cried as Declan and Stellan lowered the old man's body into the grave and insisted on saying the Caelish Prayer for the Dead. It was a depressing ode filled with many "thees" and "thous," references to the Tide Star, and suggestions of the possibility of an afterlife which Shalimar would have scorned had he been here to witness his own funeral.

Declan said nothing to her, however. The little girl had never had to confront death before. Her own father had died when she was still a small child, and she had no memory of him or the rituals associated with his passing, to help her. He sensed Nyah needed to feel she was contributing something, or perhaps saying goodbye—he wasn't sure which—so he let her speak and made no comment about it.

With the formalities done, Nyah headed back along the path toward the cabin, sobbing quietly, while Stellan and Declan filled in the grave. Unable to think of anything to say that might ease the little girl's grief, Declan watched her leave, wondering why the child—who'd known his grandfather for only a few months—seemed more upset at his passing than his own grandson, who remained dry-eyed.

"She and the old man had grown quite friendly," Stellan said, tossing a spadeful of dirt over Shalimar's canvas-wrapped corpse. Perhaps he guessed the direction of Declan's thoughts.

Declan turned back to the pile of dirt beside the grave they'd dug out the day before, forcefully thrusting the spade into the cold earth. "She barely knew him."

"Is that a prerequisite for grief? Longevity of acquaintance?"

"I suppose not," Declan said, shovelling another spadeful of dirt into the grave.

They worked in silence for a time, the still, chilly mountain air silent but for the rhythmic thud of dirt landing in the grave. The hole was perhaps half full when Stellan stopped to rest, wiping the sweat from his brow as he leaned on the handle of his spade.

"Not used to hard physical labour?" Declan asked, as he continued to work.

"Not really, no," Stellan agreed. "Although since being a guest here, I've learned the value of it." He smiled wanly. "Not all of that woodpile is your work, you know."

Declan lay his spade aside and reached for the waterskin. "You still talk like you're the lord of the manor."

"Do I?"

"Can't help yourself." Declan tossed him the waterskin and picked up his spade. "And it's contagious. Arkady wasn't married to you more than a month before she started talking the same way."

Stellan took a long swig from the skin and wiped his mouth with the back of his hand before he replied. "You have a problem with that, don't you?"

Declan shrugged and continued to shovel dirt over his grandfather, although there was no sign of him any longer. "Arkady can talk any way she likes."

"I meant with me marrying Arkady."

"Arkady is free to *marry* anybody she likes too."

"You've never been happy about it though, have you?"

Declan stopped to look at him. "Tides, Desean, you've been married to her for the better part of seven years. What? You wanna fight about it *now*?"

"On the contrary, I don't want to fight about Arkady at all."

"Then shut up and keep shovelling." Declan slammed the spade into the loose earth beside the grave, irritation lending him strength.

"I want you to find her for me."

Declan emptied the earth into the grave and then leaned on the spade, turning to look at the former duke. "You want me to *what*?"

"I want you to find Arkady and bring her home."

"Why don't *you* go look for her? You're her husband. And it's not as if you have anything better to do right now."

Stellan shook his head. "I'm supposed to be dead, remember?"

"So am I."

"Perhaps, but you're not the heir to the Glaeban throne, Declan. If you miraculously return from the dead, it's not going to start the sort of trouble my resurrection will cause."

"You don't think Arkady wouldn't like to know you're alive?"

"Even if I wanted to announce it in the town square of Herino, I don't have anything close to the discreet contacts you have, particularly in Torlenia, to find her."

The reminder that Arkady was currently missing somewhere in Torlenia silenced the objection Declan was about to make. Not only was she in Torlenia, but last he'd heard, the immortal Kinta was Arkady's newest best friend. She could be anywhere by now.

"I don't know what's happened to her, Declan. And I have no way, any longer, of ensuring she's well. When I left her at the palace with the Imperator's Consort, she was safe enough, but news of my arrest—"

"Whoa!" Declan said, wondering if he'd misheard the duke. "You left her *where*?"

"With the Imperator's Consort in the Royal Seraglium. You know what Torlenia is like. I couldn't leave her at the embassy on her own, and Lady Chintara was kind enough to offer . . . What's the matter? You look as if I left her camped on a street corner."

"Tides!" Declan swore. "She might have been better off if you had."

Stellan frowned, clearly puzzled by Declan's reaction to his news. "But that's my point, don't you see? Her status as the Ambassador of Glaeba's wife would have been thrown into doubt the moment I was arrested. I've had no word from her, Declan. I don't know if the Torlenians have offered her asylum, if she's been thrown out on the street, or if Jaxyn's had her arrested and she's already on her way back to Glaeba."

"It may make little difference," Declan said, picking up his shovel.

"Why?"

"Because the Imperator's Consort is an immortal."

Stellan stared at him in disbelief.

"Oh, you think that's not possible? You, who brought the Lord of Temperance home and kept him as a pet for nigh on a year without realising what he was?" Declan shovelled dirt into the grave as he spoke, glad of something physical to do; glad of something else to do with his spade other than crown Stellan Desean with it. "You who didn't even know his own flesh and blood well enough to spot that his niece had probably been murdered and replaced by an immortal?"

Stellan shook his head. "I had no idea . . . Declan . . . Tides, I'm still trying to adjust to the idea that immortals exist at all."

"Well, now that you've got your head around that little dilemma, try to get your head around this one. Your precious Lady Chintara is the immortal Charioteer, Kinta. As far as we can tell, she is the Imperator of Torlenia's

Consort because that's the best place to be if you're planning to topple him, so you can hand the entire country to your boyfriend—a fellow with the reassuring moniker of the Lord of Reckoning, by the way—just as soon as the Tide turns. Just like Jaxyn and Diala have lined themselves up to take Glaeba by the throat, as soon as the time is right. Just like Syrolee and her lot are doing in Caelum, which is why we're hiding Nyah here in the mountains, remember. In case you'd forgotten."

"How do we stop them?"

Declan kept on shovelling. "We can't."

"Can't or won't?"

"What's that supposed to mean?"

Stellan studied him for a moment before carefully suggesting, "You're one of them now, Declan. Perhaps you're no longer as dedicated to seeking the destruction of the immortals as you once were. I mean . . . their doom is now your doom too."

Declan was disgusted by the very suggestion. "You think a freak accident has turned me into some sort of power hungry monster? Is that it?"

Stellan shrugged. "I have no idea what it's done to you. All I know is Arkady is missing and you're the only man I know—mortal or immortal—with the ability, the resources and more importantly the *will*, to find her and bring her home."

"What makes you so damned sure about that?"

"Because you love her, Declan, probably more than I do."

Declan didn't bother answering that one. He kept on shovelling for a time and then glanced over the half-filled grave at Stellan. "You planning to move any more of this dirt or just stand there, like the lord of the flankin' manor, making profound announcements on shit you know nothing about?"

Stellan picked up his shovel. "You know I'm right, Declan."

"What I *know*, Desean, is this," he said, putting all his effort into filling the grave, his words punctuated by shovel after shovel-load of falling dirt. "Arkady married you because you offered her wealth and comfort and safety and a chance for her father to go free. I never agreed with what she did, but I understood *why* she did it. And now, because of that deal, she's stranded in a foreign country with no money, no protection and probably the captive of an immortal who's very pissed off with the *last* immortal your wife made friends with. She is neither safe, comfortable, nor wealthy, and just to make things really interesting, there's a warrant out for her arrest, is-sued by the immortal *you* brought into your palace, because you were too blinded by lust to recognise the danger a menace like Jaxyn is to everything you hold dear, including your wife." He straightened, tossing the spade aside. "So don't you dare stand there and tell me I'm the one responsible for rescuing Arkady, your *grace*. She wouldn't *need* rescuing if it wasn't for you."

Declan turned to leave, deciding Desean could finish the job. Besides, if he stayed much longer in his present mood, Shalimar might not be alone in his grave for long.

"*You* sent her to interview the Immortal Prince," Stellan called after him. "I'll admit my culpability for allowing Jaxyn into our lives, Declan, and for not realising Kylia was not who she claimed, but don't blame me for all of it. You're the one who introduced Arkady to Cayal."

Declan hesitated, glancing back over his shoulder. "So we're equally to blame."

"I don't think we are," Stellan said, shaking his head. "I might have endangered our position by bringing Jaxyn home, but you're right—I *was* blinded by lust. You, on the other hand, apparently knew all along that Kyle Lakesh was actually the Immortal Prince. And yet you sent her to him, for your own selfish reasons, even knowing the danger he represented."

That was a charge Declan couldn't deny, so he didn't bother trying. Instead, he turned from the path leading back to the clearing where Maralyce's cabin was located and headed into the woods, letting his anger and frustration guide him.

"You know I'm right, Declan!" Stellan called.

Declan ignored the duke, certain that if he turned back to confront Stellan now, only one of them would emerge from the encounter alive.

As Declan couldn't die, that really left only one likely outcome.

He'd heard Nyah's wretched Prayer for the Dead enough for one day.

Chapter 7

"Tides, will you be careful with that stuff!" Tryan called impatiently as Warlock felt his way down the bouncing gangway from the barge carrying two suitcases, a hat box and his lordship's malletball clubs. He surprised himself by making it to the luggage wagon parked at the end of the dock without tripping over something, where he handed over the luggage to the two canines loading the wagon. Lady Elyssa stood beside her brother, watching the unloading of the barge with vast disinterest.

"I'll take the female," Warlock heard the immortal tell his sister. Although they were posing as Caelish nobles, Warlock still thought of them by their Immortal names, Tryan and Elyssa, not the assumed names they were currently using, which were Lord Tyrone and Lady Alysa of Torfail. The stink of the suzerain could not be wiped away by taking a different name.

Elyssa glanced over to the wagon where a very pregnant Boots stood waiting for the unloading to finish. She'd arrived about an hour earlier on another barge sent from Lebec, laden with gifts for both the Caelish queen and her future son-in-law. Boots's expression, for anyone who could read Crasii faces, was thunderous.

"What do you want with her?"

"Females are easier to manage," Tryan said with a shrug.

"She's pregnant. What about her pups?"

"I'll drown them."

Warlock slowed as he passed the suitcases up to the canines loading the wagon, determined to hear the rest of this conversation. Tryan's casual threat to murder his pups made his blood run cold.

Curse you, Declan Hawkes, he thought. *I agreed to come here as your spy because you promised Boots and our pups would be safe, and we could still be together.*

They hadn't been here half an hour and already that was looking unlikely. Worse, his pups might be killed, while Boots became the pet of a monster. Warlock glanced at Boots and then eyed the lake warily, judging the distance, wondering if he could grab her and make it to the water before they cut him down.

"But they're a matched set," Elyssa said, crossing her arms petulantly. "They're only worth half as much if you split them up."

"I don't need a personal servant. Besides, he's probably Jaxyn's spy, anyway. Why else would he gift us with something as valuable as a matched breeding pair of canines?"

"He was trying to bribe us into leaving Herino. That's all."

Tryan shook his head. It seemed wrong to Warlock that such a dark heart could reside in such a handsome and noble-seeming exterior. "You're too gullible, Lyssa."

"I won't let you break them up. Besides, King Mathu gave them to me."

"He gave them to *both* of us."

"He gave *everything* to both of us. So I'm taking the Crasii. You already said you don't need them."

"And that they're probably spies," he reminded her.

"All the more reason to keep them together," the immortal said. "Once she's had the pups, neither the female nor her mate will betray me for fear of what might happen to them." Elyssa turned to Boots and stroked her head affectionately. "Isn't that right, Tabitha Belle?"

"To serve you is the reason I breathe, my lady," Boots managed to mutter without betraying her fury.

Elyssa smiled, which had the unfortunate effect of making her chin disappear. "There! You see!"

Tryan grabbed the reins of the mount the grooms had brought him from the palace after he'd sent word their barge had docked. Gathering up the reins, he shook his head. "You're a fool, Lyssa."

She shrugged, unconcerned. "They're Crasii, Try. It doesn't matter what Jaxyn's ordered them to do. They have no choice but to obey me. I'll just countermand his orders."

"Only until someone other than you orders them to do something different." Swinging up into the saddle, the immortal glanced out over the lake, back toward Glaeba, where another immortal plotted to take that country's throne, just as these two, with the rest of their power-hungry family, were plotting the overthrow of Caelum. "We're going to have to fight him and Diala eventually, you know. This continent isn't big enough for us *and* them."

"Jaxyn's probably thinking exactly the same thing about us."

"And *you* want to keep his spies as pets," Tryan said. "Hope you know what you're doing, Lyssa."

Without waiting for his sister to reply, Tryan turned his horse and headed up the steep road away from the docks, back toward the palace. Elyssa watched him leave, scowling at his retreating figure, and then she turned and beckoned her new Crasii to her.

"You heard that?" she asked, although Warlock doubted she wanted an answer. They both nodded wordlessly. "Understand this, creatures. I am the only thing keeping you alive, together, and with your pups. Serve me well, and I'll see you're taken care of. Listen to the orders of another . . ." She hesitated, checking to see who was in earshot. Every Crasii present would know what she was, but it was not yet common knowledge among the human population that the immortals were abroad once more. ". . . another like *me*, and I will dine on your pups. And I mean that quite literally," she added with an unpleasant smile. "I'm quite partial to dog meat."

Warlock wanted to tear her throat out. Beside him, he could tell Boots felt the same. That's what made them different from other Crasii. They were Scards, and not a single fibre of their being wanted anything to do with this monstrous immortal who was not only threatening their pups but was the figure of legend credited with creating their race.

If they wanted to live, however, there was nothing they could say, nothing they could do. It took Warlock more strength than he thought he owned to mumble, "To serve you is the reason we breathe, my lady."

Elyssa smiled even wider. "Excellent! Then let's get to the palace, shall we? I can't wait to show you off to my mother."

The biggest difference between Caelum and Glaeba, Warlock decided after a few days in the country, was the mountains. In Glaeba, the mountains marked the horizon—a misty blue wall of towering, often snowcapped peaks, protecting the fertile farmland on the valley floor that stretched from the shores of the Lower Oran to the foot of the majestic Shevron Mountains in the east.

The horizon in Caelum, on the other hand, seemed to start at the lakeshore. The world here was defined by the vast expanse of the Great Lakes on one side and the towering Caterpillar Ranges on the other. The streets of Cycrane were steep and narrow, winding around the natural contours of the foothills. The closed-in feel of the city was reflected in the closed expressions of its people.

Warlock knew he wasn't going to like it here for any number of reasons, not the least of which was that Boots wasn't speaking to him.

Not that he really blamed her. Since being rushed from the security of Hidden Valley without much more than a sketchy explanation about joining her mate, Boots had found herself enslaved, packed off to Caelum as one-half of a breeding pair, and spying for the Cabal of the Tarot.

All without anybody actually stopping to ask her what *she* wanted.

And then, just to make things really interesting, she was due to give birth at any moment. Her pups, far from being safe, were now at the mercy of a fickle immortal who might decide, at any moment, that she no longer wanted the inconvenience of a breeding female.

Warlock sympathised with her plight, but wished she'd stop blaming him for it. The Cabal of the Tarot had placed them in danger, and Boots had just as willingly joined their cause as he had. In fact, she'd probably accepted their aid even *more* willingly than he had.

Their current predicament was the cost of that aid. Warlock wished she'd accept that and stop cursing him.

And things could have gone much worse for them, given their circumstances. They were well fed and housed in decent quarters in the basement of the palace with the almost unheard-of luxury of a room of their own. With Boots so close to her confinement, Elyssa had let her off everything but the most basic duties, and she treated them more kindly than any master he'd had since Lord Ordry—although he doubted the immortal was doing so out of any innate goodness; Elyssa was just proving a point to her brother.

Was she trying to ensure the loyalty of her Crasii?

It seemed a futile thing to attempt, really. Either the Crasii were magically compelled to obey or they weren't. There didn't seem much point to Warlock, to attempt to make them *more* loyal. Perhaps it was proof the immortals were just as ego-driven as any self-aware creature. Warlock had seen it many times among the racing dogs Lord Ordry bred on the estate where Warlock had served before his imprisonment: even when warned away from a savage beast, there was always someone who stepped forward, hand outstretched, convinced they alone could inspire such trust in a wild animal that it would override the creature's instincts.

He'd seen many men almost get their hand bitten off, believing that.

Fickle, mercurial and given to unexpected outbursts of temper, Elyssa nonetheless understood the value of love, if her twisted version of it could be called that. The Crasii were magically compelled to obey all the suzerain. She knew that as well as they did. But she lived in close proximity to a half-dozen other immortals, any of whom had the power to countermand her orders.

So Elyssa treated her Crasii like beloved pets, probably because—like the men who believed they wouldn't get bitten—she hoped it meant they would stay on her side, no matter what.

It was Boots who pointed out this harsh reality to Warlock, the day they'd arrived and been shown their quarters.

"This isn't so bad," Warlock had remarked, looking around the clean, dry—albeit quite small—room, they'd been informed was their new home.

"For slaves," Boots said unhappily.

"It could be worse, Boots," he said, closing the door on the feline who'd shown them the way from the slaves' common room on the floor above.

"My name is Tabitha," she corrected. "And I don't see how it could be any worse."

"Tryan could have taken you."

She turned on him furiously. "Tryan wouldn't have even known I'm alive, *Cecil*, if you hadn't promised Declan Hawkes you'd be his willing lap dog if only you had your mate and your precious pups by your side."

"Shh! Someone might hear you!"

"In this place?" she asked, looking around. "Tides, the walls must be two feet thick. It's like a dungeon in here, which is kind of fitting, really, don't you think?"

"What was I *supposed* to do?" he hissed, not quite as confident as Boots about the insulating effects of thick stone walls.

"You could have left me in Hidden Valley. Left *us* there," she corrected with a protective hand on her swollen belly. "But no, you had to get all noble and paternal on me and decide I couldn't possibly raise your pups as well as *you* could. So you have them drag me to Lebec and then ship me off into slavery in the service of a Tide-forsaken suzerain, who now has the power of life and death over all of us. Great plan, Farm Dog. Can't wait to hear what your next move is."

Warlock winced at her tone. And her words. She hadn't called him Farm Dog for months.

"I won't let anything happen to our pups. I swear."

"You don't have the power to make a promise like that, you big fool," she said. "Elyssa is a suzerain. She doesn't care about us. She only cares about retaining our loyalty and she'll do it with kindness only while ever it suits her. But you mark my words, Farm Dog, that bitch will turn on us some day. I just hope when she does, you're the one who has to serve the gravy she pours while she's dining on our babies. Maybe then you'll realise you're not nearly as clever or heroic as you think you are."

Chapter 8

"I want your word that you won't try to commit suicide."

Arkady nodded. Cydne Medura said the same thing every time he left the cabin. Even after nearly two weeks, he still wasn't sure of her intentions. "I promise I'll not kill myself until you get back."

Cydne glared at her, not very amused, but he let the comment pass. "How do I look?"

He was dressed in his best clothes: embroidered pants and vest, frilly shirt, puffy sleeves and many-buckled sandals. By Glaeban standards, with his long, dark, elaborately curled hair and lace cuffs, he looked ridiculous. If fact, she wasn't the least surprised the crew were picking on him, given the way he dressed. Arkady knew better than to say so, however. This was, apparently, high fashion for a sharp young man about town in Port Traeker.

"You look very handsome," she assured him. And then she added for good measure, "And manly. I'm sure the captain will be impressed."

"I'll settle for him ignoring me," Cydne sighed. And then he squared his shoulders manfully. "Well, into the fray, I suppose."

Before his courage could fail him, Cydne turned toward the door and stepped outside, revealing a glimpse of the guard—more proof he didn't trust her—who waited in the hall. She heard the lock turn on the cabin door and took a deep breath.

For an hour or two at least, while Cydne dined with the captain, Arkady would be alone. Time to wash, brush her hair; time to stare wistfully at that tray of scalpels, wishing she'd given her word because she was honourable and not just a coward.

If she was dead when Cydne got back, what difference would it make?

Arkady stepped up to the tray and picked up the longest of the wickedly sharp blades. Two weeks ago she'd been prepared to risk everything for a split second of opportunity. And yet, here she was, standing in front of all the shiny, sharp implements of death she could ever desire, debating whether or not she had time to wash her hair.

"Coward," she said aloud, placing the scalpel back on the tray.

Death is a last resort, she consoled herself. *The only way out of an untenable situation.* These days the situation wasn't nearly so fraught. She was still a slave, certainly, but she wasn't doing the rounds of the crew like the other women from the slave cabins. She was protected, safe from the crew, and while she wasn't exactly unmolested, Cydne Medura was so inexperienced and shy, their couplings were hasty, silent affairs that rarely lasted longer than a few tense moments while he vented himself inside her with all the finesse of a rutting canine Crasii.

Arkady didn't waste energy agonising over the time she spent in Cydne Medura's bunk. She was prepared to do whatever she must to keep him satisfied—a split-second decision she'd made when she'd impulsively thrown herself on his mercy, reasoning the attentions of one unwanted lover had to be marginally more bearable than the unwanted attentions of the entire crew.

Arkady consoled herself with the belief that this was the lesser evil. Letting Cydne Medura have his way with her meant saving herself from something far worse than the fumbling attentions of a painfully inexperienced young man who seemed, in the cold light of day, mortally afraid of her.

When Cydne told her he had trouble dealing with women, Arkady soon discovered he wasn't joking. The young doctor—odd that she thought of him as the *young* doctor when he was actually a year older than she was— stammered and blushed and couldn't look her in the eye most of the time. He was far less worldly than his newly acquired chattel and, she soon realised, burdened with almost crippling shyness around women.

Arkady smiled, and turned from the instrument tray. There was no need to kill herself yet. So long as Cydne Medura needed her to protect him from the jeers and contempt of his crewmates, she was in no danger of being handed around the crew for sport.

Perhaps she'd find a way to escape this nightmare yet.

Several hours later, Cydne returned to the cabin, his face flushed with the effects of too much wine. Arkady snapped awake at the sound of the key in the lock, her sense of danger heightened to the levels she hadn't known since living in the slums of Lebec. She scrambled off the bunk where she'd been dozing and hastily straightened the covers. Cydne allowed her to sleep on the examination table after he was done with her; she didn't think he'd be pleased to discover her stretched out on his bunk.

"You're shtill awake," he remarked as he stumbled against the door.

Arkady wasn't sure if it was the wine or the ship's heaving deck that made, him fall. She hoped it was the latter. That was another lesson she'd learned long ago—drunks, even basically nice ones, couldn't be trusted.

"Are you all right?"

Cydne nodded and stood up straighter, clinging to the doorknob for balance. He nodded. "I'm not ushed to this."

"The ship's motion?"

He shook his head. "Drinking with the captain," he said, pushing off the door. "You were right."

"About what?"

"About him thinking I'm a real man, now I have my own . . ." he stumbled across the cabin and slammed into the bunk, ". . . whore."

Arkady chose to ignore the insult and helped him up. "So . . . what? You tried to drink him under the table to remove all doubt?"

"I didn't mean to. Oh, Tides . . . I think I'm gonna be . . ."

Arkady snatched the wash bowl from the cabinet by the wall and thrust it under Cydne's head before he could finish the sentence. He vomited up what looked like an entire carafe of red wine and not much else.

Once he'd retched a few more times, he seemed a little better. Arkady carefully placed the bowl on the floor, helped him to sit, and then opened the porthole. She emptied the bowl into the ocean and left the window open, hoping to air out the smell.

"Fank you," Cydne mumbled, as she swirled some clean water into the bowl to rinse it out.

"We whores can be quite useful, you know," she replied in her own language.

He looked up, somewhat sobered now his stomach was no longer full of wine. "I've offended you, haven't I?" he asked in Glaeban.

"I can't be offended," she said, handing him a towel. "I'm a slave, remember?"

"I don't have a problem with Crasii being slaves, but I don't agree with human slavery, you know."

Arkady looked at him in surprise, as much for his comment as for the fact that he delivered it without stammering. The alcohol had relieved him of his shyness, apparently.

"Pity your father doesn't agree with you." She sat on the examination table opposite him and studied him for a moment in the flickering light of the shielded candle burning by the door.

"I did broach the subject with him once," Cydne said, dabbing at his mouth with the towel. "After I returned from studying in your country. He didn't appreciate me pointing out that Glaeba got along just fine with only Crasii indentured servants."

"Given his entire fortune seems to be based on the trade in human flesh, I can't say I'm surprised."

Cydne smiled sourly. "Yes, well you can probably imagine his reaction to my suggestion. After he stopped spluttering, he made me promise never to even think such a thing again. I suspect he was afraid the merger might be endangered if word got out about my radical views on slavery."

"He's merging with another slaver? Oh, goody. Even more Senestran privateers preying on helpless people. You all must be beside yourselves."

Cydne was too drunk to notice her sarcasm. "You have no idea. My marriage to Olegra will make my father's company the largest slave brokerage in Senestra, possibly the whole world."

The idea that this young man was the heir to the largest slaving empire on Amyrantha intrigued Arkady far less than the notion he was engaged. "You're getting *married*?"

He nodded unhappily. "Hence the reason I have been sent on this journey to purchase slaves from the markets of Elvere."

Arkady stared at him. She didn't see the connection.

"A few months ago," the young man explained, "my father arranged a marriage for me with Olegra Pardura."

"And?" she said, when he stopped and waited expectantly for her reaction.

"I forget, you know nothing of my country. The Pardura name means nothing to you."

"That's hardly my fault."

He continued as if she hadn't spoken. "You can't imagine what a stir it caused, both in and out of the family. The Parduras have interests all over the eastern hemisphere, you see, right up into Tenacia, and . . ." He smiled as he realised how little of that meant anything to Arkady. "Well, suffice to say, our engagement had both families salivating over the opportunity to increase their wealth and power."

"Had you ever met this girl before?"

Cydne shook his head. "No. But that never bothered me. I have always expected an arranged marriage, and Olegra Pardura comes from a fine family, is quite pretty, and of a reasonable age to bear healthy children."

"Which is all that really matters, I suppose."

"Trading dynasties can be more important than royalty in Senestra, Kady," he said. "So, yes, it matters a great deal. Besides, for any number of reasons other than the commercial benefits, I was looking forward to getting married."

Arkady found that hard to believe, but she didn't bother to say it aloud, preferring to hear the rest of his story while he was in the mood to talk. By tomorrow, when he'd sobered up, she doubted he'd be able to manage more than her name without blushing and stammering like a fool.

"You see, once I'm married, I'll be allowed to settle down and continue my work as a physician. My future bride has several brothers who are far more interested in trade than I am. The merger effectively gives me three brothers to carry the weight of my father's expectations."

"You keep calling it a merger. Shouldn't you think of it as a marriage?"

"Yes, well . . . you see that's where we ran into trouble. I'm not good around women . . ."

"I had noticed that."

He threw his hands up helplessly. "It's not that I don't *like* them. Tides, I just don't know what to *say*. Or *do*. And . . . and then parts of me start reacting on their own, as if I have another brain below my belt that doesn't listen to a word the one above it is saying, and I get embarrassed, and I start to stammer . . ."

"What happened?" Arkady asked, guessing they were getting to the crux of the story.

He sighed heavily. "The first time they left me alone with Olegra, I was so nervous I threw up in her lap."

"Oh."

"Oh, indeed." He shook his head sorrowfully. "You have no idea the trouble my anxiety caused. The insult to the Padura family nearly brought about a trade war, the likes of which we haven't seen in Senestra for centuries. It was only by my father refunding a sizable chunk of the dowry and promising that I would arrive at the wedding—which is scheduled a few days after our return from Torlenia, by the way—a 'real man,' that he was able to placate Olegra's family."

Arkady nodded in understanding. "Hence the beatings by the crew and your willingness to play along with my subterfuge."

He nodded. "I owe you a debt of gratitude, Kady. Your suggestion that I claim a woman for my own use—however selfishly motivated—has convinced everyone I'm now a *real* man. I find that vaguely disturbing, actually."

"I find it a great deal more than *vaguely* disturbing," Arkady said. "Still, I shouldn't complain, given how I've benefited from it. How long before we reach Senestra?"

"The captain says less than a week."

"And then you're getting married?"

He nodded. "Hopefully, I'll be able to keep the contents of my stomach down until *after* the ceremony."

She shook her head in wonder. "How does an educated, wealthy, well-mannered, good-looking young man get to be your age, in a society that has female human slaves catering to his every whim, and still be a virgin?"

Cydne blushed crimson. "I never said . . ."

"You didn't have to. I was there for your first time, remember?"

He glared at her, not so drunk that he had forgotten his place—or Arkady's—in the general scheme of things. "It is bad enough that you pity me, slave. I will not tolerate you scorning me as well."

"I didn't mean to—"

"Say not another word," Cydne warned. "I fear I have said too much and you most certainly *have* said enough." He lay down on the bunk, quite deliberately turning his back to her. "Please extinguish the lamps before you go to sleep."

He pulled the covers up, not bothering to take off his boots or his vomit-stained shirt, too embarrassed, or too shy, perhaps, to face her, now he knew she'd guessed his deepest and most humiliating secret.

Arkady stared at his back for a time, wondering if he really did mean to go to sleep in that state, until his soft snores filled the cabin. With a sigh, and more sympathy than she ever thought she would feel for a man who called himself her master, she slipped off the table and blew out the candles by the door.

In the darkness, she felt her way back to the hard, unrelenting surface of the examination table where she stretched out, wedged herself against the wall to prevent falling out of bed while she slept, and finally, after an interminable time, drifted off to sleep.

Chapter 9

"I miss Declan Hawkes."

Queen Kylia of Glaeba looked up from the table where she was lying, scandalously naked, while the blind masseur she'd recently imported from Torlenia worked out the knots in the muscles of her back. If there *were* any knots in her muscles. Being immortal, her muscles probably didn't knot up in the first place. Jaxyn couldn't even remember the last time he'd suffered a stiff neck.

She probably just liked being touched like that, he decided. Had he not been here, she might well have ordered the hapless young man to massage more than her muscles. Then again, this was Diala. Jaxyn's presence in the room probably wouldn't have made a difference one way or another, had she wanted more than the simple pleasure of a brisk rub-down.

"Why would you be missing Hawkes?" she asked. "Fancy him, did you?"

Jaxyn leaned against the windowsill with his arms folded. "He was a little too . . . leader of the pack . . . for my liking. But he was an ambitious son of a whore. Literally. And he wasn't overburdened with a conscience. Bridgeman's a flanking loyalist."

"Then get rid of him. He's only a stopgap spymaster until you find a new one anyway, isn't he?"

"That's the problem," Jaxyn said. "Good spymasters don't grow on trees, you know. They take years to develop their contacts, their networks. If I dispose of Bridgeman, I lose the spy network that comes with him."

"Doesn't he have a deputy?"

"That *was* Declan Hawkes. When Bridgeman retired and he took over, seems he didn't think he needed to start training his replacement just yet. Guess when you're young, even if you're mortal, you think you're going to live forever."

"So we're stuck with the old man," Diala said with a shrug. "Deal with it."

"But I want to know what Tryan and Elyssa are up to in Caelum. I need Bridgeman's cooperation for that."

"I thought you said you'd taken care of it?"

"I've got a couple of canines in their service," he said. "But they're not much use to me if they have nobody to report to."

Diala murmured appreciatively as the masseur found a particularly sensitive spot and then said, "Tides, Jaxyn, how hard can it be? *He's* the spymaster and *you* have the spies. Surely you can work something out."

"Bridgeman's more concerned about the coronation, at the moment. My desire for intelligence from Caelum is a long way down his list. If it's even *on* his list."

She smiled. "Well, I'm with Bridgeman there. I can't wait 'til the coronation is done with and I'm irrevocably the Queen of Glaeba."

"I'm sure you can't."

She turned her head to study him. "Is that a note of jealousy I hear in your voice, my dear?"

"And what would I have to be jealous about?"

"Well, I'm going to be queen, and you're going to be . . . hmm . . . what *are* you going to be, Jaxyn, dearest? My minion?"

Jaxyn smiled. "I haven't been your minion for a very long time, Diala."

Damn, he'd called her Diala in front of the masseur. The man might be blind but he wasn't deaf.

Oh well . . . nobody except Diala will lament his passing in some tragic accident.

Jaxyn was very good at arranging tragic accidents.

"But I remember when you *were* my minion. We had fun together."

"Until you screwed me over."

She smiled even wider. "I screw everybody over, Jaxyn. Don't take it personally." She glanced over her shoulder at the masseur. "Lower," she ordered. The man did as she asked and she sighed happily before turning her attention back to Jaxyn. "The point is, we're in this together and for once, I have the upper hand. I'll be queen and you'll be my right-hand man. There isn't a lot we can't do with that arrangement in place."

Having decided the masseur would have to die, Jaxyn no longer worried about what the man might overhear. "Or we could get rid of that idiot child you're married to, you and I could wed and—"

"You would be king." She turned her head away. "I don't think so."

"You'd rather stay married to the idiot child?"

"I find myself growing quite fond of the idiot child," she said. "Mathu worships me, Jaxyn. It's been quite a while since I was worshipped. I'd forgotten how nice it is."

"You're prepared to risk him interfering with our plans, just so you can be worshipped? Tides, you haven't changed much in the last few thousand years, have you?"

His open admission of their immortality in front of her servant surprised Diala. She turned back to him with a warning look, and then she must have realised what his words meant and glared at him instead. "Tides, Jaxyn, it took me ages to find a decent masseur."

"Make sure the next one is blind, deaf *and* mute," he suggested. "Or find a Crasii to do the job."

"Half the pleasure of a massage, Jaxyn, is the feeling of skin on skin. Not *fur* on skin. Besides, the canines can never keep their nails short enough, a feline is likely to shred you with her claws and an amphibian . . . well, they're just too damned slimy."

"Maybe you should teach Mathu how to touch you properly, then. It would give him something useful to do."

"Or *you* could learn. You are my minion, after all."

Not for much longer, you controlling little bitch, Jaxyn thought, entirely fed up with Diala's attitude. Her command of the Tide was moderate at best. He was a Tide Lord. She had no right to lord it over him like this. But for a lucky accident, she wouldn't even be here.

Tides, that day Arkady told me to bring her back a virgin, I should have come home and confessed to raping her. That would have put paid to Diala's plans to marry the Crown Prince of Glaeba, quick smart.

But he was stuck with her now, still regretting doing a deal with the Minion Maker instead of finding a way to remove her. Were it not for the politics of the situation, he would have declared himself long before now, and Diala be damned. But the Tide wasn't back enough for that yet, and in truth, until he knew where the other Tide Lords were, he really didn't want to announce his return.

For a fleeting moment, he regretted Stellan Desean's death too. Perhaps, if he'd removed Mathu sooner, things would be more to his liking. Diala would certainly have far less power than she wielded now, and be a few steps further removed from the throne, making Jaxyn's life much easier.

With Mathu gone, Stellan could have been king.

Then again, Jaxyn realised, even with Stellan as king, that would have made Arkady queen, not him.

Which reminds me . . . where is the magnificently disdainful Arkady?

It was more than a month since he'd sent his people to Torlenia to bring Arkady home. According to their last message, they still hadn't found her. He wasn't surprised she'd gone into hiding on learning her husband had been arrested.

He was astonished, however, that she remained at large.

Arkady had no resources, didn't speak the language and was altogether too inflexible to survive in a foreign country on her own, Jaxyn believed. Which meant either some ill had befallen her and she was dead, or she'd had help.

But who would help her? She hadn't been in Ramahn long enough to make the sort of friends who would court war with a neighbouring nation to aid her, and no Glaeban citizen living in Torlenia would risk a charge of treason by helping her, either.

Were it not for the fact that Jaxyn was certain Declan Hawkes was dead, he might have confronted the spymaster about her, knowing that—even ambitious as he was—his long history with Arkady and his unrequited love for her, might be enough to tempt him into betraying the crown.

Did Hawkes set up something before he died? An escape route, perhaps, in case something went awry while Arkady and her husband were in exile?

Was the dead spymaster's hand in this, even from beyond the grave?

"Tides, Jaxyn, are you even listening to me?"

Jaxyn blinked as he realised Diala had been talking to him all this time. "Pardon?"

"You haven't heard a word I said, have you?"

He shrugged, hoping she considered his inattentiveness a sign of boredom rather than worry. "Perhaps if you said something worth listening to, I'd take the time to pay attention."

"I was telling you that if you want Mathu to declare war on Caelum, you're going to have to produce something resembling solid evidence that they're planning to attack us first."

"Well, I would," Jaxyn said, "if I could get word from the spies I've planted in their palace." Jaxyn pushed off the windowsill and began to pace the room. "Why does he care, anyway? Caelum has insulted us. They've accused us of kidnapping their wretched princess. We've plenty of reason to go to war with them."

"I've told Mathu that. You've told him too. All he says is 'Stellan would pursue a diplomatic solution first before he'd start banging the war drums.'"

Jaxyn rolled his eyes impatiently. "How noble of our young king to worry about Stellan's opinion now, when the last thing he did for his cousin was to trump up charges against him, disinherit him and put him on trial for treason."

Diala smiled nastily. "You're the one who trumped up the charges against Stellan, Jaxyn. Now his poor, dear cousin is dead, Mathu's feeling quite remorseful about the whole sorry episode."

Jaxyn didn't doubt for a moment who had planted the notion of remorse in Mathu's easily impressionable head.

This has gone on long enough, Jaxyn decided. He needed to speak to Mathu. It was time Diala learned the influence *he* had over the young king was as powerful as her own.

"Well, just be sure you don't console him too well," he said, heading for the door. "We're going to have to do something about Syrolee and her wretched clan soon. War may be our only option."

"If Tryan and Elyssa decide to stop squabbling long enough to work in concert," Diala called after him, "they'll destroy this place and every mortal in it and you won't be able to do a thing to stop them. What will happen to your sorry little kingdom then?"

Jaxyn stopped, his hand on the latch. "That'll only happen if we don't get in first and declare war on them before the Tide peaks. Oh . . . but we can't go to war now, can we, because *you've* decided to prove your power over the idiot child, by advising against it."

Diala pushed herself up on her elbows, glaring at Jaxyn. She hadn't thought about the likelihood of a confrontation with the immortals scrabbling for power in Caelum in those terms, apparently.

"Get out."

"Gladly," he said, opening the door. Then he smiled as he drew on the rising Tide and added, "By the way, I don't think your boy there is looking too healthy."

He closed the door on a stream of most un-queen-like profanity, as the blind masseur collapsed against Diala, bleeding from his eardrums as the unbearable pressure Jaxyn had induced made them explode up into his brain.

·

Chapter 10

Declan vanished for two whole days after his grandfather died, leaving Stellan alone in the cabin with Nyah. The little princess fretted the whole time Declan was gone, worrying that something had happened to him.

Stellan fretted too, but for entirely different reasons.

The Duke of Lebec had never had to survive on his own before. Since birth, the slaves and servants who took care of his every want, his every need, had surrounded him. As the only adult here, and with the responsibility for an eleven-year-old girl suddenly thrust upon him, Stellan found himself having to learn how to cook, how to clean and—even more difficult than that—how to deal with a precocious, homesick child.

Despite Stellan's awkwardness around the physical act required to make a child with Arkady, he had always wanted to be a father. At least he had come to that realisation over the past few years.

Pity I didn't realise it sooner, he decided, mentally kicking himself for his naivety. He might have been less eager to follow the advice of all his well-meaning friends, from the king down to his Crasii servants, who'd all agreed he was too young for such a responsibility. They'd all encouraged him to send Kylia away when she was the same age Nyah was now, after her parents were killed in a boating accident and he'd found himself her guardian. Of course, he'd been much younger then, much less sure of himself, and desperately afraid that if he let his young niece stay in Lebec, sooner or later she would discover his secret and, however innocently, expose him.

The guilt resulting from that selfish decision haunted Stellan. Declan's revelation that Kylia was more than likely dead, and the young woman he had welcomed into his home was the immortal Diala, had all but gutted him. He was devastated to think he'd not recognised his own niece, riddled with remorse that he had opened his home to an impostor, and unreasonably jealous to learn that she and Jaxyn were in cahoots with each other.

Against all reason, that hurt the most. The idea that while he was swearing his heart to a young man he considered his soul mate, his *soul* mate was conspiring against him, and possibly even sleeping with the creature posing as his niece.

How they must have laughed at his ignorance, at his earnest desire for something that had proved even more unattainable in reality than it had in even his worst nightmares.

How many times had Arkady warned him to be careful?

That made him an even bigger fool, he feared. His wife had spotted Jaxyn for a fraud from the first moment she met him, and yet she'd tolerated his presence and lied to protect them both. Had she laughed about him too, behind his back? Had she shared her amusement at the antics of her foolish husband, blinded by love and the charming good looks of a young man over whom he was making a complete fool of himself?

And if she had shared his folly with someone, was that someone her childhood friend, Declan Hawkes?

It was that thought—more than finding himself responsible for Nyah; more than realising he was now a dispossessed pauper and would likely have a death sentence hanging over him, had the rest of the world not believed him to be already dead—which gnawed at his gut: the idea that behind those all-knowing eyes, Hawkes was blaming him for the fate that would now befall Glaeba.

Or he was laughing at him. Stellan wasn't sure which was worse.

He had no more time to dwell on his misfortune, however. The door slammed open and Nyah pushed her way into the tiny cabin, lifting the bucket onto the table with a slosh of chilly water.

"That cascade is *sooo* cold," she complained, dropping the rope handle. "It nearly gave me frostbite."

"It's probably fed from snowmelt coming from further up the mountain," Stellan said, smiling at her exaggeration. He held up the remains of the turnip he'd been chopping for their dinner while mentally berating himself for all the foolish decisions he'd made over the past ten years. "Did you want turnip stew, turnip stew or turnip stew, this evening, your highness?"

Nyah pulled a face. Like Stellan, she was used to much finer fare, and heartily sick of turnips, which seemed to be the only vegetable Maralyce bothered to store in her larder. "Is that all that's on the menu, Lord Desean?" She rolled her eyes. "Tides, and I was *so* hoping we could have turnips for dinner too."

Stellan frowned. "You should watch your language, young lady. It ill becomes a princess to speak like that."

"Declan says 'Tides' all the time."

"Declan's not a princess."

"Glad you noticed."

Stellan jumped a little at Declan Hawkes's unexpected reply. Nyah hadn't closed the door behind her, so he'd had no warning they were no longer alone. He certainly hadn't realised Declan was back from wherever it was he'd been.

"You've returned."

"Two piercing observations in as many minutes," Declan said, sounding impressed. "Pity you weren't so sharp a year ago when you met your new Kennel Master."

Stellan gripped the handle of the vegetable knife a little tighter, and chose not to rise to the provocation, mostly because he knew the criticism wasn't undeserved.

Declan shut the door and turned back to the table, leaning forward to see what Stellan was chopping. "Oh, look, turnips. Who'd have thought?"

"You didn't catch us anything edible then," Stellan inquired, "while you were off in the woods, communing with nature?"

"No."

"You've been gone for days, Declan," Nyah said. "Didn't you get hungry?"

"Apparently I don't have to worry about starvation any longer."

There was an odd note in Declan's voice, something that spoke of barely contained anger; maybe even fear.

It put Stellan's own woes into perspective. He was worried people thought him a fool; at worst that they might consider him a traitor. Declan Hawkes was having to contend with the unexpected and unwanted realisation that he was now a member of a very exclusive club that he not only despised, but had been actively working against for most of his adult life.

"Did you find anything?" he asked, although they both knew he didn't mean food. Declan was searching for answers, even more than Stellan was. His dilemma, in the general scheme of things, was far more traumatic.

"No, but I've made a decision."

"You're leaving." Stellan didn't know how he knew that. He just did.

Declan nodded. "I'll do what you asked. Or part of it, at any rate. I'll go to Torlenia and try to find Arkady."

"And the part you're *not* planning to do?"

"Bring her back."

Stellan nodded. He was neither surprised nor particularly disturbed to learn of Declan's plans. He could offer his wife nothing now, except a life of hiding, as the world unravelled around them with the rising of the Tide.

Declan, on the other hand, was one of the rare few now, one of the power-brokers. The tables had turned completely. The duke she'd married for protection was powerless and penniless, while the childhood friend without connections or wealth could now stride the halls of power with impunity. Declan had the power to protect Arkady.

And he loved her—whether he was willing to admit it or not.

"You're not coming back?" Nyah understood what Declan was saying, even if she didn't pick up on the undercurrent running beneath the adults' words.

"Isn't much point really," he told her, taking a seat at the table.

"But what about me?" she asked. "I can't just stay here in the mountains until I die of old age."

"I was thinking about that too." Declan looked up at Stellan. "You should take her home."

"Me? I'm a wanted man. And take her home to what, exactly? I thought you took her from Cycrane in the first place to save her from a marriage to an immortal with his eye on the Caelish throne? If I take her back, wouldn't that just be handing her over to her enemies?"

"Let's *not*!" Nyah suggested vehemently.

Declan was unmoved. "One way or another, the immortals are going to try to take the Caelish throne, and Nyah's absence, which has probably slowed them down a little, has only staved off the inevitable rather than prevented it."

"But we *can't* prevent it," Nyah said. "That's why Ricard Li asked you to hide me here in Glaeba in the first place."

"And the longer you're gone from Caelum, the more chance people start believing you're dead. Once they believe that, the throne is anybody's for the taking."

Stellan nodded in reluctant agreement. "I take your point, Declan, but I still don't see the reasoning behind it. How will returning Nyah to Caelum prevent precisely what you removed her to avoid?"

"We took Nyah from Caelum to prevent her getting married to Tryan. If we send her back and she's already married, then there isn't a problem. She can't get married to two men at the same time."

"No, but widows can marry whenever they want. And I imagine that would be the fate of any young man foolish enough to accompany Nyah back to Caelum and announce he's her husband. Who did you have in mind as this walking corpse, anyway?"

"You."

Stellan put down the vegetable knife. "You cannot be serious."

"I've never been more serious."

"I'm already married."

"Actually, you're dead, Desean. You don't even own that name any longer. So we'll make one up for you. We'll give you a history. I can get word to a few people I can rely on and can probably even send you over the lake with a few trustworthy retainers. You can grow a beard. I can show you how to bleach your hair. Tides, now I'm immortal, I can probably command a whole bunch of Crasii to lie about who you are and claim they've been in your service for years."

"But there are people in Caelum who know me, Declan. The *queen* knows me."

Hawkes dismissed his concerns with a wave of his hand. "People see what they want to see, Desean. Trust me—you're dead and died in prison a suspected sodomite. Nobody will associate the crown princess of Caelum's new husband with the dead and dishonoured sodomite from Glaeba."

"What's a sodomite?" Nyah asked.

Stellan gave Declan a look and then turned to Nyah, but before he could say a word, Declan said, "It's the reason you'll be safe with Stellan as your husband."

"Safe from what?"

"I believe Declan is trying to tell you I won't force myself on you, Nyah, because even if I could come to terms with the Caelish custom of having sexual relations with children, my preferences lie elsewhere." He met Declan's gaze defiantly. One thing this nightmare of recent months had taught him was that he was over lying about who and what he was, even to a child.

Nyah looked at him in disgust. "You mean you prefer . . . like . . . *old* people?"

Declan choked and turned away.

"*What?*"

"Well, you said you don't agree with our custom of marrying when we're still children, and that your preferences lie elsewhere. Does that mean you'd rather, you know, *do* it, with old women?"

Declan looked fit to burst something. And despite himself, Stellan smiled. Good intentions were one thing, but sometimes the reality was just too difficult.

"I'm afraid so," he said with a sigh, not daring to look at Hawkes, who was trying desperately not to laugh. "My wife . . . she was . . . almost thirty. And still it wasn't enough for me."

"That's really quite sick, you know, Lord Desean."

"I know. But I just can't seem to help myself."

"As for you," she said, punching Declan in the arm as she turned away from Stellan, the matter apparently disposed of as far as she was concerned. "How does a man know something like how to bleach hair?"

"My mother was a whore. I lived in a brothel until I was ten." He leaned a little closer and said with a conspiratorial smile, "I can tell you all manner of ladies' beauty secrets."

Nyah's eyes lit up. "Really?"

" 'Course, it won't be enough to tempt your new husband, what with his sick preferences and all . . ." Declan was talking to Nyah but he was grinning from ear to ear, and looking straight at Stellan.

Stellan glared at him, but decided not to buy into the argument. Nyah had an explanation and Declan was having a little fun at his expense. This could have gone a lot worse.

"Can you pierce my ears? Mother would never let me do it."

"Ears? Tides, I can show you how to pierce your nip . . . well, maybe not. But I suppose we can't do much damage if we just do your ears."

"Then do it elsewhere," Stellan commanded, as much to gain some time to think as from his desire to have some space to prepare dinner. "I'll call you when the food is ready."

They needed no further prompting to leave. Declan seemed to understand he wanted time alone, and Nyah was now set on having her ears pierced.

"Did you really grow up in a brothel?" Nyah was asking as Declan herded her outside.

Stellan didn't catch his answer. Declan closed the door and left him alone in Maralyce's small mining cabin with his turnips and the spectre of a future filled with lies, deception, a sham marriage and the threat of constant discovery.

Except for the turnips, he decided, *nothing much has changed.*

Chapter 11

"I wish to speak with you," Cydne Medura announced on the evening of their last night onboard ship. "About your future." The Senestran coast was in sight, the weather muggy and warm and the crew busy preparing the ship for their trip through the reefs and into the sheltered harbour of Port Traeker, on tomorrow's tide.

Arkady looked up from the tray of surgical implements she was gingerly retrieving from the bowl of boiling water she was using to sterilise them. He'd spoken in Glaeban, something he only tended to do if he wanted to have a meaningful discussion with her. Although she'd been learning the language, Arkady's Senestran still wasn't good enough to hold a conversation of any substance in it. "You mean I *have* a future?"

"You must stop answering back like that," he scolded. "Such a response when we get home will get you whipped."

"Yes, master," she replied.

"And taking *that* tone with your betters will only make things worse."

"Well, that's my problem, you see," she said. "I'm not used to having *betters.*"

He stared at her for a moment with a puzzled frown and then shook his head. "I see, you are being funny. This is your Glaeban sense of humour, yes?"

"I'm sorry, master," Arkady said, nodding meekly. Cydne had been remarkably good to her, and she didn't want to alienate him. It was just with Senestra so close and the future so uncertain, she was desperate.

Now was not a good time, she reminded herself, to let her desperation manifest itself as sarcasm. She had been remarkably lucky so far. Cydne Medura treated her with cautious disdain, torn between her status as a slave and his attraction to her obvious education, something unheard of in his world, where female slaves in particular usually didn't know how to read.

"I have been thinking about what to do with you when we make port."

"Your wish is my command, my lord."

Cydne shook his head. "I wish I could believe that, Kady."

"What do you mean?"

He shrugged, choosing his words carefully. "You are not a slave, Kady.

Not in your heart. You speak the words of obedience, but you don't mean them."

"I've done everything you've asked of me."

"You've humoured me, Kady, because, in your mind, I am the lesser of two evils. I worry about what will happen to you when you are confronted with a less understanding master."

"That's kind of you, sir, but you really don't have to worry about me. I'll find a way to . . . survive."

His eyes narrowed suspiciously. "You were going to say escape, then, but thought better of it."

"No I wasn't."

"Kady, I'm not sure how to impress this upon you, but you really must watch your attitude in Senestra. You are no longer a noblewoman. You are no longer a physician's daughter. You are a chattel and you must behave as such. There is no escape. You are a branded slave and you will always *be* a slave. You must begin to accept this."

"I'll try to bear that in mind."

Cydne shook his head. "No, you won't. I can see the defiance in you, just in the way you stand. You will not survive, unless . . ." He hesitated, and then, for no apparent reason, he blushed crimson.

"Unless what?"

"Unless you learn to do as you're told."

Arkady was fairly certain that wasn't what Cydne had been planning to say, but she didn't press the issue. Rather, she decided to get the conversation back on track.

"You said you wanted to talk about my future."

He nodded, as if glad for the change of subject. "I have it in my power to see you are placed in my care when we leave here."

Arkady stared at him in surprise. "But I thought I was just a wretched batch-bought slave? Aren't we the lowest of the low in your country?"

"Naturally—being *makor-di*—you would not be permitted to serve in the household, but I have duties as a physician that take me into the more . . . undesirable parts of the city on occasion, to treat those less fortunate."

"You mean Crasii slaves."

He nodded. "Among others. Admission to the Physicians' Guild in my country requires proof of one's altruistic intentions. I am always in need of a well-trained assistant to work in my clinic and accompany me on my requisite visits into the rural areas of Senestra. With your skills, you would be suitable. Although you would have to learn to speak our language better."

"So they make you take turns in treating the poor?" Arkady was surprised to hear it. Except for Cydne Medura, her experiences with the Senestrans thus far had been less than favourable. She was astounded to learn they could be compassionate. "That's not a bad idea, really."

"You see, you cannot help but judge us. You will not last long as a slave, Kady."

"Unless you decide to keep me in your service?"

"Exactly."

Given the alternative, Arkady didn't need to think about it for long. "Fine. Sign me up."

Cydne let out a woeful sigh. "Even now, you speak as if you have a choice; as if I am discussing options with you. Whether you approve of this plan or not is entirely irrelevant, Kady. You must understand that."

"I'm sorry."

"If only you were," he sighed. Then he squared his shoulders, as if bracing himself for something unpleasant. "There is, however, a task you can perform to prove your reliability. If you perform it adequately, I will consider allowing you to accompany me as my assistant when we reach Port Traeker and you will be spared the fate you are so desperate to avoid."

"So . . . what . . . this is some sort of test?"

"If you like."

Arkady couldn't see the harm in that. She even sympathised with Cydne's position. She knew she was going to make a lousy slave. She could hardly blame the young doctor for wanting to make sure of her before taking on the responsibility of such a fractious servant. And she was prepared to do whatever it took to avoid becoming a batch-bought slave slated for an early death after being shipped to a mining camp or a slave compound as a concubine.

"What is this test, then?"

"In four days, I am to be married."

"Yes, you told me that."

"I am expected to . . . know certain things . . ." He was all but cringing with embarrassment. "About women . . ."

Arkady frowned, not sure what he meant. And then she noticed he was blushing crimson again and she realised what he wanted from her. The idea seemed so absurd, she couldn't help but smile. "Are you serious? You're asking *me* to show you what to do?"

"Again you assume this is a request."

"You are a doctor, aren't you? I mean, you know the basic—"

"Do not mock me, Kady," he warned. "You have no status here or any right to question me. I have kept you with me up until now because your presence gives me status among the crew, and you appear to be disease free. There is nothing more to it."

"And *that's* your idea of being romantic, is it?"

Her question clearly puzzled him. "What?"

"Is that what you're planning to say to your blushing bride on your wedding night? *I have chosen you because your presence gives me status, dear, and oh, you appear to be disease free?*" She shook her head in wonder. "I'd be gearing up for that family feud you're so desperately trying to avoid, if I were you, Cydne. Once your new wife reports back to Papa about your bedside manner, you're going to be in big trouble."

He glared at her. "I am not asking you to comment on my . . . my bedside manner; simply to show me the most appropriate . . . you know . . . the physical things that might make my wife, perhaps . . . enjoy—"

"Why do you assume they're two different things?"

"What?"

Arkady sighed, finding it hard to believe she was having a conversation like this with anyone, let alone the man who currently considered himself her master and had shown little inclination to do much of anything in his bunk but get it over and done with in the shortest time possible. "There's a difference between making love and just having your way with someone, you know. And I'm assuming, since this is the woman you're planning to spend the rest of your life with, your goal is the former, not the latter."

"Well . . . yes . . . I suppose . . ."

"And I'm guessing Senestran custom insists your new bride will be as inexperienced as you are."

He nodded, looking very uncertain. Arkady thought he might be regretting ever raising the subject with her. He was asking for a lesson in technique, not a lecture. But this was a subject close to Arkady's heart. She had been in the place Cydne's future bride would soon be forced to go, and it wasn't pleasant. "Then put yourself in her shoes for a moment. Try to imagine what it must be like to be young and innocent, and in the power of a man you barely know, aware he can do anything he wants to you, and you have no way to stop it."

"Marriage is a woman's sacred duty!" he objected. "You make it sound as if I will treat her no better than a slave."

"If you march into the bridal chamber on your wedding night and the best compliment you can come up with is 'you're disease free,' I'm pretty sure that's what you'll be making her feel like."

The determined set of Cydne's shoulders began to sag. Arkady wondered how long it had taken him to work himself up to even mentioning this. He was a proud—albeit painfully shy—young man. The pressure of his upcoming nuptials, the weight of his family's expectations . . . all of it must be eating him up inside.

Desperation had made him bold, and she wasn't doing anything to help, she supposed. She felt a momentary pang of pity for him. It surprised her to discover she was even willing to consider helping him.

Arkady had never expected to feel sorry for someone who was, effectively, her gaoler.

"So, let me get this straight. In return for lessons on how to please your new bride, you'll keep me in your service as your medical assistant? Is that right?"

Cydne nodded. "It's a fair bargain, don't you think?"

Arkady shook her head. "Only a Senestran would think that."

He seemed to be growing impatient with her. "We dock in the morning, Kady. Either we have a deal, or you may return to the slave quarters now and await whatever the fates have in store for you in Port Traeker tomorrow."

When he put it like that, Arkady didn't think she had much choice, but he was asking a lot of her. This wasn't the same as lying there, blocking out what was happening to her body by detaching herself from the physical experience. Being able to lie there and convince herself this was happening to someone else, allowed her to survive.

What he wanted of her now was different. This would require her active participation. "How do I know you'll keep your promise?"

"Tides, woman! That I'm even offering you a choice is more than you should expect!"

That was the stone cold truth, Arkady suspected. The trouble was, in her entire life she'd had only one experience of making love she would count as pleasurable, and she certainly did *not* want to relive the intimate details of the one surreal night she had spent with Cayal in the Shevron Mountains so this inhibited young man could do the right thing by his bride on his wedding night.

On the other hand, she didn't want to be shipped off to a mining camp either.

Arkady sighed as she contemplated this impossible choice, wondering if this would be her life from now on.

Or maybe not. Those scalpels were right there on the tray, after all.

"What's her name? Olegra, isn't it?" *Coward*, she added silently to herself.

"Yes," he said, nodding his head.

"Then that's the first thing you should, do—say her name."

"What? Olegra?"

"Like you *mean* it," Arkady said. "Like the word tastes of . . . of pleasure . . . of delicious torment, even. You must say it as if the very mention of her name is a prayer, and you're worshipping at the altar of her body."

"What is the point of that?" he asked, a little annoyed.

Arkady resisted the temptation to slap him. "The point is to make her feel *desired*. Men don't need to be loved to take pleasure from a woman; they just need somewhere to plant their seed. Women aren't like that. To truly enjoy making love, they need seducing, coaxing. They need to feel as if they're *loved*, not just a convenient receptacle. They need to feel there are other reasons you desire them that don't involve treaties, mergers or exciting commercial opportunities."

This news seemed to be something of a revelation to the young doctor. "And this is more pleasurable for women? This emotional involvement?"

For a moment Arkady allowed herself to remember what it was to feel that, and then nodded with the wisp of a smile. "Oh, yes. It's much better that way."

"Then you will also instruct me in what to say."

Arkady nodded and took a deep breath. "Then, for the Tide's sake," she said, as she began to remove her shift, "the first thing you're going to have to do is learn to say her name without choking on it."

Chapter 12

"Cecil, bring me more wine."

Warlock bowed silently and brought the carafe to the table where the Lady Elyssa sat bent over a deck of Tarot cards, studying them intently. Outside, a rainstorm beat against the windows, punctuated by the occasional flash of lightning and the low rumble of distant thunder. It seemed to rain all the time here in Caelum, even more so than in Glaeba, and the palace, set high in the hills overlooking Cycrane, was a dark, dank and depressing place, which the relentless damp did nothing to enhance.

Warlock topped up her wineglass, glancing surreptitiously at the cards as he did so. He was surprised to discover Elyssa wasn't trying to read her Tarot. She had all twenty-two of the major cards laid out, and was sorting them into some kind of order he couldn't quite discern. The immortal glanced up as he approached and then ignored him and went back to sorting the cards.

He bowed again when the glass was full and retreated to his post by the door, not wishing to give the impression he had any interest in her game. That was a lie, of course, because Elyssa spent hours each day studying every card in the Tarot, and Warlock had never been able to figure out why. It drove him mad trying to work out what she was up to.

"In Crasii lore," Elyssa said without warning, "who came first, Cayal or Jaxyn?"

"I believe it was Lord Jaxyn, my lady," Warlock said, hoping he didn't sound taken aback by her unexpected question.

"Then that would mean *this* one goes *there*," she said, mostly to herself, as she rearranged the cards. She squinted at them for a time, staring at them with unmoving patience, as if she had all the time in the world and nothing better to do, which was—Warlock had to admit—probably the case.

"Cecil, according to your lore, who are the First?"

"Lord Kentravyon," Warlock answered, hoping she hadn't noticed his slight hesitation. "Lord Pellys and Lady Maralyce. They are the First."

"Why?"

"I don't know, my lady."

Elyssa pursed her lips. "And the Chaos Crystal? What do you know of that?"

Warlock shook his head. "There is no such thing in Crasii Lore, my lady. At least not that I've heard."

"You probably know it as the Bedlam Stone."

He shook his head. "I know nothing of any stone, my lady. Or any crystal." *But I'd very much like to know why you're so interested in it,* he added silently to himself.

"That's not surprising, I suppose," she sighed. "The Chaos Crystal probably long predates your existence. Have you ever served any others of . . . my kind?"

"I've not had the honour, my lady."

"You're very lucky, Cecil. Every Crasii alive would kill to be in your position."

"The Tides have blessed me with luck beyond imagining," he replied, hoping she took his words at face value and didn't hear the irony in them.

Fortunately, she was distracted by a knock at the door. Warlock opened it to Speckles, a dour and misnamed canine who'd been here in the Cycrane Palace since he was a pup.

"I have a message for my lady," Speckles announced.

Warlock stood back to let him enter. The tricoloured Crasii stepped into the room and bowed obsequiously to his mistress. "My lady, I have come to inform you that the bitch has started to whelp."

Warlock stiffened, his tail betraying his interest—and concern.

"Tabitha Belle?" Elyssa asked, looking up from the cards.

"Yes, my lady."

"Oh, goodie!" the Tide Lord announced. "I love watching them being born. How far along are they?"

"The Kennel Master says they should be born within the hour, my lady."

Elyssa stood up from the table, smiling delightedly. Her excitement over the imminent arrival of his pups worried Warlock a great deal. Elyssa's interest in their future was nothing short of remarkable. She had argued with her brother over keeping the pregnant female slave, and even defied her mother's wishes when Syrolee had tried to intervene on Tryan's behalf.

But why? Warlock couldn't imagine what she had planned for them. *Or why you're so interested in my pups when surely your Kennels can give you all the pups you want . . .*

"Cecil, are you listening to me?"

"My lady?" he said with a start, when he realised he was letting his concern distract him from the matter at hand.

"I said . . . did you want to come down to the Kennels and watch your pups being born?"

"Of course, my lady."

"Then we'll all go," she said, clapping her hands. "The change of scenery will do us good."

Warlock followed Elyssa and Speckles through the palace and down into the courtyard where the relentless tattoo of rain on the cobblestones made them slick and dangerous. Elyssa walked in the lead, untouched by the rain, while the two Crasii, wet and bedraggled, followed along behind her. When they reached the Kennels—which were more like dungeons than living quarters—Elyssa led them down a narrow staircase to where the isolation chambers were located.

Warlock heard Boots before they reached her; she was howling in pain and snapping at the midwife who was trying to tend her. When she spied Elyssa she snarled, but the Tide Lord didn't seem to notice. Her eyes were alight as she took in the scene; the smell of blood lay heavy in the air. Warlock knew humans couldn't smell things a Crasii could, but from listening to Cayal he'd learned how much the Tide enhanced the senses of those able to ride its magical waves. The reek of fear, pain and birthing fluids would have been almost as strong to Elyssa as they were to the canines in the room.

The canines, however, did not appear to be aroused by them.

"How are you doing, Tabitha Belle?" Elyssa asked, kneeling beside the pallet where Boots knelt facing the wall, panting in pain. The immortal reached forward to stroke her back, smiling. "There, there, girl. You're being very brave, aren't you?"

Boots nodded wordlessly, but her eyes fixed on Warlock with a look he took to mean roughly: *Get this evil bitch away from me and my pups before I tear her throat out.*

If only I could, he wanted to tell her. *I would get rid of her, Boots, if only I could.*

"The Kennel Master says you might have as many as three pups," Elyssa said. "Won't that be nice?"

"Yes . . . my . . . lady," Boots managed to gasp as another contraction ripped through her.

Warlock winced in sympathy, glad the fates had decided he be born male. Was it really necessary for the creation of new life to be so . . . so fraught? Maybe it was the Tide's way of ensuring one knew the value of the gift it had bestowed upon them, if one had to suffer for it.

Still kneeling by the bed, Elyssa turned to look up at him. "Have you thought about names yet, Cecil?"

"We've talked about it, my lady, but we've not decided on anything."

"Good," the immortal said, turning back to Boots as she raised her head and howled in pain. "Then I shall name them for you. Be brave, Tabitha Belle; it'll all be over soon."

There was something in the tenor of Boots's last cry that alerted the midwife to an impending change in the status quo. Pushing Warlock aside in a business-like fashion, the human midwife employed to attend birthing slaves pulled a stool up to the end of the bed, took a seat and raised a candle higher to facilitate a better look. She nodded.

"First one's crowning," she announced, as Warlock stood by helplessly, watching his mate writhe in pain.

No, she was more than writhing in pain. Boots was howling in agony, her hands gripping the rough fabric of the pallet until it was bunched and torn. The room was close and dank and smelt of blood. Watery blood trickled down Boots's thighs, pooling on the bed beneath her.

Elyssa stayed beside Warlock's mate, stroking her pelt comfortingly, doing nothing more than muttering useless platitudes.

Evil bitch, he thought. *The Tide is on the rise. You have the power to ease her pain. But you won't, will you? You're enjoying it.*

"Here comes the first one," the midwife said, as Boots's tortured screams grew even more agonised.

There's something wrong, Warlock decided in a panic. *This can't be normal.*

"Tides, help me!" Boots cried out in between her howls of pain. "It *hurts!*"

"There, there," Elyssa said. "It's supposed to hurt, girl. That's what makes it special."

Boots snarled at the immortal in reply, something no magically wrought minion of the immortals should be able to do. Warlock stiffened in fear, waiting for Elyssa to realise Boots was a Scard and order her and her pups immediately put to death, but she didn't react. Perhaps she thought Boots's growl was just another symptom of her labour and had not seen it for what it really was—the snarl of a creature who loathed and despised the suzerain and would cheerfully have mauled her, had she not been otherwise engaged.

"Push!" the midwife commanded, her voice barely audible over Boots's howls.

"I *am* pushing!"

"Then push harder," the woman said, her tone lacking anything even remotely resembling empathy for her patient's plight.

Boots howled again, even more tormentedly, which Warlock wouldn't have thought possible.

"Here it comes!"

He leaned forward in time to see a small, dark head appear. It hesitated for a moment, as if debating whether or not it wanted to leave the safety of the womb, and then Boots howled again as another contraction expelled the tiny creature, robbing it of the choice.

The midwife caught the pup expertly, wiped its face, stuck her finger roughly in its mouth to clear it, then turned the pup over and slapped it on the rump. The pup responded with a healthy howl of complaint. Nodding with satisfaction, the woman tied off the umbilical cord, unceremoniously severed it with a small dagger, and then thrust the pup toward Warlock.

"Take him!" she ordered impatiently. "I don't have three sets of hands, you know, and the next one's already crowning."

With a great deal of trepidation, Warlock took the pup, cradling it gently in the crook of his arm, unable to suppress the wave of paternal pride that washed over him at the thought that his firstborn was a healthy male.

Boots howled again as the next one appeared, even more rapidly than its brother. It too proved to be male, and was dealt with by the midwife, efficiently and impersonally, before being thrust into Warlock's arms to hold, once the cord was cut and the pup had demonstrated the strength of his lungs.

"Will there be another?" Elyssa asked. She wasn't ready, just yet, for the entertainment to be over.

The midwife stood up from her stool and walked to the side of the pallet. Boots was still on her hands and knees, panting in pain, but her howls had eased momentarily. The midwife poked her belly for a bit and then nodded. "Feels like there's another one yet."

Tides, three pups, Warlock thought. Rare, but not so rare it was remarkable. Under different circumstances he might have been happier to get the news, but given Elyssa's interest in his offspring, he suspected the fewer pups he and Boots produced, the better.

I was a fool to ever listen to you, Declan Hawkes. I should have taken Boots away from Lebec and headed out on our own.

In his arms, one of the pups he was awkwardly holding stopped crying. He looked down at it and for a moment the pup seemed to meet his eye, almost as if he knew who Warlock was. Then the pup sighed, closed his eyes, and promptly went to sleep.

Only to wake with a start as Boots howled in pain again.

"The third one's crowning," the midwife informed them.

"Three healthy puppies," Elyssa said. "Aren't you a clever girl, Tabitha?"

The last pup seemed rather more reluctant than its brothers to leave the womb, but eventually, in a whoosh of sticky blood and amniotic fluid, the pup slipped free. This one lay limp and exhausted in the midwife's arms and took considerably more encouragement than its brothers had needed to start breathing on its own. It was female, smaller and much more delicate than her ginger-coated brothers, with white paws and belly. Elyssa took it from the midwife once the cord was severed. The midwife then turned back to Boots and the soon-to-be expelled placenta.

"Who's a proud daddy, then?" Elyssa asked, grinning up at Warlock. "Three live pups. What a stud you must be, Cecil."

He had no idea how to respond to that; he just wished he had another arm so he could take the pup from her. He didn't like the way Elyssa was eyeing his daughter as if she was a particularly tasty morsel the suzerain couldn't wait to dine on.

"One more push," the midwife was telling Boots. "Then you can rest." It was the closest the midwife had come to expressing any sort of sympathy for Boots's agony.

Elyssa leaned forward to take a closer look at the two male pups. "Aren't they handsome boys?"

"Yes, my lady."

"Did you want me to name them for you?"

Like I have a choice . . . "I'd be honoured beyond words, my lady."

Elyssa thought on it for a moment and then smiled. "I shall name them for their birth," she said, reaching to touch his firstborn on the forehead. "You shall be Despair." To the second pup, she said, "You shall be called Torment." And then, to the tiny creature she held in her arms, she added, "And you, my sweet, shall be known as Misery."

Warlock was stunned. On the pallet behind Elyssa, Boots howled again, a cry of anguish Warlock suspected was in response to the immortal's dreadful names for their children, not the expulsion of the afterbirth that shortly followed. As soon as the placenta landed on the bed, Boots fell upon it and began to devour the bloody mess, her body craving the nutrients stored in it.

"Do you like their names, Tabitha Belle?"

Warlock's gaze fixed on Boots, her face bloody and savage, willing her to agree. The names Elyssa had inflicted on their pups were nothing compared to the fate of all of them, if the immortal ever realised they were Scards.

Boots hesitated, the primal instincts of her canine ancestors very much to the fore. Warlock held his breath.

"To serve you is the reason I breathe, my lady," Boots snarled after a long, tense pause.

And then she fell on the remains of the afterbirth again, devouring it with such vicious savagery Warlock was quite certain Boots was wishing the bloody mess was not a placenta, but the Immortal Maiden herself.

Chapter 13

"It's hot here."

Azquil turned from studying the green overhanging waterway they were slowly traversing, to look at Tiji. He smiled at her in that uncomfortable way he had of making her feel as if she was the only other creature on Amyrantha besides him. "I know. Isn't it wonderful?"

"Torlenia was hot too. You didn't seem nearly as keen on the heat there."

"Torlenia is a dry heat. Our kind prefers the humidity."

Our kind. The phrase was still new to Tiji, one she'd still not grown accustomed to in the weeks since they had found her, crossed the Docilae Ocean, and brought her here to the northwestern coast of Senestra—the last enclave of her own kind.

"You're looking very pensive again."

Tiji shrugged and felt her skin tone flickering once more. She wasn't used to being around people who could read her expressions, or her body language. Even Declan hadn't known her that well. Thinking of Declan made her think of Arkady—a thought followed, as usual, by a wave of guilt.

She'd let Declan down. She'd failed to help Arkady. She'd not been able to get a message to him to let him know that Cayal believed he'd found a way to die.

And yet, she'd found her own kind—something she had never dared hope she might do someday.

Tiji felt guilty then, for not feeling *more* guilty about not helping Arkady, or getting a message about the Immortal Prince to Declan. She turned to study the green leafy tunnel through which they silently sailed, the sharp-prowed boat slicing through the murky water. The three amphibious Crasii towing their boat swam swift and sure along a route they obviously knew well. Tiji admired their skill, quite certain that left to her own devices she would be hopelessly lost in the wetlands in a matter of minutes.

"I was just thinking of a couple of people."

"More human friends?"

"Sort of."

He shook his head in amazement. "I've never met a Lost One with so many humans they consider friends."

"I've only mentioned two."

"That's two more human friends than most of us will ever have."

"You don't like humans, do you?"

"I don't trust them, Tiji. Friendship doesn't really come into it."

"I'd trust Declan Hawkes with my life."

Azquil smiled and put his arm around her, squeezing her comfortingly. "Well, you won't have to any more. You're home now, and the Trinity will protect you."

Her new companion spoke a lot about the protection of the Trinity that the chameleons enjoyed. And he quoted them a lot too. It seemed the Trinity had a quote suitable for every occasion. Not wishing to constantly remind him of her ignorance, she'd never asked him exactly what the Trinity was, assuming the chameleons had their own set of gods, in much the same way the canines and the felines prayed to The Mother, the goddess credited—according their lore—with the creation of the Crasii.

"I still wish you'd let me get a message to him."

Azquil shook his head. "Our protection lies in few humans knowing we exist, even fewer knowing where we live. We cannot risk this spymaster of yours learning about us."

"But I have something very important to tell him. And Declan wouldn't betray us."

"You can't be sure of that, Tiji. He may even promise not to, and fully intend to keep his word. But there will come a time . . . some vital matter of state will lie in the balance—perhaps even this information you claim is so important—and he'll be forced to choose between his own kind and ours."

"But—"

"Trust me, my friend, the location of the last enclave of Chameleon Crasii is something a lot of humans would pay a great deal to learn. I know what *I'd* do, if I was human and put in that position."

Azquil's assessment of Declan's character was disturbingly accurate, so she decided not to pursue the matter. Maybe, once she'd been with her own people a little longer, they'd decide to let her send him a message.

The boat sailed on, emerging from the leafy tunnels of overhanging branches into a strange landscape of chequerboard greenery. She looked around in amazement as they emerged into bright sunlight and what seemed to be scores of surprisingly rectangular islands dotting a shallow lake that stretched for several miles in every direction.

"What is this place?" she asked, her eyes wide.

"Our farmlands."

It was then she realised the islands weren't islands at all, but floating platforms filled with topsoil, upon which the Crasii grew their crops. As they sailed nearer, she spied movement in the tall reeds of the nearest island, which had already been partially harvested. She wasn't sure what crops they were and it took her a moment to realise there were chameleon Crasii working the platforms, naked and almost completely hidden by their ability to blend with their surroundings.

It was a clever idea. If some adventurous humans stumbled across these strange floating fields, the workers only had to remain still and they'd never be spotted.

About a half-hour later, during which time Tiji's head swivelled constantly in wonder at the complexity of the network of floating fields, they reached the first sign of civilisation since sailing past the Delta Settlement several hours ago. It appeared to be an inn of sorts, a large house on stilts that doubled as tavern, store and trading post.

"Welcome to The Outpost."

"The Outpost, eh?" she said, studying the ramshackle building curiously. "Is everything in your homeland so poetically named?"

"It's your homeland too, Tiji," he reminded her.

"Then why does it feel so strange?"

"It will begin to feel like home soon enough." Azquil smiled. "And I'll agree, *The Outpost* is not exactly the most imaginative name for such an important place, but it serves its purpose. Once we're past here, you'll be treading ground that's never known anything other than the Trinity and Crasii footprints."

Tiji glanced over the side of the boat. "Seems more like I'll be treading water."

"Actually, from now on, we'll be on foot," Azquil said, as the amphibians rose out of the water and pulled the boat toward the small dock in the shallows. Tiji struggled to keep her balance as they tied up the boat, and then, with a nod to Azquil, the amphibians slipped back into the water and swam away.

"Where are they going?"

"They have their own settlement not far from here. They'll come back when they're needed."

Accepting Azquil's hand, she stepped up onto the dock, catching a whiff of something familiar and decidedly rank on the air—something she knew but couldn't quite place. "How will they know when they're needed?"

What is that smell?

"Lady Ambria knows how to call them."

"Lady who?" she asked, tormented by the familiarity of the odour she couldn't quite place.

"Lady Ambria. She's the left hand of the Trinity."

She frowned. "You keep talking about that. What exactly is the—"

Tiji stopped, staring in horror as a figure emerged from the trading post. It was a woman, a human woman at first glance, who seemed in her thirties, perhaps; certainly no older than forty. The newcomer was pleasant enough to look at, although there was nothing remarkable about her. She was dressed in a simple sleeveless shift, her long dark hair braided and hanging loosely over one shoulder.

The woman smiled as she approached, wiping her hands on her apron.

Tiji took a step back in fear.

"Azquil!" the woman explained. "You're back! And with a new friend I see."

The chameleon bowed respectfully. "It's good to see you again, my lady. This is Tiji."

The woman held out her hand, smiling. "Welcome home, Tiji."

Tiji backed away from her. She knew now what it was she could smell. "Don't touch me!"

The woman looked at Tiji for a moment and then turned her gaze on Azquil. "Silly boy. You didn't warn her, did you?"

He shrugged. "I didn't want to frighten her, my lady."

The woman nodded in understanding and turned to Tiji again. "I'm sorry. Azquil should have warned you about us."

"Us?" she spat, backing up so far along the dock that her next step would land her in the water. "There's *more* of you here?"

Azquil held out a soothing hand. "This is not what it seems, Tiji . . ."

"Not what it *seems*?" she said, glaring at the pair of them. "She's a *suzerain*, Azquil. Is that what your precious Trinity is? *Three* of them? You haven't brought me home to be free. Tides, you've brought me here to be *enslaved* again. *We find the Lost Ones and bring them home*, you said. Well, now I understand why. You don't want to help me. You're in league with the immortals."

Chapter 14

"He's here."

Declan glanced up from his ale at Clyden's warning and turned to see a man's silhouette in the open doorway; he was bending a little to avoid banging his head on the low lintel of the entrance to Clyden's Inn. Declan breathed a sigh of relief. Not only had he come, but as requested, he'd come alone.

The Lord of Summerton took off his cape, shook the raindrops from it and looked around the gloomy taproom. He spied Declan and made his way through the rough-hewn tables to the hearth where Declan was sitting, nursing his third ale of the morning. Apparently, now he was immortal, it was next to impossible for him to become intoxicated. Clyden finished wiping down the table, nodded a greeting to Aleki and headed back to the bar to wipe that down again too. This early in the day there were few customers and little else to occupy him.

"It would seem the people who attended your funeral were misinformed," Aleki said, sliding into the seat opposite Declan.

Declan forced a smile and signalled Clyden for another ale for Aleki. He'd been waiting for three days for Aleki to get here, hoping his message didn't fall into the wrong hands, hoping it was Aleki who answered his summons and not Tilly or another member of the Cabal he didn't trust quite as much. Although Tilly Ponting was Aleki's mother, and the Guardian of the Lore, Aleki managed to live his own life without feeling the need to let her dictate to him at every turn. That Aleki was yet to marry the woman his mother had chosen for him was proof enough of that.

"Do they miss me? All these mourners who took the trouble to attend my funeral?"

"A few of them might. How did you survive that prison fire?"

"Desean pulled me out and threw me into the lake. By the time I came to, we were halfway to Lebec in a rowboat."

"So Stellan is alive too?"

Declan nodded.

"And he's safe?"

"For the time being."

Aleki frowned, but said nothing more until Clyden had delivered his ale and returned to polishing the bar. "We haven't heard from you in weeks, Declan. It never occurred to you to get a message to someone before now, to let us know you were both alive?"

"I really haven't had the chance until now. Shalimar . . ."

"Is he all right?"

"He's dead."

Aleki was silent for a moment and then he said, "I'm so sorry, Declan. I know how much your grandfather meant to you."

"He's not suffering any longer."

"That's some small comfort, I suppose." An awkward silence descended on them for a moment, which Declan was in no mood to break. Better Aleki think any discomfort on his part was due to Shalimar's demise. It would stop him probing any deeper.

And it seemed Declan's explanation was enough to satisfy the nobleman. "So you're heading back to Lebec to tell my mother about Shalimar?"

"No," Declan said, with a shake of his head. "That's why I sent for you. I'm heading for Torlenia. You'll have to tell Tilly there's a vacancy in the Pentangle yourself."

"You're needed here, Declan—in Glaeba. Particularly with Shalimar gone."

"I'm dead, Aleki," Declan reminded him. "If I miraculously reappear now, it'll set off far too many questions—about Desean's fate as well as mine. It's better I *stay* dead."

Although he clearly wasn't happy about it, Aleki nodded in reluctant agreement. "So what's in Torlenia?"

"The Lord of Reckoning, for one. Somebody needs to find out what Brynden and Kinta are up to." It was a plausible reason to go south; one he didn't think the Cabal would find suspicious. "And I'm curious about something else too."

"Something important enough to defy the orders of the Cabal?"

"I don't believe I've been ordered to do anything different yet, Aleki. And this might be important."

Aleki took another swig of ale. "What is it then, that's so important you want to run off to Torlenia to search for answers?"

"A few months back, we caught a Caelishman in the sewers beneath the Herino Palace. He claimed he was looking for something. He didn't know what it was, but this ancient artefact is supposed to hold the key to ultimate power."

Aleki allowed himself a small smile. "So naturally, the first place one would look for it is in a sewer."

Declan smiled. "You know, that's exactly what I said."

"What's the connection with Torlenia?"

"Lord Torfail—or as his friends affectionately think of him, Tryan the Devil—sent this spy to look for it." Declan took another swallow of ale, hoping Aleki wasn't good at spotting a liar. He'd told the truth up until now, but the rest of this tale was going to be a complete fabrication. "Apparently, this artefact was last heard of in Torlenia, in the keeping of the Lord of Reckoning."

"That still doesn't explain what this man of yours was doing in the Herino sewers."

"From what I gleaned from our Caelishman during the interrogation, Tryan thinks Jaxyn got a hold of it from Brynden and brought it to Glaeba. And I don't think he was searching the sewers looking for it; he was looking for a way into the palace."

Aleki nodded, not convinced perhaps that this warranted investigation, but obviously believing Declan's tale. "I don't suppose the fate of the Duchess of Lebec has in any way influenced your decision to follow this tenuous lead?"

"Of course I'm worried about Arkady. And if I can help her when I get to Torlenia, I will. You know that, Aleki, and that I'd be lying if I denied it. Tides, your own mother would run me through if I did anything less."

Aleki nodded. "That's true enough. But what of Desean?"

"Ah, now that's where I need your help. I have a plan, you see, about the problem we have in Caelum with the succession."

Aleki took a deep swallow of Clyden's ale. "Tides, you worry me when you say things like that, Hawkes."

Declan smiled. "Just wait 'til you've heard the plan . . ."

Several hours later, as the tavern was starting to get busy, Declan walked out to the stables with Aleki. The Lord of Summerton was leaving for Hidden Valley, having agreed to send his men to Maralyce's Mine to retrieve Stellan and Nyah, to arrange a new identity and disguise for the former Duke of Lebec, and to get him and Nyah back to Cycrane with the news that the crown princess of Caelum was now legally wed. Married, Nyah would be able to take her throne, effectively blocking Tryan's attempts to do the same thing. It had stopped raining, but low thunder still rumbled in the distance. Declan glanced up at the sky. It wouldn't be long before the next downpour.

"You know, there's a good chance the first thing Syrolee will do is order Stellan Desean killed," Aleki said, as he opened the stall where his horse had been stabled during their meeting. "And not because he's an impostor, or someone recognises him. It'll be because regardless of his identity—real or imagined—that's the fate awaiting any man fool enough to get between the Empress of the Five Realms and her ambitions for her son."

"Not if you wait until Tryan marries the queen."

"How do you know Tryan's going to marry the queen?"

"What else can he do? The longer Nyah is missing, the more people believe she's dead. The only way to secure the throne after that is to marry the current queen and get a child on her. I give it another month with no sign of Nyah and Tryan will be announcing his engagement to the current Queen of Caelum."

Aleki didn't seem nearly as optimistic about Declan's reading of the situation as he was. "If Tryan marries Jilna and Nyah returns, surely they'll just kill the queen *and* Stellan and we'll be right back where we started."

Declan shook his head. "That's too many unexplained murders for even the Emperor and Empress of the Five Realms to explain away."

"You've got to wonder why they bother," Aleki said, leading his horse out of the stall. "I mean, they command the elements. They control Tide magic, for pity's sake. Why go to all this trouble? Why not just bend the world to their will with a wave of their arms?"

"Maybe it's not that simple," Declan suggested.

"I don't know," Aleki said, swinging up into the saddle. "In my experience, most people don't give a rat's arse who rules them, provided they've got food on the table and a roof over their heads."

"You see, that's the problem," Declan said, stepping back as Aleki gathered up his reins. "It's only *most* people who don't care. But there's always the people like us—the people who *do* care. We might be few in number, but we can make an awful lot of trouble for an evil despot who really just yearns for a cooperative world full of malleable minions to lord it over."

Aleki pursed his lips thoughtfully. "Better to go through channels so everybody thinks you're legitimate? Is that what you're suggesting?"

Declan nodded. "A bit more trouble in the short term, but a whole lot less work in the long run. Less of those pesky secret societies devoted to securing your downfall too."

That made Aleki smile. He leaned down, offering Declan his hand. "Take care, my friend."

"I will," Declan promised. "Torlenia's a strange, barbaric place."

"I had the road between here and Whitewater in mind, actually. A lone rider is a tempting target to a hungry bandit. And I'm a busy man. I haven't the time to attend another funeral for you, you know."

"Don't worry, Aleki," Declan said. "You won't have to attend my funeral again. I promise." It was as close as Declan could come to admitting the truth.

Aleki didn't know that, of course. "When you get to Torlenia, make contact with Ryda Tarek," he suggested. "If there is anything to this arte-fact story, I'm sure he'll know of it. At the very least, he can keep the rest of the Cabal informed of your progress."

"Good idea. I'll be certain to look him up," Declan said, making a prom-ise he had no intention of keeping. He didn't like Ryda Tarek. He definitely wasn't going to risk the man learning his dreadful secret.

"And if you find Arkady, give her my love."

"I will."

Aleki turned his gelding's head toward the entrance to the stable and walked him outside. Declan watched him leave, relieved beyond words that his meeting had gone so well. Aleki obviously couldn't tell there was anything different about him. He hadn't been suspicious at all.

But why would he? Declan thought. *In what wild nightmare would you imagine one of your most trusted and highly placed associates in the organisation devoted to destroying the immortals, had become one himself?*

There was no answer to that question, and Declan didn't have the time to find one, anyway. As Aleki rode away, another person entered the stable. This one was a canine Crasii dressed in a tailored tunic, indicating he was probably a manservant. The Crasii was leading two horses, one of them fine enough to belong to a nobleman, the other a much more ordinary beast that was probably his own mount. This was, in fact, the first Crasii Declan had encountered since the night he'd been immolated and made immortal.

Before he could say a word to him, however, the canine's eyes widened in shock. Letting go of the horses he fell to his knees in front of Declan.

"To serve you is the reason I breathe, my lord."

Tides, Declan thought in annoyance. *Every Crasii I meet is going to act as if I'm a flanking Tide Lord.*

To which a small, ominous voice in his head replied . . . *That's because you are.*

PART II

A single breaker may recede; but the tide is coming in.

— Thomas Babington Macaulay
(1800–1859)

Chapter 15

Arkady was invited to Cydne Medura's wedding, along with every other slave, human and Crasii, belonging to the Medura and Pardura clans. The whole of Port Traeker, a city comparable in size to Herino, turned out for the celebrations, wearing either the blue of House Medura or the bottle green of House Pardura.

Cydne's father even had some slaves brought in from his country estate. Under no circumstances would the Pardura family be allowed to suffer under the misapprehension that they owned more of anything than the Meduras.

From her seat far back in the grand hall of the palace belonging to Olegra's family—a building so grand and opulent it made Lebec Palace look like a cosy country cottage—Arkady could barely make out the wedding party, let alone the expressions on the faces of the bride and groom. She could imagine them, though. Cydne would be looking pained, his father relieved and his bride . . . well, it was hard to say. The closest Arkady had come to her was earlier in the day when she passed by as Arkady was lined up along the route from the Pardura Palace to the Town Hall—where all marriages were formalised—along with all the slaves belonging to both families, who were under strict orders to cheer the couple until they were hoarse.

Olegra had seemed a pleasant enough young woman from a distance. Dark-haired, brown-eyed and a little plump, something prized here in Senestra, particularly among the powerful and ridiculously wealthy merchant class, who considered a woman with "a bit of meat on her" to be proof of both her wealth and her ability to appreciate fine food. For Arkady, who was naturally slender, this proved to be an unexpected boon. After a lifetime of being the first woman in a room a man would look at, she was now the last, which meant she was, for the most part, left alone. There were plumper, more desirable slaves to lay with than the strange, skinny Caelishwoman, who didn't even speak the language properly.

"Did . . . you . . . want . . . that . . . fish?"

Arkady turned her attention from the wedding party and looked at the man who was speaking to her. He was a large, hirsute man with a thick black beard, a well-muscled body and a brand identical to Arkady's on his chest. He was sitting on her left and spoke haltingly, almost yelling, as if he could overcome her lack of comprehension with volume.

"Pardon?"

He pointed to the dish in front of her. She'd only eaten half of her meal, finding the battered fish too spicy for her palate. "You want?"

"No," she said, offering him her plate. "You can have it."

The man took the leftovers from her and wolfed down the remains of her meal, handed her the empty plate, and without so much as a thank you began looking around for anybody else who'd not finished their dinner.

This feast, Arkady had learned, might go on for days, and because the Parduras were trying to impress the Meduras, the fare—even the meal served to the slaves—was quite spectacular. Arkady might have even enjoyed it had it not been for the fact she was sitting at the slaves' table and that—like every other slave in the hall, male or female—she was naked from the waist up.

It was clear now, why she'd been branded on the breast. It wasn't to hide her status as a slave; it was to display it. In Senestra, clothes were the privilege of free men. All slaves, regardless of race or species, wore a short linen loincloth and skirt, the coloured edging on the hem denoting their house and their rank. Arkady's skirt was banded in blue—the colour of the Medura family—and a single thin band of black, which apparently indicated that she was a *makor-di*, the lowest of the low, fit only for menial labour in the worst jobs.

She was still uncomfortable walking around in what was—by her standards—pretty much nothing at all, but with everyone else dressed (or undressed) in the same fashion, it was a little less harrowing. She had overcome her initial mortification when the slave-master at Cydne's palace had taken her shift and handed her a short skirt and nothing else to replace it, but sitting here in a hall crowded with hundreds and hundreds of people with her breasts bared, still left her feeling queasy.

The other slaves, sensing her embarrassment, laughed among themselves at her prudishness. When she glanced down the table, Alkasa, one of her companions on the journey from Torlenia, caught her eye. She cupped her large painted breasts—this was a wedding, after all, and they'd all been daubed in blue and green designs to symbolise the union between the two great houses—with both hands and pointed them at Arkady, waggling the nipples at her. Then she said something Arkady didn't catch to the women around her, and they all began to do the same.

"Yours are better."

She realised the man who'd eaten her leftovers was talking to her again.

"I beg your pardon?"

"You got nicer tits than Alkasa."

"How noble of you to notice," she replied in Glaeban, certain he wouldn't understand.

"You'd get laid more often if you were chubbier, though. Men don't like bangin' into a sack of bones. You gonna eat that bread?"

"Be my guest," Arkady said, as she handed him the crust of her bread, deciding starvation might be the go, if putting weight on was going to make her more desirable to these people.

"I'm Geriko," the man said, smiling at her. "What's your name?"

"Kady."

"You don't speak too good. You stupid or something?"

She smiled in spite of herself. "I'm still learning to speak your language."

"I could tell you was foreign," he said. Since learning she wasn't stupid, but merely foreign, he'd stopped yelling at her to make himself understood. In truth, she could make out most of what he was saying. She just wasn't that good at *speaking* Senestran yet.

"Really? What gave it away?" *Besides my skin colour, my eye colour, the language difference . . .*

"You're too tall. And you're too skinny. And you walk like you're proud of it. And your brand's still fresh."

And the only reason you know that is because you've been staring at my breasts long enough to establish the age of my brand and that they're nicer than Alkasa's. "You're very . . ." She wanted to say *observant* but didn't know the Senestran word for it . . . "You look well."

He smiled, totally misunderstanding her meaning. "You think so?"

Oh, Tides . . . "You *see* things well," she said, and then on the slim chance of directing his thoughts away from her breasts, she added, "Where do you work?"

"In Doctor Cydne's clinic. I keep the Crasii scum under control."

"Crasii *scum*?"

He nodded. "They get all snarly and snappy when they're sick. I'm there to make sure they behave themselves."

Arkady glanced down the hall at the tables even further from the wedding party than her own. That's where the Crasii sat. She was wrong to think the *makor-di* were the lowest of the low. The Crasii, the *celum-di*, ranked even lower in Senestra's complicated caste system than batch-bought human slaves.

"That's where I'll be working too." At least, Arkady hoped that's what she said. She might have said *the table leg has three eyes* for all she knew. Senestran wasn't an easy language to master.

Geriko smiled. "Then we'll be working together. Did you want to bunk with me too?"

Clearly tact, delicacy or any pretence of seduction weren't skills considered necessary among the slave caste. "Er, no . . ."

"You have another mate?"

"No."

He nodded in understanding. "Ah! *You* are the master's *wii-ah*."

"The master's *what*?" Arkady wasn't familiar with the word.

"His *wii-ah*," Geriko said. "It means . . . his . . . toy . . . plaything." He grinned broadly and leaned a little closer. "We heard the young master spent the entire voyage to Torlenia locked in his cabin with a foreign slave. Quite a few people lost money on that voyage."

"I thought the whole trip was quite successful."

"Oh, it was a commercial success, sure enough," Geriko agreed. "People lost money betting on Cydne locking himself in his cabin with a sailor, is what I meant."

Poor Cydne, Arkady thought, still a little amazed that she pitied the man who now effectively owned her. *They really do have it in for you, don't they?*

But there was an opportunity here, both to protect herself and do the young doctor a favour. And she owed him something, she supposed. She wasn't due to be shipped off to a mining camp as soon as the wedding celebrations were done, and that was entirely due to Cydne's intervention.

"It was quite a voyage," she told Geriko. "He was . . ." she hesitated, not knowing the Senestran word for insatiable, ". . . very hungry. At it all the time. Like a rutting stallion."

Geriko's eyes lit up to hear such valuable gossip. "Like a *stallion*?"

Arkady nodded, warming to the subterfuge. She leaned a little closer and added in a low voice, "He's built like one too. Damn near wore me out with it."

The slave stared at her in amazement and then looked toward the wedding table with new respect. "Really? *Cydne*? Who'd have thought?"

Arkady smiled, wondering how long it would take for the rumour to spread that Cydne Medura was not only well-endowed but an insatiable lover, to boot.

I think that makes us even, Cydne, she told him silently.

And then she turned and smiled at Geriko. If she was going to find a way out of here, if she was ever going to escape Senestra and her fate as a slave, she needed friends.

The big bearded slave who'd be working in the clinic with her, who didn't mind that she was skinny and who liked her breasts, was as good a place as any to start.

Chapter 16

"The city welcomes you."

Declan turned to the sailor who'd spoken to him. "How do you figure that?"

"The Crystal City has turned on her light show for you."

Declan squinted in the glare of the crystalline cliffs of Ramahn as his ship made its way through the heads. The cliffs and the city walls above them—assaulted by eons of crashing waves—were encrusted with salt which had been baked by the harsh sun into a glistening wall of crystal. As it usually did at this time of year, the rising sun illuminated the encrusted cliffs, setting the whole city alight, making it almost too bright to look upon.

"The Crystal City's a whore. She turns it on for every man."

The sailor laughed, revealing a row of unevenly coloured teeth. "You've been to Ramahn before, I see, if you know her well enough to call her the Whore."

"Once or twice."

"Then you'll not need to be warned about the Whore's habit of devouring strangers."

Declan shook his head. "Thanks, but I think I can cope."

The sailor moved off in response to a shouted command from the first mate, leaving Declan and the other passengers on the small freighter to admire the sparkling city walls. Declan fretted a little at the time he had taken to get here, as the sailors reefed the sails and the helmsman fought the rudder against the incoming tide. It was over a month since he'd left Clyden's Inn after speaking to Aleki. He hoped everything was working out as he planned for Nyah and Stellan, but in truth, he'd spent little time worrying about it.

He'd spent far more time wondering if he really did have the power to direct the wind and send his ship flying south; almost as much time as he'd spent worrying about what might happen if he tried.

Once he was disembarked, cleared by the Customs men and suitably warned about behaving himself while a guest in Torlenia—a warning delivered to all unaccompanied men on the ship—he shouldered his pack and headed into the city.

Of the many things Declan Hawkes had learned from the old King's Spymaster, Daly Bridgeman—and one of the first things the Cabal of the Tarot had taught him—the most useful tip was not to rely on official channels, which could be disrupted all too easily. The vagaries of war, the death of kings, sometimes the sheer inefficiency of bureaucrats, were all capable of interrupting the flow of information an effective spymaster needed to do his job. Because of that advice, Declan had long ago set up a series of protocols for his spies to contact him or leave information for him, which he didn't want to fall victim to the whim of chance or, worse, an overworked or corrupt government official.

The drop-point Declan had arranged with Tiji in Ramahn was in a tavern called Cayal's Rest. He'd chosen it because it was located in the central market of Ramahn and because it was a name he (or anyone in the employ of the Cabal) wasn't likely to forget. He was very glad he'd arranged the drop too, given that he was now supposed to be dead and appearing at the front door of the embassy asking if any of his spies had left a message for him, might prove somewhat problematic.

He ordered ale from the barkeep, looked around at the sea of unfamiliar faces and then asked the man if anybody had left a parcel or a letter for him. After a discreet exchange of currency, and the mention of a prearranged password, the barkeep admitted he did have such a letter and handed over a small packet with Declan's name scrawled across it in Tiji's spidery scrawl.

Declan took the packet to a booth in the back of the taproom, swallowed down half his ale and then opened the letter.

Not sure if you'll ever get this, the letter began. *But I'm leaving it here on the off-chance you'll send someone to follow. As you suspected, the person of note you thought might be a suzerain is exactly what we suspected and it is your friend's view that she's probably arranging things to facilitate her lover's return when the Tide peaks.*

Thought this might be a problem and then I got the news today that the Duke of Lebec was arrested. I don't know what this means for your friend. I thought of trying to get into the Royal Seraglium to see her, but I don't think I'll be able to, because something else has come up.

I have found the prisoner who escaped from Lebec with your friend's help.

I've seen him twice now, the first time when I was in the seraglium. Today I saw him again drinking in this very tavern. I followed him to the Temple of the Way of the Tide and heard him talking to one of the priests. I think he's heading for a certain person's stronghold in the desert, so I'm going to follow him. I'm sure your friend will be fine. Her new hostess likes her and I don't think she'll just hand your duchess over to the Glaeban authorities so they can send her home to stand trial for something she didn't do.

Or maybe she will. Who can tell with the suzerain?

I've booked passage on the next caravan travelling to the abbey. It leaves tomorrow.

I'll try to get word to you from there. Don't worry about me.

Tiji

He read the letter through twice, smiling at her attempts to be evasive, which he didn't think very effective at all. Anybody with even a passing acquaintance with the characters involved would be able to identify the people she was so desperately trying to protect.

And then he sighed, tore up the letter, and began burning the pieces, one at a time, using the candle on the table. *Tides*, Declan thought. *She went after the Immortal Prince.*

He shouldn't be surprised, really. That was too much temptation for a little Crasii with an abiding hatred of the suzerain. But what had happened to Arkady? He would have heard if she was still a guest at the palace; the whole city would be talking about it. There would have been a major diplomatic incident over the notion that a Glaeban citizen wanted by the Glaeban crown was being offered sanctuary in the Torlenian Royal Seraglium and they were refusing to hand her over.

That might mean Arkady had already left the seraglium. Maybe of her own free will and maybe not.

I could always just turn up at the palace, make an appointment to see the Imperator's Consort, and ask her what she's done with our missing duchess, I suppose.

Which was a grand plan, except for two small problems. He'd never get in to see the Imperator's Consort in the first place, and even if he did, she would be able to tell from across the room that he was immortal.

Declan wasn't ready for the news to get about among the rest of the immortals that another had joined their ranks.

He didn't think he *ever* would be ready for that moment.

The chances were good that someone at the Glaeban Embassy had at least an inkling about Arkady's whereabouts. He couldn't knock on the front door of the embassy, however, any more than he could arrive unannounced at the royal palace. He was supposed to be dead, and it wouldn't take long for word to reach Glaeba that he wasn't if he miraculously turned up in Torlenia.

That meant finding someone who might know something, outside the walls of the embassy. And while he was at it, he had to ensure he didn't betray the fact that the King's Spymaster was alive and well and lurking about the Torlenian capital, undoubtedly up to no good.

Declan sighed again as he burned the last pieces of Tiji's note.

There was only one thing for it, really. He was going to have to kidnap a stray Glaeban embassy official off the streets, frighten him into submission, interrogate him, possibly cause him grievous bodily harm and all while not betraying his own identity.

Why is there never an easy way to do these things?

Declan found a likely victim a few days later, after lurking in the street outside the embassy in the hope that someone had some social engagement or official function they were required to attend. Just as Declan was starting to think the entire embassy was under house arrest, the main gate opened and a lone horseman ventured forth, after waving to the feline Crasii on the gate and saying something Declan couldn't hear from his post behind the bushes outside what he thought must be the embassy for the Commonwealth of Elenovia. Given the garden beds on the lawn leading up to the entrance were laid out in the shape of the three nation-states that made up the Commonwealth, it was a reasonable assumption. Declan cursed his inability to hear what the man said. It would have been useful to know where he was headed, but his magical abilities didn't include super-hearing, apparently.

And then Declan slapped his forehead at his own stupidity.

He might not have super-hearing, but there wasn't a Crasii on Amyrantha—unless they were a Scard—who wouldn't now do his bidding without question.

To serve me, after all, is the reason they breathe . . .

As soon as the man had ridden a short way down the street, Declan stepped out from his place of concealment and crossed the road to the embassy gate.

The felines had come to attention before he was halfway across the street. By the time he reached the gate, they were on their knees, and sure enough, as soon as he stopped at the gate, the senior feline bowed her head and said, "To serve you is the reason we breathe, my lord."

Tides, Declan thought, *they could turn every Crasii on the planet against us.*

Declan still thought in terms of "them" and "us." He'd yet to come around to the notion of "we." But at that moment it occurred to Declan why his grandfather, and Tilly and all the others in the Cabal, worried so much about the immortals. He'd known on an intellectual level, of course, but now he understood it in his gut. It wasn't so much the cataclysms they could cause—they tended to hurt the immortals almost as much as their human victims and, as a rule, excesses were attributed to only a few of their number. It was that the viability of all the nations on Amyrantha was underpinned by the Crasii, a slave force that could, on the whim of a Tide Lord, be turned against the rest of the population.

"The man who just left here. Who was he?"

"Dashin Deray, my lord," the feline replied without hesitation.

"Where was he going?"

"To the home of Lord Nisenly, my lord, the Trade Secretary of the Tenacian Embassy. They meet each week to play cards."

"Where does Lord Nisenly live?"

The feline gave him the address and instructions on how to get there with the same eagerness as she'd answered the rest of his questions. When she was done, he glanced at the other three guards. "You will tell no one you have seen me or spoken to me. Understood?"

They all nodded fervently, leaving Declan marvelling at their need to please him. He turned to go, but the senior feline, the one who'd done all the talking thus far, called him back. "My lord?"

"What?"

"If I may presume, my lord, whom do we have the honour of serving?"

He stared at her blankly for a moment, not sure what she meant. "What?"

"Are you the Emperor of the Five Realms, my lord? The Immortal Prince? The Devil? The Lord of Reckoning?"

"I'm . . . the lord of nothing," he said, and then realising he could well wind up carrying such a ridiculous title into eternity, he added, "It is none of your concern who I am. How dare you even think to ask such a thing!"

The feline prostrated herself on the ground before him, begging his forgiveness for her temerity.

Declan didn't answer her, thinking that's what a Tide Lord would do.

Instead, he turned on his heel and strode away, hoping his arrogant manner and the strange magical compulsion under which these creatures laboured, were enough to keep them silent.

"I . . . can't . . . breathe!"

Declan eased off the pressure around his victim's neck but kept his knee planted firmly in the small of the man's back. Dashin Deray struggled weakly against Declan's superior strength. He wasn't a fighter in any case. He was a bureaucrat with a long history of good living behind him. He wasn't equipped to fight off a determined thief, which is what he thought Declan was.

"My money . . . my purse . . . take them . . ." he gasped in Torlenian.

"Thank you," Declan said in Glaeban, reaching forward to relieve him of the burden. It hadn't occurred to Declan until that moment, but some extra cash might come in handy. He glanced up and down the alley where he'd dragged the man after knocking him from his horse, relieved to find they were still alone. It was late, past midnight, and in this part of town all the decent people were long abed. "Don't mind if I do."

Realising his attacker had addressed him in his own language, Deray tried to twist around to look at him. Declan put paid to that notion by increasing the pressure on the man's kidneys. "You're . . . Glaeban . . ."

"How observant of you to notice."

"Are you going to . . . kill me?"

"I might," Declan said, hoping he sounded indecisive. He tightened his arm around the man's neck. "Guess it depends on whether or not you can tell me what I want to know."

"I won't . . . betray my country!"

"Good to know. Hate to think our embassy officials were a bunch of whining girls who give up state secrets at the first sight of their limbs dropping off. Where is the Duchess of Lebec?"

"*What?*"

"You heard me!"

"I don't know where she is!"

"Damn, I was so hoping you'd be cooperative. I'll never get the blood out of this shirt after I've—"

"Truly! I don't know!" he cried in desperation. "She was at the Royal Seraglium, and when the king's men came for her, she was gone."

"Gone where?"

"Tides, don't you think I would have told the king's men that if I knew?"

"Did the king's men offer to kill you?"

"Of course not!"

Declan pulled a long knife from his belt, holding it out in front of De-ray, where the starlight reflected off its wickedly sharp blade. "Then you probably weren't sufficiently motivated."

"No! wait!" Deray said, his voice so loud Declan was sure they'd wake the whole damned neighbourhood. "I swear, I don't know where she is now. But my wife heard a rumour . . ."

"What rumour?"

"Apparently the Imperator's Consort is a follower of The Way of the Tide. There's a rumour getting around the women of Ramahn that Lady Chintara sent the duchess into the desert. They have an abbey somewhere in the Great Inland Desert. I don't know where it is exactly, only that it's not far from Elvere."

Elvere. That was something, Declan supposed. Certainly more than he'd had when he arrived here in Ramahn a few days ago. And it was the same abbey Tiji was heading for—following the Immortal Prince.

Tides . . . that's all I need. Cayal showing up.

With a shove, Declan let Deray go. He landed on his face in the sandy lane. Declan placed his booted foot on the man's neck to keep him there. "If I find out you've lied to me, Deray, I'll be back."

"Who are you?" the man demanded through a mouthful of sand.

"Your worst nightmare if you ever mention this meeting to anyone."

"I'll say nothing! I swear!"

Declan considered his oath for a moment and then leaned forward. "Maybe I shouldn't take the risk . . ."

"No! Please! By the Tides, man, I've told you all I know. You can't kill me in cold blood!"

"I can, actually. The question you need to worry about is, will I?"

Dashin Deray held his breath while Declan made a show of considering his options. He could feel the man trembling beneath his boot. When he decided Deray was sufficiently cowed that he'd say nothing to anybody, other than mention he'd been robbed. Declan lifted his foot from the man's neck.

"Seems I'm feeling patriotic this evening. Go. Get out of my sight before I change my mind."

Dashin Deray needed no further encouragement. He scrambled to his feet and fled the lane before Declan could say anything else, leaving the former spymaster with a decision to make.

Arkady had gone to Elvere, possibly to the Abbey of the Way of the Tide. Maybe. It could be a rumour spread about to throw her pursuers off the scent. On the other hand, if Kinta had taken it into her head to aid Arkady, it made sense that she would have sent her to Brynden's Abbey. Even if she'd taken her prisoner, she'd likely send Arkady to the same place. Which meant a journey of several weeks into the desert in the hope of picking up her trail. Or he could take a ship to Elvere, be there in a few days, and try to pick up her trail from there.

Either way, he wasn't done with his journey yet. And although he had all the time in the world, he wasn't so sure of the fate that had befallen Arkady. The awful feeling she was in danger and he wouldn't be able to get to her in time refused to go away.

Chapter 17

"What do you mean we can't go any further?" Tiji asked.

Ambria placed a bowl of delicious smelling chowder on the table in front of her and stepped back, as if she knew how much her presence disturbed the young chameleon.

"The sickness is everywhere, Tiji. It would be foolish to come all this way to find your own kind, only to be struck down by swamp fever the day after you got here."

Tiji looked at Azquil, wondering if the suzerain was lying. He seemed to believe her, however, but there was no way of telling if that was because he was compelled to, or because he trusted her. They were sitting at the table in Ambria's kitchen, which led off the back of the workroom in the front, where apparently they harvested nacre from the local freshwater molluscs. The kitchen was clean and homely and, most disturbingly of all, strikingly *ordinary*. Gleaming copper pots hung from the ceiling, along with bunches of herbs and several cloth-wrapped puddings. The large table was scrubbed white by years of use, and the soft buzz of flies hovered around the windowsill.

It didn't seem possible this was the lair of a suzerain.

"Is Lady Arryl not able to heal the sick ones?" Azquil asked, accepting a bowl of the delicious fish stew from Ambria too.

Ambria shook her head. "The Tide's only just turning. Medwen's helping her, of course, but there's a limit to how much they can do. You'll have to stay here until it's safe, I'm afraid."

"So you're the Trinity Azquil speaks of? You, Arryl and Medwen?"

Ambria nodded. "Although it wasn't us who thought up the name. Come to think of it, I'm not sure how it got started."

"How long have you been here?"

Azquil's spoon hesitated halfway to his mouth. "Tiji, you shouldn't be—"

"It's all right," Ambria said. "I don't mind answering Tiji's questions. And I'm sure she has many. We've been here the better part of seven hundred years."

Tiji glanced around the ramshackle outpost. " 'Bout time you redecorated, don't you think?"

Ambria smiled. "We're not all interested in building palaces, Tiji. We have a mutually convenient arrangement with our hosts. We protect the chameleon Crasii from the rest of our kind, and they provide us with somewhere to hide from the humans who don't understand what it means to be immortal. We harvest nacre, craft buttons and beads and other trinkets from it, and we extract the mollusc fats to make a very effective topical cream that fetches a premium in Port Traeker. We trade, we earn our keep, and we help the Crasii. In return, they allow us to live here in peace, without having to vanish every score of years or so and resettle somewhere else where the fact that we never seem to age raises comment."

"But now the Tide's on the turn," Tiji said, risking a spoonful of the chowder. It didn't seem to be poisoned. In fact, it was even more delicious than it smelled. She added through a mouthful of fish, "That changes all the rules."

The suzerain nodded. "I fear it might, but we've not discussed the implications yet, either among ourselves *or* with the Crasii elders."

"You know you'll always be welcome here, my lady."

"Thank you, Azquil," she said with a smile. "We don't want to leave, but eventually we may not have a choice. That rank smell, you—and all Scards, for that matter—associate with my kind will only get worse as the Tide rises."

Tiji swallowed another spoonful of chowder as she turned to Azquil. "Doesn't the stench bother you? Or are you a proper Crasii, just tripping over his own scales to do the bidding of the suzerain?"

Ambria answered before Azquil could. "There are only Scard chameleons left here in the wetlands, Tiji. We are guests here at their pleasure and will leave as soon as they ask us to."

"You'll forgive me if I don't believe you, my lady, but this all sounds a bit too convenient to me. And it's not that I don't appreciate the food. It's just that in my experience, the suzerain aren't usually so accommodating."

"In *your* experience?" Ambria asked. "How many immortals have you met, Tiji?"

Tiji held up her hand and began ticking them off on her fingers with her spoon. "Cayal, Brynden, Kinta—although technically we never met, I was just in the same room—Jaxyn, Syrolee, Elyssa, Tryan—who threatened to kill me, by the way—"

Azquil looked dumbfounded. "Are you serious? You've met all of these immortals?"

"Told you my life was interesting."

"Where are they?" Ambria asked.

Tiji's eyes narrowed. "If you're not interested in joining them, my lady, why do you care?"

"I care because we don't want them coming here."

"If you know where the other immortals are, the elders will want to know too," Azquil told her, quite excited by the prospect.

Tiji glared at the two of them suspiciously for a moment, and then she shrugged. With the Tide on the rise, what difference would it make what she told them about the location of the Tide Lords? Soon enough, they'd announce themselves and the whole Tide-forsaken world would know where they were. "Last time I saw the Immortal Prince, he was in Torlenia. So are Kinta and Brynden. Kinta's the Imperator's Consort there and we figure she's lining things up for Brynden to take over when the Tide's up a bit more."

"That would not be out of character for either of them," Ambria agreed. "You said you'd met Syrolee and her family?"

Tiji nodded. "Some of them. In Caelum. Syrolee is posing as the Duchess of Torfail and desperately trying to marry her son off to the crown princess. Elyssa is with them, and although I never actually saw him in the flesh, I believe Engarhod is with them too."

"But not Krydence or Rance?"

Tiji shook her head, wondering why she was asking about the others, until she recalled Ambria had once been married to Krydence.

Is she asking about him because she wants to find him or hide from him?

"Where did you meet Jaxyn?"

"In Glaeba. He was the Kennel Master for the Duke of Lebec. Oh, and the girl posing as the duke's niece is probably Diala, but I never met her, so I can't be sure about that one."

Ambria frowned. "Diala and Jaxyn are in cahoots this time? That's not a very pleasant prospect."

No kidding, Tiji thought, but she didn't offer her opinion aloud. "Oh, I know where Maralyce is too. Sort of."

"In the Shevron Mountains northeast of Lebec?" Ambria asked. When Tiji stared at her in surprise, she added, "Maralyce hasn't moved from her mine for a long time. We all know where to find her."

"So that leaves Pellys, Lukys, Krydence, Taryx, Rance, Lyna and Kentravyon unaccounted for," Azquil said.

Ambria shook her head. "There's no need to worry about Kentravyon. I know where he is and he's not going anywhere."

"What about the others?"

The suzerain thought for a moment and then shrugged. "Pellys is the one to be concerned about, but having said that, he's usually only dangerous if he gets upset. The others aren't powerful enough to do any real damage. I'd be happier if I knew what Lukys was up to, though." Ambria rose from the table. "Eat up, Tiji. You've barely touched a bite."

"I seem to have lost my appetite," she said, pushing the bowl away.

"I haven't," Azquil said, pulling the bowl toward him. "Do you mind?"

"Be my guest."

He began tucking into her leftovers as a voice called out from the front of the building. Ambria wiped her hands on her apron and excused herself, leaving Tiji alone with Azquil.

"Do you believe her?" she asked.

"Ambria delivered me, Tiji, and Arryl saved my mother and my sister from the swamp fever the last time it hit us. Why would I *not* believe her?"

Tiji wrinkled her forehead thoughtfully. "Are you sure this swamp fever is real? I mean, they can do things like that, you know."

"What are you talking about?"

"Well, if you believe there's a fever only the suzerain can save you from, of course you're going to be nice to them. But suppose they're responsible for the fever? Suppose they create it to make you think you need them?"

"You've been around your human spymaster too long, Tiji," Azquil said. "You see plots where none exist."

"Or I see things with fresh eyes."

He shook his head. "Your logic is flawed. The Tide is only now returning. The Trinity have had no magical powers since they've been here, so they can't be responsible for causing it. Besides, swamp fever, once it takes a hold, affects everyone, human and Crasii, alike. The Trinity are immune because they're immortal, which means they're the only ones who can move about freely without catching the disease or spreading it."

"You said Arryl saved your mother and sister."

"Because she sat up all night with them, keeping their temperatures down with cold compresses, and making sure they didn't dehydrate, Tiji. There wasn't any magic involved."

Tiji didn't get a chance to argue further, because at that moment Ambria returned with another chameleon, a female several years younger than Azquil. The newcomer smiled broadly when she saw him. Azquil jumped to his feet, hurried around the table and embraced her, which made Tiji feel a little less special.

It seemed she wasn't the only one Azquil liked to hug.

"You're back!" the chameleon said. "Mother always worries about you so when you're away, you reckless boy. Is this the Lost One you found?"

Azquil nodded, and turned to introduce her. "Tiji, this is Tenika. My little sister."

Tiji smiled, unreasonably pleased this attractive young female was Azquil's sister and not something more . . . complicated.

"Hello."

Tenika disentangled herself from her brother's embrace so she could hug Tiji. Apparently it was a family trait, this desire to hug each other on the slightest excuse. Or maybe it was a chameleon thing? Tiji didn't know enough about her own species to be sure. And the prospect of families was quite terrifying when she thought about it.

"Oh, welcome home, you poor thing!" Tenika gushed. "Has Azquil been looking after you? Has he explained anything about us? Do we know anything about your family? Where you're from? Are you hurt? Was it awfully bad out there? What a pity you arrived just as the swamp fever is taking hold. You can't go back to the main settlement, of course, because you've probably never been exposed to the fever, so you'll catch it for sure. I'm all right, of course, because I've had it, and so has Azquil, but we don't want to risk you catching it and dying on us, just when we've saved you and brought you home. You should go to Watershed." The little Crasii had barely drawn a breath and was grinning broadly as she spoke, as if she'd only been allowed a minute to tell everybody everything she'd ever have to say.

A little overwhelmed by Tenika's verbal torrent, Tiji looked to Azquil for clarification. "Watershed?"

"She means Watershed Falls. It's a small settlement southeast of here. We passed it on the way here. The population is mostly Crasii, but there are a few humans, canines and several chameleons living there too. We won't be out of place, and they have a healer who visits on a regular basis if either of us gets sick."

"It's a good idea," Ambria agreed. "Tenika is right. You really can't risk the settlement until the outbreak is contained and it would be such a pity to lose you so soon after finding you, Tiji." She smiled fondly at Azquil.

"Although I suspect it would take something a good deal more determined than a dangerous fever to put this young lizard down."

"You see! I *knew* it was a good idea!" Tenika said, beaming. "And I've brought a boat, so I can take you now, if you want. Then I'd better get back home. Lady Arryl and Lady Medwen need all the help they can get, and it's only the survivors of the last outbreak, like me and Azquil, who can risk moving among the infected ones."

Tiji shook her head at the fundamental *wrongness* of this bizarre arrangement the chameleons had made with the suzerain, but didn't see any alternative other than to go along with it.

"Watershed Falls it is, then," she said, trying to inject some enthusiasm into her voice. A part of her wanted to flee this place, while another part of her hungered for the opportunity to connect with her own kind, even if that meant living in the shadow of these supposedly benign immortals.

Chapter 18

"Will he be glad to see us?"

Cayal glanced across at Pellys. The older man had been chattering away for hours as they rode, and Cayal had been paying little or no attention to what he was saying. The camels they'd hired were remarkably well mannered and had given them very few problems, for which Cayal was extremely grateful. He wouldn't have put it past Pellys to hop off the beast and break its neck if it gave him too much trouble. "Who?"

"Lukys?" Pellys said. "Do you think he'll be happy to see us?"

"Thrilled to the very core of his being, I'm sure."

Pellys grinned, taking Cayal literally. He had no concept of irony or sarcasm. "I can't wait to see Coron, too. Do you think he'll remember me? I remember him. Some things I don't remember, but I remember Coron."

Cayal didn't answer that one, not sure what Pellys would do if he learned Coron, Lukys's pet rat, was dead—particularly as he was supposed to have been an immortal rat. It was hard to say if Pellys could reason out the implications of such news, and right now he was being cooperative; Cayal didn't want to do anything to set him off. "He has a wife again, you know, so you'll have to be on your best behaviour."

"Where did Lukys get a wife from?" Pellys sounded genuinely puzzled, as if he'd been on the lookout for a wife himself and hadn't been able to find a merchant who could sell him one.

"Think he got this one in Ramahn."

"I'd like a wife. Do you think he'd find me one?"

"Didn't you have a wife once?" Cayal asked, wondering if he still remembered Syrolee.

Pellys thought for a moment. "I think so. I remember asking a whore in Elvere if she wanted to be my wife, but she said no, so I had to kill her."

His matter-of-fact tone was chilling, even to Cayal, who was used to Pellys's strange take on the world.

"That wasn't very nice," he said, squinting into the setting sun as they rode west along the last stretch of road leading to Lukys's Torlenian villa. "And I'm pretty sure Lukys would like to keep his wife for a while, so no killing her, even if she says something you don't like, all right?"

"All right."

"Promise me."

"I promise I won't kill . . . what's her name?"

"Oritha."

"I promise I won't kill Oritha. At least not until Lukys says I can."

"I'm sure he'll be touched by your forbearance, Pellys. And no killing anybody else without asking first, while we're at it."

"Why not?"

"Because it's messy and it leaves the rest of us with too much explaining to do."

"But we're Tide Lords. We don't have to explain anything to anybody."

And wouldn't I like to get my hands around the throat of the idiot who planted that *particular notion in your empty, impressionable, newly regenerated head.*

"But the Tide's not all the way back yet, Pellys. And it won't be for a while. We'll need to be careful for a little longer yet."

Pellys grinned from ear to ear, making him look very young—almost as young as his emotional age, which had never progressed much beyond that of a child since his head grew back after Cayal decapitated him. Looking at him now—at this dangerous, ingenuous halfwit—Cayal was glad, for the first time since he'd set out to get himself beheaded to make the memories of his interminable life go away, that he hadn't been successful.

Had the headsman been there the day he was scheduled to be executed in Lebec almost a year ago, he would now be no better than Pellys—ignorant, innocent, gullible and dangerous.

And I would never have met Arkady . . .

He pushed the thought aside impatiently. She was lost to him and it was better for everyone that way.

Oblivious to Cayal's dark thoughts, Pellys was still grinning at him. "Tide's on the turn, Cayal. I can feel it."

"I know."

"It feels good."

"I know."

"You know lots of stuff," Pellys concluded with a sage nod. "I think that's why I like you."

Cayal was saved from answering by the appearance of Lukys's villa on the horizon.

He urged his camel into a canter. Pellys flopped about in his saddle behind him, probably wondering, Cayal feared, what else he could kill now that Lukys's wife and any other humans he might encounter, were denied him.

"Lord Cayal," Oritha said, bowing respectfully as she entered the main hall of the villa.

"My lady," Cayal replied, bowing with equal respect. "This is Pellys. He is . . . a distant cousin of your husband's. I brought him here in the hopes your husband had returned from his trip?"

Oritha shook her head. "I fear not, my lord. Quite the contrary, in fact. He sent word to inform me he's not coming home."

"He's abandoning Torlenia?" That didn't really make sense. Lukys was settled here and he wasn't nomadic by nature. "Where is he staying now?"

"Jelidia." She smiled enthusiastically. "He wants me to join him."

"He's staying in *Jelidia*?" Cayal repeated, shaking his head.

Oritha nodded, but before she could answer, Pellys grabbed Cayal by the shoulder and spun him around to face him. "Isn't Lukys here?" he asked. "But you said he would be, Cayal. You said he wanted to see me. You said he was waiting for me . . ."

"And he *is* waiting for you," Cayal said, trying to placate him. "I just got muddled up where he is at the moment. I was wrong about the place, that's all. He's not here. He's gone to Jelidia."

"What's in Jelidia?"

Nothing but trouble, Cayal was tempted to reply.

"A palace of extraordinary beauty," Oritha told Pellys, smiling in anticipation. "Ryda assures me the home he has waiting for me there is so beautiful, it's impossible to imagine it, even in a dream."

Cayal turned to Oritha with interest. "Lukys isn't planning to come back to Torlenia at all?"

"I gather not." She clutched his arm reassuringly. "You needn't be concerned, though. The letter he sent me and the instructions for finding the new palace quite specifically extend his hospitality to you, Lord Cayal. He states, in fact, that you should bring any other members of your family who are willing to aid your endeavour to our new home in Jelidia, as soon as you can." She turned and smiled warmly at Pellys. "That would include you, my lord."

Pellys elbowed Cayal none too gently. "She called me *my lord*."

"I heard," Cayal muttered distractedly, trying to imagine what Lukys was up to. He doubted he'd relocated to Jelidia because he'd tired of the desert heat. And if he was just going down there to check on Kentravyon, why go to all the trouble of building a house down there?

"Did your husband's letter mention any other members of . . . the family?"

She shook her head. "No, my lord."

"I want food," Pellys said. "I'm starving."

"You only think you're starving, Pellys," Cayal told him, and then he smiled at Oritha, who was looking at Pellys with a rather wary eye. "Some refreshments wouldn't go astray, though." He wasn't hungry or thirsty, but food and drink would give both Pellys and Oritha something to do while Cayal thought this through.

Oritha bowed again. "Of course, my lord. Please, make yourselves at home. I'll arrange dinner."

"I like her," Pellys announced, dropping onto one of the couches in the main hall, as Oritha withdrew. He stretched luxuriously and looked around. "This is a nice place. And she's going to cook for us. Glad you told me not to kill her."

"I told you not to kill *anything*," Cayal reminded him, taking a seat on the couch opposite. "Do you want to go to Jelidia with her to see Lukys?"

"It's cold in Jelidia."

"You don't feel the cold, Pellys."

"But it's all full of snow and ice. There's nothing to see down there. And nothing to do. Although breaking glaciers might be fun."

"I'm sure it will be. And by the sound of it, Lukys has set himself up quite nicely down there. New palace. New everything, probably."

Pellys grinned. "The Palace of Impossible Dreams, that's what Oritha called it."

Cayal nodded, thinking that wasn't what Oritha had said at all, but if it made Pellys a little more cooperative, he'd happily go along with the name.

"Sounds like a grand place for a visit, actually."

"Will you come too?"

Cayal's first instinct was to say no, but he thought better of it. There were any number of reasons why he should accompany Pellys and Oritha to Jelidia, not the least of which was that Oritha might not survive the trip otherwise. Pellys's fascination for watching things die had not changed with his beheading. The only difference was that before he was decapitated,

Pellys at least had some shred of conscience, which meant he usually confined his fascination to small animals and other creatures whose life could be counted as cheap. Pellys's regenerated brain had lost its moral compass. He had no conscience any longer; no frame of reference for what might be good or evil.

For Pellys the world just *was* and that's all he seemed to know or care about.

Besides, Lukys's presence in Jelidia bothered Cayal greatly. The letter Lukys had left with Oritha for Cayal on his last visit had stated: "We need at least five of us to do this, Cayal, and we're going to have to do it when the Tide peaks. I can convince the other two, but you are the only one on Amyrantha who can convince Elyssa to join us."

Does the five Tide Lords he mentioned include that psychotic bastard, Kentravyon?

Kentravyon's madness was so much worse than Pellys's ingenuous savagery. Pellys was driven by childlike curiosity. Kentravyon, on the other hand, *knew* he was an evil bastard; worse, he positively *revelled* in it. That's why—for once—when it came time to do something about him, they'd all agreed the world would be better off with Kentravyon immobile, powerless and tucked out of the way, somewhere safe and isolated. Like Jelidia.

Except now Lukys was down there, possibly waking him up.

Do I want to die so badly, Cayal wondered, *that I'd inflict Kentravyon upon the rest of the world after I'm gone?*

Or was Lukys's plan, more than just a way to help Cayal die, also a way for him to be rid of a few enemies? *After all, if Lukys has the means to kill one immortal, why not kill a few more while you're at it?*

"Well?" Pellys demanded, when Cayal didn't answer him immediately. "Are you coming to Jelidia with us?"

And if Lukys is preparing to take out a few other immortals in the process of helping me die, what does he have against poor Elyssa, that he'd be so insistent on her joining us?

"Yes, Pellys," he said, deciding this mystery needed to be cleared up before he allowed Lukys to manipulate him any more than he already had. "I'm coming to Jelidia with you."

Chapter 19

"How are my babies doing today, Cecil?"

Warlock approached the bed, carrying Elyssa's tea. When he reached her side, he handed the cup to her with a subservient bow.

He hated that she called them *her* babies. He hated fearing for every breath they took, wondering when she was going to come for them. He hated that Boots was barely speaking to him, she was so fearful for them. He hated the names Elyssa had given them. They'd softened them—Dezi for Despair, Tory for Torment and Missy, for Warlock's pride and joy, his daughter Misery—but it didn't lessen the horror of what the Immortal Maiden had done by naming them so cruelly.

And as if to rub salt in the wound, Elyssa asked him the same question every day.

Every day he answered the same way. "They're doing fine, my lady."

"You tell Tabitha Belle, she's to look after them well for me."

"I'll make certain she does, my lady."

He handed her the tea, taking small comfort in watching the immortal suffer her own pain. Sunlight streamed into the bedroom, the lake visible in the distance through the windows leading onto the balcony. The view was spectacular, but he doubted Elyssa was aware of it. She seemed rather more interested in the young man in bed beside her, dark-haired, well-muscled and handsome. He was sprawled across the bed in a tangle of sheets, his neck twisted at an odd angle. His lips were tinged blue, his skin unnaturally pale, his chest unmoving. There was no telling how long he'd been dead. A few hours at least.

Elyssa must have taken her pleasure from him—or her twisted version of it—sometime during the night.

If she was lucky, in this wing of the palace nobody but the Crasii, who were compelled to obey her, would have heard anything amiss.

This was not the first time Warlock had encountered a similar scene in the Immortal Maiden's bedroom. There'd been hell to pay the last time. Until they'd secured the throne, Syrolee was adamant her children not do anything to expose their true identities, but with little Princess Nyah still missing, Elyssa was growing impatient. She had started taking young men to her bed and then punishing them for her suffering.

Engarhod had delivered a severe dressing down to his stepdaughter over the last incident, which paled in comparison to the slapping about her mother gave her. It astonished Warlock to watch these immortals interacting. He would have thought that after thousands of years, Elyssa would have found the courage to defy her mother, particularly as it was Elyssa who could wield the Tide with impunity, not Syrolee. The Empress of the Five Realms could work a little magic, sure enough, but Elyssa and Tryan were full-blown Tide Lords. Why they continued to toe the line, going along with every scheme their mother concocted over the eons, remained an unsolved mystery that was almost as old as the Tarot which charted the story of these inexplicably complicated beings.

But there was something new, and quite unexpected, that Warlock had learned about Elyssa. Something he suspected the Cabal didn't know—and would never know unless they contacted him soon.

The *Immortal Maiden* was more than just a title, more than just a name on a Tarot card.

It was its own special curse.

A virgin when she was made immortal, the curse of constant regeneration had an unexpected consequence for the young woman. Every time Elyssa made love, her hymen must be broken yet again. And then it would immediately begin to heal itself, an excruciatingly painful process in and of itself, without the added torment of being abraded by the thrusting urgency of a lover. Warlock had heard her screaming the night she'd killed the last young man she'd taken to her bed, just as he'd ignored her quiet sobbing while he and Speckles cleaned up the mess and removed the body before anybody discovered the handsome young baker's assistant missing from the kitchens.

This young man, Warlock didn't know. But he'd suffered the same fate as the last one. Whether out of pain or rage, Elyssa had snapped the poor lad's neck. Perhaps in the throes of passion, or maybe afterward, as she writhed tormentedly on the bed, her lover unable to comprehend her suffering or the reason for it, but finding himself blamed for it nonetheless.

Her eyes were red-rimmed and swollen, which meant she'd only just finished weeping. She saw the direction of Warlock's gaze and shrugged fatalistically. "Would you get rid of him for me, Cecil?"

"To serve you is the reason I breathe, my lady."

She accepted the tea and sighed. "Mother's going to be furious when she finds out."

"May I be so bold as to inquire where you . . . acquired him, my lady?"

"In the city. In a tavern near the lake. I don't remember his name."

"Did anybody see you with him, my lady? Anybody who might recognise you from the palace?"

She shook her head, her eyes narrowing suspiciously. "What are you suggesting, Cecil? That I say nothing about this?"

Warlock hesitated before he spoke. He was treading on very dangerous ground here. But this was the rush Declan Hawkes spoke of—that feeling he got from knowing something everyone else doesn't. The way his heart pounded because of the danger. The way the hairs stood up on his back because he knew something that might make a real difference. "Your lady mother's rage was a thing to behold the last time this happened, my lady. But Lord Tyrone showed us what to do, so Speckles and I could dispose of the last . . . problem . . . without discovery. Perhaps, in this case, we might be able to do the same to spare you any undue suffering?"

The immortal studied him for a moment and then smiled. "I knew I did the right thing, insisting on keeping you. Will you say anything about this to my mother or my brother?"

"If they ask me, my lady, I will have no choice. But if they have no reason to ask . . ."

Elyssa nodded, smiling at him. "You're a good boy, Cecil. I'll see you're rewarded for this."

"To serve you is the reason I breathe, my lady," he replied, and then he bowed and backed out of the room, so he could go fetch Speckles and cover up a murder.

"You *hid* the body for her?" Boots exclaimed when Warlock told her about the incident later that night in the chilly privacy of their bare cell.

He nodded unhappily, not sure if she could see his expression in the darkness. "We weighted him down with rocks and tossed him into the Lower Oran."

Her eyes were shining in the darkness, wide and horrified. "Are you *mad*?" she hissed.

"Quite the opposite, Boots. Elyssa now believes I am totally her creature. This has made things much safer for all of us." He looked down, smiling at Dezi and Tory who were sleeping off their latest feed. The males were curled up in the small, warm hollow under the blanket, between their parents. Missy was suckling contentedly at Boots's breast, cradled in her mother's arms.

"You helped a suzerain commit murder," Boots said. "You needn't sound so proud about it. Or try to make it my fault."

"I'm not proud," he told her. "I'm sick to my stomach over it. But Elyssa has to believe I'm hers, Boots, body and soul. If she ever tires of me, she'll let Tryan have us both and if Tryan ever got a hold of the pups . . ." He didn't have to say more. Boots knew as well as he did that Elyssa's particular fetish for murdering her lovers like a spider killing its mate was nothing compared to the stories of how much pleasure Tryan took from feeding Crasii pups to his hunting dogs when he was training them to tear apart a kill.

"Have you told the Cabal about this?"

He shook his head. "I don't even know who they are. Hawkes said someone would make contact with me, but nobody has."

Boots snorted with contempt. "Typical. They make all these great plans to get intelligence so they can halt the rise of the Tide Lords, and then forget to figure out a way to get the information out." She changed Missy to the other breast and once she was sucking contentedly, added, "Not that you've much to tell them. Other than where the bodies are hidden."

"I've more than that to tell them. With the little princess still missing, Syrolee is moving to have her declared dead."

"No princess, no wedding," Boots said with a shrug. "No wedding, no taking the throne. What's the problem?"

"I was there when they were discussing the problem yesterday. Tryan has suggested the queen bear another daughter to inherit her crown."

"Well, that buys us nine months at the very least."

"You don't understand," he said, keeping his voice low. Although they were alone in their cell and the walls were several feet thick, he didn't want this conversation to be overheard. "Tryan has *proposed* to the queen and with the succession so doubtful, and the Privy Council so nervous about the future, I fear she's going to accept him."

"Then more fool her . . ."

"No, you still don't understand, Boots. Tryan doesn't need to father a child on the queen. He just needs to be her husband. After that, for all intents and purposes, the throne is his for the taking."

"We should never have come here," she said, stroking Missy's forehead. "I don't know why we let those fools from Hidden Valley talk us into it."

"Because you hate the suzerain as much as I do," he reminded her. "You wanted to help bring them down."

"And yet here I am, with my pups given the worst names imaginable by the Immortal Maiden and my mate hiding bodies for her. Things aren't really going as we'd planned, I have to say."

"I'm so sorry, Boots," he said, reaching out to stroke her. "I'd do anything to roll back time and tell Declan Hawkes where he could shove his Cabal and their grand plans to save the world."

Boots nodded in agreement, and for once she didn't shirk from his touch. "Well, how about you find a way to save your family, Farm Dog. The flanking Cabal of the Tarot can take care of itself."

Chapter 20

Elvere was still recovering from an unseasonable storm that had caused serious damage to much of the city, when Declan arrived. The wharf where his ship was docked had been hastily repaired and many of the buildings were still unroofed, the gaping holes covered in tarpaulins that snapped in the sharp breeze coming off the harbour.

Declan made his way into the city, hoping to establish contact with a member of the Cabal who had a shop in the clothing district. A tailor of some note, the man served a broad clientele in the city, and was able to pass messages to foreigners without being remarked upon. When Declan found the shop, however, it was a wreck. The building had obviously been flooded and on the footpath outside the shop was a gelatinous stinking pile that might have once been bolts of material Pollo the Tailor kept in his shop.

"He's gone to his mother's house."

Declan turned to find a young boy tugging on his sleeve. He seemed to be no more than eight or nine years old.

"What?"

"The tailor. Mister Pollo. He's gone to his mother's house."

"How do you know?"

" 'Cause he told me he did," the boy replied. "For a copper bit, I'll tell ya how to get there."

Declan smiled at the enterprising lad. "Is that right?"

"For a silver bit, I'll take you myself."

Declan fished around in his pocket for a silver fenet and offered it to the lad, snatching it out of reach as the boy tried to grab it from his hand. "You get this *after* we've found Master Pollo's mother's house."

The boy glared at him for a moment and then shrugged. Clearly, his plan had been to take the money and run. "Come on, then," he said with a heavy sigh. "It's this way."

Almost an hour later, the lad stopped in front of a tidy house in a narrow street lined by identical tidy houses, all joined together in a row. Only the different coloured front doors and the occasional window box differentiated the houses. The house the boy led Declan to, had a blue front door with a brass knocker on it. Declan banged the knocker as the boy tugged at his sleeve. "You can pay me now."

"When I'm sure this really is Pollo's house."

A few moments later a swarthy woman, who looked so much like the tailor Declan was looking for that he didn't even need to ask, opened the door. He flipped the silver coin to the lad, who caught it, bit into it to ascertain its authenticity, and then disappeared down the street at a run.

"Can I help you?" the woman asked.

"I'd like to see your son, madam. Pollo the Tailor."

She frowned at him. "If you're after a refund, you're wasting your time. The shop is ruined. Everything is gone. He has nothing left to give anybody."

"On the contrary, madam. I'm here to pay him money I owe him. Is he home?"

She glared at Declan suspiciously, debating the issue, and then nodded, standing back to let him enter. The hall of the house proved to be small, dark and cluttered with what Declan guessed must be all Pollo had been able to rescue from his ruined shop.

The woman led him into the kitchen out back, where Pollo was sitting at the table, nursing a mug of steaming tea. Slender, swarthy and normally dressed to perfection, the tailor was unshaved and bedraggled, his shoulders slumped in defeat. He looked up morosely as Declan entered the room, his eyes widening in surprise as he realised who his visitor was.

"Tides! I never expected to see you again!" he exclaimed, jumping to his feet. "I heard you were dead."

"A vicious rumour put about by my enemies," Declan replied with a smile, as he accepted the tailor's handshake. "I saw your shop. What happened?"

"Terrible storm, it was," Pollo's mother said before her son could answer. "Went on for days. Ruined half the folk with shops near the seafront."

Pollo nodded in agreement. "It was worse than a hurricane. They, at least, move on. This one just sat over the city for days. Like it had a score to settle."

"A hurricane? At this time of year?"

Pollo turned to his mother. "Could you leave us for a few minutes, mother? This gentleman and I have some business to discuss."

Pollo's mother eyed Declan speculatively before she answered. "Says he owes you money. Make sure he pays up before he leaves." With that, she gathered up her skirts and left them alone.

Pollo shut the door behind her and then turned to look at Declan. "Sorry about mother. Tea?"

Declan shook his head. "No, thanks. Tell me about this storm."

"It wasn't natural," Pollo said, resuming his seat at the scrubbed wooden table, indicating with a wave of his hand that Declan should do the same. "And it stopped almost as unexpectedly as it started."

"Who was it?" There was no need to explain anything further. Pollo was a member of the Cabal of the Tarot. He knew as well as Declan did that unexplained hurricanes when the Tide was on the way back were likely to have more than one cause.

"Hard to say," Pollo said with a shrug. "I doubt it was Brynden. He doesn't usually mess with the weather like that."

Declan wasn't so sure. "The last cataclysm happened because he threw a meteor into the ocean," he reminded the tailor. "He's more than capable of it."

Pollo shook his head. "He had a reason for that. No, I think it was one of the others."

"The Immortal Prince was in Ramahn until recently, and rumoured to be headed this way."

"Then I'd say you've found your culprit," Pollo said with a nod. "Storms are his speciality, aren't they?"

"But why would he do it? Something must have set him off."

Pollo shrugged. "Who can say with an immortal? They're capable of anything and after all this time, most of them are more than a little touched in the head." Pollo grinned. "I'd kill myself if I discovered I was immortal." The tailor fell about laughing for a few moments at his own wit, and then brought his mirth under control when he realised Declan didn't seem to share his amusement. "That was a joke, Declan."

"I know."

"You're not laughing."

"It wasn't that funny."

Pollo sighed heavily. "What are you here for then? If you didn't know about the storm before you got here, I'm guessing it's not because of that."

"I'm looking for someone."

"Anyone in particular?"

"A Glaeban woman. I think she was headed for Brynden's abbey."

Pollo's smile faded as he shook his head. "She won't be at the abbey. Brynden has a strict 'no women' policy. Or at least, the monks there do. If your Glaeban woman was headed to the Abbey of the Way of the Tide, she'd more than likely have been turned back at the main gate."

"Would she have come here to Elvere?"

He nodded. "Unless she headed back to Ramahn via the Tarascan Oasis. I could find out easily enough."

"How?"

"My cousin works for the caravan outfit that makes the regular supply run to the abbey. He'll know if a woman was with any of the caravans coming out of the desert. How long ago are we talking?"

"A couple of months at most."

"Then we're in luck," he said rising to his feet. "Brell's been in charge of the passenger manifests since the new year." He walked to the kitchen door and opened it. "Mother!" he called. "I'm going out for a while."

"You make sure you get the money he owes you," a disembodied voice yelled back from somewhere upstairs.

Pollo turned to Declan with a grin. "You really are going to have to give me some money, you know."

Declan nodded. "The Cabal will see you're taken care of. That shop of yours is too convenient for them to let it go out of business."

Pollo's cousin Brell turned out to be even more like Pollo's mother than Pollo was. Short, thin and swarthy, had he been wearing a dress, Declan thought he'd be hard pressed to tell them apart.

"A woman, you say?" he said, as they followed him along a long line of kneeling camels as he ticked off things on the list he was carrying.

"She was Glaeban," Declan said, waving away the myriad flies that buzzed around the camel dung while waiting for a human to chance by. "Very beautiful. Dark hair. Blue eyes."

Brell rolled his eyes at Declan. "She would have been shrouded, particularly if she was coming from the abbey. How do you expect me to know what she looked like? Or if she was Glaeban? Or beautiful. Or ugly. Or had two heads. She could have been another lizard, for all I know."

"*Another* lizard?" Pollo asked, glancing at Declan.

Brell shrugged and moved on to the next camel. "Had one through here 'bout the time you're talking about. Tiny little thing she was. Shrouded, of course, but you could see it round her eyes. The scales, you know." He shuddered and returned to ticking things off his list. "Can't remember if it was before or after the other woman came through."

"What other woman?" Declan asked, resisting the temptation to relieve Brell of his wretched list so he could shove it somewhere that might get his undivided attention.

"It wasn't a woman," Brell said. "It was a slave."

"What did she look like?"

"Like every other wretched female slave I've ever seen," Brell snapped. "Tall and covered in a flanking shroud. Tides, man, what do you expect?"

"You say she was tall?" It wasn't much to go on, but if she was shrouded, Arkady's height might be the only thing that differentiated her from any other slave.

"Taller than me," Brell confirmed, moving to the next beast, who spat at them just on principle. "But then, that's nothing special. I have twelve-year-old nephews who are taller than me. And she might have had blue eyes, but I really can't remember."

"What happened to her?" Pollo asked.

"She was batch-bought by the Senestrans, as I recall."

Declan looked to Pollo for an explanation. "What's he mean? Batch-bought?"

"The Senestrans buy all their lower echelon slaves in bulk. They don't care about looks or skills. They just order a certain gender or age and let the slavers put the order together."

"Where would they have taken her?"

"To the slave markets, of course." Brell looked at Declan as if he was a little bit slow. "That's where they take all the slaves, you know."

Declan took a threatening step closer to the trader, who cowered back in fear. Pollo put an arm out to restrain him, and turned to his cousin. "My friend has no sense of humour, Brell," he warned. "Please, just tell us what you know."

"I *have* told you what I know," Brell said, sniffing indignantly. "I delivered her to the markets. I'm pretty sure they shipped her out within a matter of days, because Hento was anxious that he couldn't make up the order before the ship left, and those Senestran traders are tight bastards at the best of times. He paid me a bonus for delivering her the same day she arrived."

"Who is Hento?" Declan demanded, feeling sick to the pit of his stomach.

"Was," Pollo corrected. "He was a slaver. Worked for one of the biggest slave outfits in the city. He was killed in the storm. In fact, most of the slave markets were blown away. Gonna make business hard for everyone until they're rebuilt."

That was suspiciously coincidental, but hardly proof of anything. Declan turned to Brell. "Are you sure she shipped out for Senestra before the storm?"

"Not one hundred per cent sure," Brell said. "But Hento would never have paid me a bonus for merchandise he planned to have sitting around in the pens for weeks at a time."

Pollo smiled at Declan encouragingly. "Which means your friend probably wasn't killed in the storm and is still alive. That's a good thing."

"Just shipped off to Senestra as a slave. Not such a good thing," Declan said, his threatening gaze still fixed on Brell. "You said you saw a lizard Crasii. What happened to her?"

"I have no idea. I only saw her the one time. I swear."

Declan stepped back from the man, silently cursing. *Tides, what was Tiji up to? Why hasn't she contacted me? And how had Arkady managed to get herself sold into slavery?* Was Kinta responsible? Brynden? Or had Cayal found her and taken his revenge on her for . . . *what?* Declan had no idea.

"What will you do now?" Pollo asked.

Declan glanced along the long string of camels, not really seeing them, or smelling their rank aroma, or noticing the cloud of flies that had followed them down the line.

"Looks like I'm going to Senestra," he said.

Chapter 21

It was raining and bitterly cold as the amphibian-towed barge pulled into the Cycrane docks, for which Stellan was quite grateful. It meant they could remain hidden behind hooded cloaks for a while longer, perhaps even get to the palace without anybody being aware of their approach.

Stellan scratched at his new beard, still unused to his blond hair, the beard or the fact that he was posing as someone else entirely. Having met with Aleki Ponting—Tides, was *anybody* really who he'd thought they were—he had a new identity, two bodyguards named Tenry and Crowe . . .

But not, as Declan had suggested—to Stellan's horror—an eleven-year-old bride.

Nyah smiled up at him nervously as the boat approached the docks. She had a remarkable grasp of the situation, given her age, but Stellan thought Declan's plan far too dangerous to involve an innocent child.

At the outset, nobody agreed with him. It seemed the Cabal of the Tarot was willing to employ anything and anybody who crossed their path, if it looked like they were going to be of use to them. It wasn't until Stellan brought his diplomatic experience to the discussion that anybody was willing to admit the plan was not only fraught with danger, but would more than likely fail, even before it began.

"Don't look so worried, Jareth."

That was the new name the Cabal had chosen for him. Lord Jareth Dekayn. The real Lord Dekayn was—or had been—a distant cousin of Stellan's, and had died in circumstances that forced the family to cover up not just the manner of his death, but that he had died at all. There was little likelihood of someone who knew the real Jareth Dekayn turning up in the Caelish royal palace and inadvertently betraying him.

He smiled down at the little girl. "Was I looking worried? Who'd have thought?"

Nyah smiled back, sliding her small gloved hand into his. "They'll believe us. I'll *make* them believe you rescued me."

You'd better, he replied silently, as Tenry and Crowe helped throw the lines out onto the dock, all too aware that a large part of his fate rested in the hands of this precocious child.

But not all of it, fortunately. After Declan left Maralyce's Mine, Stellan had started to consider his future, something he'd been singularly reluctant to do up to that point. Declan's departure drove home to Stellan that he couldn't simply slink away and hide, just because he didn't want to face the world. The comfort of no longer existing, the release of being thought of as dead, was false security at best. He was only in his mid-thirties. He could hardly sulk for the rest of his life, despite how tempting that idea might have been when he'd first escaped Herino Prison.

Besides, he was a loyal and patriotic Glaeban. He couldn't stand by and let his king's murderer take the crown.

Stellan had managed to talk Aleki out of Declan's original ill-conceived plan, which was to pose as Nyah's husband. To arrive back in Caelum, announcing he was now the husband of the kidnapped crown princess, wouldn't secure anybody's throne. It would, however, more than likely see him killed almost immediately, as the man who'd stolen her away in the first place.

But what Declan didn't seem to grasp, nor Aleki when Stellan first proposed his alternate plan, was that he was still the blood heir to the Glaeban throne. That fact alone would confound Jaxyn's attempts to secure the Glaeban throne for himself. It might even keep Mathu alive a little longer.

"Look," Nyah said, breaking his train of thought. She was pointing to the buildings along the front of the wharves, most of which were decked out in bedraggled, waterlogged red and gold bunting. "Do you think that's left over from mother's wedding?"

Stellan nodded. "More than likely."

The wedding of Queen Jilna and Lord Tyrone of Torfail had only happened a couple of days ago. They'd waited for just that event before returning Nyah to her home. Now, unless Lord Tyrone—or Tryan the Devil, as his immortal persona was known—killed the queen and tried to wed Nyah soon after, the little princess was saved from being offered to him as a bride. Ironically, they had Caelish law on their side, for once. Despite not seeming to have any qualms about marrying off their children, they had quite strict laws about incest. Lord Tyrone was now Nyah's stepfather. Even if he murdered the queen tomorrow, Caelish law forbad him marrying his stepdaughter at any time in the future.

Of course, she wasn't entirely safe yet. The royal line continued through Nyah and, as such, she was required to take the throne as soon as she was married, an event the Caelish preferred to take place sooner rather than later. As soon as she reappeared, the hunt would be on once more for a suitable consort for the princess.

Hopefully, Queen Jilna's recent remarriage and Nyah's unexpected return should confuse things enough to stall any decision about the child's future for quite some time.

There was a lone figure wearing a hooded cape waiting for them at the docks, and behind him an unremarkable carriage with a forlorn-looking gelding waiting patiently in the rain for the command to move on. Hopefully, the man waiting for them was Ricard Li, Caelum's Spymaster. He was the only man in Caelum who knew where Nyah had been. Presumably, that meant Stellan could trust him.

Recent experience, however, had taught him not to trust anyone.

They bumped into the wharf. Tenry and Crowe jumped onto the dock to secure the ropes as one of the boatmen shoved the gangway out onto the dock. Nyah hurried across it and threw herself at the hooded man. He hugged her briefly and then turned to watch Stellan disembark. As he approached, Nyah hurried back to Stellan, grabbed his hand and dragged him forward to meet this stranger she clearly considered a friend.

"Jareth, this is Ricard Li," she said. "Caelum's Spymaster."

Messages had been exchanged between Caelum and Glaeba prior to their return, negotiating Nyah's homecoming and advising Ricard Li that she would be accompanied by someone important. Despite his disguise, Li recognised Stellan almost immediately.

The spymaster eyed him up and down and then shook his head. "I see the Glaeban gift for understatement remains undiminished."

"I beg your pardon?"

"*The princess will be accompanied by someone important*, I believe the message said." Li smiled thinly. "Still, one good heir deserves another I suppose. Did Hawkes think up this idiotic plan?"

Stellan squeezed Nyah's hand in warning. "Declan Hawkes is dead."

Nyah said nothing to contradict him, which was something of a relief. Even though Declan had made her swear on her mother's life that she'd say nothing about his survival, or his transformation into an immortal, Stellan still wasn't sure she understood the consequences of letting the secret slip. Stellan, who'd spent most of his life hiding what he was, appreciated the young man's predicament better than most. If Declan wanted to hide his immortality from his enemies, as well as his friends, knowing nobody would ever look at him the same way again, well . . . Stellan could hardly fault the man for that.

Li studied him curiously for a moment before he spoke. "Despite the rather pointless disguise, you're looking remarkably well, your grace. Considering you're dead."

Stellan wished he could tell if the man was joking. If he was so inclined, Ricard Li could—with a word—have him arrested and sent straight back to Glaeba.

He chose to assume the best. "The pointless disguise was to facilitate my journey through Glaeba to avoid casual recognition. I look forward to dispensing with it now I'm here in Caelum."

"You're assuming Queen Jilna is going to welcome you," Li said, frowning.

"I've returned her daughter to her," Stellan pointed out. "The daughter stolen away by persons unknown from Caelum, handed to the Glaeban Spymaster and kept prisoner all this time, until I was able to escape from prison, kill the man responsible for her incarceration and return her to the country of her birth."

Li stared at him for a long moment. Almost every word of Stellan's statement was a blatant lie, and Li knew it, because he was the one who had arranged Nyah's abduction—with her active cooperation—in the first place. The two men stared each other down, each judging the other, trying to work out how much the other knew, and how far they could be trusted.

It was Nyah, however, who, with a child's disregard for artifice, put things into perspective. "It's all right, Ricard. Stell— Jareth knows everything. About how you helped me and how Declan helped me too. He won't betray us. But it's only fair that we help him now, by giving him a sly gum."

Li glanced down at the princess, clearly not happy with her suggestion. "And to think, I was only just saying to myself this morning, *what will I do with this spare sly gum I just happen to have laying about* . . . "

Stellan smiled. "I believe she means asylum."

"Oh, don't worry, I know what she means. But it's a big ask, your grace. You were being tried for murder and treason in your own country, last I heard. And everyone thinks you're dead. At the very least, you're an escaped convict. Your arrival here is going to precipitate some serious trouble, should the queen decide to offer you asylum."

"Trouble I'm assuming will distract the queen and her new husband and keep them occupied and too busy to focus on other, smaller issues," he said, glancing down at Nyah, "for some considerable time to come."

A slow, devious smile crept over Ricard Li's face. "You make a valid point, your grace."

"There's a reason I was King Enteny's most favoured foreign envoy, Master Li, and I can assure you, it wasn't because of my taste in lovers." Better to get that sticky little detail cleared up at the outset too. Stellan had no intention of starting this new life he seemed to have acquired as a political agitator by continuing to pretend he was something he wasn't.

Let them take me as I am, he'd decided. *And to hell with the consequences.*

It was a pity Declan Hawkes had yet to learn that lesson.

"We heard about that too," Li said. "Are the rumours true?"

"Most of them."

To his immense relief, Ricard Li shrugged dismissively. "Well, that's your business, I suppose. We're not quite so . . . bothered . . . by things like that here in Caelum. Hell, we marry off our children to prop up thrones. Puts your particular . . . preferences . . . into perspective, don't you think?"

Relieved beyond words he'd survived his first few minutes in Caelum, Stellan nodded in agreement. "I believe it does."

Ricard Li smiled. "So . . . shall we escort her highness to the palace so we can break it to the queen and her new husband that the long-lost Caelish heir is returned and even if Lord Tyrone fathers a child on the queen tomorrow, he's no longer got any claim on the throne?"

Stellan glanced down at Nyah. "Are you ready for this, your highness? It might get a little rough."

Nyah nodded solemnly. "I'm the crown princess of Caelum, my lord. I will do whatever it takes to save my throne from the immortals."

Ricard looked at Stellan. "*Immortals?*"

Stellan shook his head and sighed as he realised it was going to fall to him to break the news to the Caelish Spymaster about the true identity of Lord Torfail and his family.

"We have a lot to talk about, Master Li."

"Apparently we do," he agreed, staring at them both in confusion for a moment before shaking his head and turning toward the carriage he had waiting to take Nyah home.

Chapter 22

"That's the third one this week."

Arkady glanced up from the narrow bed she was wiping down with lye soap and hot water. Its occupant had died several hours earlier. She was disinfecting it before the next patient arrived. "Have the family come for the body?"

Geriko shrugged, his eyes, as usual, going straight to her bare breasts. *One day*, she thought, *he'll look me in the eye and the shock will kill me.*

"Won't make no difference. Doc ordered 'em all burned. 'Sides, who's gonna care about a dead canine?"

Sadly, Geriko was right. The canine who had just died was of no value to anybody any longer. The man who owned him certainly didn't want a dead slave back just to give him a decent burial. That's why he'd brought his slave here to the clinic in the poorer part of the city, rather than pay a physician good money to visit his kennels.

"Well, hopefully that's the last of them."

Geriko shook his head. "It ain't even the beginning, Kady. If this is swamp fever, like the doc thinks it is, we're all in for a bad time of it."

It more than likely was the fever Geriko spoke of. The man who owned the dead canine was a jeweller who had recently been north into the wetlands on a trading mission to secure supplies of nacre, and his slave had fallen ill within a day of returning home.

"You've seen swamp fever before?"

Geriko nodded, lifting the corner of the mattress so Arkady could get to the base. She wrung out the rag again and kept cleaning as she talked. On average, the clinic slaves worked from dawn until dusk. If she ever wanted to see dinner or her bed tonight, then she had to finish this before Cydne got back from informing the canine's owner of his fate.

"Had it when I was a young 'un," he said. "Near killed me, it did. Took more 'n half the slaves in the Medura compound, now I come to think of it. And Lady Medura, herself."

"Cydne's mother?"

He nodded. "Swamp fever don't care who you are. Highborn, lowborn, slave or free, man or Crasii. Takes 'em all."

Arkady had vague recollections of her father speaking of some terrible pestilence that ravaged the swampy tropical regions of Amyrantha period-ically, but as she'd had no interest in the countries concerned at the time, she'd never paid much attention. The only thing she remembered was her father mentioning they should be grateful that Glaeba's much colder cli-mate seemed to keep the disease at bay.

"Is there a cure?" she asked, wringing out the cloth.

"Not that I know of. Mostly you just tries to stop people vomitin' and shittin' 'emselves to death. If you can survive that, you're usually better after a week or so."

"I never realised you were such a medical expert, Geriko," Cydne re-marked, entering the hospital wing from the other end of the room where the doctor's office was located. He removed his coat as he neared them and handed it to the feline Crasii bodyguard who followed him, before turning to check on Arkady's work. The feline, a ginger tabby with a white face and chest, named Jojo, accepted the coat and folded it over her arm with-out comment. Arkady didn't know her well. Cydne had only recently taken to bringing a bodyguard with him when he visited the clinic. It was an idea of his wife's apparently, and probably meant more as a chaperone than a protector.

Cydne looked around then nodded with approval. All six berths were empty. For fear of spreading the infection, Cydne had sent home all the other patients several days ago, when the infected canine arrived at the clinic, accompanied by his rather peeved owner.

Geriko bowed apologetically as their master approached. "Sorry, sir. I was just tellin' Kady 'bout swamp fever. She's not seen it before."

Cydne reached them and stopped to study Arkady thoughtfully. "Is that right? Well, I suppose it is, given you're not from around here. I should have thought of that before . . ." His voice trailed off, his face wrinkled with concern.

"Before what?"

"Before I exposed you to it," he said with a shrug. "Oh well, we'll know if you're infected in the next day or two. It has a devilishly short incuba-tion period, this wretched fever. Did you burn that body as I ordered?" he asked the big slave, as if the death sentence he had just informed Arkady she had been exposed to meant nothing at all.

"Yes, sir."

"Then you may return to your quarters until tomorrow. Good evening, Geriko."

"Sir." The big man glanced at Arkady and then bowed to his master and withdrew.

"You can wait in the hall," he added to Jojo.

The feline also bowed politely and left the room, taking her master's jacket with her. Cydne waited until they were alone before addressing Arkady. "You can finish that in the morning."

She nodded and rose to her feet, tossing the washcloth in the bucket of soapy water. "As my lord commands."

"Tides, you still haven't learned a shred of humility, Kady."

"Have I given you any reason to complain about my work?"

"No. But you still act as if I've hired you as my assistant, rather than bought you as a slave."

"If it helps me keep my sanity to think of it that way, what do you care?"

"People have noticed your less than humble demeanour."

"People?" she asked with a raised brow. "Or one person in particular?"

Cydne blushed crimson, a trait married life had done nothing to cure him of. "My wife thinks your attitude is too . . . precocious."

Olegra, Cydne's much-agonised-over wife, had turned out to be a thoroughly spoiled little brat of a girl. Pretty, chubby and with a screech on her like a cranky fish-wife, she was seventeen years old, convinced the world had been created purely to amuse her and that Cydne's purpose as her husband was to indulge her every whim.

Arkady wasn't really surprised to learn Cydne's bride disapproved of her husband's *wii-ah*. The Lady Medura had been to visit the clinic on several occasions, none of which had endeared her to the slaves who worked there; or the patients who came there for help, for that matter. She heartily disapproved of his occupation, even more so, of his commitment to working among the poorer citizens of Port Traeker, even though it was a condition of his membership of the Senestran Physicians' Guild. Unable to comprehend anyone wanting to help the lesser creatures of this world, she had recently convinced herself that Cydne's dedication to his work was because of his fascination for his batch-bought assistant, and not the dire health of the poor of Port Traeker.

And that, Arkady had discovered, was the strangest thing of all about this weird Senestran society of which she found herself a part. Olegra was a member of the same strict religious cult as the Torlenian ambassador of Senestra's wife—the woman Kinta had thrown into gaol for calling her a whore. They worshipped the Lord of Temperance, but their beliefs were nothing Jaxyn would have condoned. The cult abhorred sex for anything other than the purpose of procreation, considered any relationships other than one between man and woman to be an abomination and prayed an awful lot (sometimes four or five times a day) to an immortal who—Arkady knew for a fact—wouldn't have answered a single prayer, even if he could hear them.

Arkady couldn't fathom the cult's moral code, either. The complex and comprehensive rules they followed that governed the conduct of relationships between men and women, didn't apply to slaves. Leaving themselves a loophole you could sail one of their wretched trading ships through, they'd gotten around that sticky point by refusing to acknowledge slaves as real people. That way, it was perfectly permissible for a man to sleep with a slave, or keep one or two, or even half a dozen as his mistresses—his *wii-ah*—provided they were of the right stock and any children they bore remained unacknowledged as his heirs. Arkady, being both foreign and *makor-di*, was unacceptable. Their arguments, according to Cydne, weren't about him keeping a mistress.

They were about him keeping the wrong *sort* of mistress.

"Does the lovely Olegra think she'll catch something nasty if you lie with me and then her?"

"You see!" Cydne complained. "You have no sense of your place in this world at all, Kady. Again, you blurt out things any other master would whip you into submission for even thinking, let alone saying aloud." He took her hand and pulled her to him. Arkady let him, knowing there was no point in resisting.

"I'm guessing whipping me into submission is your wife's suggestion."

"You mustn't speak of my wife in that tone."

"Then how should I speak of her?"

"I'd rather you didn't." He traced a finger gently down between her breasts, before pulling her even closer and burying his face in her hair, as if the scent of it was some sort of heady nectar.

"Aren't you worried I might be infected with swamp fever?" She'd schooled herself not to flinch from his touch. If she didn't resist, she didn't get hurt, and she knew how to escape the feeling of being used, even if it was only in her own mind.

"It doesn't matter if you are. I survived the last outbreak. I'm immune now."

"Well, that's all right then."

He didn't seem to notice her sarcasm. "Olegra doesn't understand me like you do."

Tides, Arkady thought. *Where did you get the idea I understand you?*

He bent his head to her breast, murmuring, "We've time before I have to go home . . ."

"Now who's acting as if I have an opinion? Or a choice?"

He lifted his head from her breast, looking quite wounded. "Have I ever taken you against your will, Kady?"

Every single time, she wanted to reply, but survival demanded she keep the truth to herself. The only way out of here was down, if Cydne took it into his head to be rid of her. If she was thrown out of this clinic and sent back into the general slave pool, her life as a *makor-di* would get much much worse. "No, you've never taken me against my will."

Clearly, he didn't accept her at her word. "Would you lie about such a thing to me?"

"Of course I would," she said. "I'm a slave. Slaves tell their masters what they want to hear all the time. It's the basic flaw in your social system."

He studied her face for a moment, as if he suspected she was mocking him, and then lust won out. He kissed her, his tongue thrusting between her teeth, as his hands fumbled at the knot on her loincloth. Arkady didn't resist. She even kissed him back after a time, resigned to the inevitable.

There are worse ways to survive, she reminded herself, although as Cydne pushed her down onto the narrow bed reeking of lye soap and recent death, she couldn't, at that moment, think of a single one of them.

Chapter 23

"Stellan Desean is still alive."

The king and queen looked up from their breakfast, alarmed by Jaxyn's dramatic entrance and his even more startling news.

And so you should look startled, you flanking fools, he thought, striding across the dining room to the table where Mathu and Diala—still posing as Queen Kylia and looking every inch the innocent girl she was pretending to be—sat eating their breakfast as if they didn't have a care in the world. It was a rare sunny morning and the balcony doors were open, letting in the fresh air. Diala reached out and covered Mathu's hand with hers in a comforting gesture before turning to look at Jaxyn.

That she maintained the fiction she felt anything for this boy-king irked Jaxyn no end, but he didn't have time to do anything about it now.

"Are you sure?"

"No, I just thought you both needed an interesting start to your day," he said, rolling his eyes impatiently. "Of course I'm *sure*."

"You said he was dead," Mathu said. "Tides, Jaxyn, we gave him a state funeral."

"A little pre-emptively, it seems. Turns out the charred corpse we thought was the Duke of Lebec was someone else's charred corpse."

"How do you know he's alive?" Kylia asked.

"Because in a heroic gesture of good faith toward our neighbours, he's just returned the missing Princess Nyah to Caelum."

Mathu stared at him, still looking confused. "How can that be . . . ?"

Jaxyn leaned against the mantel and crossed his arms. "I don't know the details. All I know is that Daly Bridgeman got a report this morning from Caelum informing him Princess Nyah is alive and well, and returned to Cycrane a few days ago in the company of the former Duke of Lebec."

"So you fixed your little problem, then?" Diala asked, a direct reference to their last conversation on the topic of spies in Caelum, which he chose to ignore.

"Oh, and just to make things interesting, our not-so-dead duke has asked Queen Jilna for asylum."

Even Mathu knew what that meant. "But she wouldn't dare! Stellan was being tried as a traitor against the Glaeban crown. At the very least, he's an escaped prisoner. Giving him asylum is tantamount to an act of war."

"I'm quite sure Tryan knows that," Diala muttered, dropping her innocent façade for a moment.

"Tryan?" Mathu asked.

"I meant Lord Tyrone," she said with an ingenuous smile, smoothly covering her slip. "I always get those names muddled up."

"Do we know where Nyah's been all this time?" the young king asked Jaxyn with a frown, which was some small comfort. Apparently he was capable of taking *something* seriously.

"According to the story Desean's putting about in Cycrane, she was kidnapped from Caelum by agents of Glaeba. He's telling them he discovered her whereabouts in prison, broke out of gaol during the fire, saved her from a fate worse than death and then nobly escorted her home. He's making it very clear she was a prisoner of Declan Hawkes, your majesty, which, by implication, means she was being held by you. Hawkes was *your* spymaster, after all."

Mathu pushed away his breakfast, his appetite vanishing with Jaxyn's news. "But I knew nothing about any of this!"

"Won't make much difference to the Caelish, I suspect."

"Mathu's got a point, though," Diala said. "He can't be held responsible for something Hawkes did on his own."

"He's Glaeba's king," Jaxyn pointed out unsympathetically. "He's responsible for everything that happens in his kingdom, whether he knows about it or not."

"But it's all lies!" Mathu complained. "And because Hawkes is dead and not here to contradict him, Stellan thinks he can get away with it." He stood up and began pacing the room. "How could he do this to me? I thought he was my friend."

Jaxyn wondered if it was worth taking the time to remind this ignorant and mightily offended young king that the man he was accusing of lying about his involvement in the kidnapping of Princess Nyah was the same man he'd ordered his own spymaster to trump up charges against in the not so distant past. "Stellan was probably asking himself the same question about you, your majesty, while he was sitting in court listening to the line of witnesses you'd arranged to perjure themselves to convict him of a crime we all know he didn't commit."

"It wasn't my idea! You said it was better to try him for murder than accuse him of being a sodomite," Mathu said, turning on Jaxyn. "You said it would save the family from scandal."

"And it would have," Jaxyn pointed out reasonably, "had your cousin the decency to stay dead. My plan involved executing him, remember? Had we followed *that* plan, we wouldn't have *this* problem."

"What do you think they'll do?" Diala asked, the question about much more than the Caelish queen. They both knew the Empress of the Five Realms was behind this, and that Stellan had played right into their hands by giving them a perfectly legitimate reason to go to war now, before the Tide was fully up. A battle fought once the Tide Lords could all call on their full powers, served nobody, and would more than likely destroy the kingdoms they were squabbling over.

But a good old-fashioned war . . . one with human and Crasii soldiers to throw into a bloodbath . . .

Well, that would achieve the same result and leave at least the victor's kingdom intact, to be enjoyed to the full, once the Tide peaked and they became gods once more.

Damn you, Stellan, Jaxyn thought, angry at himself for underestimating both the man's political acumen and his desire for vengeance. *Fine time you pick to develop a spine.*

Fine time you pick to get even with me.

It wasn't often Jaxyn misjudged someone so badly. Certainly, he couldn't remember the last time a jilted lover had managed to get one up on him.

He turned to Diala. "They'll rattle their sabres at us for a while, I think. Tyrone won't formally declare war until he's in a position to attack us, but you can be sure that will be the moment the formal declaration is delivered."

"What do we do about Stellan?" Mathu demanded. He hadn't moved much beyond Stellan's betrayal. The fact that Glaeba was teetering on the edge of war didn't seem to have registered with the young king yet.

"Ask for him back," Diala said. "No, better yet, demand his return. List all his crimes, real and imagined, and warn Caelum they are interfering in the business of the sovereign state of Glaeba by offering to shelter such a heinous criminal."

"Will that work?" Mathu asked.

Jaxyn shook his head. "Of course it won't work. It won't do a damned thing except buy us some time to gather our army."

Mathu stared at him in horror, as if it had only just occurred to him this could actually mean war. Then he turned to Diala—she who had been counselling avoidance up until a few minutes ago. "What should I do?"

"What Jaxyn says," she advised, too smart to play games with the landscape so dramatically changed. "They'll attack us as soon as they think they're ready, and your sodomite cousin has given them the perfect excuse."

"He's your uncle, Kylia," Mathu reminded her.

"To my eternal shame."

"Tides, I still can't grasp the depth of Stellan's betrayal."

Jaxyn could. In fact, he almost admired Stellan for it. He certainly understood why he'd waited until now to wreak his vengeance. After all, he'd already been branded a traitor, so he really had nothing to lose. Jaxyn wished he'd taken the time to remember Stellan Desean was more than a man with a secret; more than a man with a claim on a throne and a very desirable wife. He was a diplomat and a brilliant political strategist.

Just exactly how brilliant, Jaxyn was only just beginning to appreciate.

Of course, that just left the question of whether Hawkes was really dead too, or if he was also a part of this plan. Given they had both died— or were supposed to have died—in the same fire, it wasn't inconceivable that Declan Hawkes had survived the blaze, just as Stellan had . . .

But what possible motive could the King's Spymaster, a man with a bright future in the service of the new king, have to fall into a plot with Stellan Desean, which was—by anybody's definition—high treason? Particularly as there seemed to be no love lost between the two men. After all, Stellan had stolen away Declan Hawkes's woman with the offer of wealth, a title and an escape from the slums of Lebec.

No, Jaxyn decided. *If anything, this is proof Hawkes is dead.* Even if he were inclined to betray the crown, he would never be a party to anything that involved trusting Stellan Desean, just on principle.

Which reminds me . . . where is the lovely Arkady?

"Did you know about this?"

Diala closed her door before answering Jaxyn, checking the hall to be certain he hadn't been observed entering her bedroom by anybody in the palace but a Crasii.

She leaned on the door and glared at him. "Of course I didn't know. Tides, Jaxyn, *you* were sleeping with him. Surely you must have known what he was capable of."

"He never struck me as the vengeful type."

"You think he's doing this for any other reason?" She pushed off the door and walked to the window to gaze out over the mist-shrouded lake. The earlier sunlight was gone, blocked out by the heavy clouds bringing yet another rainstorm to the Great Lakes.

Jaxyn shrugged, picking up the poker to stir the fire back into life. "What other reason is there?"

"Maybe he knows who we are. *What* we are."

He shook his head, overturning the red coals underneath the ashes. "Arkady tried to convince him Cayal was immortal and he laughed at her. No, this is about getting even with me and with Mathu for falsely accusing him of killing the king. He still believes you're his niece and I was his lover. Besides, for Stellan to throw himself on the mercy of Caelum's queen because he's afraid the Tide Lords are trying to take over Glaeba, he'd have to know that the Empress of the Five Realms and her wretched clan had taken up residence there—and who and what *they* are, too. How would he know that? How would he even suspect it?"

She turned to look at him, her arms folded across her body. "The Cabal would know."

"The Cabal of the Tarot?" he scoffed. "Tides, they're deader than Cayal's daughter."

"Are you sure about that?"

Jaxyn shrugged, picking up a small log and tossing it onto the fire in a shower of sparks. "We haven't seen or heard of them for the better part of a thousand years. It's reasonable to assume they're no longer with us."

"They've survived cataclysms before this," Diala warned. "Mortals can be very resourceful."

"As Stellan Desean has just proved in spades."

"So what are we going to do?"

Jaxyn tossed the poker aside and turned to look at her. "Get ready for war. And keep Mathu on the throne."

"I thought you wanted to get rid of him?"

"I did," he said, "when there was no other clear heir to Glaeba's throne. But Stellan's the next in line and everybody knows it. He'll be a focal point for every malcontent in Glaeba once word gets out he's alive. And we'd be foolish to underestimate the support he has among people who claim they're loyal to the king."

"If Mathu dies, I'll become queen."

"At which point, Stellan would be well within his rights to claim the throne as his, and with Caelum backing him, would have a better than even chance of taking it. I'll be damned if I'll make it easier for him by getting rid of the incumbent king."

"Would he do that?"

"Tides, who knows *what* he's capable of?"

"You claimed you did," she said, walking over to the bed. She kicked off her shoes and stretched out on the bed, with a malicious smile. "You screwed this one up royally, didn't you, Jaxyn?"

He followed her, looking down on her reclining form, wishing there was a point in wrapping his hands around her throat and squeezing the life out of her. "I will prevail, Diala."

"Well, if you don't," she said, folding her arms behind her head, the better to display her cleavage—which was pointless because Jaxyn had no interest in Diala. He'd gotten over wanting her several thousand years ago. "I can always go visit Syrolee. I'm sure she'd welcome me with open arms," she added.

"You might want to remember you said that," Jaxyn replied, shaking his head contemptuously at her blatant and pointless attempt to entice him, "the next time you start to wonder why I don't trust you."

"You don't trust anybody, Jaxyn," she said, still smiling. "Not even yourself. And with just cause, as it turns out. Hope it was good for you."

"You hope *what* was good for me?"

"You and Stellan Desean. I hope it was good for you, dear, because he's given you one right royal fucking." Then she added spitefully, "Mind you, I'm not sure you did enjoy it, because it's taken you until now to realise how profoundly you've been screwed."

Jaxyn shook his head. "Nobody gets the upper hand over me for long, Diala. Not you, not Syrolee and her power-grubbing family and certainly not Stellan Desean."

"Then what are you going to do?"

"What I should have done in the first place. Have him killed."

"But he's under the protection of the Queen of Caelum . . ."

"Who just married Lord Tyrone of Torfail, whose sister is Lady Alysa, whose Crasii are my spies. I don't have to get near Stellan to take care of this, my dear. I'll simply order the canine Cecil to kill him."

"Unless Elyssa's had the wit to order them to forget everything you ever said to them."

"She'll not even think of it. Elyssa's a fool."

"Well, it takes one to know one, I suppose."

Chapter 24

"Put those bottles in the back!" Cydne Medura called out.

He was shouting from the front of the small wooden house in the remote village of Watershed Falls they had commandeered as their temporary clinic. They'd been sent here by the Physicians' Guild to nip the outbreak of swamp fever in the bud.

Arkady hefted the slatted wooden crate full of the special tonic the guild had supplied for them to treat the outbreak. This room was the bedroom, furnished with a narrow pallet she knew was going to be uncomfortable, just by looking at. It would be even worse if Cydne expected her to share it with him. Sleeping in close contact with another body in this heat was going to be sticky, uncomfortable and unpleasant.

Maybe she could convince him to let her sleep on the floor once he was done with her. She was his *wii-ah*, after all, not the love of his life. He didn't need to hold her in his warm embrace all night long, just to prove his devotion to her.

"There's another crate to go out there too!" she heard him telling Jojo.

Arkady carefully put the crate on the floor by the small window and walked back out to the porch where Cydne was supervising the unloading of their supplies. Already a number of people had begun to line up, following the news that a doctor had arrived with some hope of relief from the fever, which was ravaging the population of the wetlands. She glanced out over the village, wondering how many more would come, once word got out they were here.

The village of Watershed Falls proved more substantial than Arkady was expecting. Somehow, from Cydne's description, she'd gained the impression of a swampy island with a dock and a tavern and a couple of houses, clinging to the edge of the wetlands, eking out a miserable existence in an insect-infested swamp.

It turned out to be a village of more than a thousand souls, human and Crasii alike. And while it was certainly infested with an impressive array of insects, most of which seemed to consider human flesh a food source, it had a main street, several other streets leading off it, and quite a number of prosperous businesses. The main industry seemed to be harvesting nacre. For Arkady, who came from Lebec, where pearls were prized and where the mother-of-pearl contained in the oyster shells was an almost valueless by-product, it seemed a strange occupation. Quite the opposite of her experience. Everything else here seemed related to the harvesting of flax, rice, cotton and a few other crops which thrived in this waterlogged environment.

"Lock the door once you've put the tonic away," Cydne told Arkady as she picked up the last crate. "If word gets out we have a cure, we're likely to be overrun."

"Do we *have* a cure?" she asked, wondering why, if this tonic was so special, they hadn't used it to save any of the swamp fever victims they'd treated at the clinic in Port Traeker.

"Oh, yes," he assured her. "Believe me, that stuff will stop swamp fever stone dead."

The pragmatism of the Senestrans continued to amaze Arkady. She'd been surprised enough to learn the Physicians' Guild insisted their members treat the poor as well as the rich, but when a delegation arrived at the clinic to inform Cydne he was being sent north to deal with a swamp fever outbreak, she'd been thoroughly impressed. Not only was the guild funding the trip, but they'd supplied all the tonic required, free of charge, and assured Cydne if he needed any more, all he had to do was ask for it.

Their logic, of course, was that if they could stop the fever at its source, then it wouldn't reach the cities, and countless lives would be saved. Arkady wondered how, in a society so driven by trade and profits, such an altruistic outlook could flourish. In the end, she decided not to question it. Besides, Senestran altruism was very selective. They might be here saving countless lives for the greater good of Senestra, but that didn't alter Arkady's circumstances one iota.

Arkady put the last crate in the bedroom next to the one Jojo had brought in, locked the door and then walked back outside with the feline bodyguard where they were confronted with a totally unexpected sight. Standing in line was a creature she at first mistook for Tiji, until she realised, on closer inspection, that the silver-skinned Crasii was male.

"That's a chameleon Crasii," she said in wonder as she handed Cydne the key.

He glanced up uninterestedly, took the key and pocketed it. "So what? They're as common as fleas around here. Most likely they're the ones responsible for the fever."

"I wish Tiji was here now." Declan's little spy—irritating and judgemental as she was—had hungered to know if there were others of her kind. Arkady finally had an answer for her . . . and nobody to share it with.

"Who's Tiji?" Jojo asked.

"A chameleon I knew once. She belonged to a friend of mine."

"Well, I hope he didn't catch anything from her," Cydne said. "You can make up those pallets in the front room next. We'll treat the humans inside and the Crasii out here on the veranda."

Arkady and Jojo spent the next hour setting everything up, by which time the line outside had grown considerably. Surprisingly—and to Arkady's intense relief—there weren't many suffering from swamp fever. She was somewhat consoled by the notion Cydne had, if not a cure, then at least a method of treating the disease should she become infected, but the thought did little to ease her mind. For this first afternoon, they saw patients with a variety of other ailments this rare visit from a Port Traeker physician had afforded them the opportunity to attend to.

They worked solidly until dusk, Cydne dispensing medicines—and often quite pointless advice—to the patients lining up to see him. He was much more confident in his role as a doctor than he was socialising with his father's trading partners or his wife's inane friends. He still stammered and blushed when called upon to examine female patients, though, and didn't know where to look when one largish, heavily pregnant woman appeared with a nasty fungal infection. He'd blushed thirteen shades of crimson by the time he was done examining her, and then glared at Arkady as if he knew she was silently laughing at his embarrassment.

Still, he managed to get through the line of patients, seeing the human patients first, regardless of their condition. The Crasii were forced to wait, Jojo hissing at a few of the more impatient ones to keep them in order. When the last of the human patients filed out—none of whom appeared to be suffering swamp fever—Cydne moved out of the front room, set himself up on the veranda and told Jojo she could start to let the Crasii come.

The first Crasii was a feline. She had a battle-scarred pelt and was suffering from an abscessed scratch acquired in a recent fight, which had swollen the left side of her face to twice its normal size. In a business-like fashion, Cydne lanced the abscess, drained it and dressed it and sent her on her way with a poultice which Arkady suspected would do nothing to aid the healing. Still, with the pressure relieved and the swelling reduced, the feline was grateful enough, and left quite happy with her treatment.

The next two patients were canines and just as easily dispensed with. And then the chameleon stepped up to be treated.

Arkady stared at him, marvelling at how much like Tiji he looked. She'd never seen a male of the species before, and was surprised to see his skin colour remain quite solid, not flickering the way Tiji's did when she got excited or upset. She wondered if it meant the male chameleons couldn't change their skin tone the way females could.

Arkady led him to Cydne, smiling at the reptilian Crasii reassuringly. "What's your name?"

"What does it matter what his name is?" Cydne snapped. "I'd rather know what's wrong with him."

"There's nothing wrong with me," he said to Cydne. And then, as if he appreciated Arkady's attempt to be civil, he added to her, "My name is Azquil."

"Why are you wasting my time if there's nothing wrong with you?" Cydne asked.

"We've been told you have a tonic that will treat swamp fever."

"What of it?"

"Well, there are other villages, sir—villages further inland where you'll not be visiting that are suffering from the fever," he said.

"And . . ." Cydne prompted impatiently as he mopped his brow. For the first time, Arkady was grateful for being able to wear so little in the heat. Cydne, in his embroidered shirt and vest, was hot and cranky and in no mood to be nice to anybody—which was probably why he'd left the Crasii until last, Arkady thought. Being subhuman, his bedside manner with them, or lack thereof, was hardly an issue.

"I've been sent to ask if we could buy some of the tonic and instructions on its use for dispensing to the inland villages."

"Who asked you?"

Azquil hesitated for a fraction of a second. "The village elders."

Cydne might have missed the hesitation, but Arkady didn't. She was fairly certain Azquil was lying, but couldn't think of a good reason he'd need to. Unless he was making up this story about the village elders because he was planning to sell the tonic on the black market . . .

"I don't have money but I have these." He opened the small pouch he was carrying and spilled the contents into his palm. The pouch was full of small, square, iridescent nacre tiles, all carved and polished to perfection.

Cydne wasn't interested in the Crasii's bag of trinkets. He fished the key from his pocket and held it out to Arkady. "Give him three bottles."

"Are you sure?"

"Don't question me."

She took the key, bowed obsequiously and replied in Glaeban so only he would understand her, "As you command, O peerless and most worthy master."

Cydne glared at her for her insolence but said nothing. Arkady retrieved the three bottles of tonic from the bedroom and went back to the veranda, where Cydne sat stiffly, ignoring Azquil.

The chameleon rose to his feet as she approached, looking very relieved.

"I can't thank you enough," he said, taking the bottles from her. "How much do I owe you for them?"

"Consider them a gift from the Senestran Physicians' Guild," Cydne told him, waving away the pouch full of polished nacre. "The dose is one spoonful every three hours. Now take the tonic and go. I have genuinely sick people to see."

Azquil nodded, spared Arkady a sympathetic smile and then bowed to Cydne before hurrying off the veranda and their makeshift consulting room.

"You weren't very nice to him," Arkady said as she handed back the key.

"I'm not paid to be nice," he said. "And it's not your place to comment on my behaviour, in any case." He pocketed the key, adjusted his vest, and sat a little straighter in his chair. "Tell Jojo to send the next one over. And tell her I said to make sure this one is actually sick."

"Yes, master."

"And, Kady," he added in an ominous voice, "if you ever take that tone with me again in front of another living soul, I will slap you until your ears bleed. Is that understood?"

Arkady hesitated and then nodded. She'd not heard him threaten anyone like that before and wasn't sure enough of herself to test his mettle.

"Of course. I'm sorry."

"So you should be," he agreed grumpily. "Now fetch the next wretched animal or we'll be here all night."

Chapter 25

"He just *gave* it to you?"

Azquil nodded, staring at the three precious bottles of creamy-coloured tonic sitting on the bench in the small cottage outside Watershed Falls where they'd been staying these past few weeks, waiting for the swamp fever to settle. "He barely even glanced at the nacre I offered him, and there was a fortune in the pouch. Said to consider it a gift from the Senestran Physicians' Guild."

"Does the Senestran Physicians' Guild usually do things like that?"

"Not so's you'd notice. Mostly they go about cursing our very existence, telling everyone we're a pestilence responsible for all the woes in the world."

"Perhaps this doctor is different," Tiji suggested.

"Maybe," Azquil said, not convinced. "His *makor-di* seemed nice enough. But he struck me as being just as stuck-up and disdainful of the Crasii as the rest of his kind."

Tiji smiled reassuringly. "Well, whatever his motives, you have the tonic. Now we can take it back to the villages the suzerain . . ."

"Please don't call them that."

"Very well, the villages the *Trinity* can't get to in time, and help them too."

He smiled. "Yes, we can. Only *we* aren't going anywhere, Tiji. *I* will deliver the tonic with Tenika. You have to stay here. You're not immune to the fever."

"But if I catch it now, you have the tonic . . ."

"We don't know how well the tonic works."

"I'm prepared to take the risk."

"I'm not," Azquil said, looking at her so intently Tiji's skin began to flicker.

He looked at her like that a lot, and in the close confines of the cottage, it was somewhat problematic. She was intensely aware of him. And knew he was aware of her. His skin tone flickered too, whenever they accidentally touched, either in the cottage or when they walked to the village. If they stopped along the way, apparently by accident Azquil always seemed to be standing next to something bright—a flower or a brilliantly plumaged bird—as if the reflections off his silver skin would make him brighter to look upon.

Tiji knew little to nothing about the mating rituals of her own species, but she didn't need a lecture in the birds, the bees and the lizards to tell when a male chameleon was coming on to her. The idea excited her and terrified her all at once. Until now, the only male of any species she had ever felt any sort of affection for was Declan Hawkes. Her feelings for Azquil were nothing like the feelings she'd had for her human master, though. This felt primal. Exciting. And right.

"You don't have to watch over me all the time, Azquil," she said.

"I do," he said. "It's my job. And even if it wasn't, I'd want to." He hesitated, the silence laden with unspoken tension, and then he smiled even wider. "Have you ever been swimming in a hot spring?"

Tiji looked at him oddly, wondering at the abrupt change of subject. "No."

"Would you like to? There's one not far from here. And I'll have to leave tomorrow to take the tonic to the Outpost, so tonight is our last chance to have a bit of fun before I go."

Tiji wasn't game enough to ask Azquil to define exactly what he meant by *a bit of fun*, but the idea of spending the evening in his company was a decidedly pleasant one.

"I'd like that."

"Good! I can show you how to catch Genoa moths."

"What's a Genoa moth?"

"The best tasting treat on Amyrantha."

"You eat them?"

He nodded. "Sure we eat them. What did you think? We were going to read poetry to them?"

"How do you cook them?"

"Well . . . you don't," he said, looking at her with a puzzled expression. "That's what makes them taste so good. And I swear, there's *nothing* like the feeling of moth wings fluttering in your mouth in that moment before you bite into them." He sighed with pleasure at the very thought of it, and then looked at her in surprise when she didn't seem to share his enthusiasm. "Don't tell me you've never eaten a Genoa moth?"

"I've never eaten any sort of moth," she said. "Or any sort of insect, come to think of it. Are you serious? You eat them raw?"

Azquil shook his head sadly. "Oh, Tiji, what have they done to you? How can you not have eaten an insect until now? That's the staple food of our diet here."

"I thought you'd been cooking meat stews."

"Well . . . stewed insects . . . yes. What did you think it was? Chicken?"

"It tasted like chicken."

"We've been eating all manner of six-legged creatures ever since you arrived," he informed her. "Tides, what do you normally eat?"

"Well, you know, meat . . ."

He pulled a face. "You mean you don't mind the dead flesh of animals, but you're worried about eating live insects? Tides, at least if they're alive, you know they're fresh. Who knows how long a cow has been dead before a human eats it? We're not carrion eaters, Tiji."

She looked at him doubtfully. "You don't lie in wait on rocks and catch them with your tongue too, do you?"

He laughed and offered her his hand. "Of course not. We trap them, same as humans trap rabbits. Come on."

"Humans don't trap rabbits, bite their heads off and then eat them while they're still squirming," she pointed out, taking his hand, a little less enthusiastic about an outing with Azquil now she'd discovered it might involve eating live insects. "Where are we going?"

"To have a swim in the hot spring," he said, "and then we'll find a nice, sun-warmed rock to lie on, light a fire, stare up at the stars for a while, and wait for the moths to come to us, at which point, trust me, I will introduce you to delights you have never experienced before."

Warily, Tiji let Azquil lead her out into the gathering darkness that was filled with the sound of singing insects, thinking the delights she had never experienced before—the ones she was looking forward to, at least—had not, even in her wildest dreams, involved swallowing live insects whole.

"Do you suppose there are other Tide Stars besides ours?" Tiji asked.

She was lying on her back staring up at the sky, letting the warm air dry her silver skin. The night was scattered with stars, shining like sprinkled ice-chips in the darkness. Against her back, the day's stored heat from the large flat rock they lay on seeped into her, the warmth both relaxing and seductive. The springs burbled in the distance and the warm air was damp, reeking faintly of sulphur, its comforting sound almost drowned out by the chirruping of the myriad nocturnal insects inhabiting the wetlands.

"I don't know," Azquil replied, lying beside her, also staring up at the crystalline sky. A few feet away, their small fire crackled, a beacon calling out to the insects of the wetlands to come hither and meet their doom. "Maybe all Tide magic comes from our sun."

"What about the hot springs?"

"What about them?"

"Where do you suppose the hot water comes from?"

"Underground volcanoes, probably," he suggested. "That's what Lady Arryl says, anyway."

"How would she know?"

"She comes from Magreth. They had hot springs there too, she told me. It was the volcanoes that warmed the water, so I suppose we have the same thing underground around here, somewhere. Only I hope they're a little safer than the ones in Magreth."

Tiji shook her head, uncomfortable with the casual mention of an immortal she instinctively despised. "It wasn't volcanoes that destroyed Magreth, Azquil. It was a Tide Lord. You know . . . like the ones you seem to be such good friends with."

"We're friends with Arryl, Medwen and Ambria, because they are friends to us. Why can't you accept that?"

She sighed, wishing Declan was here to explain it. He knew why they couldn't be trusted. And he could articulate it so much better than she could. "We're probably never going to defeat the immortals, are we?"

"That's why we need to find a way to live with them," he said. He rolled onto his side to look at her, resting his head on his hand. "Your skin looks very pretty that colour, you know."

Without her realising it, her silver scales had taken on the mottled brown hues of the rock they lay on. As soon as he brought it to her attention, however, the colour flickered and vanished.

He smiled apologetically. And he was *looking* at her like that again . . .

"I'm sorry, I've embarrassed you."

"No . . . really, I just . . ." *Tides, I'm turning into a blabbering fool . . .*

"Shhh!" he whispered, cutting her off before she could make a complete fool of herself. He placed a gentle finger on her lips and mouthed the words: *don't move.*

Tiji lay rigid, wondering if they were in some sort of danger as Azquil carefully leaned across her still damp body, his arm outstretched. He stayed like that for a long time, still in a way only a creature with reptilian blood could manage, his body pressing down on hers. Not knowing what he was doing, or why he was doing it, Tiji lay rigid beneath him, waiting for something to happen.

Unexpectedly, it did. Azquil's arm shot out as he grabbed at something, then he sat up with a triumphant expression. "Got one!"

She pushed herself up and stared at him. "You got what?"

"A Genoa moth! See." He opened his hand to reveal a large moth nestled in his palm. The colour of its wings was hard to determine in the darkness, perhaps dark blue or brown, but they were marked with two distinct, lighter coloured elliptical circles on each wing that made it seem as if there were two eyes staring out of the creature's back. Its pale body was slightly thinner than Tiji's little finger and about as long. It quivered fearfully in Azquil's grasp. "The Tide's gift to the chameleon Crasii."

"You're not seriously going to eat that, are you?"

He grinned, his slightly pointed teeth white against his handsome silver face. "Come closer. I'll show you how."

"It's disgusting."

"It's delicious."

With a great deal of trepidation, Tiji leaned forward. Azquil lifted the moth to her mouth. Certain she was going to choke on it, she resisted opening her lips, but Azquil's encouraging smile—and the almost irresistible desire to do whatever it took to impress him—finally coaxed them open. Azquil gently slid the moth into her mouth, sideways, so only one of its large wings touched her tongue, which tingled with exquisite sweetness as the acid in her saliva reacted with the moth's wing.

Shocked and delighted by the sensation, the moth's thick body wiggling against her chin, Azquil slipped the other wing into his own mouth until they were separated by nothing more than the moth's delicately ribbed torso. Giddy from the sensation of the dissolving wing on her tongue, her body tingling, Tiji moved even closer, inadvertently crushing the insect between them. The heady sweetness of the moth's wings were bland compared to the creature's meat, which tasted like nothing Tiji had ever experienced before. Hungrily, urgently, she licked at Azquil's face, as he licked hers, anxious not to waste a precious drop of the moth's sweet nectar.

As their tongues met, and before she had time to register what was happening, hunger for a taste of the crushed moth turned to hunger for each other. Their licking turned to kissing. With Azquil soon astride her, Tiji willingly lay back down on the warm rock, intoxicated by the heat and whatever strange freak of nature had turned the juice of a relatively common moth into an aphrodisiac of almost irresistible power. Her skin flickered through every colour she was capable of imitating, as did Azquil's skin, which simply added to her arousal. Azquil rubbed his body against hers, their scales hissing with a soft sibilant sigh, the vibration of scale on scale almost too sensitive to bear.

His tongue flickered over her scales, as the rising heat of her body seemed to sharpen the effects of the moth's juices. Murmuring sweet nothings, Azquil slid down her body, delivering such exquisite torture with his flickering tongue as he went that Tiji wanted him to stop almost as much as she wanted it to never end. When he finally reached between her legs she cried out in delight, not sure if this was love, or simply lust, or even if she was hallucinating under the effects of an intoxicating moth, simply living out a fantasy in her mind that was too delicious to be real.

Then he moved and was kissing her mouth again and Tiji felt the sharp pain of being entered for the first time. And then she knew that not only was this real, but it was wonderful, and for the first time since coming to the Senestran wetlands she felt as if she'd found her true home.

Chapter 26

"Tides! Will you look at that!"

Cayal glanced across at Oritha—or at what little he could see of her under her furs—and then turned back to look at what she was so excited about. On the glittering white horizon, a building had appeared . . . or perhaps materialised out of thin air would be a better description. It hadn't literally done that, of course; it just seemed as if, as they topped the rise of the snowy, gently sloped plain they were traversing, a palace made of crystal had suddenly appeared before them.

"Look!" Pellys said, his eyes lighting up with almost as much delight as Oritha's. "Lukys's Impossibly Dreaming Palace." He slapped her resoundingly on the back, almost knocking her over. "I knew Lukys was clever."

Oritha staggered under the force of Pellys's blow and then turned to look at Cayal once she'd regained her balance. "Why does he insist on calling my husband Lukys? His named is Ryda."

"Pellys is easily confused."

Oritha frowned, not entirely convinced. Cayal didn't blame her for looking at them oddly. Immune to climatic extremes, he wore a shirt, leather trousers, boots and a summer-weight coat that did little more than soak up the stray snowflakes floating on what passed for a gentle summer breeze in this frozen landscape. Pellys was barefoot and bare-chested, oblivious to the cold, the ice or the snow.

"Do you think he's expecting us?" Oritha asked their guide.

Struggling a little to restrain the dogs pulling the sled carrying Oritha's luggage, Taryx turned to her and nodded. "Of course, my lady. That's why he sent me to meet you."

That was the only reasonable explanation Cayal had heard out of Taryx for two days. Immortal like Cayal and Pellys, Taryx wasn't a Tide Lord. His power was limited, his one strength the ability to manipulate water in all its forms, which—given Lukys had apparently constructed a palace made of ice—might explain what he was doing here in Jelidia.

It didn't explain what else he might be doing here, though.

Taryx was an opportunistic little bastard, and he usually latched on to whichever Tide Lord seemed most likely to prevail during a High Tide. Of course, since his affair with Elyssa, and that whole business with creating the Crasii, he wasn't all that welcome in the halls of the Emperor and Empress of the Five Realms. In fact, his most recent playmate, if Cayal remembered things correctly, was Jaxyn. Last High Tide, the two of them had been inseparable.

"Did you do that?" Cayal asked, jerking his head in the direction of the ice palace on the horizon.

"Most of it," he said. "It was Lukys's idea. And he helped me with the really heavy stuff. He can wield more power than me."

"You called him Lukys too," Oritha said with a frown. "My husband's name is Ryda."

"Of course, that's who I meant, my lady. Shall we? I'm sure you'd like a closer look at your new home."

Oritha nodded and took her seat in the sled once more. Pellys, who'd been itching for a chance to drive the sled, snatched the reins from Taryx. Before he could protest, however, Cayal laid a restraining hand on Taryx's arm. "Let him do it. It'll keep him occupied."

Looking more than a little doubtful, Taryx nodded reluctantly and stepped back to allow Pellys to drive the sled forward.

"Didn't expect to see you here, Taryx," Cayal said as they watched the sled careening toward the distant palace. "What's going on?"

He tore his eyes from the sled and looked at Cayal. "What do you mean?"

"Is Lukys up to something?" It was a silly question. Lukys was *always* up to something.

Cayal believed Lukys had found a way for him to die, and needed several Tide Lords to help him accomplish the task. Lukys had told him as much back in Torlenia. That was much of the reason Cayal had brought Pellys here. He might be simple and more than a little dangerous, but he could wield the full power of the Tide, as could Kentravyon. Cayal had assumed the only reason Lukys risked waking up *that* madman, was for the same reason.

Taryx's presence here spoke of other plans afoot. Lukys didn't need Taryx to wield the Tide. He could do little more than freeze water, or make it steam. Lukys didn't need him to build his ice palace for him, either. He was more than capable of doing that on his own. No, Lukys was playing his own game here, and Cayal wasn't at all sure helping him die was the Tide Lord's ultimate goal.

Taryx shrugged off the question and headed in pursuit of the sled, saying, "Why don't you ask Lukys?"

Cayal strode after Taryx, annoyed at his evasiveness. "I will."

"Then that's all right then."

Cayal fell into step beside him. "How did you meet up with Lukys again, anyway? I mean, it's a big world. Odd that you just happened to stumble across him."

"I didn't find him," Taryx said. "He found me."

Cayal absorbed that news silently. Lukys had sought him out too.

"Thought he'd lost his mind, to be honest, when he asked me to come down here and help him build a palace made of ice."

"But you came, anyway."

Taryx shrugged. "Didn't have anything better to do. And with the Tide on the turn, the fun and games will start again soon. Elyssa's a bitch, Tryan's an animal, Jaxyn can't be trusted, Maralyce is a bore, Brynden's a self-righteous prick, Pellys is an idiot, Kentravyon is crazy and you're a pain in the arse. Really just left Lukys, this time 'round, if I was going to find a safe place to sit it out."

"Lukys never was the type to keep minions."

Taryx jerked his head in Oritha's direction. "Not the type to take a young wife and build her a palace in the middle of nowhere, either. But here she is. And here we are." He looked at Cayal disparagingly, adding, "And who are you calling a minion, anyway? At least I *know* the limits of my ability. I can't hope to compete with you Tide Lords, and I'm smart enough not to try. But you? You're powerful enough to challenge any one of the others, and yet here you are, trudging along in the snow, just as I am, ready to do Lukys's bidding."

There was little Cayal could say in response to that, so he remained silent, thinking it better to wait and ask Lukys in person what he was up to, because Cayal was starting to suspect his own death might prove to be a serendipitous side effect of Lukys's plan—whatever it was—rather than the main event.

Lukys greeted Oritha first, kissing her fondly and then asking one of his servants to show her to her quarters. Even more surprising was that the servants were Crasii; two score canines that Cayal could see. Lukys had never been fond of the Crasii. Cayal could think of no good reason why he'd have them here now.

They were greeted by a rush of warm air as they entered the palace, although warm was a relative term. It wasn't really warm; it was simply the temperature inside the palace was somewhat higher than outside, the wind-chill factor reduced by the solid ice walls.

Lukys looked surprised to see Pellys, but he did nothing more than greet the Tide Lord warmly and ask Taryx to escort him to one of the guest suites. Taryx acquiesced without complaint. Pellys was too taken with this fabulous crystal palace to notice he was being fobbed off. As they left, Pellys's head swivelling in amazement at the towering ice walls, Cayal turned to his host.

"You have *guest* suites?"

Lukys nodded. "Of course. One never knows who might drop in."

Cayal's eyes narrowed. "Of course. Because down here at the bottom of the world, we're at the crossroads of civilisation, aren't we?"

Lukys smiled. "More than you know. Come with me."

Still no more enlightened than he had been when he arrived, Cayal did as Lukys asked and followed him through the grand main hall, along an icy corridor and up a set of stairs carved of ice which let out onto a narrow battlement.

"Never thought I'd see you with Crasii slaves," Cayal said as they climbed the stairs.

"I don't like the way they were created, Cayal," Lukys said, glancing over his shoulder. "There are other, much less traumatic ways of manipulating life into the shapes you want, without having to go to all the trouble of making Crasii. You just need to be rather more patient than Elyssa was. But that doesn't mean they don't have their uses."

They reached the battlements and stepped outside, the whole icy vista laid out before them. From here, it was easier to get an idea of the scale of the place. It was huge. Far more than was needed for one man who'd sent for his young mortal wife. "And what's Oritha's purpose?"

"My wife?" Lukys looked surprised Cayal was questioning her place in all this. "I happen to like her, Cayal. There's nothing sinister in her presence here."

"She thinks your name is Ryda Tarek."

"That is my name. In the Cabal."

Cayal stared at him for a moment and then shook his head with a thin smile. "You didn't . . ."

Lukys laughed. "Oh, yes I did."

"You joined the Cabal of the Tarot?"

"I didn't just join it, Cayal. I'm a member of the Pentangle."

"You are shameless."

"Patient beyond description, more like it. Tides, this lot have got to be the most irritating bunch of would-be do-gooders I've ever had the misfortune to deal with. Probably because the Cabal is centred in Glaeba, these days. All that rain does something to their brains, I'm sure." He smiled even wider, stopping on the narrow walkway to lean on the icy battlements while he admired the view. "Can you believe Jaxyn and Diala were living right under their noses and they never even noticed? Although they pegged *you* for what you are quick enough. But that could be because you, well, *told* them . . ."

"They have no idea who *you* are?"

"Of course not. You know how this works."

Cayal did know. He and Lukys had had a high old time infiltrating the Holy Warriors once before, and doing exactly the same thing to them as Lukys was doing to the Cabal of the Tarot.

"But enough about my exploits. Tell me, did you talk to Brynden?" Lukys was braced against the wind, almost as if he was tempting it to blow him off the tower.

Cayal nodded. "He wasn't interested."

"I did warn you about that, didn't I?"

He shrugged. "It was worth a try. Where's Kentravyon?"

"I believe he's gone ice fishing." Lukys staggered a little as the air gusted around them. Cayal stared at Lukys but said nothing, concentrating on maintaining his balance. Up here the wind was much stronger, with an icy bite that even Cayal and Lukys, with their immortal immunity to the cold, could feel. Either one of them could have calmed it, of course, but Lukys rarely fiddled with the weather without good reason, and apparently being blown off a drop of several hundred feet, wasn't good enough.

"I'm serious!" Lukys said, when he saw the look Cayal was giving him. "Since coming back to life, the simple pleasures seem to amuse our madman almost as much as mass-murdering innocent mortals used to."

"Why did you wake him?"

"We need him," Lukys said. "Or rather, you need him."

"That's not what you said in Torlenia."

"I've had time to rework my calculations," Lukys said. "This is going to take more power than I first thought. And it's why we're here, by the way. We need to do this close to one of the magnetic poles."

"Why this one? Why not the north magnetic pole?"

"Kentravyon was already down here. Seems a bit of a wasted effort to retrieve him from the south magnetic pole just to drag him north. Besides, that would mean taking him through other places with living people in them, Cayal. Not a good plan."

"And Taryx? What's he doing here?"

"Same as Kentravyon. This is going to take every bit of power we can summon."

"Then it's a good thing I brought Pellys here."

Lukys shook his head. "He may not be as much help as you think. We need to focus our power for this, and I'm not sure Pellys is capable of that. But we'll see."

"Focus on what?"

"Pardon?"

"You said we need to focus. On what?"

"The task at hand," Lukys said so glibly even Cayal knew he was lying. "Which brings me to my next point. We need more people."

"Tides, Lukys, I'm not seducing Elyssa for you. If you think you need her help, *you* ask her for it."

"Actually, *you* need her help more than I do," Lukys said. "After all, you're the one who wants to kill himself. But we've time yet before the Tide peaks, and we need to deal with the empress and her clan. Did you know Jaxyn—with Diala's help, believe it or not—is only a hairsbreadth away from owning Glaeba?"

"I heard something about it."

"Well, while he's keeping Syrolee and Engarhod occupied—and that means Elyssa and Tryan as well—we're free to pursue our own plans." Lukys turned to look out over the spectacular icescape. "Tides, this place is awe-inspiring, isn't it?" He glanced back at Cayal with a thin smile. "Ah, that's right. Nothing inspires awe in you any longer, does it, old son? That's why you want to die."

Cayal ignored the question, certain the crux of the matter lay not in his ability to appreciate the landscape but in something else Lukys had just said. "And what exactly are our *own* plans?"

"To help you put an end to your suffering, of course," he said with an ingenuous smile.

"And make yourself God in the process?"

"Don't you just love a plan where everyone wins?"

"You've been swimming too deep in the Tide," Cayal said, shaking his head. There was no point arguing about this, and in the end, what did he care about what Lukys was really up to, anyway? If it involved his death, what happened afterward was irrelevant. "It's driven you mad too. What else do you need me to do?"

"We need as many of our kind as we can muster, down here near the magnetic pole. Even the lesser immortals like Taryx."

"Why?"

"Because we do, Cayal. Trust me."

Tides, was there ever a phrase more fraught with peril than *trust me*?

"Do you know where any of the others are?"

He nodded. "I know where at least *three* of them are."

Cayal frowned, fairly certain he wasn't going to like what came next. "Why do I get the feeling there's a reason you're telling me this and it's not just because you like standing on the edge of a precipice, making conversation?"

Lukys smiled, raising his voice to be heard over the wind. "Because I want you to go and get them for me, Cayal. Invite them here, to our . . . what did Pellys call it . . ." He opened his arms wide, to embrace the fantastic ice castle he'd created. "Our Palace of Impossible Dreams."

Cayal wasn't nearly so enchanted with the idea as Lukys. "Which three immortals are we talking about?"

"Arryl, Medwen and Ambria. All former lovers of yours, are they not?"

"I've never slept with Ambria."

Lukys looked shocked. "Who'd have thought?"

Cayal debated the advisability of going along with Lukys's plans for a moment, and then reminded himself of the one thing he must keep in mind: Lukys could help him die. "Where are they?"

"Senestra. Got themselves a very tidy little racket going, they have. They've been there almost since the last cataclysm. Call themselves the Trinity, these days. I believe they're the self-appointed goddesses of the reptilian Crasii."

Cayal was quite sure it was more complicated than that, but at least Senestra was warm. "And you think they're going to just walk away from hundreds of years of safety and security just because you're asking them to?"

Lukys shook his head, and smiled so dangerously it made Cayal's blood run cold. "No, Cayal, they'll come because *you're* asking them to. And if they refuse, you can inform the ladies of the Trinity that the next messenger I send to invite them here will be Kentravyon."

Chapter 27

"We're closed. Go see them at the clinic on Clover Street."

Declan shoved his foot between the door and the jamb to stop the big bearded slave from slamming it in his face. "I'm not sick. I just want to see the doctor."

"I know you ain't sick, so why do you want to see a doctor?" He pushed the door harder, trying to crush the intruder's foot.

The intruder, however, wasn't concerned about broken bones. "I have to see Doctor Medura."

"Why?"

"Because he has something that belongs to me."

"What?"

Still shoving against the door, Declan took a deep breath to control his anger. He couldn't afford to alienate this man, even if he was only a slave. "I believe he was inadvertently sold a slave of mine. A woman. Her name is Arkady. She's foreign, Glaeban. Or perhaps she looks Caelish . . ."

The big slave stopped trying to slam the door in his face and looked at him curiously. "You mean Kady?"

Declan felt faint with relief, both from the notion that he'd finally found her and that his foot was no longer being crushed. "You know her?"

The slave nodded warily, eyed Declan up and down for a moment and then stood back to let him enter. "Maybe you'd better come inside."

Locking the door behind them, the man indicated with his arm that Declan should follow him down the hall. It was just on dusk and the clinic was dimly lit, smelling of lye soap and disinfectant. And it appeared to be empty of patients or staff, but for this big hairy brute, which seemed very odd indeed. Like all slaves in Senestra, Declan's guide wore only a short loincloth and a chain-link brand on his chest, which did nothing but draw attention to the fact that he was probably as strong as an ox and the only way to get any information out of him was by asking nicely. Trying to beat a confession out of this man would be akin to trying to beat one out of a brick wall.

Declan followed the man through the entrance foyer, past a small hospital ward with half a dozen empty beds, and into an office which undoubtedly belonged to the ship's doctor Declan had spent the last few days looking for. The man—so the captain of the ship Declan had traced to Port Traeker, told him—who had claimed Arkady for his own on the voyage, keeping her prisoner in his cabin so he could have his way with her at his convenience.

There were many fates Declan had in mind for Cydne Medura.

All of them were excruciatingly painful.

But he had to find Arkady first. His chest constricted with anticipation as he took a seat in the office, knowing his search was almost over.

It was more than three months now since Declan had left Stellan and Nyah at Maralyce's Mine, and in that time, he'd travelled halfway round the world searching for Arkady. He didn't mind the time, in one respect, because it gave him something to think about other than his own problems. What he fretted about was the terrible things that might have befallen Arkady in the meantime, and it seemed as if his fears had not been groundless. Sold into slavery and turned into a rich man's whore.

Was there any fate more harrowing than that?

It had been no mean feat to track Arkady down, and Declan was more than a little surprised he'd even been able to pick up her trail. With Pollo's help, and a substantial bribe to several city officials responsible for the reconstruction of the slave markets in Elvere, Declan had been able to locate the slaver who'd once ruled over the vast pens before they were destroyed. It turned out he wasn't dead, despite popular rumour, but he was acting as if all his limbs had been severed.

Once they'd let the man rant for a time about how he was ruined, how the rebuilding was going to cost a fortune and how he was losing customers every day the markets remained closed, they were able to establish that only three slave ships had sailed from Elvere in the days prior to the storm that had battered the city so unexpectedly. Two of the ships, they discounted immediately. Both were headed for Tenacia and carried male slaves, destined for the mines there. The third ship was headed for Senestra, and while he didn't remember specifics, the slaver did vaguely recall there being a tall foreign woman among the batch-bought slaves one of his colleagues had sold to the Medura slaving company.

After that it had been a simple matter of finding a berth on a ship bound for Port Traeker.

The journey had taken several weeks, and most of it Declan had spent pacing the deck, wondering if he had the power to speed the ship's progress by filling her sails with wind. Or wondering if he'd inadvertently cause a disaster on the scale of the Immortal Prince creating the Great Lakes of Glaeba, if he tried to do anything so foolish.

That was the trouble with forced inactivity. He could no longer avoid thinking about his future—his very long and uncertain future.

Tides, no wonder the immortals are all crazy. It's enough to drive you mad just thinking about it . . .

Once he landed in Port Traeker, Declan was able to avoid dealing with his own problems for a while longer because he had another stroke of luck. The ship he'd followed from Elvere was in port. He'd been able to speak to the captain and get his first real confirmation that it *was* Arkady he was following. The captain remembered the Caelish slave—Declan assumed she was telling people she was Caelish to make it harder for Jaxyn's men to find her—very well indeed.

She'd been taken by the ship's doctor for sport, the captain informed Declan with great relish, and what's more, the young doctor had been so taken with her, he'd kept her as his *wii-ah* after his wedding and, as far as the captain knew, that's where she remained. In the service of one Cydne Medura, a man Declan had never met, but who he'd already decided to kill slowly and very, very painfully for what he'd done to Arkady.

He couldn't afford to let the doctor's slave know of his intentions, however. As far as the big man was concerned, Declan was here to take back—or, if necessary, buy back—the slave he rightfully owned.

"Who are you?" the slave asked, closing the door of the office as Declan took a seat.

"I am Aleki Ponting," he said, borrowing the name of Tilly's son. It was for a good cause, after all. He didn't think Tilly or Aleki would mind. "I have extensive holdings in Glaeba. The woman . . . Kady . . . is my property. She was stolen from me several months ago in a dispute and I'd like to . . . I'm sorry . . . what was your name?"

"Geriko."

"Well, Geriko, I'd like to get her back."

The slave nodded thoughtfully. "Always thought she was probably a ladies maid or something. Walks too proud to be a *makor-di*."

"Where can I find Doctor Medura? I'd like to get this taken care of as soon as possible. I've really wasted too much time on this matter already."

"He's gone."

"Then I'd like to see my slave."

Geriko shook his head. "She's gone too."

I knew this was too easy. "Gone where?"

"Up into the wetlands. Been an outbreak of swamp fever, last few weeks. The guild sent the doc and Kady went up there to help out. Nip it in the bud, you know? Before it spreads to the cities and towns again, like it did the last time."

Declan clenched his fists in frustration, unable to believe he was so close to Arkady, and yet had still missed her.

"Then I shall follow them," he said, rising to his feet. "Can you tell me where they went? I would *really* like to get my slave back."

Geriko grinned broadly, "You seem pretty anxious to get her back. What she do? Steal the family jewels?"

"She's . . . important to my family," Declan said, not sure if it was a good idea to admit such a thing, even to another slave.

The big man seemed amused. "She's gettin' to be important to a whole lotta people, that girl. Don't see that too often. 'Specially not with some-one so skinny. Still, the missus is gonna be happy if you take her away."

"The missus?"

"The doc's wife," Geriko explained. "She don't like Kady. She 'specially don't like that the doc seems to prefer his *wii-ah*'s company to hers."

Declan didn't want to think about what that meant. The idea that Arkady had been sold into slavery and was being taken against her will on a daily basis by some cheating Senestran bastard who didn't get along with his wife was horribly reminiscent of their days in Lebec.

He'd not been able to save her from Rybank. He was quite determined, however, to save her from this Cydne Medura.

"How do I find them?" he asked, hoping none of his slow-burning rage was seeping into his voice. This man seemed a reasonably loyal slave. He certainly wasn't going to tell Declan anything about how to find his master if he thought Declan's intention was to kill the man as soon as he laid eyes on him.

"You'll need to hire a boat. Down by the river docks. The amphibians know the way. I think they was headed for Watershed Falls."

"Where's that?"

"Few days northeast of here. Horrid place it is, all damp and humid and filled with lizards watching you, all the time, even though you can't see them. You can feel it though, know what I mean?" The man shuddered. "Makes ya skin crawl just thinking about it."

Declan's ears pricked up at the mention of lizards. As far as he was aware, the only reptilian Crasii to have survived through the last few Cataclysms were the chameleons, and he'd never heard of them gathered in any numbers.

"Then I shall follow them to this Watershed Falls place and conduct my business with the doctor there."

Perhaps, in addition to finding Arkady, he'd be able to offer Tiji some news about her origins. Assuming he ever found her again.

And assuming she'd even speak to him if he did, now he was immortal.

Geriko opened the office door for him. "He's not gonna be happy 'bout this. You rich?"

"Rich enough."

"You'll need to be. He likes Kady a lot."

"I'm sure I'll be able to make it worth his while to part with her."

"Kinda hope you don't," Geriko said, as he escorted Declan back through the clinic to the front door. "I like Kady too. She's got nice tits."

This time, Declan didn't even make a pretence of trying to control his fury. He slammed a punch into Geriko's face with all the force his rage-driven fist could muster.

Howling in surprise and pain, the slave dropped to his knees, blood gushing from his broken nose. Declan's hand was stinging, he may have even broken a few bones, but he didn't care.

"Don't you even think about her like that, you Senestran pile of shit," he said in Glaeban.

And then, shaking his stinging hand, which had begun to hurt out of all proportion to the injury he'd inflicted on it—a sign that he probably had broken something and the agonising healing powers of his now immortal body were at work—he left the man where he'd fallen and let himself out of the clinic.

He had a boat to catch, it seemed. And another journey ahead of him to some wetland village called Watershed Falls.

Chapter 28

"Give the youngling a dose of the tonic and then send them on their way before they infect everyone else."

Arkady smiled comfortingly at the chameleon and her young standing on the veranda, hoping her warmth would alleviate Cydne's appalling bedside manner. She desperately wanted to talk to the chameleons who seemed, if not prolific, then certainly not rare in this steamy wetland. Not that knowing anything about them would be much use to her. Who was she going to tell? The only person who'd really be interested in the fact that she'd discovered a whole region full of chameleons was Tiji, and she was probably back in Glaeba by now, apologising to Declan for losing track of his duchess.

The chameleons were looking haggard and wrung out. They were locals, these Crasii, not the visitors most of their other patients had been. The female, a small silver-skinned creature, held a dull grey pup in her arms, who was only two or three years old and almost unconscious. Arkady's heart went out to them. The older one, a slender silver male, clung to his mother's side as if he was afraid she might disappear, which, if his brother's swamp fever infected her, may well be the case.

"Come on," she said, pouring the tonic onto the spoon. "It tastes awful and it makes your eyes sting, but it will help."

The mother moved the youngling's body in her arms to make it easier for Arkady to spoon the tonic into him. Limp and unresponsive, the creamy liquid trickled into his mouth. He coughed and swallowed. Arkady waited for a moment to see if his sensitive stomach would keep the medicine down.

When it appeared he wasn't going to reflexively vomit the tonic back up again, she smiled at the mother. "Keep him cool and try to get him to take as much water as you can. He's going to be fine."

The chameleon nodded gratefully and left the veranda, her other youngling close behind her, still clinging to her side.

"That seems to be the last of them for today," Jojo said, stepping onto the veranda.

It was their second week here and as word spread through the wetlands of the presence of a Port Traeker doctor and free medicine in Watershed

Falls, more and more patients were lined up outside the house each morning, waiting to be treated.

They were seeing swamp fever victims almost exclusively now. Arkady marvelled that she'd yet to catch the disease. Maybe she was naturally immune. Swamp fever didn't attack everyone who came in contact with it. It was an opportunistic sort of disease, attacking the very young and the very old first. A normal, healthy adult had a fair chance of resisting it. Once infected, one still had an even money chance of surviving it too, if they managed not to die from dehydration.

Fortunately, Arkady also had access to Cydne's tonic. She hadn't needed to take it yet, thankfully, but intended to down a whole bottle of the wretched-smelling concoction at the first sign of an upset stomach or a loose bowel movement.

"I wish you wouldn't do that," Cydne said, rising to his feet.

"Do what?"

"Tell these creatures they'll be all better soon. You don't know that."

"The youngling seemed over the worst of it."

"It's still not your place to predict recovery," he said. "Don't do it again." With that, Cydne left the veranda and walked back inside. Arkady turned to Jojo, throwing her hands up in disgust.

"Tides, I was just trying to be nice."

"You're setting up an expectation the doctor can cure everything," the young—and tiresomely loyal—feline explained. "Patients should always expect the worst, Kady. That way, if it happens, they're prepared. If they get better, then it's a bonus."

She rolled her eyes, understanding Jojo's logic, even if she thought it absurd. "Are all felines so pessimistic?"

The Crasii shrugged. "We are pragmatic."

"That's not what I would have called it."

The feline smiled and held out the tray for Arkady. "This is why you're such a troublesome slave."

"Who says I'm troublesome?"

"Everyone."

Arkady began clearing Cydne's instruments off the veranda table so she could take them inside and boil them on the stove, ready for tomorrow.

"Well, we must be doing something right. They don't come back for a second dose. Mind you," she added, stoppering the bottle of tonic she'd used to dose that day's patients, "it could have something to do with the smell. I'd be tossing up taking a second dose of that stuff against dying a horribly painful death, if it were me."

Jojo followed her inside, shutting the door behind them against the insects that would start to swarm as soon as they lit the lamps. Cydne looked up as they entered, frowning at Arkady. "You haven't tried to taste the tonic, have you?"

"Tides, no," she said, following Jojo through the front room, past the locked door where the rest of the tonic was stored and into the small kitchen at the back of the house where the feline put the tray on the table. "I think I'd have to be dying first."

"It's not . . . not very effective for humans," Cydne said, following them into the kitchen. "I'd rather you didn't take it—even if you get infected. Sometimes, it can make things . . . worse."

She looked at him closely and then nodded in understanding. "Is that why you didn't want me reassuring the patients?"

He nodded. "The feline is right. Better they expect the worst."

She shrugged. "Fair enough. Pessimism is the order of the day from now on. Did you want to eat yet, or can I sterilise these first?"

"You can do the instruments first," he told her. "I have to finish my report for the guild and I'd rather do it in daylight. Once the lamps are lit, there are too many insects."

"And most of them bite," Arkady called after him, as he headed back to the front room. "Something people with the benefit of clothing probably don't notice!"

Jojo shook her head at Arkady's impudence, although Cydne ignored her, as she knew he would. Even for a favoured slave, even out here in the middle of nowhere, Cydne Medura wasn't going to cause a scandal by allowing his *makor-di* to dress as a free woman. Arkady was stuck with her short skirt and her bare breasts and had to settle for slathering on the foul-smelling lotion one of the whores from the Watershed tavern had given her. It protected her from the bugs, but it was a far cry from a time when she had reigned over the most fabulous social events in Glaeba wearing glorious, custom-made dresses and the Desean family jewels . . .

"Kady!"

"Yes, master?" she called, as she helped Jojo heft the large sterilising pot onto the stove.

"Make sure you bathe before you come to bed tonight," he commanded distractedly from the front room. "That stuff you're wearing to repel insects works just as well on humans."

Not well enough, Arkady sighed, as she began dropping the medical instruments into the pot to boil. *Apparently not well enough.*

It was still dark when a loud banging on the front door the following morning woke Arkady. If Cydne heard the racket, he ignored it, clearly expecting his slave to get up and answer the insistent hammering. He remained unmoving on the bed, probably faking sleep, Arkady suspected.

In fact, he almost had to be faking. The dead would waken to this racket.

With a sigh, Arkady, who, thankfully, was relegated to a blanket on the floor beside him once he was done with her each night, threw off the covers, and, still yawning, tied on her skirt as she reached the front door. Jojo had opened the door by the time she arrived in the front room. She was surprised to find the young chameleon whose desperately ill sibling they'd treated the afternoon before.

"Doctor has to come quick," the boy said, as soon as Jojo opened the door. "Pedy's real sick."

Jojo blocked the door with her body to prevent the child from pushing his way inside. "Then have your dam bring him back here when we're open."

"No!" the boy insisted. "He has to come now! Pedy's blind and he can't stay awake. Mama says he *must* come!"

Cydne's warning yesterday about giving patients false hope flashed through Arkady's mind for a moment, accompanied by a wave of guilt. She glanced at Jojo, certain the feline's unreadable white face was silently expressing "I told you so," and then nodded at the youngling. "The doctor can't come at the moment," she said, wondering if blindness was another symptom of swamp fever she hadn't heard of before. "But I'll see what I can do."

"Kady . . ."

"It'll be all right, Jojo. Tell Cydne I'll be back as soon as I can."

The feline looked unhappy, but did nothing to stop Arkady from making the house call. Arkady slipped on her sandals and followed the young chameleon through the sleeping village to a small house several streets away surrounded by a surprisingly well kept yard. Inside was not only the female Arkady and Cydne had seen yesterday, but several other females as well. The sick youngling was in the front room, laid out on a bed of woven reeds. The chameleons moved aside for Arkady, allowing her to squat beside the pallet.

As his brother had warned her, Pedy was almost comatose, whimpering softly in pain, his eyes blindly searching for his mother. His skin was deathly grey, his breathing laboured, and when she put her ear to his chest, his heartbeat seemed thready and tenuous. There was no sign, however, of him vomiting, and no evidence he'd been affected recently by the crippling diarrhoea associated with swamp fever.

"How long's he been like this?"

"A few hours," his mother told her. "He was acting as if he was dizzy when we first got home, but then he seemed to get better. But about midnight, he started to have trouble breathing. I thought it was just the fever, but then . . . when I realised he couldn't even see me . . ."

Arkady stared at the youngling helplessly. Whatever was wrong with him was taking him down fast. Even in the short time she'd been here, his respiration had worsened.

"Is there anything you can do?" the female asked. "Anything the doctor can do?"

"I don't know . . ."

"What if you give him more tonic?" one of the other chameleons crowded into the room behind her asked. "Maybe the first dose wasn't enough."

Arkady looked at the reptilian Crasii blankly for a moment and then stared down at Pedy, as a thought occurred to her that was almost too frightening to contemplate.

Only once before in her life had Arkady ever seen someone like this—dying from a combination of blindness, a weakened heart, and laboured breathing. She was about twelve at the time, with her father on one of his many trips to the mines up around Lutalo, during which she'd assisted him in much the same way she was assisting Cydne now. That time, however, it hadn't been swamp fever. It was a miner dying from drinking a bad batch of home-made spirits.

Pedy gasped painfully, his breathing growing more and more shallow. Arkady felt for a pulse at his wrist and couldn't find it.

His mother must have read her face.

"He's going to die, isn't he?" she said softly.

Arkady nodded mutely. Pessimism was the order of the day, after all.

"It was good of you to come, then," she added, scooping the limp youngling into her arms. "But you can go now."

"I'll wait with you," she said, her eyes filling with unshed tears. The female's calm acceptance of the imminent death of her child tore at Arkady's heart. "If that's all right?"

The female studied her for a moment and then nodded her permission. Her other youngling had ingratiated himself beside her, and was staring at Arkady with dark, uncomprehending eyes. Behind her, the other chameleons began to sit down. They were a family group, she suspected, and would keep vigil together.

Arkady glanced out of the small window. The sky was beginning to lighten with the onset of dawn. She settled back on her heels to wait, and realised Cydne would have to get his own breakfast.

Let him starve, she thought. *He deserves it.*

Murderer.

Chapter 29

The first stomach cramps hit Tiji just on dawn. At first, she thought it was something she'd eaten, but even as she thought it, she knew it wasn't the case. All she'd had for dinner last night was bread and cheese. Even had the cheese been bad, she would have felt the effects much sooner than this.

No, Tiji knew what it was, and cursed herself roundly for not staying out of the village as Azquil had made her promise she would, to reduce the chances of becoming infected. She hadn't, of course. There were other chameleons in the village and Tiji wanted to talk to them. She wanted to learn about her own kind—about their customs, their lives . . . and how she'd finished up in a circus where she was bought as a slave by a Glaeban named Declan Hawkes.

The chameleons couldn't answer all her questions, of course, but they were able to tell her more than she'd hoped for. Apparently, the outlying settlements in the wetlands were often raided by slavers. Chameleon younglings were prized, worth a fortune on the open market. That news made her wonder where Declan had got the money to afford her in the first place. Probably from the Cabal.

But that also meant they had a purpose in mind for her too.

Was that all she had been to Declan? Just another tool in the Cabal's armoury of weapons they might one day turn on the Tide Lords? The idea shook the very foundations of everything she believed about herself and the human she considered her best friend. Every day she wondered about it, the more she came to resent Declan, the Cabal, and everything about her previous life. She discovered she didn't care what had become of Arkady. The Cabal could all rot, for all she cared . . .

Another cramp doubled her over, making Tiji wonder if she was more fevered than she thought. She needed help, she knew that, although it seemed a bit early to pay a visit to any of her new chameleon friends in the village, even though Azquil had assured her that if she needed their help, all she had to do was ask.

Fortunately, she didn't need to bother anyone. The Port Traeker doctor was still in town.

Although she knew where it was located in the village, Tiji had kept away from the makeshift clinic until now, quite certain the fastest way to get infected with a disease was to hang around other diseased people. After writhing in pain for a while as the stomach cramps twisted her gut, Tiji finally forced herself out of the cottage and headed along the path toward the village, stopping several times to either vomit or evacuate her bowels into the undergrowth. She was feeling wretched, but was reasonably confident that if she could make it to the doctor, she'd be able to get some of the tonic he was handing out so generously.

The sun was well up by the time she reached the edge of the village, the main street stretching out before her like a quest she didn't have the strength to undertake. At the other end of that muddy street, and another street over, lay relief from the pain, and an end to the draining effects of every bodily fluid she owned trying to forcefully eject itself.

Tiji stopped to vomit again, wondering what was left inside of her to be rid of and then staggered forward. Relief was only a street away.

All she had to do was reach it.

The sun was fully risen by the time she reached the small house the visiting doctor was using as his clinic. It was too early for him to be open, so the line of humans and Crasii waiting to be treated had yet to form. She wondered if they'd make her wait or if she could see the doctor now.

It's not like he's going to have to spend much time diagnosing what's wrong with me.

She decided to try her luck. After stopping on the veranda step long enough to vomit up something that looked like a liquefied internal organ she probably needed to go on living, Tiji made it to the front door. She knocked on it weakly and was more than a little surprised when it was answered almost immediately.

"Where in the Tides have you been!" the human man—presumably the Port Traeker doctor—demanded. "I've told you about wandering off—" He stopped ranting when he realised he wasn't addressing whomever he expected to be standing there at the door. "Who are you?"

Tiji's answer was to vomit again, all over his shirt. She clung to the door frame weakly.

The doctor looked down at his shirt in disgust. "Tides, you creatures are revolting," he muttered taking a step back. "Wait there."

He disappeared for a moment and then came back carrying a bottle of the precious tonic. He pulled out the stopper and offered her the bottle. "Here, take a swig."

Tiji nodded and accepted the bottle with relief. The creamy tonic smelled foul, but she was sure that any minute now, the doctor would be wearing even more of her innards if she didn't do something. She didn't hesitate before putting her lips around the neck of the bottle and taking a deep swallow.

The tonic burned all the way down, and she gagged a little, but surprisingly, she managed to keep it down. The doctor watched her drink it, nodding.

"More," he commanded, when she lowered the bottle from her mouth. "You need a good-sized dose for it to be effective."

Grimacing, she did as he bid, taking another swallow of the burning liquid. When she was done, he took the bottle from her and stoppered it.

"Is . . . there anything else I should . . . do?"

"Don't die on my veranda," the doctor said, and then he turned and called, "Jojo!"

Unsympathetic bastard. She wondered what criteria they used in the Senestran Physicians' Guild to rate their members' compassion and charity. *Perhaps that's why they sent him here*, she thought. *To teach him some humility.*

Tiji sagged against the frame as a feline Crasii appeared behind the doctor. Had she been feeling better, Tiji might have hissed at her—she never liked or got along with felines—but she was too ill to care.

"Get rid of it," the doctor told the ginger and white feline. It wasn't until the Crasii approached her that Tiji realised she was the "it" the doctor was referring to.

"I don't . . . need help," she gasped, moving to the railing. Tiji didn't have the energy to worry about the doctor's abysmal bedside manner or the feline's intentions. She supposed the Crasii was the doctor's bodyguard. With the creature close behind her, Tiji used the wooden railing to support herself until she reached the step, and then gingerly lowered herself until she was sitting, hoping that if she waited a little, the tonic might have a chance to work its magic. After that, she might feel well enough to head back through the village to the cottage.

"You can't stay there," Jojo said behind her.

"Just gimme . . . a minute . . ."

The feline studied her for a moment, and then shook her head. "*Only* a moment. If I come back and find you here later, you won't like it."

Tiji forced herself to look up at the Crasii. "You could disembowel me right now, you wretched cat, and I'm not sure I wouldn't thank you for easing my pain."

The feline frowned, but didn't react to the insult, which was a little surprising. "Just don't be here when Doctor Cydne starts his rounds for the day," the feline warned. "Otherwise, I *will* disembowel you."

The feline turned away, muttering something that sounded like "Stupid lizard" but Tiji didn't really care what she thought. Closing her eyes, the little Crasii rested her head against the veranda post, somewhat concerned to discover she could still feel the burning in her throat from the tonic. Somehow, that didn't seem right, and her stomach was clenching as if she was about to vomit again. She hoped she didn't, and not only because she didn't think there was anything left inside her to puke up. Tiji was certain that if she sicked up the tonic, the feline *would* be back to disembowel her.

She was also fairly sure that the Crasii-hating, uncaring doctor wouldn't give her another dose.

By sheer force of will, she kept the tonic down, but stayed sitting on the step. Having sat down, she doubted she had the strength to stand up again, and the cottage felt as if it was back in Torlenia, it seemed so far away . . .

Sitting up with a jerk, Tiji realised she'd dozed off. The sun was even higher in the sky. At least, it seemed to be. It was a bit difficult to tell, it was certainly hotter, but her eyes were blurry and she couldn't seem to focus them. She looked around but nothing was clear. The street in front of the house was a strip of darkness, the other cottages vaguely rectangular shapes breaking up the green. Tiji could just make out a figure walking toward her, but couldn't make out enough detail to determine anything other than its human outline. The approaching human paid her no attention in any case. He . . . she—Tiji couldn't tell—stormed straight past her, slamming the door to the cottage open . . .

"You heartless monster!"

Tiji tried to sit up a little straighter, her head spinning. She felt drunk. The voice yelling the insult was female. Tiji silently cheered her on. Apparently, she'd witnessed the doctor's rude dismissal of his Crasii patient a few moments ago.

"You can't speak to me like that!"

"You don't deserve to be spoken to any other way, you unconscionable bastard! You and all the rest of your Tide-forsaken, murdering, Physicians' Guild!"

Tiji didn't hear the doctor's response because whatever the doctor was saying didn't matter as much as the fact the woman was yelling at him in Glaeban. Shocked to hear that language here in the Senestran wetlands, Tiji turned and crawled on her hands and knees across the veranda toward the door, to the sound of shattering glass.

"*Patients should always expect the worst*," the Glaeban woman continued scathingly. "*That way, if it happens, they're prepared.* Did he teach you that?"

It seemed as if the woman was telling off someone else besides the doctor. Maybe the feline was in trouble too.

"And so they *should* be prepared, you monstrous excuse for a human being," the woman was saying. "Because you're not *curing* the Crasii with your generous medical care and your wretched free tonic, are you? You're putting them down!"

Tiji was close enough to the door to hear the doctor's response now, the enormity of what this woman was accusing him of not quite registering in her fevered mind.

"They are diseased and their diseases spread to the human population," the doctor said. "We provide a peaceful transition into death, which is more than their Tide-forsaken swamp fever will give them and we'll save countless human lives in the process."

"A peaceful transition!" the woman cried in disbelief. "Tides, you're feeding them raw wood alcohol!"

"How could you possibly know that?"

"Because I know the symptoms, Cydne," she said. "It might look like swamp fever to the ignorant, but no swamp-borne fever ever caused someone to go blind."

Tiji heard footsteps inside the house followed by the sound of even more shattering glass and the sound of a struggle. She crawled through the open door and felt something sticky on the floor. It smelled foul, and it made her eyes burn and she cut herself on something sharp when she inadvertently put her hand in it.

"Jojo, stop her!" the man's voice was shouting from further down the hall, punctuated by the sound of even more shattering glass. "That's all we've got left!"

"Good," the female voice shot back. "That means you're done poisoning innocent Crasii." Her brave words were followed by a cry of pain. Tiji wondered if it meant the feline had attacked the human woman . . .

And then another thought occurred to her . . . *Poisoning*? Tiji smelled the stuff on her hands and realised it was the tonic. With vision too blurry to make out any detail, she felt her hand and managed to extract the sliver of glass that was stuck in it. Somewhere, in the midst of her muddled thoughts, she realised what the discussion meant.

The tonic . . . it's not a cure. Tides . . . it's a death sentence.

Desperately, Tiji stuck two fingers in her throat, trying to purge her body of the poison. It was useless. Not only did she not know how long it had been since she'd swallowed it, the fact that her eyesight was already going meant the toxins were well on the way to doing their job.

Wood alcohol. Tiji knew little about it except that it could kill you.

She heard something that sounded like a struggle and more footsteps, which seemed to be getting louder. Lacking even the strength to hold herself up on her hands and knees, Tiji collapsed into the sticky mess that was the broken bottle of tonic, not caring that it made her eyes water,

"Tides!" she thought she heard someone exclaim as they came into the room, perhaps the Glaeban woman. "Is this another one of your *patients?*"

"Leave her be, Kady," she heard the feline say. "She'll be dead soon enough."

The human woman must have ignored her. Tiji felt gentle hands turning her over, and then a horrified gasp . . .

"*Tiji?*"

And that was the last thing she heard before the blackness took away her pain.

Chapter 30

Arkady shook the little Crasii urgently, trying to revive her, but she'd lapsed into unconsciousness. Her silver skin was grey and dull and her breathing was already beginning to labour.

"Did you dose this one, too?" Arkady demanded of Cydne, her eyes filled with unshed tears. She couldn't conceive of what might have brought Tiji to this place. Torn with guilt that she might be here now, infected with swamp fever and dying of wood alcohol poisoning, because the little Crasii had somehow managed to follow her, Arkady scooped Tiji up in her arms and carried her to one of the pallets they'd set up for human patients.

Cydne stood watching her, hands on his hips, his eye watering from the reek of the spilled tonic. He was furious she'd broken the remaining bottles of tonic, and fairly sputtering with indignation over a sick Crasii being placed in a human bed. "You can't put her there!"

"The Tide take you, Cydne Medura," she said, not even bothering to look at him. She focused her attention on Tiji, ignoring the pain from the deep scratches Jojo had inflicted on her face and shoulder while trying to stop her breaking the rest of the bottles. Concentrating on the little chameleon also meant she didn't have to continue the body-count she had going in the back of her head, listing all the Crasii she'd smilingly dosed with Cydne's deadly tonic these past few weeks.

"Do you know this creature?" Jojo asked. Despite attacking Arkady on Cydne's command, she seemed to hold no ill-will toward her fellow slave.

"She used to belong to a friend of mine." Arkady rolled Tiji on her side, unsure what else she could do for her. It was one thing to recall the symptoms of wood-alcohol poisoning, quite another to remember if there was a cure. She was fairly certain there wasn't one, because she remembered that the miner her father treated who had the same symptoms had died a slow and painful death, as had poor Pedy less than an hour ago.

"You're not going to leave her to die there!" Cydne was insisting behind them.

Arkady behaved as if he wasn't in the room. She might be a slave, but she wasn't going to be a willing accomplice to any more murders.

"Did you hear what I said?" he demanded, all but stamping his foot in frustration at her continued defiance.

"Are you the doctor?"

They both looked up at the voice. Arkady hadn't noticed the door was still open. Neither had Cydne, it seemed.

Jojo inexplicably dropped to her knees.

"Come back later," Cydne snapped at the young human girl standing in the doorway. She was dark-skinned, dressed in a plain, undyed sleeveless tunic and looked no more than seventeen. "We're not seeing any more people for the time being."

"Perhaps the good doctor would see *me*?"

Another woman stepped out from behind the girl, followed by an older woman, who seemed to be in her thirties. But it was the second woman that drew Arkady's eye. She was stunning. Fair-skinned, with pale eyes and long blonde hair that reached down past her waist, she had a presence about her that marked her as someone not to be trifled with. Like the dark-skinned girl, the women wore simple homespun tunics, but that did nothing to detract from their inherent nobility. Jojo lowered her forehead to the floor.

"Get up," Cydne said to the feline, kicking her with his boot. Then he turned to their visitors. "I beg your pardon, madam," he said, realising he was in the presence of humans who might be of the same class as himself. "I thought your servant . . ."

"Medwen is not my servant," the woman said. "You are the doctor from Port Traeker who's been so generously treating the Crasii with his tonic, are you not?"

"I am."

"I'm interested in what miraculous ingredients you've discovered that can cure something as devastating as swamp fever."

"If you're looking for something to treat a member of your own family, my lady . . ." Cydne said, looking a little puzzled. "It's not good for humans, though—"

"It's not that good for Crasii, either," the older woman cut in. "Unless of course you're either ignorant beyond comprehension, or *trying* to kill them."

Arkady glanced down at Tiji, relieved to see she hadn't worsened in the last few moments, and then looked to Cydne to see what he'd do. The doctor said nothing, which could have been guilt or it might have been simply because his accusers were all women and Cydne really wasn't that good at dealing with women.

"It's poison," Arkady confessed, as Cydne seemed to have been struck mute. "I gather it's all part of the Senestran Physicians' Guild's grand plans to prevent swamp fever reaching the cities. Kill it at the source."

The women turned to look at her. "Who are you?"

"I'm his *makor-di*. He's had me doling that wretched tonic out like new-year's ale ever since we got here. I only just realised what it is. So I broke the rest of the bottles."

The blonde woman glanced down at the sticky puddle on the floor and then nodded to the dark girl, who headed into the house to look for proof Arkady was telling the truth. The older woman pushed past Cydne and came to stand by the bed. Jojo hadn't moved from her prostrated position on the floor.

The blonde woman glanced down at Tiji and shook her head. "Tides, it's the Lost One Azquil brought back on his last trip."

"Is she dead?" the dark girl asked as she came back from checking the rest of the house.

"Not yet."

"There's another crate of the stuff out back, but the slave was telling the truth. All the bottles are broken."

"Who are you people?" Cydne demanded, finally finding his voice. "You can't just barge in here like this. I am a member of the Senestran Physicians' Guild! Jojo!"

The feline made no move to respond to Cydne's command, which Arkady thought was extremely odd.

"You are a contract killer," the blonde woman said to Cydne. "And we are the Trinity. I am Arryl, this is Ambria and this is Medwen. We protect the Crasii and deal out justice to those who would harm them."

Tides . . . Arryl, Ambria and Medwen . . . No wonder Jojo has been struck dumb . . .

"You're immortals," Arkady blurted out before she could stop herself.

Arryl turned to look at her, clearly surprised. "You've *heard* of us?"

Arkady nodded mutely, not sure how she was going to explain how she knew of them.

Fortunately, Arryl didn't seem interested in explanations. "Then you'll know I'm serious when I tell you that your little expedition into the wetlands to spare the human population of the cities from swamp fever by murdering every likely Crasii carrier has earned you more than our enmity. It has earned you as slow and painful a death as you have inflicted on countless innocent Crasii until we discovered the true purpose of your tonic."

"I beg your pardon!" Cydne cried indignantly. "You can't do that. I'm a doctor. I'm a member of the Medura House—"

"You're a common murderer," Medwen, the dark-skinned girl said with contempt.

Despite the death sentence just passed on Cydne, Arkady couldn't help but stare. This was the immortal Cayal had once slept with; he'd once posed as her husband. The one he claimed he had a soft spot for. And the exquisite Arryl . . . she was the one who'd rescued Cayal in Magreth and taken him to the Temple of the Tide where he was eventually made immortal . . .

"When the guild hear about this . . ."

"You'll have been dead for several weeks," Ambria finished for him. "Both of you."

"But I had no idea what he was doing!" Arkady protested, dragging her attention back to Arryl as she realised these people intended to punish her along with Cydne. "As soon as I found out, I destroyed the rest of the tonic." And then she added thoughtlessly, "Tides, I'm only here because Brynden is furious at Cayal and wanted to hurt him so he sold me into slavery in Torlenia."

The three women turned to consider her. Arkady couldn't ever remember feeling so intimidated.

"You've met Brynden and Cayal?" Medwen asked icily.

Well, that's not the reaction I was expecting.

"More to the point, you're a bone of contention between them?" Ambria asked with a frown.

Arkady was beginning to wish she'd kept her mouth shut. She nodded warily. "Not on purpose . . ."

"Kady, what are they talking about. Do you know these people? Tell them who I am!"

"You are a dead man," Medwen informed him. "As is your *makor-di*."

"What about the feline?" Ambria asked.

Arryl looked down at the prostrate Jojo and shook her head. "She wasn't the one serving the tonic."

"To serve you is the reason I breathe, my lady," Jojo muttered.

"The poor creature is Crasii. She lacks the free will to be responsible for her actions." Arryl turned to the crowed gathered at the door. "Leave the feline. Only the humans are to be punished."

Arkady looked at the immortals in horror. "But I'm innocent!"

"That's as may be," Ambria said. "However, by your own admission, you are also likely to bring either Cayal or Brynden to our shores. With the Tide on the rise, we'd prefer they remained in ignorance of where we are—"

"I wouldn't tell!"

"And we intend to make sure of it." Arryl turned and spoke to someone over her shoulder. "Take them to the Justice Tree."

While they'd been talking, a crowd had gathered on the veranda. Made up mostly of Crasii from the village, they were led by a young male Crasii who pushed into the room and hurried to the bed as soon as he arrived. He fell to his knees beside Tiji, his expression distraught.

"Tides, Tiji, why didn't you wait for me?" he said, stroking her dull grey scales. And then he looked to Arryl with pleading eyes. "Can you save her, my lady?"

"I can try, Azquil," Arryl replied. "But the Tide's not peaked yet and she may be too far gone . . ."

"Do whatever you can, my lady." He leaned forward to kiss Tiji's pallid forehead. Then he rose to his feet and turned to look at the others, his expression hardening. "I'll take care of these two. Take them!" Before Arkady could further protest her innocence, a number of other chameleon Crasii bustled into the small front room and grabbed the two human prisoners. Azquil glanced down at Jojo with a frown. "We should destroy the feline too, my lady."

Arryl shook her head. "She's not to blame for this."

"But she's a feline. Her kind would kill us, soon as look at us. She can't stay here."

"Get up," Arryl ordered.

Jojo rose to her feet without hesitation.

"You live because we choose to let you live," the immortal told her. "But your kind are not welcome in the wetlands. You must leave now and not return. Do you understand?"

"To serve you is the reason I breathe," Jojo repeated, as if she'd lost the ability to say anything else.

"You can't order my slaves around!" Cydne protested uselessly, as he struggled against the Crasii tying his hands behind his back.

Oh, yes they can, Arkady might have told him, had she been feeling a little more generous toward him, as her hands were similarly bound. *This is the danger of the Tide Lords. Every Crasii on Amyrantha is theirs to command.*

But Jojo's fate was no longer her concern. As soon as their hands were secure, they dragged Arkady and Cydne from the cottage toward the centre of the town, accompanied by a murderous mob. Cydne complained loudly and indignantly as they pulled him along beside her. Arkady wasn't sure he fully appreciated either the enormity of his crime or that this mob was serious in their intent to seek justice for his malfeasance.

Arkady was under no such illusions. Arryl was immortal and for all that she obviously had more compassion than most other immortals Arkady had met, she knew neither Arryl, Medwen nor Ambria would balk at removing a threat to their peacefully hidden existence.

"When my father hears about my treatment here . . ." Cydne was ranting, as if the threat of some irate human from Port Traeker these Crasii had never heard of would even dent the sensibilities of this mob of grieving mothers, fathers, husbands, wives, sons and daughters . . .

"Cydne, shut up."

They finally came to a tree, a massive, ancient palm located on the very edge of the main channel some distance from the village proper. Decades of having its large leaves harvested for shelter and twine had left behind a trunk covered with sawn-off branch ends honed to savage points, stained dark with the blood of generations of previous miscreants. Arkady cried out as someone pushed her against the tree, the spikes cutting into her flesh everywhere they touched. Her arms were pulled over her head and bound to the trunk above her.

The mob quickly and efficiently stripped Cydne down to his breeches and tied him in a similar fashion beside her. With a rope around her ankles and another around her waist, there was no relief from the razor-sharp spikes at her back. Through the pain, Arkady could already feel the blood trickling down her spine.

"You cannot treat me in this fashion!" Cydne protested between screams, but his voice lacked conviction. Maybe he was starting to appreciate that this danger was real.

Azquil, the young chameleon male who had begged Arryl to save Tiji, stepped forward once the mob had secured them to the Justice Tree and fallen back to admire their handiwork. Wincing, tears running down her face from the pain of the stabbing spikes, Arkady stared at him, wondering who he was. And wondering what was to come next.

She didn't have long to wait before she found out.

"You will remain here until you die," Azquil announced in a voice so cold Arkady couldn't believe it came from such a small and harmless-looking creature, "If you're lucky, that will be sometime in the next day or so. The blood and pain you can already feel from the spikes on the trunk will attract many creatures, the most frightful of which is the gobie ant. It feeds on fresh blood and raw meat." He turned then to address the crowd. "The gobie ants will feast tonight!"

Tides, I can't believe it's going to end like this.

A cheer went up from the mob. Something hit Arkady in the shoulder, wet and slimy, and then slid down her breast. Rancid and foul, it smelled like rotting fruit, but trying to avoid it simply drove the spikes deeper into her back. That missile was soon followed by a score of others, a few of them clods of earth.

"Make them stop!" Cydne ordered, unable to keep the panic from his voice.

She glared at him. "You're joking, aren't you?"

"They're throwing things at us!"

"Be grateful we're in the wetlands . . . and there aren't too many rocks around," she said, shaking her head at his foolishness. The action pushed dozens of razor-sharp spikes further into her skin, making her cry out in pain.

The mob cheered to see her suffering. The chameleon, Azquil, studied them both for a moment with a look of intense satisfaction, and then turned away.

Please, let it be over quickly.

"They'll pay . . . for this when we get back . . . to Port Traeker."

Cydne was openly weeping, but he still didn't understand they'd been left here to die. In his mind, this was probably an elaborate charade de-signed to frighten them.

Arkady turned her head, as much as she was able, to glare at him. "You think eventually . . . common sense will prevail . . . and these wretched crea-tures will see the error of their ways . . . and . . . let us go. Is that it?" An-other chunk of rotten fruit caught her on the chin and slid down her sweat-slick body.

Tides, I don't think I can do this . . . dying shouldn't be allowed to hurt so much.

"I'll murder every . . . last . . . filthy one of them."

Grimacing as the spikes bit deep into her flesh, Arkady turned her head away. "That's what got us tied to this tree . . . and sentenced to death, Cydne."

"It's your fault for destroying the rest of the tonic."

Arkady closed her eyes, hoping to at least blot out the burning sunlight and the sight of a mob settling in to watch them die, if not the pain in her back and legs which got worse with even the slightest movement.

"Go to hell."

"You can't speak . . . to me like that."

"I can speak to you . . . any way . . . I please," she told him, gasping with the agony of the piercing spikes. "We're going to die, Cydne. In exactly the same way."

"That doesn't give you the right—"

"Oh yes . . . it does," she cut in, trying to ignore the agony of this death by a thousand small cuts designed to attract flesh-eating insects. "Because, you see, finally . . . Cydne Medura . . . we are equal."

Chapter 31

"I didn't think you'd come."

Warlock glanced fearfully over his shoulder, certain someone must have seen him sneaking down to the courtyard. The man he was meeting stayed in the shadows so Warlock couldn't see his face. In fact, he wasn't entirely sure it was a man. He might have been a Crasii. He smelled of horse manure, which he had probably applied to stop Warlock from picking up his scent and being able to identify him later.

"If I'm caught down here, they'll kill me. And my family."

Although he fretted constantly about not having heard from his contact in the Cabal, when Warlock finally received the summons to meet the man to whom he would be passing on the secrets of Elyssa's court, he found he didn't want to go. Their lives were fraught with enough danger as it was. To be caught betraying his immortal masters would result in the annihilation of his entire family.

"Should have thought about that before you volunteered," the shadowy man said unsympathetically. "What have you to report?"

That was the trouble, Warlock knew. He had so *much* to tell them.

"Lord Desean is here."

"That's no secret."

"He's been having a lot of meetings."

"Also nothing any beggar in the street couldn't have told me. You'd better come up with something better than that, Dog Boy, or the Cabal will be turning you in themselves."

"I think he knows who Lord Jaxyn is."

"That's not really surprising, considering—"

"He knows *what* he is," Warlock cut in. "And who Queen Kylia really is too."

That gave the man in the shadows pause. Warlock was sure he was a man, now. Dog Boy was an insult only humans bestowed on the canine Crasii.

"What's he doing about it?"

Warlock shrugged, glancing over his shoulder again to ensure the darkened courtyard was still empty. It was past midnight, so there were few with a legitimate excuse to be wandering the palace grounds—Warlock included. "He seems to have been having a lot of meetings. Trying to drum up support, I suppose, but he's not having these meetings with the queen. She sits in on them occasionally, but Tryan's got Jilna completely wrapped around his little finger. She's barely even noticed Princess Nyah has returned."

"As soon as her daughter marries, Nyah becomes queen," the man pointed out.

"That's not going to happen any time soon," Warlock said, shaking his head. "Elyssa has been given the task of finding her new niece a husband, but she's not even looking. It does not suit these immortals to allow the little princess to take the throne."

"Why don't they just kill her then?"

"Because Desean made her safety a condition of his cooperation."

The man was silent for a moment, digesting that information. After a time, he asked, "Cooperation for what?"

"Desean is talking war. He knows Jaxyn and Diala are immortal. He's offering to lead the Caelish troops in an invasion of Glaeba, and in return for the throne once King Mathu is dead, Queen Kylia removed and Lord Jaxyn defeated."

"He'd murder his own cousin?"

"I don't believe he thinks he'll have to. He's telling Tryan that Jaxyn and Kylia will do it for him." Warlock hesitated, wondering how he could convey the danger Glaeba was in. Stellan Desean was a persuasive, intelligent man, with a gift for offering tyrants what they wanted to hear. Worse, everything he was telling the immortals was the truth. He *was* the heir to Glaeba, and a popular man in his own country. He *did* have a large following and even Warlock knew how much of the country might prefer him as king, despite the charges of sodomy laid against him by Mathu.

Having met the Duke of Lebec once before, Warlock was having a hard time believing this was the same man. He was harder now, less trusting, and willing to go to extremes to claim a throne he clearly considered his.

And he knew things now—things Warlock was certain the duke hadn't known before. Months ago, when he'd visited Warlock in the Watchhouse of the Lebec City Watch, Stellan Desean hadn't known anything about the immortals. Now he was urging Tryan to attack, and although he'd never said it in Warlock's presence, it was as if he knew it must happen before the Tide peaked and with it, Jaxyn's full powers.

"Who's running the show? Syrolee or Tryan?"

"They battle among themselves. Constantly. I think Tryan is winning the battle because Syrolee has called for reinforcements. Engarhod is here already, and his sons, Rance and Krydence, are on their way, I gather. Soon the whole family will be here."

"I'm sure Lord Aranville has his own reinforcements he can call on," the man said. "Have you any news of the other immortals?"

"None," Warlock said. "Elyssa often speaks of Cayal. She's been counselling her brother to find him and bring him into the fold. Apparently she believes that with three Tide Lords facing him, Jaxyn will back down and cede Glaeba without a fight."

"Why Cayal? Why not one of the others?"

"They've heard Cayal was in Glaeba recently. And that he fought with Jaxyn. And I think Elyssa desires him. She is the one advocating his inclusion, most of all." That was something of an understatement. Elyssa was quite obsessed by him. It was hard, sometimes, to remain silent. Warlock would dearly love to tell her that he'd met Cayal and the Immortal Prince shuddered at the very mention of her name.

The shadowy man had fallen silent again.

"There's not much else I can tell you," Warlock said. "They talk a great deal, but nothing has been agreed upon yet. Desean's arrival has thrown all their plans into disarray."

"Which makes you wonder if that's not why the Cabal sent him here," the man mused, but he sounded more as if he was thinking out loud than engaging Warlock in conversation.

"Rance and Krydence are supposed to arrive in the next few days. I don't think they'll make any firm plans until they get here."

"Then we'll meet back here three days from now. Hopefully you'll have something more useful to report by then."

The man melted back into the shadows, leaving Warlock standing in the cold courtyard, shivering a little in the icy breeze that swirled around his legs.

Tides, I was mad to agree to this.

Squaring his shoulders and lifting his tail confidently, so he looked—to the casual observer—as if he was meant to be here at this time of night, Warlock turned and headed toward the main store, taking the key from the pocket of his tunic. He hurried along the stone path, no longer worried if anybody noticed him. He was fetching a jug of cider for Lady Alysa, after all. As her personal servant, nobody would question his right to be doing that.

Of course, he was spying for more than one master and in theory, still had to get a message to Jaxyn, but in that, his status as a Crasii had worked in his favour. He had been ordered by Elyssa to remain loyal to her. Her orders, being the most recent, overrode anything Jaxyn might have ordered him to do before they left Glaeba. Jaxyn must have known it was a risk Elyssa or Tryan would take such a precaution, but perhaps he'd believed they wouldn't. If Jaxyn had one fault Warlock could readily identify, it was that he constantly underestimated his enemies.

Warlock reached the store, lifted the torch from the bracket outside and unlocked the door, thinking he'd never imagined there would come a time when he wished—however fleetingly—that he was back, safe and sound, in his cell on Recidivists' Row.

Three days later, on a bitterly cold wet night, as promised, the shadowy man was back.

Warlock, however, had little more to report. Krydence and Rance had still not arrived. Syrolee, Engarhod and Tryan were still arguing. Elyssa was still urging her brother to find Cayal and make peace with him. The queen still acted as if she was intoxicated most of the time, and only the little princess seemed to be fully aware of what was going on around her.

Warlock explained this to the shadowy man, who seemed to take the news fairly well, all things considered.

"It's of little mind," the man said. "The important thing is Stellan Desean. His arrival here is what will cause the most grief."

"It certainly will," Warlock agreed, hoping he didn't sound too pleased about it.

"Provided he keeps his head on his shoulders."

"What can Jaxyn do to stop him?"

"He can't do anything to stop him, Dog Boy. But you can bet he's going to try."

There was a change in the man's tone of voice that spoke of plans he hadn't known of a few days earlier at their last meeting.

"You know why Desean is here, don't you?"

The man was silent for a moment, and then Warlock felt, rather than saw, him nodding in the darkness. "Turns out your news wasn't such a big surprise."

The implications of that statement were terrifying. "Do you know the reason the Cabal sent him here?"

"I can't say," the man replied, as if he regretted even giving that much away. "All I can tell you is to be on your guard. It doesn't suit our . . . superiors . . . for Desean to die."

"What do you expect me to do about it?"

"Keep your eyes open. And if you can manage it, while you're at it, stop Jaxyn's assassins from killing Stellan Desean," the shadowy man said.

Oh, Warlock thought. *Is that all?*

Chapter 32

Arkady Desean had reevaluated her definition of pain.

She'd thought being raped as a fourteen-year-old was the worst it could get. She'd thought being branded was marginally worse. Or laying there while Cydne had his way with her, to save herself from being used by the whole crew of a slave ship or being packed off to a Senestran mining camp.

As it turned out, these were now fond memories of better days. Days she could recall in detail. Days when she could actually describe how she felt.

She couldn't do that any longer.

Because there were no words to describe what Arkady was experiencing now.

The first gobie ant scouts had found them within the hour. They tickled as their tiny feet ran across her raw skin, seeking the fresh blood they could sense from the countless wounds inflicted on her flesh by the trunk's thick spikes. She only tried once to dislodge them. *That* had sent the spikes driving even further into her back, making her wounds bleed afresh. She didn't try it again.

The ants nibbled tentatively at her bleeding wounds, causing her irritation rather than pain, and then they disappeared. Arkady was faint with relief. It turned out the gobie ants weren't as bad as Azquil predicted.

Their audience dwindled after a time, as midday approached and people returned home for lunch. By mid-afternoon, the dying prisoners had lost all entertainment value and there was nobody there at all to watch them perish.

The sun climbed higher. Arkady's thirst had turned to desperation by the time her body stopped sweating, a sign of how quickly her dehydration was progressing. The sun scorched Arkady's skin. As sunburn competed with the stabbing spines in her back and legs, it was debateable which caused the most pain. She entertained herself with dreams of rescue. Jojo had been sent away, after all.

She would have gone for help, wouldn't she?

The immortals didn't specifically *forbid* her to say anything of their fate. *Isn't that what a loyal Crasii would do? Go for help?*

Of course, the nearest help was probably at the Delta Settlement and that was hours away . . .

And who, in this Tide-forsaken country, would launch a rescue based on the word of a lone feline Crasii slave anyway?

Arkady was finding it hard to concentrate and she knew her dreams of rescue were just that . . . dreams . . .

Cydne had fallen silent some time ago, his cracked lips and parched tongue preventing him from keeping up his rant against these uncivilised wretches who didn't understand who he was and how important his father was. Arkady no longer cared what happened to him. It hurt too much to move her head to look at him, and in her mind he deserved everything he was getting anyway.

At some indeterminate point, someone offered her water. Arkady tried to open her eyes to see who it was, but the pain of even that much movement proved too much. Every muscle she owned was burning from the need to keep her body rigid and unmoving to prevent the spikes driving deeper into her flesh.

"Try to drink something."

The voice was vaguely familiar. Arkady wondered if it was Jojo. Or maybe Pedy's mother? Her cracked lips hungered for the liquid, even while a detached voice in the back of her mind reminded her that to take fluid now simply meant delaying the inevitable.

Better to refuse and have this done with, the voice in her head suggested.

Her parched throat disagreed. She lapped hungrily at the cool water, which all too quickly stopped flowing.

"I'm sorry," her anonymous benefactor whispered. "I know you meant well. But that's all I can do for you . . ."

Arkady realised after a few moments that she was alone again, except for the softly groaning Cydne beside her. The pain had blurred into something so real, so solid, that she was able to step away from it.

The agony was still there, it was happening, but it was happening to somebody else. It made her torment bearable. It gave her the strength to tolerate it.

And then, just after sundown, the ants came back.

The first few ants had been a scouting party and when they came back, they came in force. She heard them more than saw them, felt them crawling over her feet and swarming up her body. Someone screamed. She supposed it was Cydne.

She wondered how he had the strength left.

When the first of the ants reached the stab wounds in her legs, Arkady discovered a new definition of agony. Delirious, parched and sunburned to the point of blistering, she could feel the ants biting into the raw flesh of her wounds, feel them marching inexorably up her body, seeking other portals into the meat beneath her flesh.

She could no longer remain still. Arkady could feel every tiny set of pincers tearing the flesh of her bloody wounds apart. Every movement caused more damage, either by slicing the spikes deeper into her flesh, or by forcing desiccated muscles frozen in place by hours of inactivity into moving, which rubbed her sunburn raw . . . The fresh blood didn't run freely. By now, she was dehydrated to the point of delirium. The blood was sluggish, leaking from her skin like tree sap from an axe-cut trunk.

Arkady screamed. She screamed as the ants swarmed up her legs, as they bit into her back and across her belly. She screamed as they found her bleeding lips, the cuts on her shoulder and face Jojo had inflicted when she was trying to destroy the tonic, her open mouth, crawled into her dried-up eyes . . .

And then, out of nowhere, a wall of cold water slammed into her, as if a wave had risen out of the channel of its own accord to wash her tiny tormenters away . . .

A second wave hit with savage force, pushing her back onto the spikes, making her cry out, and then a third. She spat out a mouthful of the rank water along with the drowning ants, and then screamed anew as her arms, tied over her head for so long, were cut free and the agony of stillness replaced the anguish of movement.

Her throat was raw. Unable to speak, she collapsed into the arms of her rescuer as he cut away the ropes that bound her waist and feet. As least she *hoped* he was rescuing her. For all she knew, this was just part of their punishment and she'd been cut down simply to be taken somewhere else, so they could add another layer to her torment.

Perhaps the idea isn't to let us die yet, but to revive us and torture us all over again, and again, and again, again . . .

Arryl was here, after all, and she'd brought Cayal back from the brink of death. There was no real reason she couldn't do the same for Arkady and Cydne. Particularly if it meant she could arrange to have these callous murderers from Port Traeker tortured for days, even weeks, until they'd repented their sins sufficiently.

More likely, Arkady decided, *I'm delirious.*

She wasn't being rescued at all. *Maybe*, Arkady wondered, as she imagined being doused with cool water again to rid her body of the last of the flesh-eating gobie ants, *I'm actually being devoured by them.*

She'd stepped out of her body before to survive intolerable pain. This could easily be more of the same.

"Arkady . . ."

Tides, that's Declan's voice.

She knew now that she had to be delirious; wishing for something that could never be. Something that *would* never be. It was a pity really. Declan had loved her all her life. Until she'd been forced to put aside her own feelings to save her father by marrying Stellan, she'd never imagined spending her life with anyone else.

Funny, how at the moment of death, we can finally admit our deepest secrets, our most heartfelt desires, even if it's only to ourselves.

"Tides, Arkady, speak to me . . ."

There is truth in dying. Who'd have thought . . . ?

If she was imagining this, if her fevered mind had created this illusion to distract her as the ants devoured her body, she decided she might as well enjoy it. Imagining Declan running to her rescue again—as he had so many times when they were children—was better than feeling gobie ants eating their way down to her bones with their tiny little pincers and their tiny little feet and the excruciating pain they brought with them . . .

I knew you'd come for me. Arkady wasn't sure if she said the words aloud, or even if it made a difference. This was all in her dying imagination, after all . . .

"Tides, Arkady . . . I'm *so* sorry I didn't find you sooner . . ."

His words made no sense, and in any case, she didn't care, because they were followed by unimaginable pain ripping through her. It felt as if the ants had returned and were gnawing on her raw nerve endings.

The pain went on and on, wave after wave of it, until, even in her dying hallucination she couldn't take it any longer and she sought refuge in oblivion.

When Arkady's eyes fluttered open an indeterminate time later, a number of things struck her almost simultaneously.

It was night, she was no longer tied to the Justice Tree, she was parched, her throat so dry she could hardly speak . . .

And the pain had gone.

"You're awake."

Apparently death wasn't so bad, after all. Languorously, Arkady turned in the direction of Declan's voice and smiled. The grass under her body felt cool, her skin supple and whole. There was no pain. Not so much as a twinge. She'd never felt better.

"Awake? No. I'm delirious. Or I'm dead. The latter, I think, given it's not hurting any more."

Declan placed a cool hand on her forehead. It felt so deliciously real. She turned her face and kissed his palm. Perhaps the Crasii were right and there really was a heaven, and in her heaven it was cool and dark and Declan was there to look after her . . .

"You're not dead, Arkady," Declan said, carefully extracting his hand. "But you might well be if we don't get out of here before someone comes down to check on you."

That took a few moments to register. Pushing herself up on one elbow, Arkady stared at the vision of hope and wonder and began to doubt that this *was* a vision.

"*Declan?* Is that really you?"

He smiled. "Don't you know I'll always be around to haul you out of these terrible scrapes you somehow manage to get yourself into, Kady Morel?"

"Tides!" Arkady sat bolt upright, as the day's events crowded in on her along with the startling realisation that she wasn't actually dead. "Cydne!"

"You mean him?" Declan asked glancing over his shoulder.

There was little left of the Port Traeker doctor, at least that Arkady could see of him in the darkness. Although he appeared to move occasionally, it was the gobie ants that covered him completely which created the illusion. His eye sockets were empty and there didn't seem to be any skin left in the places where the mass of insects moved enough for her to see. Arkady looked away. Cydne deserved to suffer for what he'd done, but nobody deserved that fate . . .

"Why didn't you save him, too?"

Declan's expression hardened. "Isn't he the man who kept you as a slave?"

She nodded and looked away, unable to meet his eye. *Tides, how am I going to explain the last few months to you?*

"Then he deserved to die," Declan said with little emotion, although Arkady didn't really pay much attention, because when she tried to avoid his eye, she looked down at her bare breasts and realised that not only was she all but naked, but something else was missing.

"It's gone."

He looked at her, puzzled. "What's gone?"

"My slave brand." When he did nothing but look at her blankly, she added, "They branded me, Declan. With a branding iron. On my right breast. Here. And now it's gone. For that matter," she added, holding her hands out, turning them over and over, examining them in wonder, "there's not a mark on me. Tides, you didn't ask Arryl to heal me magically, did you?"

"Arryl?" Declan repeated, looking puzzled. "Arryl *who*?"

"The immortal, Arryl, of course," she said. "She was the one who condemned us to death. How did you get her to change her mind?"

Declan paled. "Arryl is *here*? In Watershed Falls?" He stood up quickly and offered her his hand. "We have to get out of here, Arkady. *Now*."

She let him pull her to her feet, full of questions and things she had to tell Declan. About what had happened to her. About Cayal finding a way to die. About how she'd survived. About finding Tiji and the other chameleons . . .

And she wished she was wearing something more than a loincloth.

"But surely, we can . . ."

Declan held up his hand to silence her, as if he was listening for something. He stood like that for a moment, still as a reptilian Crasii, and then he grabbed her hand. "Trust me, Arkady, we need to get out of here before—"

"Before any other immortals find you?"

They both spun around as a third person Arkady hadn't known was nearby, answered his question. The woman who finished Declan's sentence was walking toward them from the direction of the village, carrying a torch which shed a circle of light around her and made the shadows all the more sinister for it.

Arkady stepped closer to Declan, expecting the woman to turn on her, but Arryl acted as if she didn't exist.

Her attention fixed on Declan, who, for some reason, didn't seem surprised.

Arryl raised the torch a little and studied him curiously. "Yes, I can imagine *you* would rather be gone before another immortal arrived."

Declan remained silent.

"Although if you were planning to keep your presence in Watershed Falls a secret," Arryl added, "it was foolish of you to call on the Tide."

"I wouldn't have had to," Declan replied cryptically, "if you weren't going about torturing innocent people."

"What is she talking about?" Arkady whispered to Declan, but she might as well have been addressing Cydne's corpse for all the notice he was taking of her.

"Do you mean *her*?" Arryl asked, pointing to Arkady. "Tides, ask her how many innocent Crasii *she's* killed in the past few weeks, before you go accusing *us* of torturing innocents. Who are you?"

He hesitated, and then squared his shoulders a little. "My name is Declan Hawkes."

"You're Glaeban?"

He nodded.

"And you've not been long in our ranks, I'm guessing." Arryl studied him in the flickering light. "You're fair bristling with raw power, though, aren't you?" She glanced at Arkady. "I couldn't heal anyone that fast with the Tide only partially up, and I've been practising for thousands of years. Who else knows about you?"

"Only Maralyce."

"Declan, what's going on?"

"She a particular friend of yours?" Arryl asked, jerking her head in Arkady's direction, speaking about her as if she wasn't actually there. "Or do you just make a habit of rescuing damsels in distress?"

"She's a friend."

"Seems you know a few more immortals than you let on, young lady."

Confused and totally at a loss to explain what was going on here, Arkady glared at the blonde immortal. "I'm sorry, but you condemned me for knowing *two* immortals. Telling you I knew more of them wasn't likely to help."

"I'm not surprised you didn't mention this one, though."

Arkady looked at Declan who seemed very uncomfortable with this odd and totally inexplicable conversation.

Arryl smiled. "Tides, she doesn't know."

"I don't know what?" Arkady demanded. "Declan? What is she talking about?"

"Your friend here is not what he seems, my dear," Arryl said.

"What do you mean?"

"Exactly what I said," the exquisite blonde immortal replied. "This man—this friend of yours who would defy the wrath of the Trinity, just because he knows he can, I suspect—this Glaeban you know as Declan Hawkes, is one of us."

"One of *you*? What do you mean—*one of you*? How could he be *one of you*?" Arkady looked to Declan, waiting for him to protest, waiting for him to deny Arryl's ludicrous suggestion, but he said nothing. "*Declan*?"

His eyes were focused on Arryl, as if he was seeing something Arkady couldn't. And then he turned to look at her. "I'm sorry."

Comprehension dawned on her slowly. The remembrance of her pain, her rescue and the agony of being completely healed . . .

She took a step back from him. "Tides, you're immortal."

"Not by choice."

"Few of us are," Arryl said, lifting the torch a little higher. She stepped forward and did something completely unexpected. She extended her hand toward Declan. "And I'm guessing you've a lot of questions Maralyce wouldn't answer."

Declan nodded, studying her outstretched hand with caution. Arkady kept staring at him, trying to see if there was anything different about him, but there was nothing. In the flickering torchlight he was the Declan she remembered. Her friend. The Declan she'd loved since childhood.

How could he possibly be immortal?

"You'll make enemies of most of us, eventually," Arryl warned. "But for now, before we jump to conclusions about each other, let us—for a time, at least—be friends."

"I want your word no harm will come to Arkady."

"You have it."

Warily, Declan accepted her hand. "Then for a time—friends."

Arryl smiled. "And now, since that's taken care of, let's go somewhere we can talk. The Eternal Flame has been extinguished for six thousand years, Declan Hawkes of Glaeba. I want to know how you managed something nobody has been able to do since then."

Declan nodded and then turned to Arkady, his eyes full of fear. She knew him so well; it wasn't hard to guess what he was thinking. *Will she hate me? Will she look at me differently?*

Arkady stepped closer and put her hand in his. Since she'd seen him last she'd been sold into slavery, willingly whored herself to a mass-murdering member of the Senestran Physicians' Guild to keep herself out of a brothel and murdered a few score innocent Crasii herself.

On balance, Declan's new status as an immortal seemed quite tame by comparison.

PART III

What fates impose, that men must needs abide;
It boots not to resist both wind and tide.
—William Shakespeare (1564–1616)

Chapter 33

"Where are we?"

"Back at the Outpost."

Tiji pushed herself up on her elbows and looked around. It was dark, a single candle flickering on the table beside the bed, but sure enough, the walls of her small room were the rough planking of the Outpost, rather than the bamboo walls of the cottage in Watershed Falls. Her head was pounding, she had a gnawing emptiness in her belly and felt completely wrung out, but the cramps and her blurry vision were nothing more than a distant memory.

"What are we doing back here? What happened? Last I thing I remember was visiting the Port Traeker doctor."

Azquil sat on the edge of the pallet and smiled comfortingly. "Well, you won't have to worry about him or his *makor-di* again. The Trinity took care of them."

She gave him a puzzled look. "What are you talking about?"

"That tonic they were handing out so generously. It wasn't a cure, Tiji; it was mostly wood alcohol with a bit of cream and a few herbs thrown in to mask the smell."

"But that's a poison . . ."

"Which is what they were counting on. Apparently, the Physicians' Guild's plan was to kill the disease at its source. Literally."

"That's monstrous!"

Azquil nodded and took her hand in his. "Thank the Tide we arrived when we did, or you'd be dead by now."

She stared at him for a moment, and then her eyes widened as she remembered at least one thing that had happened in Watershed Falls that morning. "Tides! The doctor. He gave me the tonic! I drank it! Lots of it!"

Azquil nodded. "I know. By the time we arrived you were already unconscious."

Her eyes widened in surprise. "How did you know to come looking for me?"

"I didn't," he said. "It was just luck we found you when we did."

Luck. Or perhaps fate. Tiji wasn't so dismissive of either, lately. "I thought you and Tenika would be gone for weeks."

"We planned to be. After I left you at the cottage, I brought the tonic here, with the intention of helping the Trinity with their healing work. Arryl and Medwen started using the tonic on the less serious cases in some of the nearer inland villages, hoping it would ease the burden on their healing powers. The Tide's still on the rise, you see, and there's a limit to what they can do magically. But everyone who took the tonic died, and much more rapidly than one would expect swamp fever to take them. It took us a few days to realise why, and as soon as we did, we headed back to Watershed to confront the doctor. By the time we got there, you were almost dead."

Tiji tried to recall what had happened this morning—Tides, was it *only* this morning—after she arrived at the clinic, but she couldn't remember much beyond the doctor giving her that burning tonic and that wretched feline telling her to move along. "What happened to him?"

"The doctor? We strung him and his wretched *makor-di* up on the Justice Tree for the gobie ants to feed on," he said, with unaccustomed savagery.

"And how is it that I'm still alive?"

"Arryl saved you."

"With Tide magic?"

He nodded.

"You let a *suzerain* use *Tide* magic on me?"

"The alternative was to let you die, Tiji."

She was horrified. "What if they've done something to me? What if they've changed me so I have to obey them, or something? What if . . ." Azquil silenced her fears with a kiss. It took her so completely by surprise, she forgot what she was going to say. "Um . . . what if . . . they made me . . . not love you anymore," she added lamely, when they came up for air.

"I didn't know you loved me in the first place," Azquil said with a grin.

Oh, Tides, I didn't mean to say that . . . "Well, it's just I . . . I mean, I meant . . ."

Leaning forward and taking her gently by the shoulders, he kissed her again, his delightfully flickering tongue making her heart pound. "It's all right, Tiji. You don't have to apologise," he breathed against her skin. "But you do have to get better." He let her go, stood up and offered her his hand. "And I'm guessing you're probably starving, given you've kept nothing down for the past day or so."

Tiji nodded, as she realised the gnawing emptiness in her stomach really *was* hunger and not just a reaction to Azquil no longer kissing her. "I think I *might* be a bit peckish, now you mention it."

"Then let's go fix some food," he said, pulling her to her feet. "Ambria's still in Watershed Falls with Arryl and Medwen. I'm not sure they'll be back tonight, so we have the run of the place. Let's go raid the Trinity's larder."

Tiji smiled and nodded, feeling her skin colour flicker. Azquil was too much of a gentleman to remark on it, though.

Smiling at him, she let him take her hand and lead her back through the house to the Outpost's large, homely kitchen, where—as if they were an old married human couple—he began to fix her dinner.

"So . . . what is this?" Tiji asked, as Azquil placed the steaming bowl on the table in front of her.

"Grasshopper and cockroach stew," he said. "With a bit of small human child thrown in for good measure. Ambria has a couple of them hanging in her larder."

Tiji hesitated, then spooned a healthy portion of the spicy stew into her mouth. "You're mocking me, aren't you?" she said, her words muffled by her mouthful of food.

He smiled and took the seat opposite her. "Just a little bit. And the truth is, I'm not sure what it is. I did find the meat in Ambria's larder. It could be a small human child, for all I know."

"Just so long as it's not cockroach," she said, reaching for the bowl of salt. "I draw the line at eating cockroaches."

"But small human children are fine?"

"With enough salt." She said it with a grin, deciding to play along. Tiji had never really had someone like Azquil to trade silly banter with before. Except Declan.

Tides, I should get a message to Declan . . .

Azquil laughed, and began eating his own meal. Ravenous, Tiji put all thoughts of her former life out of mind and wolfed down the stew, wondering how she'd go about asking for seconds, when she caught a whiff of something rank.

"Ambria's back."

Azquil sniffed the air for a moment and then shook his head. "I can't smell anything."

"You're used to the scent of them," she said. "Trust me, there's a suzerain coming."

"I really wish you wouldn't call them that," Azquil said, frowning. "The Trinity are our friends."

"*Your* friends, Azquil, not mine."

"Arryl saved your life."

"I didn't ask her to."

"Are you saying you'd rather die than accept help from an immortal?"

Yes! Tiji wanted to reply emphatically, but she had a feeling this was such a pivotal issue between them, she would ruin whatever hope she had of a future with this handsome young lizard if she said it aloud. So she shrugged, spooned the last of the stew into her mouth and hedged around the issue with a noncommittal, "Maybe."

"You'll change your mind once you get to know them." His head came up and he sniffed the air again. "You're right, though. They are coming."

"They?"

"Arryl, and Medwen must be with her. The scent is too strong to be a lone immortal."

Tides, that's all I need. A whole clutch of suzerain.

"I can't wait," she forced herself to say with a smile. "I suppose I should thank Arryl for saving my life while I'm at it."

"It would be a good start, Tiji. Are you finished?"

She nodded, showing him her empty bowl.

"Then let's take a torch down to the dock to meet them."

Tiji smiled through gritted teeth. "Good idea."

The nights were loud, raucous affairs out here in the wetlands, Tiji had discovered, and this night was no exception. The chirruping of insects filled the darkness, as millions of nocturnal creatures went about their business, apparently determined to share every intimate detail of their lives with all the other insects in the swamp.

Why else, Tiji wondered, *would they have so much to say?*

They heard the boat before they saw it, the splash of the amphibians towing it along the shallow channel only just audible over the racket of the insects. Azquil raised the torch and waved it back and forth to make it easier for the amphibians to find the dock. As the boat neared the outpost, Tiji found herself wanting to gag on the stench of the suzerain. Tides, this was worse than when she'd hidden in the Ladies Walk of the Cycrane Palace in Caelum and listened in on the plans of the Empress of the Five Realms and her kin.

There were three passengers in the boat, although it was impossible to tell who they were in the dark from this distance. Tiji thought one looked male. The others were obviously women.

So I finally get to meet all three of the Trinity. What Declan and the Cabal would give to know what I know now . . .

Not wishing to get too close to these creatures that—by virtue of both instinct and training—she so despised, Tiji hung back as Azquil helped tie up the boat, exchanging a greeting with the amphibians before they swam off toward their homes further along the channel. She couldn't understand why Azquil thought so highly of the Trinity, certain there was no power in the universe, up to and including Tide magic, that could force her to like or trust a suzerain.

There were greetings all round and apparently some introductions, and then the boat passengers turned and headed for the Outpost. Tiji watched them warily, her caution turning to delighted surprise when she realised that the tall human woman wearing only a slave skirt and a hastily tied shawl around her breasts was Arkady Desean, and the man walking a pace behind her was . . .

"*Declan!*"

Tiji flew across the narrow patch of ground between them, ready to hurl herself into his arms. She had so much to tell him . . . about her journey here, her news about the Immortal Prince, about finding the other chameleons, about the suzerain . . .

She skidded to a halt a few feet from him, as it occurred to her that he already knew about the suzerain, because he had arrived with them.

And then she noticed the stench, the rank aroma of immortality that her Scard nose could not deny.

"Tides . . ." she murmured, taking a step backward. "No . . ."

Azquil and the suzerain were staring at her in surprise. Arkady looked relieved for some reason. Declan . . . Declan just looked filled with regret.

"You know this child?" Arryl asked.

"It's a long story," Declan said, his eyes fixed on Tiji. He reached out his hand to her. "Tiji . . ."

"Don't you touch me!" she spat, her eyes filling with tears. "You're not Declan Hawkes."

Declan looked at her helplessly and then threw his hands up and glanced at Arkady, as if he'd known all along how she'd react to meeting him like this, and was telling the duchess *I told you so*. "I'm sorry, Tiji."

Sorry! She couldn't believe he was apologising to her. Declan Hawkes, her saviour, her hero . . . he stank like a suzerain. It was the ultimate betrayal.

He had joined the ranks of the enemy.

Sorry? It was going to take a damn sight more than a simple *sorry* to make things better between them.

Tiji turned away, storming back toward the Outpost, unable to bear looking at Declan. Azquil hurried after her, grabbing her arm before she could disappear inside.

"Tiji, wait . . ."

She shook free of him, her eyes blurred with tears. "You asked me earlier if I'd rather have died today, Azquil, and I said no. I lied. I wish you *had* let me die." She turned and pointed an accusing finger at Declan. "Then I wouldn't have to deal with him."

Leaving Declan to explain, Tiji fled, not into the house, but into the surrounding jungle, where the cacophony of insect noises was so much louder and might have some hope of drowning out her tears.

Chapter 34

Ambria's kitchen was a homely place, about as far from the majestic marble temples of Tide Lord legend as it was possible to get. Arryl lit a few more lamps and indicated they should sit at the long, scrubbed wooden table. She sat opposite Declan and Arkady, who hadn't left his side since he'd found her as if she was afraid that if she lost sight of him, he'd disappear. The young male chameleon had gone in search of Tiji.

"Do you think Azquil will be able to find her?" Arkady asked, as she took a seat beside Declan. He thought she was making conversation rather than genuinely inquiring about Tiji's fate. Azquil, after all, was the one who'd tied her to that tree and she was probably glad not to have to face him just yet.

Arryl nodded. "He'll find her. I'm not certain we'll see either of them again for a while, though. They can be emotional little creatures, the chameleons, and they don't forgive easily." She looked at Declan. "She appears to have quite a bit to forgive."

"I would have counted Tiji among my best friends until a few minutes ago," Declan said. "And I can't, for the life of me, imagine how she finished up here in the first place."

"I think she was following me," Arkady said.

Arryl shook her head. "She was brought here by the Retrievers."

"Who?"

"A team of specially trained chameleons," the immortal explained, standing up to poke around the stove to see if it was alight. "They search for chameleons stolen as younglings. They found her on the streets of Elvere, I believe. Would anyone else like some tea? I'm going to make a pot, anyway."

Only Arkady indicated she wanted tea. Arryl bustled around the stove for a moment, got the kettle heating and then stared at Declan in a very disconcerting manner.

He stared back and said nothing.

After a moment, Arryl shifted her gaze to Arkady. "And you. What brings you to the Senestran Wetlands?"

She hesitated before answering. "It's a long story."

"Believe me, my dear," Arryl said, "everyone here can afford the time."

Arkady glanced at Declan for a moment and then took a deep breath. "All right, then. It goes like this . . . My husband was the Duke of Lebec. For reasons too complicated to go into, we were exiled to Torlenia. Trouble is, he had a lover who turned out to be your friend Jaxyn. Oh, and the girl we thought was his niece turned out to be Diala. While we were away, the King and Queen of Glaeba died in an accident, so my husband returned home for the funeral. Kinta invited me to stay at the Royal Seraglium in Ramahn while he was gone. Then we got word my husband had been arrested and stripped of his title and estates. Figuring Jaxyn was behind his downfall, I asked Kinta for asylum. She sent me into the desert to stay with Brynden, but I met up with Cayal along the way—"

"You *what?*"

"Let her speak, Declan," Arryl scolded. She turned to Arkady. "Please . . . tell us the rest of your remarkable tale."

Arkady looked as if she was biting back what she really wanted to say, merely complying with Arryl's instructions out of politeness. Declan put his hand over hers encouragingly, but all he could think was, *Tides, she's been with Cayal again.*

"When I got to the abbey, Cayal and Brynden talked and agreed that I would stay at the abbey while Cayal went off to fetch Lukys, because Cayal thinks Lukys has found a way for him to die," Arkady continued. "As soon as he was out of sight, Brynden sold me to a slaver in Elvere, because he's still angry with Cayal. That's where I was batch-bought by the Senestrans. As I didn't fancy being passed around the crew for their entertainment, I offered myself to the ship's doctor on the voyage here. After we docked in Port Traeker, he kept me on as his assistant because my father had also been a physician and I knew enough of his trade to be useful to him. About three weeks ago the Senestran Physicians' Guild sent us here to the wet- lands to implement their grand plans for the eradication of swamp fever." She took another deep breath. "That's about it really."

The immortal was staring at her in amazement. Declan wasn't sure what to say, but one thing he was certain of—Arkady's explanation was meant for him as much as it was for Arryl.

And she's been with Cayal again.

Arryl shook her head in wonder. "You've met all those immortals in the past few months?"

Arkady nodded. "I met Cayal first . . . actually, that's not strictly correct.

Jaxyn was the first, followed by Diala, but I didn't know who they were until after I met Cayal."

The immortal shook her head in despair as she turned to lift the boiling kettle from the stove. "It doesn't take them long, does it? The Tide's barely turned and they're already on the move."

There didn't seem to be an answer to that, and Arryl didn't seem to expect one. She filled the teapot, took two cups from a shelf, and sat down again, waiting for the tea to draw. After a moment, she turned to Declan. "And what's your story?"

"Arkady's one of my oldest friends. When I heard she went missing I came looking for her."

"Aren't you leaving out a few important details? Like you being the Glaeban spymaster?"

"How could you possibly know that?" Arkady asked in surprise.

"Tiji would have told her," Declan answered, not taking his eyes from Arryl's. "And yes, I was Glaeba's spymaster. Until . . . circumstances intervened."

"Ah," she said, pushing a mug of steaming tea across the table to Arkady before taking her own seat. "About that . . . would you like to tell me *how*?"

"I was caught in a fire."

Arryl's eyes narrowed doubtfully. "Just an ordinary, everyday fire?"

Declan allowed himself a small smile. "I'm not sure if I'd call it ordinary or everyday. We burned the entire Herino Prison to the ground in the process."

"And somehow, you emerged immortal?"

Declan nodded. Arkady turned to Arryl. "You were the keeper of the Eternal Flame for centuries," she said. "How could an ordinary fire make an ordinary man immortal?"

"You're assuming he's an ordinary man," Arryl said, studying Declan closely.

"I think that has something to do with it, actually," Declan agreed.

"What?" Arkady asked with a thin smile, the first he'd seen since he'd found her tied to that wretched tree. "You think you're something special, do you?"

"My grandfather was Maralyce's son."

Arkady stared at him in surprise but said nothing more. The news about Shalimar appeared to have rendered her speechless.

"And your parents?" Arryl asked.

Sitting beside him, her hand in his, Arkady sipped her tea and said nothing, but he could feel her gaze on him, questioning and curious. He could sense no animosity from her, though. She'd certainly taken the news he was now immortal a great deal better than Tiji had.

Had Cayal really found a way to die?

"My mother was a whore," he said, forcing himself to focus on the matter at hand. "I could have been fathered by any one of a thousand men."

Arryl quickly came to the same conclusion Maralyce had. "But you think he's an immortal?"

"That's as near to an explanation as I can come."

"But it doesn't make sense," Arkady said, finding her voice. "I thought you could only make immortals by setting them alight with the Eternal Flame?"

"So did I," Arryl said. "And it's certainly the way *we* were all made. But all of us, as far as we know, were ordinary humans before we were immolated. If he's right about who fathered him, and he's Maralyce's grandson, then he was more than half immortal to start with."

"Or your precious Eternal Flame wasn't so special after all," Declan said. "At least, that's what Maralyce implied when I asked her about it."

Arryl looked shocked. "She *said* that?"

"She said it suited them for everyone to believe it. She wasn't nearly so surprised as you are, that an ordinary fire did this to me."

"Who did she mean by *them*?" Arkady asked.

That question silenced the room for a moment. Eventually Arryl shrugged. "I'm not really sure. There's always been a question over how Maralyce was made. And some of the others too, like Pellys and Kentravyon . . ."

"Cayal told me Pellys was made when the brothel in Cuttlefish Bay burned down because the fire was started by the Eternal Flame."

"I always believed that to be true," Arryl agreed. "But then, we always assumed Pellys was mortal to begin with . . ." She hesitated, her expression grim. "Tides, if that's true, and there really never *was* anything particularly special about the Eternal Flame, imagine the fun Diala could be having, setting fire to anything that takes her fancy."

"Perhaps that's *why* they had you believing it was magical," Arkady said. "To prevent immortals like your sister from making too many more of you. I mean, you assume so much. Accept so much. And yet there's no proof—"

"Arkady . . ." Declan said, recognising the danger signs that indicated Arkady was about to get on her high academic horse.

"Let her speak," Arryl said, her expression anything but accommodating. Declan cringed to think of what might happen if Arkady angered this woman. "I'm interested in how this death-dealing Glaeban slave who's been alive for all of an eye-blink has worked out all about us immortals, because, of course, unlike her, *we* haven't spared the idea a single thought in a thousand years."

He looked at Arkady fearfully, but Declan should have known better than to worry about her. Arkady wasn't intimidated by Arryl. "What I was *going* to say, my lady, is that you assume the Eternal Flame landed on Amyrantha when that meteor hit Engarhod's ship in Jelidia. But think about it . . . what are the chances of that particular meteorite hitting a single ship in the middle of the ocean? And then Lukys and Engarhod who—with a single rat, wasn't it?—somehow worked out it was the fire that must be responsible? Because, naturally, you'd know it was the *fire* responsible for your miraculous survival, and not any one of a thousand other factors."

"What are you saying? That we don't even know our own history?" Arryl asked.

"What I'm saying, my lady, is that immortals are just as prone to allowing facts to fall into myth as us mere mortals—and not seeing what is right in front of them. If Declan became immortal because he survived being burned alive by ordinary fire, it doesn't automatically follow that all fire will make humans into immortals. Perhaps Declan really *was* more than half-immortal to start with, and you need the right combination of ancestors before the fire will work. For that matter, are you sure you even *need* fire? If you've the right bloodline, surely drowning would be just as effective as immolation to trigger immortality."

Arryl stared at Arkady for a moment as she calmly sipped her tea and then turned to Declan. "Who *is* this woman?"

Declan glanced at Arkady and smiled, thinking even if he *was* going to live forever, Arkady lecturing an immortal on the fallacy of her beliefs of her origins was a memory he'd carry with him into eternity. "You'll have to forgive my friend. She likes logical explanations for everything."

"So do I, as a rule," Arryl said. She sighed, shaking her head. "Your appearance in our ranks is going to create more than a little stir, Declan, because your friend is correct. Your mere existence throws into doubt everything we know to be true about ourselves and how we were created."

Arkady finished her tea, and—stifling a yawn—she shrugged apologetically. "I don't mean to be argumentative, my lady, it's just ever since Cayal told me how he was made, and what Lukys told *him* about the Eternal Flame, I've been trying to find fault with his story. On your orders, remember," she added to Declan. "I've given this quite a bit of thought."

"Something I'd also like to give it," Arryl said. "Why don't you two turn in for the night? You may not need much sleep these days, Declan, but Arkady certainly does. We can talk more in the morning. There's a room out back you can use," she added, rising to her feet.

It was clear Arryl had had enough of them for the evening and as Declan got no objections from Arkady, he nodded and they both climbed to their feet. Arryl picked up one of the lamps from the table and led them down the hall to a door that opened onto a small storeroom stacked with sacks of mollusc shells and a narrow sleeping pallet tucked into the corner. Although it wasn't exactly an inn, clearly they were used to having overnight guests.

She left the lamp with them, wished them a rather insincere goodnight, and headed back to the kitchen. Seeing Arkady yawning again, Declan pointed to the pallet. "You take the bed, I'll sleep on the floor."

"Don't be ridiculous," she said. "We're both grown-ups."

Which is precisely why we shouldn't share that bed, Declan was tempted to reply. Arkady had been dressed as a slave so long, apparently she no longer noticed she was wearing next to nothing. Even with the shock of meeting up with Tiji and Arryl, sitting next to her these past few hours had been distracting enough. He wasn't sure he had the strength to spend the night with her at his side.

"But you're exhausted . . ."

"Are you *kidding*, Declan? So far today I've been sentenced to death, hung out to dry, almost eaten alive by flesh-eating insects, magically healed, discovered my best friend is now immortal and gotten into an argument with the Sorceress of the Chameleon Crasii about the origins of immortality. You couldn't stop me falling asleep if you tried."

Without waiting for him to respond, she lay down on the pallet, turned on her side, closed her eyes and then added, opening one eye, "Don't forget to put out that lamp. I'm pretty sure *my* ancestors were all mortal and I'd rather not put your 'immortal parentage makes you more likely to survive being burned alive' theory to the test."

He smiled. "I doubt the good ladies of the Trinity would have much of a sense of humour if we burned their Outpost down, either," he said, lifting the glass to blow out the lamp.

When she didn't answer, he put the lamp down, felt his way through the darkness to the pallet and lay down beside her. Without saying a word, she snuggled closer to him until her head was resting on his shoulder, her warm breath tickling his chest.

"Tides, we haven't done this since we were children," he said softly, but Arkady didn't reply and he realised she had relaxed completely. Her deep, even breathing meant she was already asleep.

Chapter 35

Jaxyn Aranville walked the majestic halls of the Herino Palace with a long, impatient stride. Servants scurried out of his path; Crasii trembled and bowed as he passed, able to sense his mood and understandably wary of it.

And so they should be. Jaxyn did not want any further trouble this morning. It wasn't enough, apparently, that Stellan Desean was rattling his sabre at them from across the lake, threatening war, and seemed to have Syrolee and her wretched clan backing him. It wasn't enough that Diala was interfering with his plans at every turn, giving Mathu ideas about being a proper king (whatever that meant) and insisting on approving every order Jaxyn issued in his name. It wasn't enough that Arkady had disappeared from Ramahn—aided by the Imperator's Consort, of all people, so his spies informed him—blatantly thumbing her nose at the King of Glaeba's authority, which Jaxyn wielded in Mathu's name.

Because now, to top it all off, another wretched Aranville cousin had turned up. One who claimed a close friendship with the real—and long dead—Jaxyn Aranville. This cousin could expose him. He didn't have time to deal with this, and despite every Crasii in the palace being compelled to obey him, even *he* might have trouble covering up a murder committed in the main reception rooms of the Herino Palace.

A rumble of thunder sounded in the distance, illuminating the grey day for a split second as the lightning battered the island city. Although he wasn't responsible for the storm, Jaxyn was glad of it. It matched his temperament perfectly this morning.

The Crasii withdrew from the atrium as he approached. The "cousin" in question was a woman, dressed in a long lavender gown with puffy sleeves. The fashion was one Diala had started as a joke, convinced that now she was queen, she could wear anything, no matter how absurd or unflattering, and every woman in Herino would shortly follow suit. The cousin had dark hair, a body even Jaxyn could appreciate and as she turned to him, her face lit up with a smile.

"Cousin Jaxyn! What a delight to see you again."

Apprehension turned to relief mixed with a sense of impending danger at the sight of her. He smiled with all the forced enthusiasm he could muster. "Cousin Aleena! What a marvellous surprise!"

They embraced briefly, kissing the air beside one another's cheeks.

"It's so good to see you again, cousin," the woman calling herself "Aleena Aranville" said, eyeing him up and down with all the calculating judgement she'd learned as a whore. There was nobody better at summing up a man's character in a glance than Lyna, with the possible exception of Syrolee, who'd also been a whore in the long distant past. "You can't imagine my surprise when I discovered *you* were living here in Herino."

"You can't imagine my surprise at seeing you here now."

"Then I'm glad," she said. "We've an opportunity to become reacquainted."

Jaxyn glanced around to be certain they were alone. The rain pattered on the high roof, the noise loud enough to give them an added level of privacy. He lowered his voice. "What are you doing here, Lyna?"

"Straight to the point, I see," she said. "Are you going to offer me a seat and some refreshments, or have me tossed into the lake?"

"Well, if I thought you'd drown . . ." he said, a little testily, indicating she should take a seat on one of the couches in the nearest alcove. "What are you doing here?"

"Looking for a home, Jaxyn."

He studied her as she sat down, wondering if she was lying. It irked Jaxyn that his magical ability allowed him to move mountains, but couldn't help him at all in detecting when someone wasn't telling him the truth.

"So why come here?" he asked, taking the couch opposite. "Syrolee's right next door."

"I'm tired of Syrolee," Lyna said. "She's only interested in making things good for her family. Besides, her way of doing things is getting boring. But you . . . you seem to have carved a very nice niche for yourself here in Glaeba."

"Not as nice as it could be."

She looked at him with a puzzled expression.

"Diala's here too," he explained. "Somewhat inconveniently married to the new king."

With a resigned sigh, Lyna rose to her feet. "Then there's not much room for me here," she said. "Maybe I will pay Syrolee a visit in Caelum, after all."

"You could marry me," he said, in a flash of inspiration.

She stared down at him, shaking her head. "You cannot be serious."

He nodded, smiling slyly, the idea forming even as he spoke. "I have acquired a bit of an unfortunate reputation around here, which is going to cause me trouble if I don't nip it in the bud. Taking a wife would do that."

"What sort of reputation?"

"The heir to the throne, with whom I used to be . . . *friends* . . . was disinherited and put on trial for treason, but only to cover up the fact he was a sodomite. Glaebans are rather narrow-minded about things like that."

Lyna didn't seem in the slightest bit surprised. But then why would she? She'd been Kentravyon's consort for a long time. Jaxyn, even at his worst, would be hard pressed to top some of the things her former lover had done.

"Let me guess, you were the one who gave up your sodomite's nasty little secret?"

Jaxyn nodded. It was a relief, sometimes, to talk to someone who made no pretence of being particularly noble or decent. "I run the risk of being tarred with the same brush unless I do something to persuade those who have a vested interest in seeing me tossed out of Glaeba, that I was the victim and not a willing participant in my former patron's games."

"You mean you're afraid Diala will turn on you?" Lyna concluded with barely a moment to think about it. "That figures. I don't know why you thought you could trust her in the first place."

"Circumstances thrust us together. I didn't set out to conspire with her deliberately."

Lyna studied him thoughtfully. "So, in return for becoming the 'little woman' and removing any doubt about your sexual preferences, what do I get out of it?"

"I'll make you Queen of Glaeba some day."

"Hasn't Diala already got that job?"

"While Mathu lives, she has. But my old friend, the sodomite-who-just-happens-to-have-a-claim-on-the-throne, has teamed up with Syrolee and Tryan in Caelum. We'll be at war within a matter of weeks." He smiled nastily. "All sorts of terrible accidents happen during wars."

Lyna thought on it for a moment, and then nodded. Jaxyn wasn't really surprised. She probably had nowhere else to go. Since they'd banded together to put Kentravyon on ice—literally—Lyna had been at a loose end. She'd hung around on the fringes of Syrolee's clan mostly, during the last few High Tides, but she had no special loyalty to them . . .

Or does she? Is that what she's doing here? Has Tryan sent her to spy on me and Diala?

Jaxyn wished he'd thought of that *before* proposing to her . . .

Still, there might be a way to turn this to his advantage, regardless of whose side Lyna was actually on. "Of course, you don't have to marry me right away. A betrothal will serve me just as well at this point."

Lyna shrugged, unconcerned. "Just so long as I'm treated in the manner befitting the fiancée of the king's Private Secretary and the new Duke of . . . well, whatever it is you're the duke of now, you can take as long as you want."

"Good, because I have a job that needs doing and I want someone I can trust to do it for me."

"What job?" she asked, taking a seat again.

"I need to find the wife of the former Duke of Lebec."

"Why?"

Because I want her. Because the bitch defied me.

"Because I can use her to slow Stellan Desean down. He's urging Tryan to declare war on us because he thinks he has nothing to lose. I'd like to dissuade him of that notion."

Lyna seemed to accept his reasons. And even Jaxyn had to admit, it sounded plausible. "What does this have to do with me?"

"I want you to find her. She was in Ramahn, last I heard, but the trail's gone cold. I need you to find her and bring her back to Glaeba. Alive."

"Won't that get in the way of our betrothal, dear?"

He smiled and reached for her hand, kissing it gallantly. "You love to shop, Lyna, and nothing is too much for my beloved. Far be it from me to object if you want to search for the perfect wedding dress, even if it means travelling to the very ends of Amyrantha to find it."

Lyna smiled. "You'll finance my *shopping* expedition?"

"Provided you bring home the parcel I want, money is no object."

"Then we have a deal." She glanced past his shoulder at the entrance to the large atrium and then fixed her gaze on his. "There's a young man approaching us," she warned in a low voice. "Dark hair, wearing a coronet."

"That will be Mathu, our new king. Kiss me."

Lyna complied without argument, too skilled at the kind of deceit they were plotting to stand on ceremony. She kissed him with all the expertise a career as a whore and a few thousand years of practice had endowed her with. It was a very long time since Jaxyn had slept with Lyna. Her kiss made him regret that a little.

"Well, aren't you the dark horse, Jaxyn Aranville!" Mathu exclaimed.

They broke apart as the king stopped before them. Lyna—accomplished actress that she was—looked mortified to have been caught in such a compromising position. Jaxyn jumped to his feet, as if he was embarrassed beyond words.

"Tides, I'm so sorry, your majesty . . ."

"There's no need to apologise," the young man said with a wide grin. "Kylia told me you had a cousin come to visit, so I thought I'd come down and greet her personally. Never realised it was such a *close* cousin."

Back-stabbing little bitch, Jaxyn thought, smiling at the king. Diala must have thought the same as Jaxyn had when he'd first been informed one Aleena Aranville was waiting in the atrium. She'd probably sent Mathu down here, thinking a real Aranville cousin had turned up and was in the throes of exposing Jaxyn as an impostor.

"I'm more than my lord Aranville's cousin, your majesty," Lyna said, lowering her eyes with a demure curtsey. "We've been betrothed since we were children."

Mathu punched Jaxyn on the arm playfully. "And you never mentioned her before? Shame on you, Jaxyn, for keeping your lovely fiancée a secret from us." He turned to Lyna. "You'll be staying here at the palace with us, of course, while you're visiting Herino? When's the wedding?"

"Not for a while yet, your majesty," Jaxyn said. "Aleena is determined not to allow me the pleasure of her company until she finds the right dress in which to be married. Apparently, the only dressmaker worthy of the task is in Ramahn."

"Then make the arrangements, Jaxyn!" the young king declared. "A man in your position needs a wife, and I know Kylia will be thrilled to have a new friend at court."

"You're too kind, your majesty," Lyna said. "But I wouldn't presume to impose my company on the queen."

"It's no imposition," Mathu assured her. "Kylia will be delighted to meet you." He elbowed Jaxyn with a grin. "She'll be stunned to learn you have a fiancée, Jaxyn."

Jaxyn smiled apologetically. "I hope the queen will forgive me for keeping Aleena a secret as generously as you have, your majesty."

"Of course she will," Mathu assured him. "Now, you must bring her to lunch today. Kylia will be desperate to meet the woman who stole Jaxyn Aranville's heart."

"I can't wait to meet her majesty too," Lyna agreed graciously. "I'm sure the look on her face when she realises that all this time Jaxyn was hiding such a secret from her will be something to behold."

Jaxyn nodded, thinking Lyna had the right of it.

Diala's face, when he realised she was no longer the only player in town, *was* going to be priceless.

Chapter 36

"My Lady Alysa requests the pleasure of your company for lunch at midday today, your grace. May I inform her you accept her invitation?"

Stellan Desean looked up from the document he was reading. The suite he'd been provided with in the Caelish Palace was cluttered with papers and books. It was snowing outside and the duke was sitting by a table near the window to make the most of the natural daylight. Clearly, Desean was researching something, but Warlock couldn't read the titles of any of the open books on the desk. "Thank the Lady Alysa and tell her I'd be delighted to accept."

It hadn't been easy for Warlock to arrange time alone with Stellan Desean. Although technically a guest in the Cycrane Palace, the former duke was under constant guard, to protect him from potential Glaeban assassins (the Cabal weren't the only ones who feared Jaxyn's wrath) as much to keep an eye on him. Warlock had managed it, however, by mentioning to his ever distrustful mistress that he'd noticed her brother, Lord Tyrone, speaking to the duke in a rather suspicious manner. He hadn't, of course, but Elyssa was quite paranoid about what her mother and brother might be plotting behind her back, particularly since her stepbrothers, Rance and Krydence, had arrived in Cycrane. She'd swallowed the bait whole and immediately sent Warlock to invite the duke to lunch in her apartments, so she could pump him for information about what her brother was up to.

Warlock bowed in acknowledgment of the duke's acceptance, but made no move to leave, hesitating on the brink of doing the most foolish thing he'd ever done, which—given some of the things he'd done of late—was no mean feat.

Desean looked at him curiously. "Was there something else?"

Here goes nothing. "Do you remember me, your grace?"

"Is there a particular reason why I should remember you . . . Cecil, isn't it?"

"We've met before, your grace. In Glaeba."

That got the duke's attention. He put down the document he was reading and rose to his feet, studying Warlock closely for a moment, before shaking his head. "I'm sorry, but I can't recall . . ."

"It was in the Lebec Watch-house, your grace. You questioned me about the actions of your wife after she went missing."

Desean glanced at the door, perhaps wondering if he called out, how long the guards would take to get to him. It was an optimistic hope. Warlock—had he been an assassin—could tear his throat out long before help arrived. And Desean was probably expecting a Glaeban assassin sooner or later. He was too shrewd and much too smart to be unaware of the reaction in Herino to his treasonous actions here in Caelum to think it would go unavenged for long.

"I remember you now. Only your name wasn't Cecil then. It was, if I recall it correctly, Warlock."

"You gave me my freedom that night, your grace," Warlock said, mostly to assure the duke he *wasn't* here to kill him. He didn't want him calling out to the guards. "You could have revoked my pardon with a word."

"And this is how you repay me?" Stellan Desean seemed neither impressed nor particularly comforted by Warlock's declaration. But he did look ready to defend himself. "By coming here to slit my throat?"

"Of course not," Warlock objected, before Desean changed his mind and raised the alarm. "I'm here because not only do I owe you a debt of gratitude, but because there are others who are relying on me and I need to ensure they are safe and—"

"You're planning to talk me to death then, are you?" the duke said with a smile, cutting off his attempts to explain himself, which, even to Warlock, sounded implausible.

Tides, the man is acting as if this is a joke. He shook his head, wondering how the duke could find any humour in the dangerous situation in which he currently found himself. "Lord Aranville sent me here to Cycrane believing I'm his creature, your grace. Lady Elyssa believes I'm her creature too. I am not."

"So you're *not* planning to kill me?"

"Not unless I'm ordered to by Declan Hawkes."

The duke pointed to the chair beside the desk. "I think you'd better take a seat, Warlock. You have some more explaining to do, my lad."

Warlock did as the duke bid, sitting on the edge of the seat, after pushing his tail aside, never comfortable sitting like an equal in the presence of men he'd been raised to consider his betters.

"If you were working for Hawkes, then I assume you know something of his . . . extra-curricular activities?"

"If you mean, do I know of the immortals who move among us and his work with the Cabal, then of course I do." Warlock stared at the duke, looking for a reaction. "And I gather you know about them too."

"More than I ever wanted or expected to, Warlock. How is it you know Hawkes?"

Warlock hesitated, wondering for the millionth time since Boots suggested he seek out the duke and reveal his connection to the Cabal, about the wisdom of confiding in a man who was willingly plotting to invade his own country with a foreign army at his back. Stellan Desean, after all, was the one stirring up the war between Caelum and Glaeba by spreading the story it was Declan Hawkes who'd been responsible for kidnapping Princess Nyah.

"I met him in Lebec."

"And he recruited you into his Cabal too, I suppose? Tides, the man's worse than a jellyfish. He has tentacles everywhere."

There wasn't anything Warlock could really say to that, so he remained silent.

"So Lord Aranville thinks you're his creature?"

Warlock nodded. "All the suzerain believe my kind are theirs to command, your grace. Sadly, most of us are."

"But you're one of these Scards Declan spoke of? One of the few Crasii who can defy the orders of an immortal?"

Warlock nodded, not expecting the duke to speak of the spymaster with such familiarity. "I was sent by Master Hawkes to serve Jaxyn Aranville in Herino because the Cabal promised me and my family sanctuary."

"How is it you finished up serving the Lady Alysa?"

"Lord Aranville sent me here to spy for him."

"And act as his assassin when the occasion calls for it?" Desean said. "That would seem an optimistic plan, given your orders can easily be over-ridden by another immortal."

"I believe he was hoping they'd not think to countermand his orders."

Desean frowned. "That sounds like Jaxyn—arrogant to the point of stupidity. What are you planning to do?"

"Keep my family alive until I can get them out of here. And for that, I need your help, your grace."

The duke shook his head. "My power is limited, Warlock. I'm barely in a position to help myself. What do you want me to do?"

"My mate is here in Cycrane, along with our pups. I want you to help them get back to Glaeba and safety."

"How do you expect me to achieve that?"

"I have no idea, your grace, but that's the cost of me not betraying your involvement with the Cabal to my mistress."

Desean studied him thoughtfully. "I could call out to the guards now and have you—and your family—executed on the spot for being Jaxyn Aranville's spies. What makes you so certain I won't?"

Warlock met his eye evenly, pretending a level of confidence he really didn't feel. "Because Jaxyn doesn't know Elyssa has countermanded his orders. So I am in a position to feed Lord Aranville whatever information you need, your grace. Your war for control of Glaeba will be much easier to prosecute if your enemy's intelligence is flawed."

Desean stood up and began to pace the room, rubbing his chin pensively. He had shaved the beard he'd arrived in Caelum wearing, but his hair was still blond at the tips as the darker hair grew back. After a few moments, he turned to face Warlock, his expression thoughtful. "What would happen now, if you confessed to Lady Alysa that you were Jaxyn's spy?"

"She'd have me killed," Warlock said without hesitation. "And then she'd torture and kill my mate and my pups. Most likely she'd do it in the reverse order, just so I could watch."

"Are you sure about that?"

"Yes."

"But don't the immortals believe all the Crasii are compelled to follow their orders? You could tell her you had no choice."

"You don't understand the compulsion, your grace. The very act of confession *implies* I had a choice."

"I suppose *I* could expose you . . ."

Tides, I knew this was a mistake. Before he could stop himself, he growled low in his throat.

The duke turned to him, but oddly enough, he was smiling. "I didn't mean that the way it sounded, Warlock. What I mean is, if you cannot confess to your orders to spy for Jaxyn, because to do so alerts the immortals that you're able to exercise free will, then to expose you—to do what *you're* suggesting, in fact, which is to feed Jaxyn misinformation about what's happening here in Caelum—we would need to convince the immortals *here* you could be useful as his spy."

"Yes . . ." Warlock agreed warily, not sure where the duke was going with this.

"What if *I* were to recognise you? I could bring your service to Lord Aranville to the attention of the immortals here. I could be the one to suggest that you be used to mislead him, which leaves your status as a loyal Crasii minion unsullied."

"Except for the part where you expose me as a potential Glaeban spy." Warlock shook his head. "Recognising me will achieve nothing, your grace. I was a gift to Lord Tyrone and Lady Alysa from the King of Glaeba. They know I was in his service. Lord Tyrone has already suggested to his sister that I'm a spy, and she didn't care."

"That's because they don't realise how arrogant Jaxyn can be."

"I'd not be too sure about that. They've known him for thousands of years."

"I've known him most recently," Desean said. "I can convince them I probably know him better."

Warlock wondered if he could trust the duke. The only thing he really knew about this man was that he'd not sent him back to prison in Lebec when he had the chance. It was a flimsy basis for a conspiracy involving such a high level of trust.

"Do you promise to help my family if I help you?"

Stellan Desean nodded. "I do, but you have to appreciate how limited my power is here, Warlock. I'm constantly guarded and have very little freedom of movement. I may not be *able* to help them."

Warlock knew that, but even the notion that if anything happened to *him* there was someone who might care what happened to Boots and the pups, allowed him to breathe a little easier. After all, he was the one who'd dragged them into this mess.

"This is a very dangerous game we're playing, your grace."

"It's no more dangerous than the games both you and I are already involved in," the duke replied. "And, having said that, there's no guarantee it will work. Are you sure you want to try?"

With some reluctance, Warlock nodded. "If it means getting Boots and the pups out of here eventually, I'm prepared to do anything. The only problem with your plan, however, is how to convince Elyssa . . . and the others . . . that this is a viable way to confuse Jaxyn."

"That's the easy part," the duke said.

Warlock shook his head. "Syrolee won't want to take the risk."

"I can handle the Empress of the Five Realms." Then the duke smiled, shaking his head ruefully. "Tides, I can't believe we're even having this conversation."

Warlock shrugged. "Such is the price of the games we play, your grace."

"I wish I'd known you in the old days, Warlock. Back when I was the master of all I surveyed and you were the steward every lord wishes for. I would have enjoyed having you in my service."

Warlock appreciated the compliment, but wasn't sure, given the complicated web of lies Desean must have woven about himself to survive, that he would have wanted to have been caught in the middle of them.

"Thank you, your grace, but . . ."

"I know." Desean turned to gaze out of the window at the rain pattering silently against the thick glass. After a moment he turned to Warlock. "I will speak with your mistress when we meet for lunch. I'll tell her I remember you from court, and suggest she uses you to feed false intelligence back to Herino."

"You'll need to be very persuasive, my lord."

"I can be persuasive. Although this whole compulsion to obey the immortals thing . . . which one you should obey, whose orders overrides whom . . . Tides, it confuses the blazes out of me."

"Imagine how I feel."

Desean smiled sympathetically. "We make an odd pair of conspirators, Warlock, but it's nice to know there's at least one friendly face in this place. I'll do what I can to help you."

"And my mate?"

"That's a harder nut to crack, but I'll see what I can do."

Warlock nodded, content he'd done all he could, for the time being, to protect his family.

It wasn't much, but it was something.

Chapter 37

Declan lay awake until dawn watching Arkady sleep, holding her, wondering if, in the cold light of day—once gratitude for saving her life and healing her wounds had lost its veneer—she would ever willingly spend another night in his arms. Although she seemed to have taken the news about his immortality in her stride, a lot had happened yesterday. He was half-expecting Arkady to wake up and have a reaction similar to Tiji's.

So he savoured this night, and held her close. In sleep, her face was peaceful—the alertness, the coiled-spring awareness of her relaxed, for once. Her long dark hair drifted down her back. The pre-dawn light revealed only a little of the pale perfection of her skin; the rest of her body was hidden by the sheet he'd thrown over them for protection from the insects of the wetlands.

The fabric had draped itself around the mounds and hollows of her body, only one long, perfect leg poking out from underneath the sheet where she had kicked it aside in her sleep. Her head lay on his shoulder, her face toward him.

He couldn't remember ever loving her more.

Eternity is not going to be a pleasant prospect, he thought, *once Arkady is gone.*

It was the first time he'd allowed himself to consider the reality of his situation—the bitter flipside of living forever.

"Tides, Declan," she murmured sleepily, "you look so miserable, anybody would think your grandfather just died."

He hadn't realised she was awake. "He did die, actually, only I wasn't thinking about him."

She lifted her head to stare at him. "Shalimar is *dead*?"

He wished he'd broken the news a little less bluntly, but it was too late now. "A couple of months ago."

"I'm so sorry, Declan."

He shrugged, not sure what else to tell her, lamenting the fact he wasn't better at delivering bad news. "He's not suffering anymore. That's something, I suppose."

Arkady fell silent, and lay her head on his shoulder again, but made no attempt to move out of his arms, which was remarkable because he was expecting her to leap across the room in fright the moment she realised where she was. But she stayed put and when she finally spoke again, it wasn't to ask after his grandfather.

"Are you really immortal now, Declan?" she asked softly.

Tides, how do I tell her about this? "I'm afraid so."

She seemed much less concerned about it than he was. "I thought I'd dreamed that bit. Actually, I was kind of hoping I'd dreamed *most* of the past few months."

He let out a short, bitter laugh. "I know *that* feeling well."

"Are you angry with me, Declan?"

That question took him completely by surprise. "Me? Angry with *you*? Tides, Arkady, what have I got to be angry at you about?"

She sighed forlornly. "Where do I *start*? I got caught up with Kinta and Brynden. I ran into Cayal again and because of that, I got myself sold into slavery, and you don't want to even think about how I survived *that*. And then you had to follow me halfway around the world to rescue me, the irony being I probably wouldn't have *needed* rescuing, except apparently I was mass-murdering innocent Crasii in my spare time, your little pet, Tiji, among them." She smiled sadly. "Tides, Declan . . . *angry* at me? I can't believe you're still *speaking* to me."

"Take more than a few dead Crasii to make me hate you, Arkady," he said. On impulse, he bent his head to hers and kissed her briefly on the lips, if only to reassure her that he meant what he said. He knew he'd made a mistake the moment he did it, because she went rigid in his arms.

"Declan . . ."

Tides, here it comes . . . you're my best friend . . . you know I love you . . . but you're my friend . . . And I really can't deal with you being immortal . . .

"It's all right, Arkady. I understand."

She pushed herself up until she was leaning on his chest. The thin shawl across her breasts that Arryl had given her in Watershed Falls had slipped during the night. It was doing little to conceal them and nothing to lessen the feeling of her body pressing against his. With her face only inches from his, she looked him in the eye. "I'm not the person who left Glaeba, Declan. You wouldn't believe some of the things I've had to do to survive."

He was amused by the notion that he'd worried every day since leaving Glaeba about Arkady's reaction to discovering he was immortal, and now when he had finally found her, she was worried about what *he'd* think of *her*. "I don't care what you've done, Arkady. If you and I start judging each other, neither of us is going to come out of the exercise looking too good."

"Do you forgive me?"

He kissed her forehead and squeezed her comfortingly. "There's nothing to forgive. You did what you had to do to stay alive. Nobody can ask more of a person than that."

"So, is this new-found tolerance because you're immortal now, or because I'm lying on top of you half naked?"

"Oh, you noticed you were half naked, did you?"

She smiled at him. "You know, when I was dying, tied to that wretched tree in Watershed Falls, I only wanted to see one person."

"And you ended up with me. I'm sorry."

Arkady's smile faded. "Don't tease. I'm trying to tell you something important here. If you're going to make light of my epiphany, I won't share it with you."

"I'm sorry," he said. "By all means, share your epiphany."

"Well, I was thinking about Cayal."

Oh, I so wanted to hear that . . .

"I was thinking about him and Gabriella. About how sad it was he was never able to be with the one true love of his life, even for a short time."

"Didn't she drop him like a hot rock at the first sign of trouble and then marry his brother after his sister exiled him? Sounds to me like he was better off without her."

"But that's just it. Do you think he'd be quite so suicidal or depressed now if he'd known love, even once, rather than lost it?"

"I have no idea," he said, looking at her with concern. She wasn't kidding when she said she wasn't the same person she'd been in Glaeba. The Arkady of old would have scorned the notion of a man pining for lost love for thousands of years. He wondered if it was her recent brush with death or her months in slavery that had affected her so profoundly. "And to be honest, Arkady, there aren't words to describe how little I *care* about whether or not the Immortal Prince still has a broken heart after eight thousand years."

"I know, and that's not why I'm telling you this. It just got me to thinking, you see, about life in general. And some of the decisions I've made. Some of the things I've done and what I'd do if I had my time over again. I don't want to end up like Cayal."

He studied her curiously in the faint dawn light seeping through the cracks in the walls, a little uncomfortable with how intimate this conversation was getting. "So, let me see if I've got this right. There you are, tied to a tree covered in thorny spines, slowly bleeding to death from a score of stab wounds, delirious from dehydration and sunburn, just waiting for the flesh-devouring ants to come eat you alive, and you decide you don't want to be suicidal. Fair enough. Probably not how *I* would have handled it . . ."

She slapped his chest in annoyance. "Stop it."

"I'm sorry."

"No, you're not. You're making fun of me."

"You're right. I'm not sorry. I am making fun of you. I promise to stop interrupting."

She flopped down beside him and crossed her arms grumpily. "I *was* going to tell you I was sorry I'd never told you how much I loved you," she said. "But you're being a bastard about it, so now I don't think I will."

Ah, but do you love me as a friend or a lover? That's the question . . .

"I wouldn't have believed you anyway," he said aloud, fairly certain being flippant wasn't helping his cause but unable to think of anything more profound to woo her with. Declan wished he had even an ounce of romance in his soul. *That's probably what attracts her to Cayal. He's had thousands of years to think up exactly the right things to say . . .* "You don't love me at all. You're always marrying other men, running off with them . . ."

"That's a terrible thing to accuse me of!"

"But true, nevertheless, you'd have to agree."

She turned to look at him again, grinning. *Tides, why does nobody else understand me like she does?* "You know, Stellan told me once I should take you to my bed and put you out of your misery."

"A good wife would have listened to her husband," he said. "Shame on you for not doing as he commanded."

She smiled briefly . . . and then the moment was lost, her thoughts turning to her husband. "Tides, poor Stellan. I wonder what's happened to him? I wish I knew whether he was alive or dead."

Declan debated lying to her and then figured there wasn't much point. Besides, Stellan's *power* had always been the thing Arkady lusted after, not Stellan himself. Arkady was here in his arms, after all. He doubted her husband could come between them now.

"He's alive," Declan assured her. "And safe for the time being. Everyone in Glaeba thinks you're a widow, however."

"You've seen him?"

"He's the one who pulled me out of the prison fire."

Her brows shot up in surprise. "Does that mean he's finally admitted to himself that the Tide Lords exist?"

Declan nodded. "Between what happened to me and meeting Maralyce, he really didn't have a choice."

"You took him to meet *Maralyce*?"

"Stellan's had a few epiphanies of his own, lately."

"I'm becoming quite taken with epiphanies. And I don't ever want my life to flash before my eyes like that again . . ." she punctuated her words with a kiss that was neither chaste nor friendly and Declan thought he might die from wanting her, immortal or no, ". . . and see it filled with so much regret."

Declan couldn't think of a single thing to say which didn't sound either trite or ridiculous, so he didn't even try. Instead, he wrapped his fingers in her thick, dark hair, drew her close, and kissed her again, relishing the feel of her in his arms, in his bed, her body pressed against his, wondering how this reality could be so much better than his dreams. Whatever had happened to her these past few months—however profound her epiphany— the change in her was remarkable. The Arkady of his youth would have slapped him had he tried to kiss her like that. The new Arkady seemed much less reticent, much more anxious to make up for lost time.

She kissed him back so wantonly it left him gasping . . . even as a small, insidious, unwelcome worm of doubt crept in . . .

Suppose she's just doing this out of relief? Out of gratitude?

Out of some misguided notion that she somehow owed him something?

Tides, suppose she really is taking Stellan's advice and "putting me out of my misery"?

Declan wanted Arkady to love him, not pity him, or feel indebted to him for all his years of faithful service. And he wasn't entirely certain that Arkady was simply treating him the same way she must have had to treat her slave master these past few months. She might well do something like that. It certainly hadn't taken her long to work out how to survive as a slave.

In his dreams there had never been any doubt about Arkady's love. When she finally came to him, it wasn't supposed to be like this. There wasn't supposed to be any questions . . .

Overwhelmed by suspicion, he pushed her away. *Tides . . . I can't believe I'm doing this . . .*

Arkady looked surprised, hurt, and more than a little embarrassed. "Declan . . . Oh, Tides, I'm so sorry . . ."

"For what?"

"I didn't mean to throw myself at you like that . . . I only meant to . . ."

"What? Put me out of my misery?"

She sat up and retied the shawl around her breasts, a gesture that was as disappointing as it was final. "That's a cruel thing to suggest."

Declan studied her closely, wondering what self-destructive impulse was making him do this. He didn't know and couldn't stop himself, in any case. "You could have had me any time you wanted me at the mere crook of your little finger, Arkady. Why now?"

"Because I thought you loved me."

"I've loved you all your life and you've known it too. It never did me any good before now."

"You saved my life, Declan."

"And you're happy to sleep with me to discharge the debt, is that it? Or does saving your life mean I own you now, and you're doing what's required of you to keep me happy?"

Arkady's eyes glistened. "You know, I thought immortality hadn't made the slightest difference to you. But I was wrong. It's turned you into a heartless, selfish prick." She scrambled over the top of him, climbed to her feet, straightened the tiny slave skirt and shawl she wore and let herself out of the storeroom, slamming the door behind her so hard the whole wall shook with the force of it.

Declan watched her leave without saying a word. Once she was gone, he folded his hands behind his head to ponder the stupidity of what he had just done.

What had possessed him to question her like that? To question his good fortune?

He had, for a fleeting moment, had everything he ever wanted, in his arms, willing and wanting him . . .

And then he'd pushed her away for . . . *what?*

Declan cursed himself in every language he knew. He had, quite possibly, ruined any chance he had with Arkady.

Why? For an assurance she loved him? When had *that* ever mattered?

Declan couldn't think of words to describe what kind of fool he was. Even more painful was the knowledge that when she was astride him and he was drowning in the taste of her, for the briefest of moments—in what he feared would be a very long, tormented life—he'd been utterly and completely happy.

Chapter 38

"Ah, you're awake, I see."

Arryl was in the workroom, pouring water from the large, cast-iron kettle into a deep tub filled with molluscs. There was no sign of Tiji and her chameleon friend.

The immortal looked up from her work as Arkady entered the workroom. She looked no older than twenty-four or twenty-five. By Arkady's reckoning, she had to be at least ten thousand years old.

"Did you sleep well?"

Arkady nodded. "Like the dead."

The immortal smiled. "Well, I wouldn't know about that. But I know how exhausting magical healing can be, for both the person wielding the Tide, as well as the recipient. I'm not surprised it wiped you out for a time. Is Declan awake?"

"I'm not sure he slept."

Arryl didn't seem surprised. "Did you want some tea? Feel free to help yourself in the kitchen."

"Thank you, my lady. What I'd really like is some decent clothing, if you can spare it."

Arryl cast her gaze over Arkady's slave skirt and nodded. "I don't blame you, dear. You're fortunate—or perhaps, unfortunate—to cast a rather striking figure dressed as a Senestran slave. It must have caused you quite a bit of trouble in Port Traeker."

Cydne's orderly, Geriko, and his endless compliments about her breasts—not to mention his unsubtle hints about sharing his bunk—immediately leapt to mind. She nodded. "That's one of the reasons I latched on to Cydne Medura."

"He was the lesser evil?"

"So it seemed at the time," Arkady said, taking a seat at the work table.

"*That* assessment proved to be spectacularly wrong, didn't it?"

There was no way to deny Arryl's accusation, so Arkady didn't try. She wasn't sure what time it was. Not long after dawn, she guessed, wondering if Tiji had come back to the Outpost or spent the night in the wetlands. She sighed as she remembered what she'd done to Tiji's new-found people. *Tides, how many did we kill?*

Arryl didn't seem too concerned with apportioning blame, fortunately. She finished filling the bowl with boiling water and returned the kettle to the small stove in the corner of the room. Having been born and bred in Lebec, where freshwater pearls were one of the province's major industries, Arkady recognised the tools of Arryl's trade. She was harvesting nacre, the iridescent lining of oyster shells, known in Glaeba as mother-of-pearl.

The room was filled with sacks of mollusc shell, containers of beads and tiles and shelves of beautifully wrought trinkets, waiting to be set into silver or gold for the ladies of Port Traeker. There was another table against the wall that looked suspiciously like an apothecary's workbench, which seemed curious. The nacre made sense, though. Arkady remembered Cayal telling her once that Medwen, in particular, was a glass craftswoman of some renown. Apparently, during this low Tide, she'd decided to add the craft of making nacre jewellery to her repertoire.

Arryl smiled at her reassuringly as she studied the workshop. "I'll speak to the chameleon elders. I'm sure we can convince them you were as much a victim in this unfortunate affair as they were."

She frowned at the immortal. "Will they be all right, my lady? The chameleons, I mean. Cydne was right about one thing: he does come from a very important and wealthy family. They won't let his execution go unavenged when they learn how he died."

"Don't worry about it," Arryl said, stirring the molluscs with a long stick to ensure they were completely submerged. "Medwen and Ambria are already on their way to Port Traeker to explain to his family and the Physicians' Guild too, I suppose, the circumstances surrounding the tragic accident that killed the scion of House Medura. They'll deal with any potential trouble his family might cause."

"I didn't think the Lady Medwen, or the Lady Ambria, was that magically gifted."

Arryl laughed.

"Did I say something funny, my lady?"

"Who told you that? Cayal, I suppose? Tides, that man sees the world through such self-absorbed eyes."

"I'm sorry, but what I meant—"

"You meant you don't believe either of my immortal sisters has the power to wreak the sort of vengeance Cayal indulges in when he wants to bend the world to his will," Arryl said, not letting Arkady finish her apology. "And I laughed, Arkady, because you seem to assume that's the only thing we do. Did it never occur to you that ten thousand years of experience teaches one skills *other* than the wanton destruction of civilisation as we know it whenever we don't get our own way?"

"To be honest, my lady, I don't think I did." Arkady smiled sheepishly. She knew better than to make assumptions like that.

What happened to Arkady the reasoning, careful academic? she wondered. *Did I lose her along with my clothes and any morals I once used to own?*

Arryl appeared to be quite forgiving. "Then let that be the *first* thing you do now the Tide is on the turn, Arkady. Start thinking about us immortals as people, not only gods or monsters."

"And what is Declan now?" she asked curiously. "A god or a monster?"

The immortal shrugged and threw a handful of salt into the bowl from a small sack on the shelf behind her. "That's really up to him, I suppose. I imagine, like the rest of us, he'll end up a little bit of both."

Arkady looked at her uncomprehendingly. "Declan's not *evil*."

"Not to you, perhaps, but I'd hazard a guess it wouldn't be too hard to find plenty of people who disagree with you. He was the King of Glaeba's spymaster, wasn't he? At least that's what Tiji told Ambria." When Arkady didn't deny the accusation, she nodded, her point proved. "Trust me, he didn't hold down *that* job because he was filled with the milk of human kindness. Your friend may be a good and noble man to you, Arkady, he may even believe that of himself, but based on his past, I'd not be holding out any great hopes for his future as an immortal."

Arkady shook her head. She couldn't imagine Declan doing the sort of terrible things Cayal and his ilk had done. "You don't know him, my lady. He wouldn't deliberately hurt anyone." She knew it was a lie, even as she said it. Tides, he'd just cut *her* to the quick with his callous rejection.

And Arryl was right about Declan and his role as the King's spymaster too. He'd been frighteningly good at his job.

The immortal seemed to know Arkady was lying to herself as much anyone else. "You're hoping he'll only use his powers for good, aren't you?" she said. "Tides, there is *nothing* more dangerous than a misguided soul thinking he's doing good."

"I think Declan knows enough about the immortals to understand the danger," she said, not sure why she was defending him. It wasn't as if he'd done anything to deserve her loyalty lately. *Except perhaps saving me from death by flesh-eating ants. And healing my wounds . . . dropping everything to track me halfway across the world to find me . . .* And then another thought occurred to her. *Tides, what will the Cabal do when they find out?*

"Declan's got a fair idea about what it is to be immortal, my lady. And what it can do to a person."

Arryl shook her head. "No, Arkady, he doesn't. He hasn't even begun to understand what's happened to him and you'll be long dead before he does. And the trouble is, he's not *just* immortal. He's a Tide Lord, which means he has the power to do just as much damage as any of those other fools."

Typical, Arkady thought. *Declan never does anything by halves.*

"He can learn, my lady. And he has the benefit of seeing what immortality has done to others."

"He still sees the world through mortal eyes, Arkady. Believe me, immortal vision is quite different to the way *you* see the world." She picked up her mixing stick and stirred the salt into the molluscs for a moment and then she put it down and sighed. "I hate to say it, but probably the safest thing for him to do would be to find Lukys."

"Why?"

"Lukys is the only one of us who's ever been willing to spare the time to teach another immortal anything other than a lesson in what happens when you cross them. I don't know if it's because he's generous or because he has an ulterior motive, but whatever the reason, he's helped all of us at one time or another. He's probably the only one who can help Declan understand what he's become."

"He told Cayal he'd found a way for him to die."

Arryl shrugged. "I'm sure Cayal believes that, Arkady, but it doesn't make it real. Lukys's games are more sophisticated than most, but they're still games. Declan will need to be careful."

"Why does he need to have anything to do with any of you?"

Arryl smiled knowingly. "He won't be able to avoid it. And I'd rather have a High Tide come and go that didn't involve millions of deaths and humanity having to start from scratch all over again."

For all that she was mad at him, Arryl's insistence that Declan was likely to turn into something as dangerous as Jaxyn or Cayal was starting to wear on Arkady. She felt she had earned to the right to be mad at Declan, but the Tides help anybody else game enough to think ill of him. "You don't know he'd do anything of the kind, my lady. He may decide not to use the Tide at all."

Arryl laughed sceptically. "Not use the Tide? Look at yourself, woman. You should be dead and there's not a mark on you. Declan can't help himself. He probably swore every which way from yesterday that he'd never touch the Tide. And what happens? First time someone he loves is in danger he's drawing on it like there's no tomorrow." She threw her hands up, as if Arkady's ignorance appalled her. "He healed you almost instantly; don't you understand that, Arkady? Even I can't do that, and I've been practising for thousands of years. And I'll bet he doesn't have the faintest notion of how he did it, either. He just willed it to happen and there you are, all nice and shiny new again." She picked up a large wooden disk and placed it over the top of the tub to cover it, shaking her head. "Tides, it's the well-intentioned ones that cause the most trouble."

She was talking from experience, Arkady suspected, not theoretically, and it intrigued her. Arryl, of all the immortals, was the one credited with having some humanity left; the kindest of a cruel race. What had she done to cause such regret in her voice, even after all this time?

"Are you talking about Cayal?" Arkady prompted. "About how he extinguished the Eternal Flame?"

Arryl looked up. "Told you about that, did he? Or his version of it, at least. But no, I'm not talking about Cayal's rage. I speak of a classic example of how the highway to oblivion is paved with the well-meaning deeds of noble fools."

"What happened?" Arkady asked.

Somewhat to Arkady's amazement, the immortal told her . . .

Chapter 39

If you know how Cayal was made immortal, then you probably know what happened next. He left with Tryan to win his beloved Gabriella back. The failure of that mission, the subsequent destruction of Lakesh and indeed all of Kordana, devastated him.

We heard about the destruction of Kordana, of course. Felt it too for a time. That much smoke and ash in the atmosphere affects the whole planet, no matter how localised the source of the trouble. And we *all* heard about it. When he got back, Tryan couldn't wait to tell us what they'd done.

Cayal was less anxious to brag about it. In fact, it was years before anybody in Magreth saw him again.

I wasn't there, so I can't tell you exactly what happened in Kordana, but I'm sure it was the first time Cayal truly appreciated the power that was his to wield and I'm certain it frightened the living daylights out of him too.

Unfortunately, it didn't stop him wanting to do something else noble with his power. Perhaps he wanted to makes amends. But two global catastrophes don't make the first one better. But Cayal, being Cayal, had to find that out the hard way.

I'm not sure what it is with some men, but they seem to think they were given immortality for a divine purpose; that there is some reason for their very existence beyond the ken of ordinary men. Brynden suffers the same affliction, thinking his immortality was awarded for some higher purpose. Jaxyn thinks so too, although he's far less likely to admit it to anyone these days, least of all himself.

I felt Cayal before I saw him. He's a powerful Tide Lord and his presence on the Tide is unmistakable. It grows with time too; the more you draw on the Tide the more you affect the Tide around you. That's why we can't always tell if a new immortal is going to be a Tide Lord. You have to dip your toe in the water a few times, so to speak; learn how far out you can swim before you discover how deep you can go and still return with your sanity intact.

And if you're wondering what happens when you swim too far, ask me sometime about Kentravyon . . .

But I was speaking of Cayal. I sensed the ripples of a powerful Tide

Lord in the Tide and hurried to the main hall of the temple, expecting Lukys. We were still in Magreth in those days, the Tide was up and I think, by then, Cayal was nearly three hundred years old. He didn't look it, of course. Then—as he does now—he looked no older than the twenty-six years he was when Diala made him immortal.

"Cayal!" I exclaimed in surprise.

He turned to look at me. He was dressed like a native—in a simple patterned wrap tied around his waist—so I assumed he'd been back in Magreth for a while. I had no notion of what brought him here, but he was staring at the Eternal Flame as if it offered the answer to the meaning of life. He was starting to show the weariness of age, by then. Not physically, of course, but a certain weariness of the soul that afflicts us all, sooner or later. None of us are immune.

You can tell yourself you're immortal until you're breathless, but until you've outlived everyone you know, it doesn't really hit you. I think that's why Cayal had come back to Magreth. Despite knowing he was immortal, it had only just occurred to him he was going to live forever.

"Hello, Arryl."

I stared at him, looking for some change—the Tides know why—but he seemed exactly the same as the last time I'd seen him. "Why didn't you send word you were coming? Diala's not here but . . ."

"But they'd like to know up at the palace that the Immortal Prince has returned?"

"They'll learn you're here, Cayal. Either someone will tell them or they'll come close enough to the temple to feel you on the Tide."

"Is Tryan here?"

"In Magreth? No, I haven't seen him in years. I believe he's in Fyrenne somewhere. With Elyssa."

He was obviously relieved. "I'm glad to hear it. I'm not sure I've the patience to deal with Tryan at the moment. Or Elyssa."

I smiled sympathetically. Elyssa's fascination with Cayal is well known to all of us. "She is quite taken with you, Cayal."

"Are you sure Tryan's not here?" Clearly, he didn't want to discuss Elyssa.

"Positive."

"So who is here in Magreth, keeping the empress company?"

"Engarhod's here, of course. Rance and Krydence come and go. So do Medwen and Lyna. Ambria's long gone, but then she'd left before you came here the first time, I think. I haven't seen Lukys for several years. Bryndcn has settled in Torlenia, I hear, with Kinta. I'm not sure what Kentravyon, Taryx or Jaxyn are up to. But Pellys is here at the moment."

Cayal smiled. He'd always had a soft spot for Pellys. "How's the fish population?"

"Suffering, I fear. He'll be pleased to learn you've returned, though. He's not been happy of late."

"Immortality weighing him down?"

Cayal's question surprised me, both for its perceptiveness and its accuracy. "I think it might be. How did you know?"

He shrugged. "Call it an educated guess. How are you holding up?"

I smiled. "Holding up? Against what?"

"I don't know . . . life . . ."

"Is something wrong, Cayal?"

Cayal shook his head and forced a smile that didn't fool me for a moment. "Not a thing in the world, Arryl. We're young, we're beautiful and we're going to live forever. Where's the problem in that?"

There was an edge to his voice that should have warned me he wasn't happy. Or maybe I'd just like to imagine there was. "Are you planning to stay a while?"

"If you'll have me."

"I'll always welcome you, Cayal, wherever I am. You know that."

"Immortality's been much kinder to you than the rest of us, Arryl," he said, taking my hand. "Or maybe you were just a better person than the rest of us to begin with."

I wasn't really sure how to answer that, so I just smiled and kissed him to welcome him home. He kissed me back like a lover, which surprised me a little, although I can't say I minded. I've never been in love with Cayal, but he's hard to resist, particularly when he's being vulnerable; and with Diala away, I didn't have to worry about upsetting my sister.

"You came back for *me*?" I asked, finding myself a little breathless, I have to admit, by the unexpected intensity of his kiss.

"I came back to remind myself why I'm still alive," he said.

I understood that in a way only another immortal can, so without another word I took his hand and then led him out of the temple and down to the terrace where Pellys was killing my goldfish.

There's something about Pellys, an innocence that belies his appearance. To look at him you'd think him a man in his thirties. Talking to him, you find yourself quickly revising that opinion. It's like talking to a child. Even before the incident that destroyed Magreth, he wasn't much brighter. If you know how Cayal was made immortal, then you probably think my sister a monster, but I sometimes wonder if her method wasn't the less cruel way of being made immortal. Diala tempted and tormented the men she immortalised, but they all had a choice, even if they weren't entirely clear on what it was they were choosing. Pellys, on the other hand, was made by accident. At least we've always thought he was. He survived the fire that burned down the brothel where Syrolee worked.

The Tide is both apathetic and remorseless. None of us was singled out, I fear, for our nobility of spirit.

Pellys was beside himself when he saw Cayal. He'd hung around the temple for years, on and off, waiting for Syrolee to summon him. She never did, of course. She'd chosen Engarhod the Sea Captain over Pellys the Half-witted Brothel Bouncer more than a thousand years before and nothing had happened in the meantime to change her mind. I do believe she'd have put Engarhod aside in a heartbeat if she thought Lukys might have anything to do with her. He's a powerful Tide Lord, after all, and Syrolee loves power more than life. But Lukys, even before they became immortal, thought her a crass and irritating whore, and I'm fairly certain neither immortality nor the intervening thousands of years has done anything to change his opinion of her.

But I digress. I was talking of Pellys and how glad he was to see Cayal.

Cayal smiled when he saw the pile of fish on the ground beside the pond and how engrossed Pellys was in his game. "I hope you're planning to restock Arryl's fountain when you've killed all that lot."

I'm not sure why, but Cayal seems to have endless patience when it comes to Pellys. Perhaps that's why, despite some of the things he's done, I still think essentially, he's a decent soul, albeit a somewhat confused and, at times, exceedingly dangerous and irritating one.

Pellys looked up from his game, dropped the fish he'd just caught—back into the pond, thankfully—and rushed to embrace Cayal.

And then he burst into tears.

Cayal embraced him uncertainly as Pellys wept, looking over his shoulder at me.

I shrugged. "He's been like this ever since he got back from Euland."

You've probably not heard of Euland. It's long gone, now. It was a small island off the northern coast of Magreth, on the other side of the equator. We had trade dealings with them, but not much else. I certainly hadn't been there for centuries, and neither, I'm confident, had any other immortals.

Cayal disentangled himself from Pellys and studied him curiously. "What's the matter, big fella? Nobody in Euland have any goldfish for you to play with?"

Pellys has no concept of irony or sarcasm. He just shook his head, taking Cayal's question at face value. "They wouldn't let me keep my wife."

Cayal's eyes widened. "You have a *wife*?"

"Not anymore. They wouldn't let me keep her."

He looked to me for clarification, but I knew as much as Cayal did. When Pellys had returned to the temple several months ago, after an absence of more than a century, he'd told me the same thing, but never explained what he meant.

"I always thought you were hoping Syrolee would come back to you?"

Pellys shook his head. "She looked like Syrolee."

"You found a wife who looked like Syrolee?" Cayal repeated uncertainly. "While you were in Euland?"

"That's right."

"And they wouldn't let you keep her, you say? Who is *they*?"

"The people what got upset."

"Upset? What people got upset?"

"The ones who found her. She was mine, Cayal," he sobbed, "and they wouldn't let me keep her."

He was having far more success than I'd had in getting the story out of Pellys. But I listened to Cayal interrogating him with a growing sense of dread. Nothing which upsets a Tide Lord—particularly one with Pellys's power and limited understanding—could possibly be a good thing, I thought. Especially not during a High Tide.

Cayal seemed to share my concern. "Pellys, why wouldn't they let you keep her? She wasn't someone else's wife, was she?"

Pellys shook his head, tears coursing freely down his face. "No. She was mine. She was so pretty. Just like Syrolee. And I fixed it so she'd stay that way. But they took her from me."

Tides, I thought, *he tried to make her immortal.*

Cayal was obviously thinking the same thing. "You set her alight?"

Pellys shook his head, sniffing loudly. "Of course not. That would have ruined her. The flames would have burned her hair and messed up her face . . . Tides, I wouldn't do something like that."

"Then what did you do?" Cayal said, glancing at me with growing concern.

"I filled her with spirits to preserve her."

At first I thought he meant *spirits* in the ephemeral, divine sense. Cayal, however, sees the world differently to me, or perhaps he knew Pellys better than I thought. He looked at him in utter disbelief. "You tried to preserve her, Pellys? With *alcohol*?"

The older man nodded and wiped his nose on his bare arm. Clearly, he saw nothing wrong with the notion. "It would have worked too, if they hadn't taken her from me."

"Was she . . ." Cayal hesitated, a little afraid, I suspect, to put his suspicions into words. "Was she alive when you tried to replace her blood with alcohol, Pellys?"

He glared at Cayal as if he was a little bit stupid. "Well, of *course* she was *alive*. That's what I was trying to preserve."

I felt physically ill at the notion. Tides, he'd bled some girl to death and tried to fill her veins with alcohol. Who was this poor girl he'd taken a fancy to? And who were the people who'd taken her from him?

More importantly, what had happened to *them*?

Cayal must have read my mind. Or at least the horrified look on my face. "What happened when they took her from you, Pellys?" he asked gently.

"I made them go away."

"How?"

"I don't know . . . I just called on the Tide and made them go away."

Tides, it sounds so trite and harmless now. *I made them go away*, he said.

We didn't know it then, but that was the first hint we had of the destruction of Euland and the fate of the several thousand people who called the island their home.

He hadn't just made them go away. Pellys had wiped Euland off the face of Amyrantha.

I had to leave. I couldn't bear to look at him, let alone contemplate what he'd done. I was still coming to grips with the death Tryan and Cayal had unleashed in Kordana, and that had been centuries in the past. I left Cayal to coax the rest of the story out of Pellys and returned to the temple, sick to the very core of my being.

At that moment, I was tempted to put an end to the Eternal Flame myself.

Cayal found me later, kneeling in front of the Eternal Flame, praying for guidance. I don't know why I did that. It's not like the Tide ever answered back or offered any sort of enlightenment . . .

Anyway, it was dark by the time Cayal found me. I'm not sure what Pellys was doing by then, but Cayal was alone and looking worried when he knelt on the cool marble floor beside me.

"Does it help?"

"Does what help?"

"Praying?"

"Sometimes," I said, sitting back on my heels. "How's Pellys?"

"He wants me to kill him."

I turned to stare at Cayal, wondering if he was trying to be funny. "*What?*"

"He wants me to kill him."

"But . . . he's *immortal* . . . "

"He wants me to cut off his head," Cayal explained. "Apparently, if I do that, it'll grow back without all the memories he's burdened with now. Clean slate, clean mind . . . even if he can't die, I suppose it's as good as being born again." He seemed to be taking the suggestion quite seriously. And wasn't nearly as upset about the idea as I was.

"You're not seriously thinking of agreeing to this, are you?"

"Why not?" he asked with a shrug. "If Pellys loses his memories, he'll stop pining for Syrolee. That might also prevent him from murdering any more wives. Or villages full of innocent bystanders. Or whole islands full of innocent bystanders, come to think of it."

"Do you really think he destroyed Euland?"

The temple was dark, Cayal's expression lit only by the flickering shadows of the Eternal Flame. "Why not? Tryan and I destroyed Kordana without even trying. It's not that hard to do if you can draw enough power."

It chilled me to hear him so casually refer to the destruction of his homeland. But I knew better than to open that particular jar of woe. "We should send someone to investigate."

"What would be the point? It's either gone or it's not. Nothing either one of us can do at this point is going to change that." His practicality was disturbing. I was ill just *thinking* about what Pellys might have done. Cayal appeared completely accepting of it.

"You speak as if Euland was no more than a lifeless landmass. There were nearly twenty thousand people living there, Cayal."

"Do you think I should do it?"

It took me a moment to realise he wasn't talking about visiting Euland, but Pellys's desire to be decapitated. "Pellys is disturbed and depressed, Cayal. Why do you want to buy into his troubles?"

"Maybe I want to know if it works."

"Why?" I asked. "Do you think there'll come a time when you need to be . . . what did you call it . . . born again?"

He smiled. "You can never have too much knowledge, Arryl. Lukys says that all the time."

I didn't think anything about this was amusing. "That doesn't mean you should cut off the head of a man who thinks you're his friend, Cayal, just to satisfy your morbid curiosity."

"Not even if it means putting an end to that friend's pain?"

It's hard to argue with logic like that. And it was clear Cayal had all but made up his mind. "You're going to do it, aren't you?"

"Maybe . . ."

"Don't lie to me."

"All right, then yes, I'm thinking about it. But why are you looking at me like that? Tides, you've seen him, Arryl. When he's not destroying entire countries full of unsuspecting mortals, he's pining after Syrolee, looking for a replacement for her, or hanging around here killing your ornamental fish for entertainment. Would it be so cruel to give him a fresh start? A chance to begin again without any of the baggage of the past?" He rose to his feet, offering me his hand. I accepted and let him help me up. "Far from hurting him, it might be the biggest favour one friend can do for another."

"It might not work," I warned.

"But if it does?"

I hesitated, tempted by the prospect of a new beginning. I didn't want to die and had no desire to forget my past—and I still don't—but there's something frightfully seductive about the idea of knowing that if worse comes to worst, we might have a way out.

"You'd have to do it quickly."

"I know."

I searched his face, but in the darkness I couldn't see anything in his eyes other than concern for Pellys's pain, and the idea that he might be able to relieve it.

Tides, it's the ones with the best intentions who always bring us down.

"The others won't like this."

"I won't tell them if you don't." He smiled encouragingly. "It'll just be between the three of us. The rest of our immortal brethren need never know."

In hindsight, I like to think he sounded convincing, but the truth is, I *wanted* to believe him. I know the pain Pellys suffered and the idea of relieving it made me feel like I'd be doing something noble too.

So I agreed to go along with Pellys's absurd request and the very next day—before any of us could have second thoughts—Cayal took an axe, and with Pellys's active cooperation, he cleaved his head from his shoulders with a single, powerful blow.

Almost immediately the ground began to shake. As Pellys's decapitated head rolled across the terrace, we could feel the swelling Tide. I think it occurred to both of us that at that moment, Pellys's body wasn't just magically repairing itself; with no controlling centre, his body was randomly drawing on the Tide. There was no restraint, nothing to temper the swell. I felt Cayal trying to counteract the force, but there's no way any sane Tide Lord can draw that much power to themselves deliberately. There was no focus, no point he could attack, and no way to make Pellys stop. Within minutes the ground was shaking so hard we could no longer stand. I heard a crack and realised the temple was starting to go. The waterfall beside the terrace had begun to boil. Clouds were building up in the sky at an unnatural pace as he unconsciously began to affect the weather. In the distance, a long dormant volcano began to creak and groan as Pellys unknowingly woke it from its slumber . . .

Tides, even now I shudder to recall it. It took less than a day for his head to grow back, and he knew nothing when it did—not even how to speak.

By the time Cayal made him understand he must stop what he was doing, Magreth no longer existed.

Our good intentions destroyed the entire country and the aftermath plunged Amyrantha into anarchy. The twenty thousand souls Pellys destroyed in Euland proved pitiful by comparison.

We never thought, Cayal nor I, of what a regrowing mind, blank, empty, and able to draw on the Tide, might be capable of. We never realised he'd have no memory of asking for oblivion afterward. Tides, until the ground began to splinter under our feet and the volcanoes began to rumble and spew, we never even imagined what all that undirected magical energy could do.

We thought only of Pellys's pain; of being able to banish it for him. And selfishly, that maybe, one day, we might be able to ease our own.

Chapter 40

"So your good intentions almost destroyed the world," Declan said. "Is that what you're trying to tell us?"

Arryl nodded, her gaze fixed on Declan. She'd spied him coming into the workroom not long after she began talking, he knew. Arkady didn't seem to notice him, however, and not wishing to interrupt Arryl, he'd stayed leaning by the door until she'd finished her tale.

"Meaning well won't protect you from unintended consequences, Declan. It's important to remember that."

Arkady glanced over her shoulder at him, but her gaze was cold. "Good morning, Declan. I didn't realise you were up."

Tides, she is so angry with me.

Arryl looked from one to the other, sensing the tension between them, but not understanding the reason. Declan wasn't surprised she looked confused. Last night, he and Arkady had been the best of friends and she'd probably thought them lovers. Now Arkady's voice dripped icicles when she spoke to him.

"Arryl was suggesting you seek out Lukys," Arkady added. "Apparently you're going to need lessons on how to deal with your new-found immortal powers."

"Why?" Declan asked, directing the question to Arryl. "I've no interest in becoming *one of the gang*, my lady. Far from it."

"You *are* one of the gang, Declan," she said, "whether you like it or not. And I'm not suggesting this lightly. This isn't about what you want, or even your ego. This is about learning to control something that will soon be uncontrollable. You need guidance."

"Maralyce didn't seem to think so."

"Maralyce hadn't seen your little trick with the instant healing, I suspect," Arryl said. "I'm quite certain, had she realised you were capable of something like that, she'd have taught you herself."

Declan shook his head. "I'm not interested in socialising with any more immortals, my lady. Running into you was an accident, and while I appreciate your hospitality, I'm not interested in becoming friends."

"You'll have to excuse Declan's manners, my lady," Arkady said. "He's trying his damndest to ensure he has no friends at all this morning."

Arryl looked at Arkady curiously, as if wondering about her harsh tone, and then shrugged. "Well, that's his choice, I suppose. Did you still want me to find you something a little less exposed to wear? You're taller than me, but there should be something in Ambria's room that will fit you."

Arkady nodded and rose to her feet. "Thank you, my lady. I'd like that very much."

Arkady pushed past Declan and followed Arryl back through the kitchen, leaving Declan alone in the workroom.

He turned to look at the kitchen, wondering if he should eat something. Despite not having eaten for several days, he was neither hungry nor thirsty, something he'd still not gotten used to. Declan ate and drank now out of habit, rather from necessity. Rather than hang around the house, he walked through the cluttered workroom and stepped out onto the veranda.

A faint mist hovered over the channel, one he expected would burn off as soon as the sun rose fully. The morning was loud, filled with the chirruping of millions of insects and the calls of birds yelling to each other across the swamp. Declan let the noise wash over him, feeling the edge of the Tide lapping at his consciousness. It had been gnawing at his awareness like an annoying tic ever since he'd spied Arkady tied to that tree, covered in ants.

Arryl was right about that much. Declan had no idea what he'd done or how he'd done it. He vaguely remembered thinking he needed to get the ants off Arkady when he found her, a thought that moments later had turned to a series of violent waves rising unexpectedly out of the channel to splash over her, washing the ants away. He remembered berating himself for being too late as he cut her down. He vaguely remembered wishing he could make her better . . .

And then the Tide rose in him and she was healed . . . and he'd alerted every flanking immortal in the vicinity that he was in Watershed Falls.

Declan caught a movement out of the corner of his eye. He turned to find Tiji and Azquil, walking along the shoreline toward the Outpost.

Oh, great . . . Tiji's back . . . as if I don't have enough trouble going on with Arkady . . .

Tiji and Azquil were holding hands. Or maybe they weren't. On closer inspection, it looked like Azquil was ever so subtly dragging a very reluctant Tiji toward the Outpost.

He waited on the veranda until they stopped a few feet from him, on the grassy hummock below the house.

"Good morning, my lord," Azquil said politely.

"I'm not highborn, Azquil," Declan said. "You've no need to address me as if I am."

"You are an immortal, my lord," the chameleon pointed out. "I could not conceive of addressing you any other way."

Tides, but I'm going to get sick of this . . .

"Good morning, Tiji."

She glared at him and said nothing.

"Tiji would like to apologise, my lord," Azquil said. "She did not mean to act the way she did last night."

"The hell I didn't," Tiji muttered under her breath, but still loud enough for Declan to hear.

"It's all right, Azquil," he said, pushing off the railing. He took the two steps down from the veranda and walked toward them. "I understand why she's mad at me. And I don't really blame her. It'd be nice if she gave me a chance to explain, though, before she starts cursing the very ground I walk on."

"Don't talk about me like I'm not here."

"Then stop glaring at me like that."

Azquil tugged on Tiji's hand until she was standing in front of Declan. "She'll be happy to listen to you, my lord." He turned to Tiji. *"Won't you?"*

Somewhat to Declan's surprise, Tiji nodded.

Azquil let go of her hand and stepped back. "I must speak with the Lady Arryl," he said, "if you and Tiji want to take this opportunity to talk."

Without waiting for either of them to reply, Azquil headed into the Outpost, leaving them alone.

Declan watched him leave and then turned to Tiji with a faint smile, hoping to make light of this awkward situation. "You never struck me as the sort of girl who likes the forceful type."

"Put up with *you* for long enough, didn't I?" she said angrily.

Fair comment. "So, are you and the chameleon lad . . . you know . . . ?"

"Mind your own business. And it's not like you don't have plenty of business to mind now you're one of *them*."

Her hostility was starting to wear a little thin. "Tides, Tiji, can you cut me a *little* slack? I didn't know this was going to happen to me, and I'd give anything to reverse it, but apparently that's not an option."

She turned from him and began to walk away from the house. "So you say."

He fell into step beside her, wondering if this ability to alienate every friend he'd ever owned was something newly acquired with immortality, or a gift he'd always been in possession of. "What do you want me to say?"

"I don't want you to say anything," she said.

"Tiji . . ."

She stopped and looked up at him, the pain in her eyes almost too much to bear. "All right, Declan, do you know what I want you to tell me?"

"What?"

"What did you get?"

He gave her a puzzled look. The question made no sense.

"What are you talking about?"

"What did you get out of this, Declan? What did they offer you? I would have thought you knew enough about the immortals to know the cost of eternal life. So what was it? What did they promise you . . ." Her voice trailed off as she looked past him and her eyes fixed on the veranda of the Outpost. Azquil was standing near the door, talking to Arryl, who'd been joined by a much more demurely clothed Arkady. Tiji studied the trio on the veranda for a moment and then shook her head. "Tides, you are so pathetic."

"*What?*"

"Is *that* what they offered you?" She pointed to the veranda.

"I have no idea what you mean, Tiji."

"Your girl up there," she said, her voice full of contempt. "Is that what it took for Declan Hawkes to betray everything he ever believed in? The chance to finally have the girl of his dreams?"

He stared at her uncomprehendingly for a moment, until her accusation began to make sense. "You think I traded my mortality for a chance to be with Arkady?"

"Can't think of any other reason you'd do it."

"Tides, Tiji, I never had a choice. I was caught in the fire that destroyed Herino Prison and woke up immortal. You can't possibly think I sought this out deliberately. Or that I want anything to do with the immortals."

She frowned at him, unconvinced. "So you were made immortal by accident, eh? What happened to that whole Eternal Flame legend?"

"According to Maralyce—"

"According to Maralyce? Yeah . . . I can see how you've not got any interest in socialising with the other immortals . . ."

He took a deep breath, forcing himself to remain calm. "According to Maralyce, it was just that. A legend they propagated so people wouldn't realise it took nothing special to make immortality happen."

"That's absurd," she said. "Anybody caught in a fire could become immortal if you follow that reasoning."

He shook his head. "Not just anybody, Tiji. Only somebody with enough Tide Lord blood in them to make them more than half-immortal."

"I still don't buy it," she said. "Your grandfather is the Tidewatcher in the family. You are . . . were . . . what . . . only one-eighth immortal at best."

"Not if my father was an immortal too."

Tiji paused to consider that for a moment, her frown softening a little, as if, for the first time since discovering his new status as an immortal, she was willing to contemplate the notion that he hadn't done it deliberately. "You always said you had no idea who your father was."

"And I still don't," he said. "But given what happened to me in that fire, it's a fair bet he was an immortal."

She searched his face with a worried expression. "Are you *sure* this was an accident?"

"Yes, Tiji, I'm sure."

The little chameleon glanced back at the trio on the veranda. "And you really didn't sell your soul for a chance to be with your girlfriend?"

"If I did, then it was a lousy deal, Tiji. Arkady's not actually speaking to me at the moment."

"Why not?"

"Long story. And none of your business. Are we still friends, Slinky?"

She frowned. "You smell wrong, Declan."

"I can't help that."

Tiji shook her head. "You don't understand. Immortals smell . . . *off* . . . to the Scards. Like something rotten. You learn to recognise the smell and associate it with danger." She looked up at him apologetically. "You smell like danger, Declan."

"So we're friends, only if I stay downwind?"

Tiji wasn't amused. "You're not making this any easier, you know. And the smell of you all is driving me mad. Tides, the three of you stink like something died in you, and is rotting from the inside out."

"There's only two of us here," he reminded her. "Me and Arryl. The others have gone to Port Traeker."

Tiji lifted her nose and sniffed the air. "Then one of them is on the way back," she said. "Because I can smell three of you."

Even before she'd finished speaking, Declan felt it too—the disturbance on the Tide that meant another immortal was near. This was different to anything he'd felt with Arryl, Medwen or Ambria, however. This wasn't a gentle rippling of the Tide; it was much more violent, much more powerful.

Arryl must have felt it too, almost as soon as Declan had. She looked up, and then hurried down from the veranda toward the dock, much more experienced than Declan at picking the direction the disturbance was emanating from.

Arkady and Azquil followed her. Arkady, who could sense nothing about the approaching immortal, looked curious rather than worried, as she stopped beside Arryl on the small wooden dock to greet the newcomer. Azquil, on the other hand, had adopted the same alert stance Tiji was holding—his posture hovering somewhere between absolute stillness and panicked flight.

"Who is it?" Declan asked, wondering if Tiji had encountered any other immortals during her time in the wetlands.

"I don't know."

That worried Declan. He'd been trying to kid himself for months now that if he kept his head down he might be able to go through eternity without ever encountering another immortal. But he was wrong, and this just reminded him *how* wrong he was.

Tides, it's as if we attract each other . . .

The boat Arryl was obviously expecting resolved out of the mist a few moments later, pulled toward the dock by two amphibians who were barely visible in the murky water. As it neared the dock, the single passenger rose to his feet, nimbly jumping to the dock without waiting for the boat to be secured.

Despite being too far away to hear what was being said, Declan's blood ran cold at the sight of him.

He recognised him immediately. This was not just any immortal come to visit his sisters in the Senestran Wetlands. He walked straight past Arryl, said something Declan was too far away to hear and then stopped in front of Arkady.

If Declan was in any doubt about the identity of their visitor, it was gone the moment the man, after exchanging a few words with her, took Arkady in his arms and kissed her like a returning lover.

It was Cayal, the Immortal Prince.

Chapter 41

"So, is Desean dead yet?"

Jaxyn turned to face Queen Kylia, surprised she'd ask something so dangerous where anybody could overhear her. Fortunately, the hallway of the Herino Palace was deserted, the distant rumbling of another thunderstorm the only thing likely to interrupt them.

Things had been tense between Jaxyn and Diala since he'd introduced Lyna as his fiancée. To add to Diala's frustration, he refused to explain why no sooner had he announced he was marrying his cousin, he let her run off to Torlenia, supposedly on a shopping expedition. Diala was too conniving to ask him outright, of course, but it gave Jaxyn a small measure of comfort to realise that not knowing what he and Lyna were up to was driving her quietly mad.

"You're not very familiar with the concept of subtlety, are you, your majesty?"

Diala smiled and looked around. "There's nobody here but us immortals."

"You hope." He took a step closer, wishing there was a way to be rid of her, frustrated beyond words that he couldn't think of one. Until there was, he had to keep pretending she was a part of his plans. But the Tide came back a little more each day. There would come a time, very soon, when he no longer needed to play these games with her. "Apparently Elyssa has taken Cecil into her service, rather than Tryan."

"And the first thing she did was countermand any order you gave the wretched creature? Tides, Jaxyn, I can't believe you imagined that wasn't going to be the first thing she did."

"There was a chance she wouldn't. Or that Tryan would have claimed them. Tides, they could have finished up serving Engarhod."

"The chance was slim to none."

"I still don't know for certain that she has countermanded my orders." He shrugged. "But to be on the safe side, I'll arrange his assassination by more conventional means. It'll take a little longer, but he'll be dead soon enough."

"So you gave away a pair of perfectly good breeding canines for nothing."

"Maybe not. They were a gift from Tilly Ponting, remember. That sly old bitch isn't as stupid as she likes to make out. I'm not sorry to be rid of any gift of hers."

"They weren't a gift to *you*," Diala pointed out with a pout. "They were meant for me and Mathu."

"Then I probably did you a favour. Was there anything else? I have work to do, you know."

"Aren't you always the busy one these days?" Diala smiled condescendingly. "I find your conscientiousness quite marvellous, actually. Mathu and I can't thank you enough for working so hard to keep Glaeba safe for us."

There will come a time, you stupid, shallow little bitch, when you'll regret treating me like your minion. "I live only to serve, your majesty," he said with a mocking bow, making no attempt to keep the scorn from his voice. "And now, unless you're here to report the Caelish are sailing across the Lower Oran in battle formation, I'll be on my way."

"Hmmm . . . about that," Diala said. "You don't seem to be putting much effort into preparing us for war. I mean, shouldn't we be gathering the fleet or something?"

"I have everything under control."

"So you say," she said.

"I have everything under control," he repeated. "When the time comes to attack, we'll have everything we need, where we need it."

"So we're going to attack Caelum, then, and not wait for them to attack us?"

"We'll do what we have to."

"That's not an answer."

"But it's all you're going to get from me, my dear, so you might as well stop asking." And with that, he turned and continued down the hall to the office of the King's Private Secretary without waiting for her reply.

Patches was waiting for him when he let himself into the office. The canine had been sorting the mail and arranging it for his lord's perusal. This was the part of his job that Jaxyn despised. It was also the part that he knew he couldn't risk neglecting. One learned a great deal about how a nation was faring going through the mundane correspondence of the king.

"Tides, how much more is there?"

"This pile here, Lord Aranville," the canine scribe replied, pointing to a depressingly large stack of papers on Jaxyn's desk. "And I have the latest dispatches from Lebec."

Jaxyn sighed heavily and took a seat at the desk. Taking on the duties of the King's Private Secretary may have given him almost unlimited power to act in the king's name, but he'd failed to take into account the amount of work involved. Added to the responsibility he now had for the Duchy of Lebec, he often found himself at his desk from dawn until close to midnight. It irked him no end, the problem made worse by the fact that the one person he should have been able to entrust with some of the load was too busy playing at being queen.

Jaxyn would remember that when the time came. If Diala thought he was going to put up with her lounging around the palace, amusing herself by tormenting the Crasii and making Mathu dote on her, she had another think coming.

"Is there nothing there from my fiancée?"

Jaxyn itched for Lyna to return. Even if she didn't find Arkady, giving Diala a rival should be enough to shake her out of her torpor. And it would be good to have somebody he trusted to delegate some of the more delicate matters involved in securing oneself a kingdom. Assuming of course that he *could* trust Lyna, which remained to be seen. The last he'd heard from her she was heading for Elvere. That might mean she was on Arkady's trail, or it might mean she'd decided to throw her lot in with Brynden. He thought that unlikely, however. Brynden was a self-righteous and unforgiving bastard. Lyna's former profession as a whore meant she was sullied in his eyes, even if she hadn't taken a penny for her favours in several thousand years.

"No, your grace. Nothing. There is a missive from Lord Devale in Port Traeker, however, congratulating you on your appointment as Duke of Lebec, and assuring you of his family's continuing loyalty and support."

"Why in the name of the Tides do I care about Devale's continuing loyalty and support?"

"Lord Devale is our ambassador to Senestra, your grace. I believe his wife, Lady Loriny, is also a distant cousin of the Desean family."

Ah, that made sense then. About once a week Jaxyn received a similar note from some nobleman he'd never heard of, assuring him they were loyal supporters of the crown. It didn't mean they were, of course, only that they did not wish to be tarred with the same brush as Stellan Desean.

The former Duke of Lebec had died an accused murderer and risen again as a traitor. Even if they were secretly sending him money, publicly these people wanted everyone to believe they were firmly behind the new Duke of Lebec and supported the king's actions in this matter. To do anything else would be treason and these men were anxious not to be seen to commit treason—even if they were up to their necks in it.

"Do you think Devale knows Stellan's still alive?"

"The letter doesn't mention Lord Desean at all."

"He's what prompted it though, I'll be bound." Jaxyn shrugged and turned back to the pile of correspondence on his desk. "Draft a letter for me to sign. Tell Devale the king appreciates his support and never doubted his loyalty. You know what to say . . . Tides, we must have sent a score of them by now."

"Of course, my lord. What about the rest of the Lebec dispatches?"

Jaxyn sighed again. The scribe was holding the letters from Lebec, a packet of documents that didn't seem nearly as large or depressing as the pile on his desk. "Is there anything interesting in that lot?"

"I'm not sure what his grace would consider interesting."

Curse these wretched creatures and their desire to please. It interfered significantly in getting a straight answer out of them.

"Is there anything in the pile out of the ordinary," he amended, hoping that would prompt a useful answer.

"Only the letter from the Warden at the Lebec Prison."

"What does he want?"

Patches rifled through the letters and withdrew the document in question. He placed the rest of the pile on the desk and opened the letter. "My dear Lord Aranville . . ."

"I don't want you to read the whole flanking letter to me. Just tell me what he wants."

The scribe was silent for a moment while he scanned the contents of the letter. "It seems the Warden wants to know what to do with Prisoner Two-Eight-Two."

"What's so special about Prisoner Two-Eight-Two?"

The canine read on for a moment and then shook his head. "The letter doesn't say, your grace. It merely states: *'as you are no doubt aware, Prisoner Two-Eight-Two has been held at the pleasure of the former Duke of Lebec for some seven years now. With the demise of the former duke, I would like to know your intentions regarding this man's continuing incarceration. Should I continue to keep him incommunicado? Shall I arrange a trial? Should I release him?'* He signs off with *'hoping to receive your orders in this delicate matter as soon as possible,'* your grace. That's all it says."

Jaxyn leaned back in his seat thoughtfully. "Do you have any idea who he's talking about?"

The scribe shook his head. "The Duke of Lebec, or of any other province for that matter, has the power to incarcerate any person they consider a threat to the crown, and may incarcerate them for as long as they wish without trial, if they consider it to be in the best interests of their province or of Glaeba."

Jaxyn's eyes lit up. "They *do?*"

"It's a seldom-used power, my lord. One has to be very sure the confinement will pass the court's scrutiny if the prisoner or their family appeals to the king."

What a pity Jaxyn hadn't known about that tidy little loophole when they'd caught Cayal. He'd have advised Stellan to do exactly that—lock him up and throw away the key—and then the Immortal Prince would never have met Arkady and managed to escape.

In hindsight, it probably wouldn't have worked. Cayal had been posing as a Caelishman, so there was all that nonsense going on with the Caelish ambassador. And Declan Hawkes had got involved when the immortal didn't die after they tried to hang him, which messed everything up, because Hawkes was the one who'd recruited Arkady . . .

Tides, it would have been nice if somebody had thought of it, though . . .

"If this man has been locked up for seven years, then I'm guessing there's nobody on the outside willing to make too much noise on his behalf. Does the king know about this?"

The scribe shrugged. "There would be no need for a duke to advise the king in such a matter, unless he believed the prisoner was a threat to the crown."

"So the righteous and oh-so-irritatingly-upstanding Stellan Desean threw someone in gaol without a trial and threw away the key? Who'd have thought? Does this prisoner have a name?"

"The letter only refers to him as Prisoner Two-Eight-Two, your grace."

"Write back to the Warden. Tell him he's to continue the current arrangement with Prisoner Two-Eight-Two until I've had a chance to interrogate him myself, the next time I'm in Lebec."

"As you wish, your grace."

"And when you're done with that, tell the new spymaster I want to see him."

"To serve you is the reason I breathe," Patches said with a bow.

Jaxyn wasn't listening, however. All he wanted to know was if Rye Barnes, the man he'd elevated from the ranks of torturer to spymaster, knew where to get his hands on a reliable assassin.

Chapter 42

Eight thousand years of immortality had taught Cayal to be sceptical of fate or destiny. When he stepped off the small boat and onto the Outpost's tiny dock expecting to find Arryl, Medwen and Ambria, and found Arkady waiting for him instead, he wondered briefly if he'd been wrong all this time.

There didn't seem to be any other way to explain what she was doing here.

Arryl was standing a couple of steps in front of the Glaeban duchess, which meant Lukys's directions had been spot on, although there was no sign of either Ambria or Medwen, and no sense of them on the Tide, either. He hardly cared about that, given who he *had* found in this Tide-forsaken place.

He leapt out of the boat and jumped onto the dock, drinking in the sight of Arkady, who seemed almost as shocked to see him as he was to see her.

"Cayal!"

It was Arryl, and not Arkady, who found her voice first. The Sorceress of the Tide sounded stunned, which wasn't surprising. Her presence here, and that of her sisters, was supposed to be one of the best kept secrets on Amyrantha.

"Hello, Arryl," he said absently, his gaze fixed on Arkady. He didn't care that he'd found Arryl, or where the others might be hiding. The sight of Arkady drowned out all other concerns, making him blind even to the pull of the Tide which was warning him there was another immortal in the vicinity.

"Tides . . . how did you find us?" Arryl's voice trailed off when she realised he wasn't listening to her. Given how long she and her friends, Medwen and Ambria, had been hiding out in the Senestran Wetlands, he guessed she was probably appalled at how easily he had located them. He imagined it would come as an even greater shock to her when he informed her that Lukys had known of their whereabouts for centuries.

But at that moment, Cayal didn't care about Arryl's distress or what she thought of his arrival. With eyes only for Arkady, he walked toward her instead. She made no move to come closer, but neither did she shy away from him.

Cayal stopped when he reached her, searching her face for some hint of what she was thinking; what she was feeling. *Why was it every time I think I've put this woman out of my mind, she reappears?*

"Hello, Cayal," she said after a time.

"Arkady."

"You're starting to develop a talent for turning up in the most unexpected places, aren't you?"

"I bow in deference to the master."

That comment brought a faint smile to her face, which was all the encouragement he needed. He took her in his arms and kissed her on the mouth. She hesitated for a fraction of a second, and then her arms tightened around him and she kissed him back.

After a time, he touched his forehead to hers, drinking in the nearness of her. "Tides, you've no idea how many times I've dreamed about you," he said in a voice only she was close enough to hear.

He expected her to respond in kind, but she just shook her head. "You've a very dull life, indeed, Cayal, if that's all you have to dream about."

"I missed you."

"*Missed* me? You told me you were trying to forget me. Why so glad to see me now?"

"I'm fickle," he said with a shrug. "So don't worry. I'll probably go back to despising you soon enough." He smiled again, kissed her briefly, took her by the hands and then turned to Arryl, only then noticing there were others waiting at the Outpost. Two of them were chameleon Crasii he dismissed as unimportant. The other male, at first glance, appeared human, and vaguely familiar . . .

And then he realised the powerful ripples he felt on the Tide couldn't possibly come from Arryl.

Cayal pushed Arkady away and turned to confront the stranger, drawing the Tide to him, ready to strike. "Who are you?"

"His name is Declan Hawkes," Arryl said behind him, before the stranger could answer. "And he's here at my invitation. Settle down." She would be feeling the power Cayal had gathered to himself, just as he could feel this strange immortal clumsily drawing on the Tide. She looked past him and glared at Hawkes. "*Both* of you."

Cayal studied this new immortal warily, waiting for him to do something, wondering why his name sounded familiar. The man said nothing, just watched Cayal with the same cautious mistrust, as he gathered the Tide to himself.

"Tides, you're the Glaeban spymaster," Cayal said after a few tense moments when he finally recalled where he'd seen this man before.

"Cayal . . ."

Laughing bitterly at the irony, Cayal suddenly understood why she was here. He turned to Arkady, "*This* is the man you wanted to save me from in Glaeba? The one you feared would torture and kill me? Funny how you neglected to mention he was immortal. He certainly wasn't the last time we met."

"Declan's only been recently elevated to your ranks," Arkady told him.

Cayal had been alive a very long time and he could read most people like an open book, particularly when they were angry about something. There was an edge to Arkady's voice that spoke of a bitterness running far deeper than mere surprise or concern at his own unexpected appearance or that this spymaster for the Glaeban king was now an immortal. Was that the reason she'd greeted him so warmly, with such uncharacteristic passion? Arkady, as a rule, was as ambivalent about her feelings for Cayal as he was about his feelings for her. The tension in the air around this isolated Outpost spoke of something far more complicated going on here. Something Cayal had a feeling had little to do with him.

Arkady's animosity toward Hawkes concerned Cayal less, however, than the realisation that somehow this man had found a way to *become* immortal, which was more than a little vexing. Cayal had killed several million people making sure something like that *couldn't* happen, ever again.

"How?" He didn't direct the question to anyone in particular. He just wanted an answer.

"We don't know," Arryl said.

Cayal fixed his gaze on Hawkes. "*You* know, though, don't you?"

"And what makes you think I'd share the knowledge with you, even if I did?"

"Stop it!" Arkady said.

"Stop what?" Cayal asked, his gaze locked with Hawkes, the Tide swelling around them. The man had little control of what he was doing, but that didn't really matter. It was like standing next to Pellys when he was upset—he was full of raw, undirected, unfocused, and potentially dangerous power too.

"Stop snarling at each other like a couple of canines facing each other off over a bitch on heat."

Cayal held back, although not because Arkady asked him to. Hawkes was radiating power, but clearly had no idea what to do with it. Cayal felt torn between curiosity and rage. This immortal's very existence threatened everything he was working toward. Here he was, desperately looking for a way to die, and somehow this man had found a way to live forever.

Lukys needed to know about this.

If he doesn't already know. The thought popped unbidden into Cayal's mind along with another random thought: Oritha telling him why Lukys had gone to Glaeba. "Tides, Lukys," he muttered to himself. "What have you done?"

"Cayal?" Arkady said. She heard him speak but not caught the words, he supposed.

Cayal didn't answer her. Instead, he turned to Arryl. "How long have you known about this?"

"About a day longer than you, Cayal. What are you doing here?"

"I came to extend an invitation to you and the others."

"On whose behalf?" Hawkes asked, bristling with animosity. "Your immortal friends in Caelum?"

Cayal turned to look at Hawkes. *Tides, he's ready to explode.* "Oh, so you know about them, do you?"

"I know a great deal more than you think."

The anger in Hawkes was evident even to those not able to draw on the Tide. *Something very interesting was going on before I got here,* Cayal decided.

Beneath his feet, he could feel a slight tremble in the dock. Hawkes, out of either fear or ignorance, was about to let loose a natural disaster. A part of Cayal was horrified. Not because he particularly cared about an imminent natural disaster, but mostly because the Tide was still on the way back. It would be months, perhaps years, before it peaked. It might be that inexperience hadn't taught him subtlety yet, or the wisdom of masking the true depth of his ability, but this freshly minted Tide Lord was among the most powerful Cayal had ever encountered.

Cayal would get no answers if Hawkes let loose and dropped northern Senestra into the ocean. And there was a very real danger he might. Cayal had been where Hawkes was now—brimming with power, uncertain about what was happening to him. And absolutely no notion of what he was capable of doing.

Kordana had been wiped off the face of Amyrantha as a consequence.

"I doubt you know much of anything at all, Hawkes," Cayal said, wondering if there was anything he could say that might head off this impending disaster. "You certainly don't know as much as you think you do. And sure as the Tide is on the rise, you don't know what to do with all that power you're clinging to." He turned to Arryl for help. Hawkes was here at her house, after all, so perhaps she had some influence over him. "Would you like to tell your little friend here what's going to happen if he *doesn't* let it go? Got a feeling he won't believe anything I tell him."

"Cayal's right, Declan," Arryl said soothingly. "You're dangerously close to doing something truly disastrous. Relax. The people of the wetlands don't deserve that."

Although she'd not be able to feel him, gathering the Tide, even Arkady could feel the ground shaking. She took a step toward the spymaster. "Declan . . . please . . ."

The Tide surged around Hawkes. The channel started to foam around the dock. Far from placating him, Arkady's appeal seemed to be having the opposite effect. She stumbled backwards as if pushed, falling into Arryl, who caught her clumsily as she struggled to maintain her footing. The amphibians who'd brought Cayal's boat to the Outpost disappeared into the churning water with a squeal of fright.

"Declan, stop!" Arryl cried out, helping Arkady up. She clutched at Cayal's arm. "Do something!"

Do what? was his first reaction, as the Tide welled up inside him to match the threat he could feel from the other man. He could stop Hawkes from unleashing the Tide, sure enough, but that would require him to give free rein to an equal amount of power. If they both let loose at the same time, the effect would be disastrous. Hawkes wouldn't know that, Cayal was certain, otherwise the fool wouldn't be trying to protect himself by drawing all the Tide he could manage to shield himself from the danger he clearly thought Cayal represented.

And then another thought occurred to Cayal. *Tides, with that much power to burn, we wouldn't need Elyssa to put an end to it all . . . With me and Lukys, a few of the lesser immortals, Pellys, Kentravyon, and the power this unexpected immortal can draw on, we'd be able to do anything . . .*

Even die, perhaps.

The thought stayed Cayal's hand.

He took a deep breath. "Let it go, Hawkes," Cayal said, as calmly as he could manage. He let the Tide drain away, certain Hawkes would feel the gesture and hoping it would placate him. "We need to talk."

"I have absolutely nothing to say to you, Cayal."

"Then you can listen to me," he said. "Now let it go."

"You have absolutely nothing to say that I want to hear."

"I think I have something you'd very much like to hear."

"Cayal, please," he heard Arkady urge softly behind him. "Don't make this worse."

Cayal took a step toward Hawkes. The channel churned beneath the dock. Hawkes wasn't letting anything go.

"Just out of curiosity, what's your father's name?"

The question caught the Glaeban off-guard. Hawkes hesitated before answering. "Why?"

"Do you even *know* your father's name?"

"He doesn't," Arryl answered for him. "But we think he might have been an immortal. Declan is apparently Maralyce's great-grandson. We were trying to figure out how this might have happened. We've been speculating that if his father was an immortal too that would explain how *he* became immortal."

Cayal's suspicion that Lukys was somehow involved in this solidified into a certainty. "*I imagine his business in Glaeba had something to do with gems,*" Oritha had told Cayal months ago when he returned to fetch Lukys after he'd spoken with Brynden. "*And he probably wanted to visit his son.*"

"*Ryda Tarek has a son in Glaeba?*" he recalled asking. He'd thought the story about a son in Glaeba was just a tale Lukys had spun to keep Oritha from asking too many awkward questions about his past.

Tides, it all makes so much sense in hindsight . . .

"So you think his father was an immortal, do you?" he said to Arryl. Cayal turned back to Hawkes, who was visibly trembling with the force of the power he was trying to contain. "In that case, I most definitely have something you want to hear, old son." He took a step closer, deciding a show of fearlessness here might be the only thing Hawkes responded to. "Now let it go before Senestra goes the way of Magreth."

Hawkes glared at him and asked through gritted teeth, "What could you possibly have to tell me that I'd be interested in, Cayal?"

"Let's start," Cayal suggested, "with who your father is."

Chapter 43

Lunch with the Lady Alysa was served in her rooms, a warm fire crackling merrily in the fireplace, giving the room a very convivial atmosphere which was at complete odds with the discussion Stellan knew would soon be going on between the diners. Warlock, the Crasii ex-convict sent here to spy for the Cabal, served the meal as if nothing was amiss.

"Your steward seems familiar," Stellan said, as Warlock cleared the empty plates from their second course. Until now, the discussion over lunch had been quite inane. If the Immortal Maiden was trying to pump him for information about what he was really doing here in Caelum, she was either very subtle or hadn't got around to it yet.

Elyssa smiled and nodded in agreement. "You probably saw him in Herino. He was a gift from King Mathu and Queen Kylia."

"Then he's probably spying for them," Stellan said, folding his napkin as he leaned back in his seat.

"No," Elyssa said confidently. "He's not."

"How can you be certain?"

"I inspire undying loyalty in all my Crasii," she said. "None of them would ever betray me."

Stellan looked sceptical. Or at least he hoped he did. He wasn't supposed to know, after all, that this woman was an immortal and that her confidence in Warlock's loyalty came from the magical compulsion on all Crasii to obey their immortal masters.

"Jaxyn Aranville will have found a way, my lady. You can be certain of it."

She smiled. "You speak with such bitterness when you mention his name. Is that something my brother should be wary of?"

"I'm not here to push my own personal agenda, my lady. Glaeba is under threat and I believe that only an external force can deal with the problem."

"You want Caelum to go to war for you, in other words?"

"I want you to take action against the people who kidnapped your princess and kept her prisoner for their own nefarious purposes. That those same people are, I believe, responsible for killing my king and plan to take the throne of Glaeba from its rightful heirs just means we have a common enemy."

"And your enemy's enemy is your friend?"

"Precisely."

"I've had . . . previous dealings with Lord Jaxyn," Elyssa said carefully. "In fact I know him quite well. Are you sure you want to confront him head on? He doesn't play nice at all."

"Something I've learned through bitter experience."

"You were lovers, according to popular rumour."

"Do you listen to rumours, my lady?"

"I do when they're as juicy as this one."

Stellan shrugged; the stories circulating about his sexual preferences the least of his problems, these days. "As you say, my lady, Jaxyn doesn't play nice. He does what he must to get what he wants. I was foolish enough to be standing between him and his prize for a time."

Elyssa smiled. "And now you want to stop him getting his hands on it at all?"

"The throne of Glaeba isn't something one can take a fancy to and decide to take, just because one can, my lady." He looked at her earnestly, as he realised the lifetime he'd spent living a lie was probably the best training he could have had for the situation he now found himself in. "I mean . . . how would *you* feel if some stranger came along and decided to snatch the throne from Princess Nyah?"

Elyssa, to her credit, didn't even blink. "It would be a terrible thing."

"Then you understand my position."

"I do, your grace," she agreed. "But if I understand you correctly, you've been advocating an immediate invasion of Glaeba. It may have escaped your notice, but the legal heir to the throne of Glaeba currently occupies it. Jaxyn hasn't made a move on the throne and doesn't appear to be planning one. Why invade now?"

Because the Tide isn't all the way up yet! Stellan wanted to jump to his feet and yell at her. *Because there's still some chance we can win this war without destroying Caelum and Glaeba in the process. Because if you and your inhuman kind get involved in a land war, you might not be so keen to get involved in a magical one . . .*

The reasons were endless, and not one of them could he mention aloud without betraying his new-found knowledge of the immortals.

"Because Mathu is still alive, my lady," he said, picking the most plausible excuse. "If Caelum invades now, Glaeba must keep the incumbent king alive, because the moment Mathu dies, I am the legal successor, and your invasion force owns the moral high ground. Far from being seen as invaders, if Mathu died you'd be seen as the saviours bringing the rightful king home. Jaxyn can't risk that happening."

Elyssa frowned, her expression thoughtful. She was not, Stellan suspected, quite as stupid as everybody believed. But neither was she as clever as she imagined herself to be. "Let me see if I have this straight—you want us to go to war so Jaxyn can't dispose of Mathu and take the crown?"

"I think you know, my lady, that Queen Kylia would take a new husband as soon as the mourning period is done with. I certainly don't want Jaxyn Aranville on the throne of Glaeba when she takes a second husband. Do you?" Not that he needed her to answer the question. *I know you suspect that's what will happen, because you* know *Queen Kylia is Diala.*

Jaxyn sitting across the border as king of a more powerful country, in cahoots with another immortal as morally bankrupt as the Minion Maker, is pretty much your worst nightmare.

The immortal studied him curiously. "Why do you care what happens to Mathu anyway? The little ingrate had you charged with murder and treason."

"That doesn't alter the fact that he's the rightful King of Glaeba."

Elyssa rolled her eyes. "The Tides preserve me from another noble man," she muttered.

"I beg your pardon?" he said, pretending he hadn't quite caught her words.

"Nothing. Has my brother agreed to go to war?"

"He said he would take my proposal to Queen Jilna."

"Do you think Jaxyn's heard that you're here in Cycrane?"

"I'm almost certain of it."

That seemed to amuse her. "I'll bet he's furious."

Stellan allowed himself a rare, genuine smile. "I'll bet he is too."

"Of course, he'll know you're up to something. Do you think he's already preparing for war?"

"He'd be a fool if he wasn't," Stellan said, "which brings me to an interesting point. You really believe Cecil is loyal to you, don't you?"

She didn't even glance in Warlock's direction. "Of course."

"Would Jaxyn be suffering under the same misconception?"

Her brows knitted together in puzzlement. "What do you mean?"

"Well, if Jaxyn sent Cecil here to spy on *you*, and he is now so loyal to you that you're confident he isn't, then aren't you ignoring a golden opportunity to feed Jaxyn false information?"

"You mean I should let Cecil report back to him? What would be the point? He'd know any information that came from me was likely to be false."

Stellan made a show of thinking about it for a moment and then looked up with a smile, as if he'd been struck by a brilliant idea. "What if the information came from *me*?"

"How?"

"Suppose . . . I don't know . . . you didn't trust me . . . or perhaps there's a way to convince Jaxyn you don't trust your brother? I'm not suggesting that you don't, my lady, of course, but just let's pretend for a time . . . Suppose you placed Cecil in *my* service? And suppose you allowed him to report back to Glaeba? Jaxyn would believe you've done so for reasons totally unrelated to *him*, and you could then instruct Cecil to feed anything you wanted back to Jaxyn. Tides, you could give him false troop numbers, inaccurate placements, incorrect dates . . ." He stopped, a little embarrassed at how he was letting his enthusiasm run away with him, and leaned back in his seat. "I'm sorry, my lady . . . it's a silly plan. To set something up like that would take years, and it's unlikely Jaxyn would fall for it. Forgive me. My desire to see that man brought down gets the better of me at times."

Elyssa smiled, but her expression was thoughtful. "It's all right, your grace. I can appreciate how much you must hunger to get even with someone who has betrayed you so heinously."

"It wasn't me he betrayed, my lady; it was Glaeba."

"Still, your plan has some merit. And I can see the benefit of having a spy in the meetings you have with my brother." Elyssa laughed then, a forced, silly laugh that was as false as it was telling. "I mean, I can see how *Jaxyn* would think he might benefit from having a spy in the meetings you have with my brother."

"Of course, my lady. I never assumed you meant anything else."

Elyssa smiled brightly, apparently taking him at his word. "Then shall we have dessert? All this talk of war and spies has made me quite peckish."

"By all means."

Elyssa glanced up at the door where Warlock had stood throughout the entire discussion without moving a muscle.

Tides, that creature has more courage than I do, thought Stellan.

"Cecil! You can serve dessert now."

The canine bowed and moved to the table, the very picture of docile submission. It was only as he turned to offer Stellan the plate of delicate pastries his hostess had ordered for lunch that the Crasii allowed himself a faint nod of approval.

Stellan wished he shared the big canine's confidence. He might have planted the idea in Elyssa's head about using Warlock to feed false information to Jaxyn, but there were two parts to his deal with Warlock.

And Stellan didn't have the faintest idea how he was going to save Boots and Warlock's newborn pups from the Tide Lords and get them back to Glaeba.

Chapter 44

Arkady had thought the first meeting between Cayal and Declan was tense, but other than the slightly lessened risk of a natural disaster, things did not noticeably improve once they'd retired inside.

Azquil and Tiji had wisely made themselves scarce, leaving Cayal, Arryl, Declan and Arkady to sort things out among themselves. It was midmorning by the time they took their seats around Ambria's incongruously normal kitchen table to discuss the fate of the world.

Not that Arkady didn't have her own share of worldly concerns. She was already regretting letting Cayal kiss her that way on the dock when he arrived so unexpectedly. She probably wouldn't have, had she and Declan not argued earlier. And she was having no luck at all convincing herself it was just shock and not a perverse desire to get even with Declan that had prompted her to respond so willingly. The trouble was, even if she'd done it to annoy Declan, in the process she'd sent a message to Cayal she hadn't meant to give him. She wasn't in love with Cayal. Her feelings for the Immortal Prince were far more complicated than that. She was fascinated by him, horrified by him, afraid of him, grateful to him and even attracted to him. None of those feelings, however, even taken as a whole, constituted love.

Of course, the problem was, having greeted him like a long-lost lover, Cayal was acting as if that's exactly what she was, which was doing nothing but irritate Declan. On the other hand, Declan had made it quite clear this morning that he wanted nothing to do with her, so the Tides take him and be damned.

I miss Stellan, Arkady decided wistfully, as she took a seat at the table an equal distance from both men, for fear of giving either one of them ideas. *At least when I was married to him, I knew exactly where I stood.*

"Who wants to go first?" Arryl asked as she took a seat opposite Arkady. Now the men had let go of the Tide and the Senestran Wetlands were no longer in imminent danger of annihilation, she seemed a lot happier.

"You said you know the identity of my father," Declan said to Cayal. "Why don't you start?"

Arryl nodded in agreement. "I'd like to know what you're doing here first."

"I'm here because Lukys asked me to come," Cayal said, glancing at both of them. "He wants you to join him in Jelidia, Arryl. You, Medwen and Ambria. Have you got anything to drink around here?"

"I'll make some tea," Arkady offered, glad for an opportunity to do something useful, however banal. It also meant she didn't have to look either Cayal or Declan in the eye.

"Why would I want to leave Senestra for Jelidia?" Arryl asked. "Why would any of us want to leave, for that matter? We're quite happy here, thank you very much."

"We . . . I . . . need your help with something."

"Exactly what do you mean by *something*?" Declan asked.

"He's found a way to die," Arkady answered for him, certain Cayal would find a way to avoid the truth if he was able.

Cayal glared at Arkady, but didn't contradict her.

Arryl looked astonished. "Is that true?"

"Lukys seems to think so." He smiled a little sheepishly. "I had a really good story worked out about needing your help with one of Lukys's experiments to create a portal to another world. Thanks, Arkady, for spoiling all my fun."

"How?"

"Well, she told you—"

Arryl shook her head impatiently. "I mean how can Lukys kill an immortal?"

Cayal shrugged. "I don't know the details. I only know Lukys says he's found a way and that Coron is already dead. He says we need all the immortals we can muster to do it. That's all I know."

"And you expect us to drop everything, to walk away from hundreds of years of peace and security, just so you can die?" Arryl shook her head in amazement. "Tides, but you're a selfish bastard, Cayal."

"More selfish than you know, Arryl," Cayal agreed without apology. "And if you refuse me, Lukys will just send someone else to fetch you."

She smiled sceptically. "Lukys thinks force will work if the charms of the Immortal Prince fail him, does he?"

"I think the next messenger he sends will be Kentravyon."

Arryl visibly paled. "But he's . . . Tides, you're not telling me Lukys revived Kentravyon, are you?"

Cayal nodded. "Like I said, we're going to need all the immortals we can find. This will take power, Arryl, not sanity or a particular nobility of spirit."

Arryl rose to her feet and began pacing the kitchen. "You can't be serious, Cayal. Surely Lukys knows how dangerous he is? And it's not like you'll ever get the opportunity to put him on ice again. Kentravyon won't fall for the same trick twice."

"Maybe he wants to try it out on him first," Arkady suggested, spooning tea into Ambria's chipped earthenware teapot. She wrapped her skirt around her hands and lifted the heavy kettle from the stove and turned back to the table to find everyone staring at her. "*What?* I was just thinking out loud, that's all. I mean, if Lukys has found a way to kill an immortal, why stop at the one who *wants* to die? Why not get rid of a few more while you're at it?" She filled the teapot and replaced the kettle on the stove with a loud thump and turned back to the table. Cayal was shaking his head.

"That's insane. Lukys would never . . ." He hesitated and glanced at Arryl. "Or maybe he would, now I come to think of it." The Immortal Prince shrugged, unconcerned. "And so what if Lukys *does* want to kill Kentravyon? It's not like any one of us—you included, Arryl—wouldn't have taken out the psychotic bastard eons ago, if we'd had the means."

Arryl accepted the cup of steaming tea Arkady poured for her without looking at it. "If you can die, Cayal, we all can."

"Which means you're not immortal any longer," Declan added. "Better yet, *I'm* not immortal."

His comment seemed to amuse Cayal. "You know, you sound so happy saying that. It's almost enough to make me like you, Hawkes."

"That's interesting," Declan replied. "Because I can't imagine a single thing you could say that would make me like you."

"Enough!" Arryl snapped impatiently, as Arkady handed Declan and Cayal their tea. She had no idea if they still wanted it or not, but at least it had given her something constructive to do for a while.

Cayal ignored the comment anyway; he was too interested in securing Arryl's cooperation. "So, are you interested?"

"In coming to Jelidia with you to help you die? Absolutely not."

"I need your help, Arryl."

"And I've helped you, Cayal," she reminded him. "Plenty of times. For thousands of years I've been helping you. But this is too much. The Tide is on the turn. You can't expect me to walk away now from the people who've sheltered and protected us for almost a thousand years, at a time when they'll need our help the most."

"We need every bit of the Tide we can channel to do this, Arryl."

"Then convince your new friend here to go with you," Arryl said, pointing at Declan. "Anyway, he can channel more than me, Medwen and Ambria put together. And I have a feeling he'd be quite happy to watch you die."

"I'm more interested in your claim about knowing who my father is," Declan said, although his tone of voice suggested Arryl was right and he'd happily take part in any venture liable to result in the end of the Immortal Prince.

Cayal shrugged, as if the matter was of little or no concern to him. "It's probably Lukys," he said.

"How do you know?"

"He told his wife he had a son in Glaeba. If what you say is true, and you're related to Maralyce, then it stands to reason he was talking about you. Although it doesn't explain how you managed to become immortal."

"He was caught in a fire," Arkady said, when Declan seemed disinclined to answer. "It happened by accident."

"The Eternal Flame is long gone."

"Declan says Maralyce claims there never was an Eternal Flame. She says they just told everybody that to keep the numbers down," Arkady added.

Cayal stared at Declan in amazement. "Are you serious?"

Declan shrugged. "It's what she told me. I've no idea if it's true or not."

"Well, you can ask Lukys when you see him, I suppose."

"I'm not going with you to Jelidia to meet Lukys."

Cayal gave Declan a puzzled look. "Why not?"

"Because I don't care to meet him, any more than I care to help *you* or have anything to do with any other immortals."

"But he's your father."

"You *think* he's my father, Cayal," Declan said, rising to his feet. "And even if he is, I'm not interested in getting to know him." He glanced around the table, his look of disgust meant for Arkady along with the other two immortals. "The Tide take all of you *and* your plans and schemes. I'm not interested in getting involved with any of this."

Declan left the kitchen, leaving the others staring after him. Arkady pushed her tea away and stood up. "Let me talk to him."

Cayal studied her suspiciously. "Is there some particular reason he'll listen to *you?*"

"He's my friend."

"How good a friend?"

"Leave it alone, Cayal," Arryl said. "Let her talk to him."

Cayal shrugged and picked up his tea, feigning indifference. "Talk to him then. He needs this more than I need him."

That was an outright lie, Arkady suspected, but she didn't bother to say so. Instead, she turned and followed Declan outside, wondering what she could possibly say to him, after everything that had happened today, that was going to make things better and not a thousand times worse.

Declan was standing on the small dock watching a distant speck on the channel that was probably another boat heading for the Outpost. He turned at the sound of footsteps on the wooden planking, and then turned back to stare at the water when he realised it was Arkady.

"Declan . . ."

"Leave me alone."

"I've never seen you lost before."

"I'm not lost."

"Yes you are," she said, coming to stand beside him. "You were always the strong one, when we were children. You always made me feel safe. And now you're floundering for the first time in your life. I want to return the favour and help *you* for a change."

He glanced down at her sceptically. "Not flaunting your affair with the Immortal Prince might be a good place to start."

"You made it quite plain how you felt about us this morning, Declan."

"I'm glad you were able to get over the disappointment and move on with your life in such a timely manner. Tides, it must have taken you . . . oh, an hour, at least . . ."

Arkady knew Declan well enough to know he was trying to pick a fight with her to avoid facing the real issue. He was the master of distraction. He always had been, even when they were children.

"I'm not going to fight with you, Declan."

He folded his arms across his body and looked away. "Then go away, Arkady. I'm not really interested in doing anything else with you right now."

"Cayal is offering you the chance to meet your father. To find out something about what you are . . ."

"I don't care."

She wanted to stamp her foot at his stubbornness. "Well, if you won't do it for yourself, do it for your grandfather's memory."

He glared at her. "Don't you dare bring Shalimar into this. He has nothing to do with it."

"He has *everything* to do with it, Declan," she said, lowering her voice a little, although it was unlikely they would hear her inside the house unless, she was shouting. "You spent your whole life working for the Cabal, looking for a way to end the Tide Lords. And here you are, with the answer being offered to you on a silver platter, and you don't want anything to do with it."

Declan stared at her for a moment, as if the idea of helping the Cabal had never even occurred to him, and then he shook his head. "You think I can go back to the Cabal now, after everything that's happened to me?"

"I think you're about to discover the very thing your wretched Cabal has been seeking for the last five thousand years, and you're going to turn your back on the knowledge because you're angry at me."

"You think I'm that petty, do you?"

"Frankly, yes."

"Well, then, it's a good thing the Immortal Prince is here for you. Clearly, I don't measure up to your high standards."

Arkady wanted to slap him. She might have, had not the single passenger in the boat heading for the Outpost chosen that moment to stand up and begin calling out to them urgently. She turned toward the water, a little surprised to discover that the passenger waving at them so frantically was another chameleon. Before Arkady could work out what the little Crasii was yelling, Azquil and Tiji appeared from behind the Outpost, pushing past Declan and Arkady in their haste to reach the water.

"Tenika!" Azquil called, as the boat approached. "What happened? Where are Lady Ambria and Lady Medwen?"

The amphibians put on an extra burst of speed to bring the boat into the dock. Arkady gasped when she realised that not only was the little chameleon frantic, but she was bleeding from a nasty head wound. Azquil helped her out of the boat without bothering to secure it. Declan and Arkady hurried forward but stopped when Tiji turned and warned them back with a look.

The little Crasii burst into tears as the male hugged her, whispering soothing nonsense words to her. Tiji knelt beside them, stroking the wounded chameleon's silver scales in an equally comforting, if somewhat redundant, gesture. After a moment, the sobbing Crasii seemed to get a grip on herself and pushed Azquil away.

"What happened, Tenika?" he asked.

"They arrested Lady Medwen and Lady Ambria," the little Crasii said.

"Who arrested them?" Arkady asked.

"The Merchant Marines, probably," Azquil said, although he seemed a little annoyed he had to explain. "They're the only ones in the wetlands who'd bother arresting anyone." He turned back to Tenika. "Why were they arrested?"

Tenika sniffed loudly before she answered. "We were on our way to Port Traeker to tell them about the doctor. About him dying, and you know . . . about it being a terrible accident. But when we reached the Delta Settlement, there was a Medura ship already in port, and the ship's captain was the doctor's brother or something."

"Brother-in-law, probably," Arkady corrected. "Cydne didn't have any siblings." She remembered the Delta Settlement too. She'd passed through the port on her way to Watershed Falls with Cydne. Ten times the size of Watershed, it was the main port on the complicated network of channels and floodplains that made up the wetlands. It was also as far as the deep-draughted trading ships could go.

Everything that traded out of the Senestran Wetlands came in by raft or small boat to the Delta Settlement, where it was loaded onto the larger trading vessels belonging to the great merchant houses like the Meduras and the Parduras, and then taken back to Port Traeker. It made sense that one of Olegra's many brothers was in port. They were all involved in trade and most captained their own vessels. That's what Cydne had liked about them so much; all those brothers-in-law that came with his marriage to Olegra Pardura meant he was free to practise as a physician.

And to murder innocent Crasii, as it turned out.

"I'm not sure who this captain was, but I know he was related to the doctor somehow," Tenika said, her tears now under control. "Lady Medwen thought it would be faster to tell the captain and let him take the message back to the doctor's family in Port Traeker."

"And they got arrested for their trouble?"

Tenika nodded. "I managed to escape. Nobody cares much about slaves, or thinks they know anything useful. But Lady Medwen and Lady Ambria . . . That feline you let go . . . Jojo . . . she got there first. They already knew what had happened. The captain didn't believe their story about it being an accident. He was furious, Azquil, and threatening to wipe out every village in the wetlands in retaliation. He had them dragged aboard his ship and left for Port Traeker that same night. It was only because Izzy and Lenor waited for us that I got away."

Azquil turned to the amphibians, who were standing waist deep in the water, leaning on the dock as they listened to Tenika's tale. They were, presumably, Izzy and Lenor.

"I thank you for bringing my sister back safely," he said to them. "But you must be exhausted to have made it back from the Delta Settlement so quickly. Please, take your rest. Tenika will be fine now, thanks to you. I'm sure Lady Arryl will call on you again when you're needed."

The two amphibians replied in their own strange language that few non-Crasii understood, and then slipped into the water and swam away, back toward their own settlement further along the channel.

Azquil turned back to his sister and tried to help her to her feet, but whether from exhaustion or injury, she seemed unable to stand. Without saying a word, Declan pushed past Arkady and Tiji and scooped the little Crasii into his arms.

Azquil bowed to Declan respectfully. "Thank you, my lord."

Declan didn't answer, not even to correct Azquil for calling him "my lord." Instead, he turned for the Outpost and carried the wounded chameleon inside, leaving Azquil, Tiji and Arkady to follow in the certain knowledge that whatever problems Declan was having with the notion of immortality, whatever private agenda Cayal was working toward, everything was now secondary to rescuing Medwen and Ambria from the wrath of the great trading house of Medura.

Chapter 45

With Tenika's head wound taken care of and the young chameleon put to bed, they gathered in the Outpost's kitchen for the second time this morning, only now it was a council of war that convened around Ambria's scrubbed wooden table. Despite his reluctance to have anything to do with the Tide Lords, Declan found himself drawn into the machinations of the immortals. There seemed little point in fighting the inevitable. He was here and he was—however reluctantly—one of them. It would be foolish to turn his back on this opportunity, just because he didn't like what it made him.

This realisation was still very new to Declan, prompted by something Arkady had said to him on the dock earlier. *You spent your whole life working for the Cabal, looking for a way to end the Tide Lords. And here you are, with the answer being offered to you on a silver platter, and you don't want anything to do with it . . . you're about to discover the very thing your wretched Cabal has been seeking for the last five thousand years, and you're going to turn your back on the knowledge because you're angry at me.*

It horrified Declan to realise how right she was. He hadn't given the Cabal a thought when he told Cayal he wanted nothing to do with his plans to take his own life.

Idiot.

Everything the Cabal had been set up to learn, the very reason for their existence, was to find a way to put an end to the Tide Lords. And here he was, one of them, with a Tide Lord who'd found a way to destroy himself. There was no room for pride or personal feelings. Perhaps that was why fate had made him immortal in the first place. Perhaps even destiny had decided the Tide Lords had gone on long enough and had decided they must go . . .

Assuming destiny was anything other than random chance . . .

Declan's head ached just thinking about it.

But to learn the secret of destroying the Tide Lords, he was going to have to cooperate with Arryl and—worse—with Cayal. And not pay any attention to the fact that Arkady clearly preferred the company of the Immortal Prince to his, even though Declan knew the only one he could blame for that sorry state of affairs was himself.

Cayal's reaction to learning the news about Ambria and Medwen's arrest surprised Declan. He'd always thought the immortal completely selfish and self-serving. He'd assumed the Immortal Prince would consider the plight of his immortal sisters an unfortunate complication, and not want to get involved.

Cayal stunned him by announcing, "We have to get them back."

"That's going to blow our cover," Arryl said with a frown. "Particularly if you march into a Senestran prison and start magically melting the bars."

"Can you *do* that, my lord?" Azquil asked in awe.

Cayal shrugged. "Tide might not be up far enough for anything quite so dramatic."

"We've gone to a great deal of trouble to keep our presence here a secret, Cayal," Arryl said. "I won't have you endangering that."

He looked sceptical. "You don't think Medwen and Ambria healing up as soon as they're beaten—and they *will* be beaten—isn't going to give the game away? Or worse, if they try to execute them?"

"Maybe the Marines will just question Ambria and Medwen and then release them?" Tiji suggested. She sat close to Azquil. Declan wasn't sure if it was because she'd finally found another member of her own species or there was something more going on between his slave and the handsome young male she'd managed to find herself. "I mean, they just brought the news about the doctor's death, not confessed to causing it. The Senestran authorities won't just execute the messengers out of spite, will they?"

"Cydne comes from a very important family," Arkady said. "I don't think the Meduras will let this go without some investigation. Particularly if Jojo got there first with the truth."

Arryl nodded in agreement. "Medwen and Ambria were going to tell them he died of the fever. Their word will carry more weight than a feline's if only because they look human, and Senestrans think the Crasii little more than animals blessed with the ability to speak. But with two different versions of his death, and the certain news that he *did* die, this man's family will not let the matter rest."

"How *did* he die?" Cayal asked.

"We tied him to the Justice Tree and let the gobie ants eat him alive," Azquil said.

Cayal smiled. "Charming."

Arryl didn't seem nearly so amused. She frowned and turned to Azquil.

"We need to go back to Watershed. Get rid of the body and any trace of him being there."

"That won't work," Arkady said. "The Physicians' Guild know we were there. Tides, they *sent* us there."

Azquil nodded in agreement as he studied Arkady thoughtfully. Declan found himself staring at the young male, fascinated by how much he looked like Tiji. He wished he had the time to meet more of these creatures, to see how they lived. *Who'd have thought there was a whole conclave of them here in the Senestra Wetlands?* Declan could understand why Tiji had abandoned any pretence of belonging to him.

"You raise a valid point. And something else we should have thought of."

"What's that?" Arryl asked.

"The first person they will come looking for to tell them the truth about his fate is the doctor's *wii-ah*."

"Who is that?" Cayal asked.

"Me."

Cayal turned to Arkady with a raised brow. "*You* were the good doctor's *wii-ah*? That's a fairly impressive step down from duchess."

Declan wasn't sure what a *wii-ah* was. The slave at the clinic in Port Traeker had used the same word, but Declan still wasn't sure what it meant. And he certainly didn't like the way Cayal was looking at Arkady. Or the way he spoke to her.

For that matter, he wasn't particularly fond of *anything* about the Immortal Prince.

"What's a *wii-ah*?" he asked, fairly sure he wasn't going to like the answer.

"A slave," Cayal answered before anybody else could. "A body slave to be exact. Not quite a mistress, but a step or two up from a whore. A chattel with no rights, favoured by her master for all the wrong reasons. I had one once, I think. Name of Finea or Fonia, I think. Do you remember her, Arryl?"

"No," Arryl said. "But then, I don't make a habit of keeping up with your sexual exploits as a rule, Cayal."

"Neither do I," he said with the hint of a grin. "Which is probably why I can't remember her name. Still, it's quite the career change for a Glaeban duchess with a doctorate in history."

Declan was astonished when Arkady, rather than slap Cayal for the insult, just shrugged and looked down at her hands. "You've done worse to stay alive."

"Done worse, yes," Cayal agreed. "But I didn't need to do it to stay alive. Who else knew you were his *wii-ah*?"

"Everyone," Arkady said. "His wife made sure of it. She didn't like me."

"Hardly surprising," Arryl said, her expression thoughtful. "But it means they'll come looking for you. Or expect you to return to Port Traeker. After all, you're probably the one reliable witness, as far as the family is concerned, to your master's fate." She leaned back in her chair, shaking her head.

Arkady didn't seem so sure. "I don't know that they will, my lady. If Jojo told them I was tied to that tree along with Cydne, wouldn't they assume that by now I am also dead?"

"If she even brought up your fate, when she reported to the family. Being *wii-ah*, you may not have rated a mention." Cayal sighed heavily, as if he considered everything the Trinity had done thus far just a little bit stupid. "Pity Ambria or Medwen didn't think this through a little better before they went running off to report the doctor's death."

"What do you think will happen now?" Declan asked, hoping to keep the discussion on topic. Although he had a broad grasp of the structure of Senestran society, he wasn't up on the politics of the various trading Houses. And he had no idea how the Senestrans would react in a situation like this.

Or that Arkady, when she'd told him *you don't want to even think about how I survived*, was trying to explain that for the past few months she'd been some Senestran nobleman's favoured mistress. And to think, she'd claimed it was all Cayal's fault. Running into him had set off the chain of events that led her to this pass . . .

Funny, she doesn't seem to be holding it against him, though.

"I suspect they'll send someone to investigate in the first instance," Arryl said.

"And if they don't like what they find," Azquil added, "they'll probably decide to wipe out every living creature in the wetlands, just to be certain they got everyone involved in the death of one of their scions."

Declan shook his head in disbelief. "Would they really do that much damage over the death of one man?"

"Your little friend here was sent by these same people to indiscriminately deal out poison to the Crasii," Arryl reminded him, "just as a preventative measure to stop swamp fever spreading to the cities. Believe me, Azquil is not exaggerating."

"And if they harm Medwen or Ambria, by either torturing them or trying to execute them, things are going to get a whole lot more complicated," Cayal said. He looked at Arryl and smiled. "Jelidia's looking pretty attractive right now, isn't it?"

Arryl glared at the Immortal Prince. "Does that mean you're abandoning us in our hour of need?"

"Not at all," Cayal said. "I wouldn't miss this party for the world. I'll help you get the others back, Arryl. Tides, I'll save your wretched little lizard friends from the wrath of the Senestran Trading Guilds on my own if I have to. But I expect you to return the favour."

"How?"

"When we're done, you and the others come back to Jelidia with me."

"So we can help you kill yourself?" Arryl asked, clearly not pleased with the idea.

"We all have our dreams, Arryl. Don't deny me mine."

The Sorceress thought about it for a moment and then nodded reluctantly. "Once this is done, there'll be no point in trying to stay here anyway. I can't speak for Ambria or Medwen, but if you can save the others and somehow protect the Crasii of the wetlands from annihilation—preferably without causing another cataclysm—then I'll come to Jelidia with you."

Cayal nodded, seemingly satisfied with that. And then he turned his disconcerting gaze on Declan. "What about you?"

"What about me?"

"Are you in?"

"In *what*, exactly?" Declan asked.

"Our noble plan to save the Crasii of the Senestran Wetlands from their own stupidity."

"Cydne Medura was a murderer, my lord," Azquil objected. "We delivered justice."

"Which is possibly the stupidest thing you've done in your short, pitiful life, my slimy young friend." He turned to look at Declan. "Well?"

"In return for my help, you'll take me to Jelidia to meet Lukys?" he asked, determined to make certain he knew exactly what he was getting into. *Tides, Shalimar, if you could see me now.* "And I get to help you kill yourself?"

Cayal smiled, not fooled for a moment by Declan's calm demeanour. That was the problem with the Tide, Declan was rapidly learning: you could sound in control but the Tide would betray you to anybody who could read the signs. "You get to meet your daddy. I get to die. Everybody wins."

Declan refused to look at Arkady or Tiji, although he could feel their eyes on him. Arkady would know why he was doing this. *Tides, she was the one who suggested it.* He doubted Tiji would be as understanding. But there was nothing for it; the only way to learn this secret for the Cabal, the only way to ensure his *own* immortality could be defeated some day, was to find the man who had found a way to end the life of an immortal.

That the same man may or may not be his father was something Declan decided he'd deal with later.

He nodded. "Count me in then. Although I'm not sure how much use I'm going to be. I really don't know much about Tide magic. And I'm assuming that's how you're planning to help these people?"

Cayal shrugged. "You'll learn quick enough."

"What are you going to do?" Arkady asked. She didn't even glance at Declan.

"Send you back to Watershed Falls for a start," Cayal said. "Dress you like a slave and have you waiting there for when the good doctor's family comes a-calling, to find out what really happened. That should buy us a few days at least."

Arkady shook her head. "I don't know why you think I'm getting involved in this. These women you want to save from the Senestrans ordered me tied to the Justice Tree and condemned me to a slow and painful death, a couple of days ago, for the simple crime of being Cydne's slave."

"And I've since promised Declan no harm will come to you," Arryl reminded her.

"By sending me back to Watershed Falls where they think I murdered a few score of their loved ones, to await the arrival of the Medura family who'll probably blame me for the death of their only son. Yes, I can see how *that's* going to work."

Cayal smiled, which Declan didn't think would help matters much. "She has a point, Arryl."

Arryl wasn't smiling. "Then consider it repayment for not taking you back to the Justice Tree to see the remainder of your sentence carried out."

Arkady glared at Arryl and Cayal for a moment and then glanced at Declan. She said nothing, but he knew her well enough to guess what she was thinking. She'd just lectured him, after all, about refusing an opportunity to find a way to be rid of the immortals, and here she was, doing exactly the same thing. He read the internal war going on inside her head and noted the moment she gave in. She turned back to Arryl, looking resigned.

"How do I explain about the brand?"

"What brand?" Cayal asked.

"All Senestran slaves are branded on the right breast," she said. "Mine's gone."

"Gone where?"

"Just gone. Declan made it go away when he healed me after they tried to execute me."

Cayal turned his gaze on Declan and stared at him in silence for a time. But he said nothing in the end, turning to Azquil instead. "You really are impulsive little creatures, aren't you? No wonder you can't survive without immortal protection."

Azquil was unapologetic, even to a Tide Lord. "She was dealing out poison as readily as the doctor was, my lord. She deserved the same fate."

The Immortal Prince shook his head and turned to Arkady, apparently amused by something. "You really have moved on from being a duchess, haven't you?"

Arkady ignored the remark. "What do we do about the brand?"

Arryl shrugged. "We could draw one on you, I suppose, that'll pass casual inspection."

"Unless you'd like to be branded again for the sake of authenticity?" Cayal added.

"No, thank you."

"Then it's settled," Cayal said, rising to his feet. "Arkady goes back to Watershed Falls to wait for the Trading Guild, or the Physicians' Guild, or whatever wretched guild decides to deal with this. You two can go with her," he added to Azquil and Tiji. "You'll be able to bring word as soon as they arrive. And maybe stop all your cousins in the village from stringing her up a second time."

"What about me?" Declan asked, almost afraid to wonder what the Immortal Prince had in mind for him.

"You and I are going to spend the short time we have before all hell breaks loose, teaching you some control. Any attack on the wetlands will logically come via the water. I'm going to have to teach you how to use the Tide to sink a boat."

"Without harming the amphibians who are towing it," Arryl said.

Cayal sighed. "If you insist."

"I do, Cayal."

"You're far too nice to be immortal, Arryl." Not waiting for her to answer that accusation, Cayal turned to Declan. "Unlike our spymaster here, who, if his reputation on Recidivists' Row was anything to go by, is enough of a bastard to fit right in."

"Cayal . . . please . . ." Arkady said, but Declan wasn't sure if she was interceding on his behalf or asking the Immortal Prince to contain himself for some other reason.

Tides, why I am doing this? Declan thought. *It's insane.*

He glanced at Arkady, but she was looking at Cayal. It was almost as if she was deliberately avoiding meeting his eye. *What are you playing at, Arkady?* She was acting like the Immortal Prince was her long-lost lover, while advising him to follow Cayal to learn the secret of killing an immortal.

Declan wished he knew if that was because Arkady genuinely wanted to see an end to the Tide Lords, or if she was just interested in seeing the end of one in particular.

And if it *was* the latter motivating her, which immortal was she hoping would die once they'd learned the secret of killing immortals? Jaxyn, perhaps? He was still hunting her, after all. Diala? She'd made a fool of Arkady and Stellan by posing as her husband's niece. Was it Kinta, the woman who had sent her to Brynden? Or Brynden himself, who'd sold her like a piece of meat to a Torlenian slaver? Was it Cayal? The immortal who'd seduced her and then abandoned her, allowing her to be sold as a slave in the first place?

Or was it him? The childhood friend she'd loved and trusted, who had scorned her affection for no reason he could readily explain. That wound was still raw, he was certain. Was it enough to make her hate him?

The Tenacians had a saying, Declan recalled. *Even the Tide cannot hold back the wrath of a woman unwanted.*

Declan had a bad feeling he was going to find out the hard way if the Tenacians were right.

Chapter 46

"What's the weather like outside, Cecil?"

"It's overcast, my lady. And cold. But it's not snowing."

Elyssa looked up from the floor where she was sitting with the pups. She'd ordered Boots to bring them to her rooms to play with them, something she did far too frequently for comfort. She never harmed them. In fact, Elyssa seemed genuinely amused by them, but her affection for their pups drove Boots insane. She was forced to sit by and watch as Elyssa cooed and cuddled and tickled her babies. She was forced to feed them with Elyssa looking on critically, to make sure each pup was getting its fair share. And there was nothing she could do. Not a snarl, not even a faint growl could she risk, for fear of betraying she was a Scard.

"I think, tomorrow, we'll go for a picnic." She looked down at Missy, who was lying on the floor on a blanket, waving her arms and legs around to no apparent purpose. Although she was barely a month old, the pup seemed to turn her head toward Elyssa whenever the immortal spoke. "Would you like to go on a picnic, Misery?"

"I'm not sure the weather would suit taking the pups outside, my lady," Boots suggested meekly. "We wouldn't want them to catch a chill."

Warlock held his breath, fearful Elyssa would take Boots's comments as defiance. Fortunately, she didn't seem to mind, assuming it was motherly concern for her pups and not Scard-like disobedience that prompted her suggestion.

"You may be right," the immortal conceded. She smiled at Boots. "You're a good mother, Tabitha Belle."

"To serve you is the reason I breathe," Boots replied with suitable deference.

"Still, I do need to go check something out. Do you know the countryside around Deadman's Bluff, Cecil?"

"No, my lady. I'd never been to Caelum before coming here in your service."

"Never mind," Elyssa said, turning to tickle Dezi under the chin. "I know where I want to go. And your dam is right, precious," she added in a singsong tone to the pup she'd named Despair. "It's much too cold outside for my puppies."

A knock at the door distracted Elyssa, which was fortunate, because Boots's lips were curled back over her teeth in a silent snarl. Warlock hurried to the door and opened it to admit Princess Nyah. Elyssa looked up from the floor and smiled at the little princess, beckoning her forward.

"Nyah! Come say hello to my puppies. Aren't they cute?"

The little princess did as the immortal asked, kneeling on the floor beside them, smiling. "They are very cute, Aunt Alysa," she said. "Can I hold one?"

Elyssa nodded. Nyah reached forward and picked up Tor, holding him gingerly, as if he was made of porcelain. Disturbed from a peaceful nap, the pup immediately began to cry, but was silenced with a sharp word from Elyssa.

"What are their names?"

"Despair, Torment and Misery."

The little princess frowned. "They're *terrible* names. Who called them that?"

"I did."

"Shame on you, Aunt Alysa. You should have thought of something much nicer. They're much too sweet to be known by such awful names."

Hear, hear! Warlock thought. *Why does it take a human child to say it, though?*

Elyssa didn't appreciate being scolded by an eleven-year-old. She scowled at the princess. "Did you want something, Nyah?"

"I came to talk to you about my future husband. Mother says you're in charge of finding me a suitable consort."

"And I will. In time."

"I don't want it to be one of Lord Tyrone's . . . friends."

Elyssa looked at her curiously. "Who do you mean?"

"His friends, Rance and Krydence. Your mother seems quite taken with them ever since they got here, and Lord Tyrone has been telling my mother what respectable gentlemen they are. I think he wants me to marry one of them."

Warlock glanced at Boots whose expression betrayed more surprise than it should have at the little princess's words.

She knows, Warlock realised at the same time as his mate. *This child knows about the immortals.*

Perhaps it wasn't so surprising. Nyah had been brought back to Caelum by Stellan Desean, after all, and he was obviously a part of the Cabal these days. Why wouldn't they have had a hand in Nyah's disappearance? And informed her of who she was dealing with?

Still, she was handling herself remarkably well under the circumstances. And pitching her complaint where it was likely to do the most good. Even Warlock knew Elyssa had little patience with her stepbrothers and wasn't pleased they had arrived in Cycrane.

Elyssa smiled reassuringly at the little girl. "Never fear, Nyah. When you marry, I can assure you it won't be to Rance or Krydence." She reached forward and stroked the child's short-cropped hair. "I'd marry you to Cecil first."

The princess glanced at the Crasii and grimaced. "I'd like a prince, thank you. And one who'll put the good of Caelum before his own interests."

"That's very noble of you to want that," Elyssa said. "I'll see what I can do."

Nyah handed the pup back to Elyssa and climbed to her feet. "Thank you, my lady. I knew I could count on you."

The little princess curtseyed gracefully and let herself out of the room. As soon as the door closed behind her, Elyssa shook her head, her smile fading. "Precocious little brat."

There was no response to that, so Warlock and Boots both remained silent. Nyah's visit had spoiled the mood, however. Elyssa rose to her feet, turning her back on the pups. "Take them away, Tabitha Belle. I'm done with them now."

"As you wish, my lady," Boots agreed readily, gathering up Missy and placing her in the sling she wore, before picking up the two male pups. She bowed awkwardly. "To serve you is the reason I breathe."

Warlock hurried to the door to open it for her, knowing Boots would want to get the pups away from here as fast as she could. Elyssa wandered over to the window, her expression thoughtful, all interest in the pups apparently departing with the little princess.

Boots gave Warlock a look that spoke volumes as she left, but said nothing aloud. As soon as she was gone, he turned to pick up the blanket where the pups had been lying, and to tidy up after them.

"Have the cooks prepare a hamper for tomorrow, Cecil," Elyssa said without looking back at him.

"You'll be picnicking after all, my lady?"

"Visiting a site of historical interest would be more accurate," she said. "You'll be coming with me."

"I'll make the arrangements, my lady," he promised. "To serve you is the reason I breathe."

Elyssa didn't seem to be listening to him, however. She was staring out over the mountains, her expression distant, her thoughts apparently a million miles away.

When Warlock finally retired much later that evening, he found Boots in their dark, underground cell, the pups curled up beside her for warmth, silently weeping. He'd expected another tirade at the very least, which was what usually happened after Elyssa had been playing with the pups, so Boots's obvious distress left him speechless.

He hurried to her side and sat down beside her, putting his arm around her. Instead of complaining, she rested her head on his shoulder and tried to sniff back her tears.

"What's the matter? Are the pups hurt?"

She shook her head. "No, they're fine."

"I'm trying to get us out of here, Boots," he said in a low voice, guessing her tears had something to do with being trapped here in Cycrane.

Boots sniffed loudly and sat up a little straighter. "I don't know that it would make much difference if you did."

He looked at her oddly. In the light from the single lamp high on the wall above them, her expression was almost impossible to read. "What do you mean?"

"Didn't you see her with them, Warlock? She owns them."

"The pups are ours, Boots, and nobody can—"

"No!" she insisted, slapping away his arm as he tried to pull her closer. "That's not what I mean. I mean she *owns* them. I think the pups are Crasii."

"Well, of course they're . . ." He hesitated, as he realised what she was saying. "Oh, Tides, no . . ."

Boots had started crying again. "Didn't you see her with them? They stop crying when she commands it. They turn at the sound of her voice . . ."

"They're just reacting to any old noise, Boots. They're too young to understand. Besides, we're both Scards . . ."

"My parents were both Crasii," she reminded him. "And so were yours, I'll wager. That doesn't make the slightest difference. If a couple of Crasii can throw a Scard, then there's no reason why a couple of Scards can't throw a Crasii litter."

Though she tried to push him away, this time Warlock wouldn't be put off so easily. He pulled her to him and held her close, letting the implications of this dreadful news sink in. He'd never even considered the possibility his pups wouldn't be Scards, just like him and Boots. But if she was right, if the pups were pure Crasii, compelled to obey their immortal masters, their futures were all in doubt.

He glanced down at the sleeping pups, so innocently curled into their mother's body for warmth.

Tides, could fate be so cruel?

"It's too early to tell, Boots. And even if they are . . ."

"What? They'll still *love* us? No, they won't. They'll betray us as soon as look at us, Farm Dog, and you know that as well as I do. They won't have any choice."

"We can't hate them for being what they are," he said.

"But they can hate *us* for it," Boots replied. "So you'd better find us a way out of here, and soon, Farm Dog, before your own children destroy us both."

Chapter 47

It was quite a while since Arkady had felt self-conscious wearing the slave skirt of a Senestran *makor-di*. Wearing it every day, while surrounded by others wearing the same thing, had deadened her sensibilities. She no longer saw the bare flesh, no longer noticed the sagging breasts of the older slaves or the wrinkled pot bellies hanging over the skirts belonging to the well-fed scribes whose jobs required little physical labour.

But donning the skirt again after her brief stint wearing Ambria's borrowed dress and walking back out into the kitchen where Cayal and Declan waited, was more harrowing than she bargained for. Arkady tied the skirt on and squared her shoulders, scolding herself for her foolishness. Declan had already seen her wearing it. Tides, she slept the night in his arms wearing little else. And it wasn't as if Cayal had never seen her naked . . .

"Get a grip, girl!" she told herself sternly.

Taking a deep breath, she opened the door to the storeroom and headed back toward the kitchen before her courage failed her. Everyone looked up as she entered. Cayal and Declan, who'd been discussing something with Arryl, both wore expressions Arkady could have read any number of thoughts into, had she been prepared to look either man in the eye.

Instead, she focused her attention on Arryl, trying to behave as if it was perfectly normal to be standing in a stranger's kitchen wearing nothing but a strip of black-banded cloth around her hips that didn't quite reach mid-thigh. "The brand was two links of a chain," she said, as matter-of-factly as she could manage.

Arryl, perhaps sensing her uneasiness, nodded in agreement. "I know the one. It's fairly common on batch-bought slaves. Right or left breast?"

"Right."

Carrying a small bowl, she pushed past the two men. There was a gooey, gelatinous mess in the bottom that Arryl was stirring with a small stick. It smelt disgusting.

"It's hide gum," Arryl explained. "Once it's set, it should look like scar tissue if nobody gets too close or starts picking at it. And it won't wash off easily."

That made sense, Arkady supposed. She turned her head away from the fumes as Arryl began to apply the gum with the stick, in the same pattern as her now-healed brand. By turning her head, however, she was forced to look at Declan.

Arkady turned her head the other way and closed her eyes, just to be on the safe side.

"If they sailed back to Port Traeker with Ambria and Medwen," Cayal said after a moment, picking up the conversation Arkady had interrupted with her arrival, "then we have a few days before they get back to the Delta Settlement."

"Is that where you're planning to attack them?" Declan asked in the same I'm-not-interested-in-anything-Arkady-is-doing tone.

"It would be," Cayal said, glancing at Arryl, "if certain people hadn't made me promise to keep the amphibian casualties to a minimum."

"Don't start, Cayal . . ." Arryl said, without looking up from her task.

The Immortal Prince made a noise that sounded somewhere between a snort of derision and disgust, and continued explaining his plans to Declan. "We'll have to wait until the fleet reaches the shallower water around Watershed Falls. The channels around the Delta Settlement are too deep. If we take their ships down there, we'll take the Crasii with them. They've a better chance of getting out of the harnesses and swimming away in shallow water."

"Is that how you're planning to deal with this?" Declan asked. "Just sink every ship that sails up the channel?"

"You have a better idea?"

"Well . . . not exactly . . . I'm just wondering what you hope to achieve."

"Sinking their boats," Cayal said. "Weren't you listening?"

"So you sink them. What then? Won't they just send more?"

"What if they do? We'll sink them too."

"And how long can you keep that up?"

"As long as we have to. They'll get the message. Eventually."

"I don't think they will," Declan said. "I think they'll get increasingly annoyed at the loss of life and shipping—although given this is Senestra, not necessarily in that order—and you'll end up causing the annihilation of the wetland Crasii, long after they've forgotten what they came here for in the first place."

"He has a point, Cayal," Arryl said. "I'd prefer we kept the human casualties to a minimum too."

"Why not just insist nobody gets hurt?" he snapped. "Just to make things really interesting."

"Very well . . ."

"Not funny, Arryl."

"I wasn't trying to be funny, Cayal." Arryl finished with the brand and stood back to admire her handiwork on Arkady's breast. "That should do it. Try not to touch it until it dries. It'll probably itch like crazy for a while." She turned to Cayal and Declan, placing the bowl of gum on the table. "Declan is right, Cayal. Murdering anybody who comes up the channel to inquire about Cydne Medura's death will result in reprisals that defeat the whole purpose of the exercise. Defend the Crasii if you must, by all means, but there's nothing to be gained by provoking an attack."

"I may not be the one provoking it," he said. "Ambria and Medwen may have done that already, simply by still being alive."

Arkady couldn't resist it any longer. She opened her eyes and turned to look at the two of them. Engaged as they were in their discussion about tactics, the men seemed to have lost interest in her.

"Why don't you just tell them who you are?" she said.

They all turned to look at her.

"The Tide's on the rise, isn't it? And it's not as if the Senestrans haven't heard of the Tide Lords. They still have cults dedicated to your worship."

"Not in the wetlands, they don't," Arryl said. "I've made damn sure of that."

"But it's not the wetlands you have to worry about. The men coming here to punish the Crasii for Cydne's death are from the cities, and the cults there are thriving. I don't know if they really believe the Tide Lords ever existed, but they use the common-held belief in the immortals as an excuse to join the club. There's some pretty influential people involved too."

"Do you know that for a fact?" Cayal asked.

"I do," Declan said, surprising her a little with his support.

He seemed to have taken her advice and was no longer trying to distance himself from the immortals. She didn't know if he'd decided to throw his lot in with them to help the Cabal or himself, and supposed it didn't really matter. Immortality was his problem, not hers. Arkady just wanted to get this over and done with so she could be gone from this place.

But that didn't make seeing Declan Hawkes and the Immortal Prince in cahoots with each other any less disturbing to watch.

"We used to keep tabs on the cults for just that reason," Declan explained. "The Senestran ambassador to Glaeba was a member of one of them, if I remember correctly."

"So was the wife of the Senestran ambassador to Torlenia," Arkady said. "Kinta had her thrown in gaol for calling her a whore."

That made Cayal smile. "Even *I* wouldn't be brave enough to do that."

"And I'm not sure I see your point, Arkady," Arryl said. "Senestran ambassadors currently stationed across the globe aren't much use to us, here and now."

"My point is that they *believe*, my lady. Most Senestrans still believe in the Tide Lords. In Glaeba, nobody took Cayal seriously when he told us he was immortal, because we consider the Tide Lords to be nothing more than a child's myth. You have people here in Senestra—influential people with the power to call off an attack—who know you exist. Cydne's wife is a member of the same cult, which means her brothers probably are too. Given the Tide's on the way back and you can actually prove your claim, why *not* just stand up and declare yourselves? Ambria and Medwen may have already done it, for all you know, because they've had no other choice."

The room was quiet as the immortals digested her suggestion. It was Arryl who finally broke the uneasy silence. "You get so used to hiding when the Tide is out, sometimes it's hard to remember what it was like not to be afraid of who you are."

Cayal was staring at her thoughtfully. "So you think we should just ask for a meeting with the captain of the Medura flagship and ask him nicely to go home because we're Tide Lords and we don't want them messing with our Crasii?"

"The cult Arkady's talking about worships Jaxyn, the Lord of Temperance," Declan said.

Cayal looked at the former spymaster and rolled his eyes. "Tides, that's all we need."

"You could pose as Jaxyn," Arkady said.

"No, thank you. I do have my standards, you know."

"You'll need to acknowledge him, though," Arryl suggested, "if you expect his believers to take you seriously."

"You need to do more than that," Arkady said. "I think you need to put on a show. I think you'll need to demonstrate the point forcefully. And you'll need to do it in such a way that they'll leave and you can be sure they won't come back."

Cayal seemed unconvinced. Arryl seemed uncertain. It was impossible to guess what Declan was thinking.

She threw her hands up in exasperation. "Tides, what are you worried about? Every Crasii on Amyrantha knows what you are, and have done all along, even when you were in hiding. And seriously, how long do you think it's going to be before one of the other immortals announces they're back, and this whole 'secret-identity' obsession you people have is out in the open anyway?"

Cayal shrugged after a moment and turned to Arryl. "It's up to you. These are your creatures and your turf. We can give them a show if you want, but there'll be no going back if we do."

Arryl nodded reluctantly. "She's right, I suppose. If they've tried to harm Ambria or Medwen, they'll know they're immortal by now."

Cayal glanced at Declan. "What about you? You're the spymaster, the *trained* tactician. What do you think?"

"Why do you care what I think?"

The Immortal Prince let out a long-suffering sigh, designed—Arkady was certain—purely to aggravate Declan. "Because for the time being, Hawkes, I'm stuck with you. It'll be a lot less trouble for all of us if we're on the same side, at least temporarily."

Declan glared at Cayal but his answer was much less antagonistic than his expression. "Then for what it's worth, I think Arkady may be right. Go out there and tell them the Tide Lords are back. Demand they return Medwen and Ambria. Tell them Cydne Medura was executed for sins against . . . whatever . . . and tell them to back off or there'll be hell to pay. I'm sure you're up for a few random executions of innocent bystanders to demonstrate your sincerity."

"Or I could show *you* how," Cayal offered. "I think you'd be quite at home with the random execution of innocent bystanders, spymaster."

"Stop it," Arryl said. "Both of you."

Somewhat to Arkady's surprise, both men heeded her words and ceased their sniping at each other.

The Sorceress turned to Arkady. "If we're going to do it this way, then it's up to you, in the first instance, to prepare them for what's coming. When they arrive in the village looking for your doctor, Azquil can bring word. You can, in the meantime, explain to whoever is thumping their chest the loudest that sending a physician into the wetlands armed with a poison designed to murder any potential carriers of swamp fever has been looked upon very dimly by the Immortal Trinity."

"But the Trinity's not here, my lady . . ."

"There are three of us here capable of wielding the Tide," she said. "That's all they need to know."

"It'll be all right, Arkady," Cayal said. "We should get there before they string you back up on the Justice Tree. And if we don't . . . well, your old friend here seems to be a dab hand at fixing up things like chewed out eyeballs."

"Pay no attention to Cayal," Arryl said, giving him a displeased look. "Azquil and Tiji are waiting by the boat. They'll see you back to Watershed and ensure no harm comes to you until we arrive."

"Thank you, my lady." Without sparing either Cayal or Declan so much as a glance, Arkady hurried from the room, through the workroom in the front of the Outpost and onto the veranda. As promised, Tiji and Azquil were waiting for her at the dock, sitting on the edge of it with their feet in the water, talking to the amphibians who waited in their harness to tow their small craft to Watershed Falls.

Arkady straightened her skirt, squared her shoulders, resisted the urge to scratch the gummy residue on her breast and took a deep breath, relieved to have escaped Ambria's kitchen.

She was even more relieved to get away from the Outpost.

With its immortals, its tension and the unspoken words that hung between her and Declan, her and Cayal . . . even Declan and Cayal, this place was like standing in the eye of a hurricane and never being certain from which direction the wall of wind would hit, when the storm moved on.

Chapter 48

"Will she be safe?"

Arryl picked up the bowl of gum and began scraping the remains onto a scrap of cloth. "She's in more danger from the residents of Watershed Falls who remember her handing out that tonic than she is from the Medura clan. But Azquil should be able to smooth things over. And Cayal's right; we have a few days before the doctor's family arrive."

"Time enough to teach you a few techniques for the random execution of innocent bystanders," Cayal said to Declan.

"If you think it will help." Declan had no intention of letting Cayal bait him into doing something stupid. And he *was* trying to bait him. Incessantly. *This must be what terminal boredom does to you.*

Cayal smiled. "I bet you were a very good spymaster, weren't you?"

"The best," Declan agreed without hesitation.

Cayal studied him for a moment and then shook his head. "Tides, you're going to drive Lukys crazy. Come on."

"Come where?"

"Outside," Cayal said. "Arryl will get mad at us if we start throwing things around her kitchen."

The immortal looked up from the bowl she was cleaning and nodded in agreement. "Don't do anything foolish."

"Define foolish," Cayal said.

"Don't kill anyone. Or destroy anything. Or sink anything."

"You're no fun, Arryl." Cayal planted a quick peck on her cheek as he led Declan back down the hall. They passed the storeroom Declan had shared the first night here with Arkady.

The door at the end of the hall led out into a yard scattered with the debris of several hundred years of habitation. Most of it was broken furniture waiting to be chopped up for firewood, barrels no longer watertight, a couple of small boats that were long past being able to stay afloat, and various other bits of detritus that Declan couldn't readily identify.

"How long has it been?" Cayal asked, turning to face Declan.

"How long has what been?"

"Since you were made immortal."

"A few months."

"And healing Arkady is the only time you've used the Tide?"

"That I know of." And then, not sure why he'd want to confide any-thing to this maniac, he added, "I can feel it, though. All the time."

Cayal nodded sympathetically, taking a seat on an upturned barrel near a lean-to that housed another, much more seaworthy-looking craft. "That's the worst thing about the Tide being out. You feel it all the time when it's up, and you think it's irritating. But when it goes away . . . Tides, it's like you're missing a limb."

"So . . . what do I do?"

"Learn to enjoy it while you can."

"I was hoping you'd be a little more specific."

Cayal nodded and began to draw on the Tide. Not a lot of it, but enough that Declan could feel what he was doing as the Tide swirling around him reacted to the forces acting on it. Almost simultaneously, Declan discovered he was having trouble breathing.

"Tide magic is elemental," Cayal told him, as Declan began to gasp for air. "You can't make things disappear into thin air, any more than you can blink a banquet into existence, or make someone fall in love with you."

Declan clutched at his throat, gasping. It was as if the air around him could no longer sustain life. On an intellectual level, he knew he couldn't die from it, but his body reacted with the same panic any mortal man might ex-perience when he suddenly found he couldn't breathe.

"You can, however, affect the senses and the elements," Cayal continued in a lecturing tone, as if nothing was amiss, despite the fact that Declan was turning blue before his very eyes. "You can make it rain, you can freeze things, warm things up, start a fire, put one out, calm a storm, whip one up . . ."

Declan fell to his knees, choking for the lack of air.

"Or suffocate a man by taking the air from his lungs . . ."

As he said the words, the pressure on his chest faded and Declan found himself able to breathe again. He pushed himself up and glared at Cayal, who seemed unconcerned.

The Immortal Prince smiled. "Sometimes it's faster to show than tell."

"How far is the Tide up?" Declan asked, struggling to his feet. There didn't seem to be any point in trying to retaliate. Not yet, at any rate. There would come a time when Declan was in a position to even the score with the Immortal Prince. But it wasn't now.

Cayal thought for a moment before he answered. "Almost halfway, I think. It's not easy to tell. The power of the Tide increases exponentially as it rises. Sometimes we don't even know it's peaked until after the fact."

That made sense, Declan supposed. It certainly explained why the Tide Lords could only crack continents in half at the peak of a Tide.

"What you did to me just then. How did you do it?"

"I moved the air away from you. Same way as moving water—moving anything. It doesn't take long to learn. It'll take you a thousand years to be able to do it with any sort of finesse, though."

"Show me."

Cayal nodded and rose to his feet. "Close your eyes."

"Why?"

"Because it's easier to concentrate."

Declan wasn't entirely certain such a thing was necessary. Closing his eyes around Cayal was akin to turning his back on him, something Declan wasn't willing to do for any price. "If I close my eyes every time I want to use the Tide, doesn't that mean everyone will know what I'm doing?"

"You can learn to do it with your eyes open when you've had some practice. Right now, I don't want you getting distracted."

"I suppose," Declan conceded. He closed his eyes.

"Now reach for the Tide. *Gently.*"

Declan gasped as he was almost sucked into a whirling vortex of power so rich and vibrant that for a moment he was blinded by it. Cayal jerked him back to the shallows.

"Ow! That hurt!"

"Then pay attention. You're too inexperienced to swim the Tide. And for this, you don't need to. All you need to do is paddle in the edges of it. Now do it again. And remember, I said *gently.*"

Despite wanting to punch Cayal between the eyes for his condescending manner, this was something Declan found himself intrigued to learn. A lifetime of despising these inhuman beings who could wield the Tide hadn't really prepared him for the possibility that he might one day have the same ability himself. Torn between wonder at the power he now commanded and the inescapable feeling he was betraying every principle he'd ever owned, Declan did as Cayal ordered. With his eyes still closed, he took a mental step toward the shallows, letting the Tide lap at the edge of his awareness. He could feel Cayal beside him on the Tide, his presence causing ripples that stretched out endlessly into the distance. He waited, trying to emulate Cayal's calm breathing. As he did, the Tide settled, quiescent now, barely moving.

"Now think of the air around the barrel I was just sitting on."

"And then what?"

"Squeeze it."

"Is that all?"

He could feel, rather than see, Cayal smiling. "What were you expecting? An incantation in some long-dead language? Something involving eye of newt, perhaps?"

"I don't know . . . something harder, I suppose."

"It's not as easy as it looks. Try it."

Declan did as Cayal suggested. He pictured the barrel in his mind, imagined squeezing the air around it . . . and then jumped backwards in fright as the barrel exploded into kindling in front of him.

"Tides!" he said, staring at the remains of the barrel. The bands were twisted beyond recognition and there didn't seem to be a piece of wood left that was larger than his little finger.

"Now let go of the Tide."

Declan hadn't realised he was still holding on to it. The sense of loss as he let the power drain away was alarming.

"What else can I do?" he asked, hoping his expression wasn't betraying how bereft he felt. Or how excited.

Cayal shrugged. "In theory, you're only limited by what you can visualise and how far you can swim into the Tide to make it a reality. The danger lies in not knowing how deep you can go—and not knowing how to get back."

"What happens if you go too deep?"

"Kentravyon."

Declan frowned, not sure what Cayal meant. "Didn't you freeze him because he thought he was God?"

"And you think any sane man thinks he's God?"

"Fair point."

Cayal shrugged. "Swimming too deep made him crazy. And not in a good way. The God-fixation was just the latest in a long line of increasingly disturbing delusions he suffers from. Worse, we were all suffering because of him. It was better for everyone, once he was out of the picture." Cayal suddenly smiled. "Not that swimming too deep isn't a temptation we've all had to deal with, at one time or another. It's so insidious, you see."

"What is?"

"Tide magic. You start out thinking there's no practical purpose for it, and the next thing you know, you're laying waste to an entire continent."

"That's your particular hobby, Cayal," Declan said. "It won't be mine."

"You say that now, spymaster. Time will tell."

And time, Declan supposed, was the one thing he now owned in abundance. He wasn't in the mood to discuss his future, however, with the Immortal Prince.

Fortunately, Cayal didn't seem interested in making a friend of Declan, either. He walked across the yard, picked up another barrel, carried it back to the centre of the yard and placed it in roughly the same spot as the barrel Declan had just destroyed had stood.

"Let's try again, shall we? Only this time, try to leave something larger than a splinter behind."

"So you think Arkady's idea will work, then?"

"Not if you don't have the faintest idea what you're doing," Cayal said, stepping away from the barrel. "Now focus."

Declan wished he could argue the point with Cayal. He wanted to. Anything that had him disagreeing with the Immortal Prince felt right. But the Tide was there, tickling at the edge of his awareness, calling to him like a hungry lover, and this was the first time he'd consciously tried to draw on it. The feeling was beyond seductive. The urge to dive in and drown in its sweetness was almost irresistible.

Like it or not, Declan realised as the second barrel went the way of the first, he could touch the Tide now, draw on it, even plunge right into its depths if he was game enough.

And rather than scorning it as the evil force he'd been raised to believe the Tide represented, he'd discovered it was the single most exhilarating experience of his life and something he was certain he was going to have to consciously resist drawing on if he wished to retain his sanity.

And he was going to have to resist it until the end of time.

Chapter 49

The villagers had trashed the house Cydne Medura had taken over as a clinic in Watershed Falls. The shutters were broken, the contents ransacked, and the whole place reeked of the eye-watering stench of wood alcohol.

It took nearly three days to restore it to some semblance of order. Tiji was glad of something to do, something to keep her occupied and her mind off what was happening back at the Outpost. She still hadn't come to grips with the notion that Declan was immortal, and she was grateful for the time away from him to get her thoughts in order.

Of course, it didn't help matters much that Arkady Desean was here. Despite Declan's assurances to the contrary, she was not convinced Arkady wasn't somehow responsible for Declan's immortality. She could think of no other reason, no single person on Amyrantha, who could inspire him to do anything so drastic.

But Arkady seemed as confused about it all as Tiji was. She told Tiji she knew nothing about it until after Declan had rescued her from the Justice Tree. Arkady seemed genuine and Tiji wanted to believe her, but it all sounded just a little too glib for her liking.

They had other problems to deal with though, and soon even the soul-shattering news that Declan had joined the ranks of the enemy—however unwittingly—became secondary to simple survival.

Arkady's presence in the house was problematic. The village elders knew nothing about her except she was the one who'd been spooning poison down the throats of the innocent victims of the Senestran Physicians' Guild's plan for the eradication of swamp fever. Azquil had spoken to the elders. He'd explained the consequences of Cydne Medura's death and how the Trinity intended to protect the wetlands, but they weren't all that interested in hearing what they considered his excuses.

As far as the villagers were concerned, Arkady had escaped justice. And now she was back, unmarked and unharmed (which they considered merely flaunting her status as one favoured by the Tide Lords) waiting for the men who were likely to invade the wetlands in force, to seek vengeance for the death of one of their own.

"Do you think he's all right?"

Tiji turned from her seat by the window in the kitchen where she'd been staring out at the path that ran along the side of the house, and was the direction Azquil had gone when he left the house this morning to speak with the elders again. It was raining. It wasn't the gentle, incessant rain of Glaeba, but a loud and violent downpour with drops that looked big enough to fill a bucket. Of course, the rain lasted a lot less time here in the wetlands than it did around the Great Lakes. It pelted down for a while and then, an hour later, the land was steaming in bright sunshine.

"Why do you ask?"

"He's been gone a long time. And you've almost disappeared." Arkady was peeling vegetables, preparing them for lunch. Without realising it, Tiji had been sitting so still she'd taken on the colouring of the rough wooden wall.

"The elders aren't happy," she said, as her skin faded back to its normal silvery sheen. "And until one of the Trinity tells them in person that you're not to be harmed, Azquil may be having trouble convincing them otherwise."

"I'm sorry. I don't mean to cause so much trouble."

Tiji was a little surprised by the apology. The Duchess of Lebec she remembered would never have admitted fault so readily. *Mind you, the Duchess of Lebec used to wear clothes too.* The all-but-naked woman who stood at the table preparing a meal for herself and a couple of reptilian Crasii seemed a far cry from the restrained and perfectly proper duchess Tiji remembered from Torlenia. Tiji wondered if she'd offered to cook dinner to keep her hands busy and stop herself picking at the itchy fake slave brand.

"It's not your fault," Tiji said. "You didn't know what you were doing. Or what was in that tonic."

"I wonder if Jojo knew?"

"Who's Jojo?"

"The feline we had with us. Cydne's bodyguard."

"The feline who escaped back to the Delta Settlement and tipped off the brother-in-law about what happened here before Ambria and Medwen got to him? I'd say a resounding *yes* to that one."

"She's Crasii, Tiji. She probably didn't have a choice."

"I'm Crasii. I have a choice."

"No, you're a Scard," Arkady said. "That's what sets you apart. You have free will. The Crasii don't."

"The Crasii are only compelled to obey *immortals*," Tiji reminded her. "They can defy their human masters as often as they want."

"Can they?" Arkady asked, putting the paring knife down on the chopping board in order to lift the parsnips into the pot of water boiling on the stove. "If you are naturally inclined to follow, why would you seek to lead?"

Tides, this woman likes to complicate everything. What could you possibly see in her, Declan? She's too tall, too pale, too clever for her own good, and altogether far too talkative. "I don't understand what you're getting at."

"Look at the Crasii, Tiji. Feline, canine, amphibian . . . whatever species you care to name. They are slaves. Wherever you go, whatever country you're in, the Crasii are the slaves of Amyrantha. It's as though they're happiest in that state."

"There speaks a human who's used to owning slaves. Does it make you feel better, your grace? Believing we *like* to be enslaved? Is that how humans convince themselves they're doing us a favour? By making us serve them because we're only really happy as servants?"

Arkady looked a little taken aback by the force of Tiji's reaction. "That's not what I meant at all."

"Then what did you mean?"

"I meant, the moment a Crasii has free will, they *want* to be free. Every Scard I've ever encountered wants nothing more."

"I'm a Scard. I was a slave in Glaeba for most of my life. I never tried to escape."

"Is that because you didn't want to be free, or because you had a master who kept you on such a long leash, you didn't feel trapped in the first place?"

Tiji hesitated before answering, not sure Arkady didn't have a point. She'd never rebelled at being Declan's slave because he'd never treated her as one.

"Look around you, Tiji. The entire Senestran Wetlands are filled with Scards who want to be free. *Your* people—the race the Tide Lords tried to eradicate because your species wouldn't toe the line. Yet there are millions of Crasii the world over who would never even think to question their status as slaves. The Tide Lords created the Crasii as a subservient race, remember. You were *bred* to serve. They magically compelled the Crasii to make their obedience stick, but that doesn't mean it's not in your nature to serve, compelled or not."

"So you're saying I'm doomed to be somebody's servant, just because that's my nature?"

"I wasn't talking about the Scards."

"No, you were justifying that flanking cat betraying Medwen and Ambria."

"I think Jojo did what she had to do. She's as compelled to serve her masters as you are to defy them. I don't think you can hold it against her, that's all."

"Yeah, well I'll try to remember that," Tiji said, "if I ever have the misfortune to run into this feline of yours."

"She was Cydne's slave, not mine."

"According to you, she wouldn't be able to tell the difference." Tiji glanced out of the window as she spoke and then jumped to her feet as she saw a figure bent over against the rain, heading toward the house. "Azquil's back!"

"You know, you turn all the colours of the rainbow whenever you mention his name," Arkady told her with a smile.

"Mind your own business." It was bad enough to be lectured by this fallen duchess about the need of her race to serve. Tiji didn't need her giving her pointers on her love life as well. She hurried down the hall and into the front room where the recently repaired door stood locked and secure against the many grieving villagers who thought Arkady still needed to pay for the lives of their lost loved ones.

Standing on the stained floorboards in the front room that had so recently been covered in broken bottles of poisonous tonic, Tiji unlocked the door as Azquil stepped onto the veranda. He shook off the raindrops from his silver skin before he came inside.

Tiji glanced over his shoulder and smiled. "Well, you didn't come back with a lynch mob. That's a good sign."

"Not as good as you think," the chameleon said. "Where's the human woman?"

"Out back, preparing lunch."

Azquil pushed past Tiji and headed out to the kitchen. Tiji followed him, sensing something was amiss.

"So, do I get a reprieve?" Arkady asked when she spied the chameleons.

"You do, *wii-ah*," he said. "But only because there are other, more important, matters to take care of."

"They're here?" Arkady guessed.

Azquil nodded. "The amphibians have just brought word. There are three ships on their way from the Delta Settlement, full of marines and some very indignant humans of both the Medura and Pardura houses."

"How long before they get here?"

"Dusk at the latest."

Arkady took a deep breath, as if she was bracing herself for the coming confrontation.

And well she might, Tiji thought. *If the immortals don't get here before the Medura family, she may not be around to see the outcome.* Certainly no Crasii in the village was going to intercede on behalf of the woman who assisted in the murder of so many of their kind.

"Are you going to fetch Arryl . . . and the others?" Tiji asked. She couldn't quite bring herself to believe they were relying on the assistance of the Immortal Prince. Or that Declan was planning to help him save the day by using Tide magic.

Azquil shook his head. "I've sent Izzy and Lenor on ahead. They can swim faster if they're not towing me in a boat."

"And how long will it take our immortal cavalry to get back to Watershed Falls?" Arkady asked.

"A few hours," Azquil said with a shrug. "If everything goes according to plan."

"So we've got a whole evening?" Arkady asked, looking very unhappy. "Tides, they could torch the village and everyone in it long before help arrives."

"I believe that's where you come in," Tiji reminded her. "You're supposed to stall the doctor's family by giving them your testimony about what happened. You're supposed to keep them busy."

"If Jojo's already told them what happened, that could be a very short conversation." Arkady put her hands on her hips. "Tides, why didn't Cayal and Declan just come back here to Watershed with us in the first place?"

"I believe the Immortal Prince wished to instruct the Glaeban Tide Lord in the use of Tide magic," Azquil said. "In private."

"Arryl could have come."

"Arryl is not a Tide Lord," Tiji reminded her. "She can't fight off three boatloads of marines."

"But apparently *I* can."

"Talk them to death," Tiji said, losing patience with her. "You're really good at that."

Arkady glared at Tiji for a moment, but she didn't respond. She turned to Azquil instead. "What's to stop your precious village elders from trussing me up and handing me over to Cydne's family, claiming it was all my fault?"

"The elders fear the wrath of the Trinity more than the wrath of the House Medura. You're not welcome here, Arkady, but the elders will do nothing to interfere with the plans of the immortals—particularly when those plans come with an assurance they will protect the wetlands from harm."

Arkady didn't look convinced. "Next time I'm sold into slavery, I'm going to put my hand up for a transfer to the mines."

"Female *makor-di* have a life expectancy of about two years in the mining camps of Senestra," Azquil told her.

"Two years?" Arkady looked impressed. "Tides, that's about a year and a half longer than I'm likely to survive as a flanking *wii-ah* for the Medura clan. What was I thinking?"

Azquil smiled. "Don't tell me you imagined being singled out by one owner would be safer than the anonymity of a whorehouse?"

"Seems such a foolish notion, in hindsight."

"But a noble one," Azquil said, as if he had finally found something worthy in the character of this woman who had, in his opinion, done nothing but cause trouble thus far. "Misguided and ill-informed, perhaps, but I suppose I'd have done something similar in your position."

"You'd never be in my position, Azquil. Your whole race has managed to stay hidden here in the wetlands for a thousand years. You lizards are too clever to get caught the way I was."

"I got caught," Tiji reminded them, a little peeved to see Azquil smiling at Arkady like that.

"You were drugged and stolen as a small child," Azquil said, putting his arm around her. "That doesn't count." Tiji felt her skin flickering as he touched her, but made no attempt to move away. He turned back to Arkady and added, "Besides, we've had immortal help to stay hidden."

"You had the help of the only three immortals, as far as I can tell," Arkady said, "who have a shred of humanity left in them. When Cydne's family gets here, you won't be relying on the Trinity for help. You'll be counting on one immortal who's suicidal and perverse, even on a good day, and another who doesn't even understand what it means."

"But don't you count both of these immortals friends?" Azquil asked.

Arkady hesitated and then nodded, somewhat reluctantly. "Sort of, I suppose."

"Then we will have to rely on your friends, Arkady, and hope you mean as much to them as they do to you."

Arkady didn't have anything to say to that, so she turned to the pot on the stove to stir the vegetables. They probably didn't need stirring, Tiji guessed, but it gave her somewhere else to look.

Tiji, on the other hand, had quite a bit she wanted to say about Declan and Cayal; however, she chose to remain silent, realising there was nothing she could add to the discussion that would help matters very much.

Chapter 50

"So much has changed," Elyssa said, looking around the bluff with a frown. "The trees are different. Tides, until they found the bones, I wasn't even sure this was the right place."

Warlock wondered at the strange location Elyssa had chosen for her picnic. They had been gone from the palace since before dawn to get here, and it was already mid-afternoon. They'd be lucky to see Cycrane again before midnight.

They had finally arrived here at Deadman's Bluff to discover what seemed to be some sort of archaeological dig. The snow had been cleared and a series of tents had been pitched across the top of the bluff to accommodate the small but busy work crew. To the left there was something that looked like a mining headframe that stretched out over the cliff with a small cage attached to ropes reaching down the cliff to the rocks some four hundred feet below. Shivering in the chill air, Warlock followed Elyssa to the largest tent where the braziers did little to warm the air and a small mountain of weathered and bleached human bones were laid out, as a number of earnest-looking young men apparently tried to put the skeletons back together again.

"Lady Alysa!"

Elyssa stopped and waited for the man who had hailed her to catch up. When he arrived, puffing heavily from the exertion, he bowed respectfully and then beamed at her. "You honour us with your presence, my lady. But truly, there was no need for you to come all this way. I was intending to visit you in Cycrane myself, early next month."

This then, was the man in charge. Warlock was a little surprised to realise he was Glaeban, not Caelish. Warlock looked around the camp with interest as the Glaeban—a balding man in his late fifties—caught his breath. He was rugged up against the cold, his nose red, his fingers protruding from fingerless gloves. He treated his unexpected visitor with such deference it was obvious Elyssa was either financing the excavation or supporting it in some other way. It was the only reason Warlock could think of to explain why she'd been welcomed so handsomely.

What are you up to now, I wonder?

"I didn't want to wait, Professor Fawk. What do you have to show me?"

"Were you looking for something in particular, my lady?"

"I'm interested in any possessions you've found."

Professor Fawk led the way forward and walked further into the large pavilion where the tables were covered in artefacts that, Warlock supposed, had been recovered from the site.

"We've counted twenty-two skulls," the professor informed his patron, as she strolled past the tables, stopping occasionally to examine an item of interest, "ranging from children to adults. We assume it's some sort of mass grave, although it seems some of the bodies were bound together, which is fascinating."

"Maybe they committed mass suicide," Elyssa suggested, not looking up from the broken wooden doll that had caught her interest. "They could have all jumped off the cliff together."

The professor treated Elyssa to a patronising smile, which—fortunately for him—she didn't notice. "My lady, such speculation is best left to the experts."

Elyssa put down the wooden doll and picked up a small wooden disk from a pile of several matching disks. From a distance, Warlock thought they might be old coins, but then he realised they were buttons from some long-dead human's rotted-away-to-nothing shirt.

"Have you found any religious artefacts?"

The professor shook his head. "I'm not sure what you would define as a religious artefact, my lady."

"Icons, statues of the Tide Lords . . ."

"Nothing, my lady, except an old set of Tarot cards."

Elyssa's head snapped up. "You found the cards? Show me?"

Warlock couldn't help thinking this was what Elyssa had been hoping to hear. In fact, she seemed so excited he began to wonder if it wasn't the purpose of this entire expedition. If Elyssa was the patron of this dig, if she was funding it, then it was probably because they were looking for something on her behalf.

How had she known where they needed to look?

Because there was a pile of bodies at the bottom of the cliff? Was she right when she suggested this wasn't a mass grave but the site of a mass suicide?

There was a good chance, Warlock realised with a leaden heart, that

Elyssa knew where to find the bodies because she was the one who'd sent them there.

The Glaeban professor led Elyssa to another table near the back of the pavilion. On this one lay a large deck of cards. Although they were rotted around the edges and faded with age, they'd been protected by the now very fragile leather case in which they'd been stored. The professor pushed aside the young man working on slowly peeling the cards apart, so that Elyssa could see.

"This is it?"

"Yes, my lady."

"How is it they're still intact?"

"There is a small depression at the base of the cliff, my lady," the assistant explained. "It seems quite soon after the bodies were placed there, a rockfall sealed them in."

"It's been most fortunate for us," Fawk added. "One would not normally expect to find something made of paper wrapped in leather to have survived so long in less ideal conditions."

"Is the whole deck there?" she asked, eyeing the cards with awe.

"As far as we can tell."

Trying to look past her shoulder without being too obvious about it, Warlock thought he might explode, trying to contain his curiosity. After a moment, Elyssa turned and beckoned him closer. "Do you know what this is, Cecil?"

"A Tide Lord Tarot, my lady."

Elyssa shook her head. "It's much more than that," she said. "It's a Lore Tarot."

Even Warlock had heard of the Lore Tarot. It was—supposedly—the true story of the Tide Lords, not the romanticised version peddled in the markets of every city on Amyrantha, which bored noblewomen used to tell each other's fortunes. A Lore Tarot was something precious, and usually only found in the possession of a Crasii elder. Or the Guardian of the Lore, the human keeper of the Tide Lord history—one of the few in the Cabal entrusted with the truth.

But how had it finished up here? In a cave at the bottom of a cliff amid a pile of bones?

And how had Elyssa known where to look for it?

The professor seemed impressed by her knowledge, and smiled at her the way a professional would smile at an enthusiastic amateur. "You are absolutely right, my lady. It is indeed a Lore Tarot."

"It's beautiful," Elyssa said.

"We've never found a complete set before now, my lady. This is valuable beyond words. I trust your investment has paid off?"

"More than you know," she said, not taking her eyes off the fragile cards. "How long before you have them all separated out?"

"It's very delicate work, my lady," the professor told her with a frown. "It could be another two or three weeks."

Elyssa pursed her lips unhappily as she debated, no doubt, the advisability of insisting the job be finished sooner against the risk of damaging the cards. "When they are separated, before you show them to another soul, you are to bring them to me," the immortal instructed.

"But, my lady . . ."

"I am not asking, Professor Fawk, I am ordering you to do this." She looked around the camp meaningfully and then fixed her gaze on the professor. "I paid for this dig. I am paying your way and if it wasn't for me, your pathetic little university in Lebec would still be begging the crown for money to keep its doors open."

Warlock stared at the professor in surprise. *This man is from Lebec? Tides, I wonder if that means he knew the Duchess Arkady?* She was a historian too working at the university in Lebec.

Had the Duke of Lebec's fall affected so many?

He supposed it might. Stellan Desean had been known as a philanthropist, after all. It wasn't hard to imagine his money had supported a university in his city. In fact, it almost had to be the case. A city the size of Lebec would not normally have its own place of higher learning without some serious support from its provincial duke. And if that was the case, then it wasn't hard to imagine how Elyssa had been able to secure the services of a reputable academic like Andre Fawk for her excavation. With Stellan Desean no longer the Duke of Lebec, the university would have been starved for funds.

Elyssa's money must have looked very attractive.

Right up until now, when he found out the real cost.

"My lady, the Caelish authorities were very insistent about the fate of any historical—"

"What Caelish authorities?" Elyssa scoffed. "I am all the Caelish *authority* you need. My brother is married to the queen, in case it slipped your mind."

Fawk, to his credit, wasn't so easily dissuaded. "Be that as it may, my lady, this site is of significant historical interest to the people of Caelum."

"Until I told you about it, not you, the people of Caelum, or any other pitiful sod you care to name, even knew this significant historical site was here. So, I will take whatever I want from your wretched little dig, professor—the dig that *I* am paying for—and there's not a damned thing you can do to stop me."

"These cards belong to Caelum, my lady," the professor insisted. "If you want a souvenir, then we can find you something much less fragile. But these cards . . . you can't sell them. Unless they have been authenticated . . ."

"I don't intend to sell them," she said. "But I do intend to have them in my possession within the fortnight." Elyssa turned to Warlock. "And to make certain I have them, I'm leaving Cecil here to watch over them."

"There is really no need . . ."

"I believe there is," she said. "I think the moment my back is turned, you're going to try to smuggle those cards out of here in some misguided attempt to preserve Caelum's history. Or enrich Lebec University's rapidly dwindling coffers. No. Cecil stays. He will watch over these cards and any attempt to harm them, or remove them, and he will tear your throat out. Won't you, Cecil?"

"To serve you is the reason I breathe, my lady."

She smiled and reached up to pat the side of his face. "There's a good boy, Cecil." Then she turned to the historian. "Are we clear, now?"

Professor Fawk glared at Warlock and then shook his head reluctantly. "I shall have them delivered to you as soon as they are separated, my lady."

"Then the world is as it should be," Elyssa said with a smile, at complete odds with her dire threat to have Warlock tear the throat out of any man who defied her. She turned to leave the tent, but Fawk called her back, helpless to do anything about her order, but furious, nonetheless.

"What do you want with them?"

She turned to look at him. "I beg your pardon?"

"From the moment you first approached me with the location of this site, you've been talking about finding a Tarot. You knew these bodies were here. I've a feeling you knew we'd find the Tarot deck too. Do you know what happened in this place, my lady? Do you know how these people died?"

Warlock was expecting Elyssa to deny any knowledge of the event, but she surprised him. "A handful of mere mortals defied a Tide Lord," she said in a voice that chilled every man in the tent. "And it would serve you well to remember their fate, professor, before you do the same."

Chapter 51

It was just on sunset when the first of the House Medura ships arrived in Watershed Falls. Arkady didn't see them dock, but she saw their passengers, sure enough, after they landed, heading down the street toward the cottage that had so recently been Cydne's clinic.

A full troop of marines armed with swords and truncheons, wearing the distinctive bottle green of House Pardura, marched on the house in the rapidly gathering darkness. Leading the marines was a heavyset man wearing an expensive waistcoat and a heavily embroidered jacket that must be killing him in this heat. Walking beside him, under a parasol carried by a canine Crasii slave, was Cydne's young wife, Olegra.

"Tides, that's all I need."

"You know this man?" Azquil asked. They stood on the veranda, watching the delegation approach. Arkady was standing at the railing. Azquil stood behind her. Between the shadows and his natural ability to fade into his surroundings, he blended almost perfectly with the wall.

"I know the girl. She's Cydne's wife." Arkady was amazed at how calm she sounded. She didn't feel it. Her stomach was churning and she'd broken into a cold sweat.

Despite their assurances that they would be in Watershed Falls before she was in any real danger, there was no sign of the immortals. Everyone else in the village had wisely made themselves scarce too. For all intents and purposes, Arkady was facing the wrath of House Medura on her own.

"Does this woman know you?" Azquil asked softly behind her.

"Better than that. She actively despises me."

"Then you should be able to use that to stall her," he said.

Arkady didn't reply. The delegation had reached the cottage.

Taking a deep breath, she turned and walked down the two short steps to the grass to meet them. The troop fell into place with a clatter of metal and shuffling of many booted feet, followed by some more shuffling in the rear, as someone was shoved forward. The man in the jacket made several hand signals, and some of the troops dispersed, probably to search the house and its surrounds. She hoped Azquil and Tiji stayed well hidden.

Arkady stopped in front of Olegra and the man she assumed was one of Cydne's brothers-in-law, as a ginger feline, chained and bleeding, was thrown to the ground at Arkady's feet. It was Jojo, Cydne's bodyguard. There was no question now who'd raised the alarm and tipped off Cydne's family to his fate.

There was no sign of Ambria and Medwen, however. Perhaps they'd been taken back to Port Traeker. Clearly, the news of Cydne's death had reached that far already. Olegra wouldn't be here otherwise.

"This will be *your* fate, whore," Olegra announced, glaring at Arkady with undiluted venom, "unless you tell us the truth about the fate of my husband."

Not wasting any time on small talk, I see. For a girl not yet eighteen, she carried herself like she owned the world and every slave in it, including Arkady.

"He's dead."

"Who killed him?"

"He died of swamp fever."

"Lying bitch."

With a snap of his fingers, the man standing beside Olegra ordered two men forward. They quickly flanked Arkady, grabbing her by the arms with bruising force, and pushed her down until she was kneeling on the grass.

Arkady didn't resist. There wasn't any point.

Now would be a very good time, Declan, for you to appear out of nowhere and save me again. Or Cayal. Arkady wasn't really bothered at this juncture which one of them turned up.

Just so long as *one* of them did.

Olegra's brother stepped forward and pointed at Jojo. The feline was on her knees also, bleeding from multiple lash wounds and looking scared witless. Felines were tough little creatures, but they didn't take well to being tortured and restrained. *Not that anybody really relishes being tortured and restrained,* Arkady thought, *except maybe those clients who used to frequent that place in the slums near Shalimar's attic.* The one whose girls would come to her father to treat their wounds on an almost weekly basis. *The place my father forbade me to go anywhere near . . .*

Arkady forced her attention back to the present, feeling herself retreating from the pain already, even though it hadn't started yet.

"This creature claims my brother-in-law was murdered. Two village women arrived in the Delta Settlement a few hours later to inform us he died of swamp fever. As a consequence, I am sure of only two things. My sister's husband is dead and someone must pay for it."

"The village women were right," Arkady said, wondering why Ambria and Medwen weren't here, bleeding and beaten like Jojo. "Cydne died of the fever. I've been stuck here ever since, waiting for someone to come and fetch me, actually. Can we go home now?"

"Liar!" Olegra screamed, pushing her brother out of the way. She back-handed Arkady with all the force she could muster, which turned out to be not much at all. Although her head jerked backward with the slap, it didn't do much more than sting Arkady's cheek a little. "Cydne was immune to the fever. The guild would never have sent him to this Tide-forsaken swamp otherwise!"

"If you know that, why bother asking me?" Arkady said, irritated by this obnoxious young woman who'd been the direct cause of Cydne's fumbling attentions these past few months. Were it not for the impossible demands of this spoiled child, Arkady might not have had to warm her husband's bed nearly so often.

"Watch your tongue, you foreign slut! You're a slave! You can't speak to me like that!"

Arkady was sorry now that she'd allowed Ambria to replace her healed brand with a false one. She didn't feel like a slave. Part of her problem was that she never had. Although she knew she mustn't, Arkady wanted to climb to her feet and stare this girl down; intimidate her with all the withering contempt she could summon. The sort of look she used to give Jaxyn when she was the Duchess of Lebec. After all, if she could make a Tide Lord hesitate with an icy stare, Arkady was quite certain she could eviscerate this irritating child with the same look.

Olegra sensed her defiance, even if Arkady hadn't spoken it aloud.

"Don't you dare look at me in that manner," she said, her face beet-red with fury. "You are *nothing*, you hear me! Nothing but a foreign whore who tried to weasel her way into my household by beguiling my husband!"

"Maybe if you'd been more of a wife and less of a shrew, he wouldn't have been so easy to beguile." That was actually the truth. Arkady was quite sure Cydne's fascination for his foreign slave would have faded very quickly if he'd had something worth going home to.

Not surprisingly, her insolence earned her another slap. Anger had lent Olegra strength. This one actually hurt.

Tides, Cayal . . . Declan. Where are you?

"You will tell us what happened," Olegra's brother insisted. "And you will do it without insulting my sister."

Just take your time, boys, she muttered silently. *No reason to hurry. I can go for hours before I pass out from the pain . . .*

"The Trinity killed him," Arkady said, deciding there was nothing to be gained by trying to invent anything more creative. The truth was strange enough.

"Trinity? What's the Trinity? What's she talking about, Ulag?"

"She speaks of the Crasii goddesses," Olegra's brother replied. "All these wretched swamp creatures believe in them."

Olegra rolled her eyes with scorn. "Oh, so it was the will of the *goddesses*, was it? Why? Did they not like the sound of a civilised accent?"

"Actually, I think it had more to do with the few score Crasii your husband poisoned at the behest of the Senestran Physicians' Guild," she replied. "Not sure they even noticed his accent."

The charge obviously took Olegra completely by surprise. She'd raised her hand to hit Arkady again, but held back, turning instead to her brother. "What is she talking about?"

"Cydne was here helping the Crasii, Olegra."

"No, he wasn't," Arkady said. Her eyes narrowed as she studied the brother. "Tides, you knew about it too. Didn't you? That's why you're asking *how* he died, not *if*."

"My husband would never harm a helpless creature," Olegra insisted. "He came here to heal the sick."

"He came here with a couple of gallons of wood alcohol disguised as a curative tonic," Arkady told her. "And it was a curative too. Only it cured *life*. Permanently."

"You scandalous bitch!" Olegra shouted, this time pounding Arkady with small, ineffectual fists. "Don't you dare say things like that about my husband! He comes from one of the best families in Port Traeker!"

"He was strung up by the Trinity," Arkady said, directing her comments to the brother. "They tied him to the Justice Tree and let the gobie ants take him."

"No!" Olegra squealed. "I don't believe you!"

"Who delivered this sentence?" Ulag demanded. He turned and called to the rapidly gathering night, "Step forward, this fool who claims to speak for the Trinity, and show me proof of your right to pass sentence on a free man!"

Of course, nothing happened. Cayal didn't magically appear, nor did Arryl or Declan.

So much for being rescued in the nick of time . . .

"Seems your Trinity isn't here to defend themselves."

"Probably don't consider you important enough," she replied, figuring she was doomed anyway, so it really didn't matter much at this point how disrespectful she was. Arkady had been biting her tongue for months around these people. She was thoroughly fed up with all of them. If Declan and Cayal weren't going to make it in time to save her, she wasn't going to die kowtowing to these fools.

Cydne would not be the only one in Watershed Falls to die free.

"I *want* these people, Ulag," Olegra demanded of her brother, stamping her foot like the spoiled child she was. "Not just this lying slut, but every soul in this village and every other village in the wetlands who thinks they can claim their ridiculous religion justifies killing an innocent man."

"As opposed to *your* ridiculous religion?" Arkady said. "Don't you worship the Lord of Temperance? Well, I've met your precious Lord of Temperance, Olegra, and he's a right little prick, actually. Did you know he sleeps with men *and* women? And drinks. And gambles. And generally skips through life whoring around like a sailor after six months at sea."

Olegra slapped her again—as Arkady knew she would—but she was still alive, which was something to be grateful for.

It was questionable how much longer that state of affairs would remain in effect, however, if Cayal, Arryl and Declan didn't get here soon.

"Shut up!" Olegra cried. "You do not have permission to speak!"

"Don't need it," Arkady said, a little bit horrified to realise she was enjoying herself. Of course, they hadn't actually done anything to her yet, besides slap her around a bit. She doubted this would be quite as much fun if Olegra's brother was doing the hitting, but the looks on the faces of these arrogant merchants, confronted with true defiance from a slave for the first time in their smug, self-righteous lives, was really quite exhilarating. "Did you know your husband made me give him lessons on how to touch you, Olegra? *Where* to touch you . . . what to say . . ."

Olegra let out another incomprehensible squeal, but it was carried away by a sudden gust of wind. All around them, the trees began to tremble with a breeze that blew so forcefully Olegra was pushed into her brother, who was forced to brace himself or be blown over. Although she couldn't feel them working the Tide, Arkady sagged with relief, guessing nothing natural had caused this sudden change in the weather.

However tardy, rescue in the form of the Trinity—or at least, this latest version of it—had arrived.

Chapter 52

Watershed Falls had been all but deserted when Declan arrived with Cayal and Arryl as the sun sank below the horizon. Insects buzzed in the twilight, but generally ignored the immortals, an unexpected bonus Declan hadn't noticed until now.

There were three ships clustered about the dock, but only the larger vessel seemed to have disembarked passengers. It had a gangway lowered to the wharf and a number of guards posted around it. They paid little attention, however, to the three unarmed civilians disembarking from their small, Crasii-towed craft, in the shadow of the larger vessel, until they attempted to head toward the village.

"Come along, dear," Cayal said, putting his arm around Arryl. "Once we get to mother's house, you can rest."

A marine from the docked vessel stepped in front of them, hand on the hilt of his sword, blocking their way forward.

"Where do you think you lot are going?"

"To my mother's house in the village," Cayal explained in Senestran so perfect he sounded like a local. "My wife is ill. I think it's swamp fever, something she would never have caught if her half-witted brother . . ." he jerked his head in Declan's direction, ". . . hadn't got himself fired from his job in the flax fields and we had to go fetch him and bring him home. Now, if you don't mind, let us pass. My wife needs rest, and I need to have a long talk with my shiftless brother-in-law."

The guard studied Arryl, who had was leaning weakly on Cayal as she groaned, and then glared at Declan with the sort of look one reserved for shiftless brothers-in-law. "You're to go straight home, understand? No hanging around the village."

"Thank you, admiral," Cayal said. "That's exactly what I plan to do."

The marine stood back to let them pass. Arryl allowed Cayal to help her down the wharf, not moving out of his embrace until the bulk of the ship blocked them from the view of the guards.

She smiled as Cayal let her go, glancing back at the ship. "Long time since we've done something like that, Cayal."

He smiled smugly at them both. "You'll note I haven't lost my deft touch."

"Yes," Declan agreed, a little disturbed at how easily subterfuge came to these people, even Arryl, who hadn't hesitated to fall in with Cayal's lies. "You're a remarkably good liar."

"We're all remarkably good liars," Cayal said with a shrug. "As you will be too, if you're not already, spymaster, once you've had a few thousand years of practice."

Cayal didn't give Declan an opportunity to respond. He turned to Arryl, and with a courtly bow indicated she should lead the way. Declan fell in beside Cayal, seething with the need to do something about the Immortal Prince. Cayal was driving him insane with his constant needling. The only thing holding Declan back was the knowledge that Cayal was doing it for precisely that reason, and by not retaliating, he was probably having a similar effect on Cayal.

It took a few minutes to reach the street where the house-turned-clinic was located. They walked past one darkened house after another. Apparently, the residents of Watershed Falls were staying out of the way of this potentially nasty confrontation. Many of them had probably fled the village and made their way further into the wetlands, seeking shelter with friends and family in other settlements until the fuss over the death of Cydne Medura died down.

The street and the small grassed yard at the front of the cottage was crowded with troops when they turned the corner. Arryl stopped, still unnoticed by the men ahead of them, and turned to Cayal.

"How do you want to do this?"

"You do the talking," Cayal said. "That'll leave me and the sprog here free to wreak some havoc." He glanced around, spied a reasonably straight fallen branch by the side of the road, picked it up and handed it to Arryl. "Here. Take this. Goddesses always look more impressive when they're wielding fire."

The Tide surged and the end of the impromptu staff burst into flame. Squinting against the sudden brightness, Declan wasn't sure if it was Cayal or Arryl who'd made it happen, though.

"Shall I tell them who you are?"

"Tell them I'm the Immortal Prince?" Cayal shrugged. "Sure. They want to name their silly Tarot after us, let's play along." He turned to Declan. "What shall we call you, spymaster? You're not in the Tarot, are you?" Cayal made a show of thinking about it and then turned back to Arryl, smiling brightly. "I know, he can fill in for Coron, seeing as how the rat is dead. Tell them this is The Rodent."

"Cayal . . ."

"It's all right, Arryl," Declan said. "I think I'd rather be named after a rat than some other immortals I could name."

Cayal didn't miss the dig, but chose to ignore it. He turned toward the house with a sweep of the cloak he was wearing—and had insisted the others wear as well—and plunged into the Tide.

The breeze picked up as they approached the house, the marines looking around in confusion. As with the guards at the wharf, they made no attempt to reach for their weapons, considering three unarmed strangers no threat. But there was something about them that worried the men, because they opened ranks to allow the newcomers through, without being asked. Declan wasn't sure if that was because they looked so impressive with their billowing cloaks and Arryl's blazing staff, or if, as soldiers, they were just conditioned to respond to anybody who looked as if they were in command.

When they finally found Arkady, it was to discover she was on her knees before a Senestran man and woman, their backs to the new arrivals, who'd probably been interrogating her.

"She's still alive," Arryl remarked, sounding a little surprised.

"Told you we'd make it in time," Cayal added in a low voice.

At that moment, Arkady spied the immortals coming up the street and looked at her captors. "Might be a good idea to kneel," she called, loud enough for the immortals to catch her words. Declan guessed she was yelling to make sure her warning carried on the unnatural breeze. "You're about to meet a few of *your* gods."

The man and woman both turned to look behind them as the marines fell back. Declan wondered at the sight this impromptu Trinity made, coming up the road with the last of the sunset behind them. The burning staff Arryl carried, blazing far too bright for mere man-made fire . . . the Sorceress of the Tide, flanked by two dangerous-looking men, cloaks billowing theatrically in Cayal's magically induced breeze . . . Declan didn't know where the cloaks had come from—who even *owned* a cloak out here in this wretched heat? He guessed their entrance was likely to impress even the most cynical non-believer.

Arkady smiled at them, looking mightily relieved, as the wind died down and Arryl stepped forward into the sudden calm.

"Release them!" she commanded, pointing at Arkady and a wounded ginger feline who lay on the ground beside her, using what was, Declan assumed, her very best Sorceress of the Tide voice. It certainly wasn't the way she'd spoken to anybody back at the Outpost.

The marines holding Arkady did as she bid without any further encouragement, reacting instinctively to the authority in her voice. Nobody moved to release the chained feline, however, who lay a few feet away.

The man in charge recovered first, obviously annoyed by the lack of resistance from his men. "I am Ulag Pardura," he said, pushing his sister behind him, "of the House Pardura, here representing the House Medura. I don't know who you are, but this is a company matter. You have no business here."

"I am Arryl, Sorceress of the Tide."

"I don't care if you're the Lord of Temperance himself," the man replied, unimpressed. "You have no business here."

Arkady climbed to her feet, rubbing her bruised arms. "She is, you know. You'd better pay attention."

Olegra turned to Arkady, forced to look up at her now her slave was standing. "Silence, whore!" Then she added to the guards who had just released her, "I did not command you to let the slave go."

"I'm not your slave, you stupid little bitch," she told Olegra, grabbing the edge of the fake slave brand where she'd been picking at it. She tore the brand off and tossed it at Olegra.

"Lay another hand on that woman and you will regret it," Arryl warned, before Olegra could react. "She is a disciple of mine and under my protection."

Wisely, the men didn't move.

The young woman was livid. "Don't listen to her! I commanded you to arrest this murderous slut!"

The men wavered with indecision for a moment and then nodded to their mistress. Declan struck as soon as they moved toward Arkady. He plunged into the Tide as Cayal had instructed earlier, pushing the air away from the two marines, who began to suffocate before his very eyes. He felt the Tide surge and every man present began to gasp and pull at their collars. Cayal was doing the same to the rest of the marines. Within moments, the only mortals in the vicinity still able to breathe were Arkady, the wounded feline on the ground, Ulag Pardura and the young woman beside him.

Pardura looked around in a panic as his men began to fall. "What's happening! What are you doing?"

Interesting, Declan thought, *that Pardura knows the source of the trouble without asking.* Perhaps he was one of the men who'd tried to torture the truth out of Medwen and Ambria and discovered the immortals were still among them.

"You will leave the wetlands," Arryl said. "And you will not return, except for one ship, which will bring my sisters—whom you currently hold prisoner—back to me."

"I don't know what—"

"If you fail," Arryl continued, as if he hadn't spoken, "then I will allow my brothers to wreak the punishment they believe you and your people deserve. You will agree to this now, and without conditions, or your men will die, followed by you and your young lady friend here." Arryl glanced around at the choking marines dispassionately. "Make up your mind, puny mortal. You have about thirty seconds before your men begin to die."

Ulag Pardura looked as if he was going to quibble about it, so Declan pushed a little harder, sucking the air away from the young woman as well.

The moment she began to choke, the mortal surrendered. "All right! Stop it! I agree!"

Exhilarated by the surging Tide, Declan stopped pushing the air away with some reluctance, allowing it to rush back into the void. The young woman began to cry inconsolably. The soldiers he'd been restraining began to cough and splutter as their starved lungs gulped in the precious air.

Arryl turned to Cayal and smiled. "You see. I told you mortals could be reasonable." Then she turned back to Ulag Pardura. "Leave now. You have two days to return with my sisters. If you fail, the last swamp-fever epidemic to devastate Port Traeker will seem merciful by comparison to the destruction my brothers will rain down on your pitiful lives."

"What about my husband?" the girl asked, through her tears.

"Your husband has paid for his crimes, child," Arryl said. "Be grateful I don't hold you responsible for them too."

The doctor's wife looked like she might argue the point, but the man grabbed her by the arm and pulled her close, whispering something in her ear, after which she visibly calmed down. He then turned and ordered his men to withdraw.

A few moments later, with a canine slave on her heels whose sole function seemed to be to hold her parasol, the young Lady Medura headed back through the village with her marines and her brother in tow.

Declan hurried to Arkady to see if she was harmed, but she was kneeling on the ground, pulling the chains from the wounded feline.

"Are you all right?"

"I'm fine. This is Jojo. Can you help her?"

He squatted down by Arkady and studied the feline curiously. "Isn't she the feline who betrayed you to the doctor's family?"

"She's Crasii, Declan. It wasn't her fault. She wouldn't have known what else to do."

Declan frowned, not sure he was quite as forgiving as Arkady. The feline pushed herself onto her knees, clearly in agony, but nonetheless determined to kneel before him. "To . . . to serve you . . . is the reason I breathe . . ."

Tides, I wish they'd stop doing that . . .

"Are you unharmed, Arkady?" Arryl asked, coming up behind them.

She nodded. "Jojo's in a bad way, though. I was just asking Declan to help her."

Arryl shook her head. "Let's not go *there* again, for a while. Not until your friend here figures out what he's doing. I'll heal your little friend. In the meantime, Declan, why don't you and Cayal follow our friends back to their ship? Just to make sure they leave."

Declan nodded and rose to his feet. "Do you think they'll be back?"

"For certain."

"Will they bring Medwen and Ambria?"

"Probably."

He studied Arryl's face in the light of her blazing staff. "But you don't think they plan to surrender them?"

"Not without us having to make the point much more forcibly the second time around," Cayal said, his back to them as he watched the mortals cautiously retreating toward the village and their ships.

Arryl nodded in agreement. "Mortals often need to be told things more than once, Declan, before they absorb the lesson. Not a trait uncommon among *im*mortals, either."

Declan was fairly sure she was having a dig at him, but not entirely certain what he'd done to deserve it. He turned to Arkady. "Will you be all right?"

She nodded. "Go. Help Cayal rid us of all those *puny* mortals."

Arryl smiled. "Can you believe I said that without cracking so much as a smile?"

Declan was astonished at how smug Arryl sounded. He smiled at her childlike glee.

"You were very convincing," Cayal assured her.

"Kentravyon does it better."

"I thought you said he was a psychotic murderer?" Declan said.

"Which is *why* he does it so much better," she replied. "Now go, Declan, and give Cayal a hand. Arkady, you can help me get this poor creature inside so we can fix her. Where are Azquil and Tiji?"

"I told them to hide until the soldiers left."

"Then they should be back soon. As soon as they reappear, have them boil some water."

"You'll need it to bathe her wounds?"

"Not at all," Arryl said to Arkady, lifting the feline between them, as Declan headed off with Cayal in pursuit of the fleeing marines. "I can heal her injuries with the Tide. The water is for me, dear. I'd like a cup of tea."

Chapter 53

They waited on the dock until the last of the ships had been towed out of sight by the amphibians before Cayal judged it safe to return to the house where Arkady and Arryl waited. It was well and truly dark by then, the night filled with the chittering song of a million hungry insects, none of whom, Cayal had been delighted to discover, considered him edible.

Declan Hawkes waited beside him, hands thrust deep into his pockets, full of questions, full of doubt, full of anger and full of awe. Cayal vaguely remembered feeling the same way once, several eons ago. Discovering the Tide was a dangerous yet wondrous time for a new immortal, and while he mistrusted and disliked the spymaster, he couldn't help but envy him his journey.

At least until the poor sod realises it's a journey without end, he amended silently. The voyage lost its allure when one came to understand what eternity *really* meant.

But this new immortal was still in that halcyon phase of discovery all immortals went through, no matter how unwillingly.

Declan Hawkes *knew* he was immortal, but he didn't *understand* it yet.

Which raised the question, yet again, of how Hawkes could even exist.

Cayal wasn't sure how he felt about that. Instinct told him Hawkes would be a dangerous adversary, but knowing Lukys needed all the power he could muster to end Cayal's life, finding a new Tide Lord, one who wasn't yet involved in the politics of immortals, was beyond good fortune. Cayal was fairly certain it wasn't luck, though. The likelihood of this new immortal being the result of random chance was so remote it was effectively impossible. Lukys learning Maralyce had borne a child was much more plausible. That he'd waited until the child had fathered a daughter he could impregnate was much more likely too than the idea of another immortal just happening by a brothel in Lebec, to do the deed by accident.

What probably *was* chance, Cayal figured, was Hawkes being caught in a fire that, had he not been more than half-immortal already, should have killed him.

Cayal knew Lukys had gone to Glaeba looking for his son. He wondered now if that's why he returned early. Was it because when he got there, his son was gone? Had Lukys heard the news of Declan Hawkes's death and written off his experiment as a failure?

Is that why he'd gone to Jelidia and awakened Kentravyon? Because he needed the power of another Tide Lord for his plans, and thought the new, much more malleable (not to mention sane) one he'd been trying to manufacture, was lost to him?

It was going to be interesting to see the look on Lukys's face, Cayal decided, when he returned to Jelidia with Hawkes, all bright and shiny and alive—and immortal.

Of course, that raised another question Cayal had been carefully avoiding until now. If Lukys had been responsible for this, what was he really up to? Not for a moment did Cayal believe Lukys would go to all this trouble just to help him die.

Lukys telling Cayal he wanted to be God didn't seem so far-fetched these days. Not if he was out there making new immortals.

"So what happens when they return in force?"

Cayal pushed aside that alarming thought to answer Hawkes. "We'll have to give them a memorable lesson in the perils of pissing off a Tide Lord."

Hawkes cracked a rare smile. He was slowly being seduced, Cayal knew, by the power he now commanded. "And how do we do that? By choking every man they send after us?"

Cayal shook his head. "Tide's not up far enough to do anything on that scale. Besides, you start sucking the air out of anything but the most localised area, it'll affect the weather. And that never seems to work well for anybody."

"I'm surprised something like that bothers you."

"That's because you're a narrow-minded, judgemental son-of-a-bitch," Cayal replied pleasantly, "who thinks all immortals are evil. How are you coping with that, by the way? You know . . . being evil?"

"I'm thinking of growing a moustache and maybe wearing an eye patch," Hawkes replied without missing a beat. "So I can look the part too."

Cayal smiled. Hawkes might be a narrow-minded, judgemental son-of-a-bitch, but he was quick. "Sorry, old son, but that's not going to happen unless you had one the day you were immolated. Whatever hair you had the day you became immortal, that's pretty much what you're stuck with until the end of time."

"Good thing I didn't get immortalised with a bad haircut," Hawkes said with a faint smile. "But still, that would explain why I haven't had to shave in months. Why is that, do you think?"

"I have no idea."

"But you must have wondered about it?"

"Wondered, yes," Cayal said. "Cared about it? No."

Hawkes fell silent for a time, staring out over the dark water of the channel. After a while, he turned to Cayal. "Do you think they've gone now?"

He nodded. "Certain of it. I ordered the amphibians towing the boats not to stop until they reached the Delta Settlement. No mere human is going to be able to override that compulsion any time soon." He turned from the water to look back at the darkened village. "We should probably get back to the others."

Declan nodded in agreement, falling in beside Cayal as they turned toward the town. "And when they come back? What then?"

"We'll give them something else to think about other than murdering the inhabitants of the wetlands."

"Can you do that, though?" Hawkes said, unconvinced. "Like you said, the Tide's not all the way up and Pardura didn't strike me as the type to give up easily. If he comes back here in force . . ."

"Then so much the better," Cayal said.

"I don't understand."

"That's because in addition to being a narrow-minded, judgemental son-of-a-bitch, you appear to be quite stupid."

Hawkes stopped walking. Cayal took a few steps further, realised Hawkes was no longer with him, and then turned to find out why.

The spymaster was glaring at him.

"*What*?"

"You done?"

Cayal smiled. "Oh, dear, I've hurt your precious little feelings, haven't I?"

"You're starting to piss me off, Cayal."

"And what are you planning to do about it, Rodent?" Cayal asked. He'd been needling Hawkes for days now and this was the first time he'd gotten any sort of reaction out of him. "Call me out over it? Challenge me to a duel, perhaps? To the *death*?"

"No," Hawkes said. "I'll leave."

"Now I'm really quaking in my boots."

Hawkes shrugged. "I don't care whether you're quaking or not. Fact is, Cayal, you need me a whole lot more than I need you."

"I *need* you?" He laughed at the very idea. "Tides, Hawkes, I could lay waste to these entire wetlands without raising a sweat. You think I need *your* help to get Ambria and Medwen back? You don't even know which way in the Tide is up." He turned and headed back up the street.

"You're the immortal who wants to die, Cayal," Declan said to his retreating back.

Cayal stopped and slowly turned to look at him.

"You're the suicidal maniac who needs all the Tide Lord power you can muster to make it happen," Hawkes added with the certainty of a man absolutely sure of his position. "I don't even know if all those things you said about Lukys being my father are true. What I *do* know is that you need my help a whole lot more than I need yours."

"You need my help to find Lukys."

The spymaster shook his head. "I'm immortal, Cayal; I've got the time to find him on my own."

Cayal stared at the spymaster, mentally kicking himself for overlooking the fact that Hawkes's quick wit was more than likely the result of above-average intelligence. It was a foolish mistake to make. And it wasn't that he didn't *know* the two went hand in hand.

Tides, this man made a living out of lying, spying and manipulating people.
Like father, like son?

"So what are you offering?"

Hawkes smiled. "What am *I* offering? You're the one who should be offering me a deal. I found what I came for and I can leave with it any time I please."

"*Arkady?*" Cayal smiled at the bald-faced gall of the man. "Is that your price?"

"You'll only hurt her, Cayal."

"And you won't?"

"I care about her."

"Funny, she doesn't seem to care too much for you that I've noticed. Actually, she seems to hate your guts."

"That's for me and Arkady to work out. You do nothing but distract her. And let's face it, she's nothing but a distraction to you too."

Hawkes was right about that. Arkady made Cayal want to live. And this man had the power to help him die.

When he thought about it like that, it was a pretty tidy package, really.

"Fine," he said with a shrug. "She's yours."

Hawkes seemed suspicious of his quick capitulation. "Just like that? You're not even going to argue about it?"

"What would be the point?" Cayal asked with a shrug. "You're right. What's even more annoying, you *know* you're right. I *want* Arkady, but I *need* you. And I want to die more than I want Arkady."

"Then it's settled," Hawkes said, taking a step closer. "You leave Arkady alone . . . no, you make it quite clear you have no interest in her, and I'll come with you to Jelidia and help you die."

Cayal thrust his hand forward to shake on the deal. "Done!"

Somewhat more cautiously, Declan accepted his handshake. Cayal wasn't going to let it rest there, however. It was one thing to let the spymaster win this argument, quite another to have him feeling smug about it.

"You help me die, and I leave your girl alone," he agreed, and then added with a jaded smile, "Suits me, anyway. I've already slept with her. Your turn now."

Hawkes's fist slammed into his face, sending him flying, almost before he finished speaking. Cayal didn't retaliate. He didn't have to. He'd made his point and they both knew it, so he lay on the ground on his back, the metallic tang of blood filling his mouth, and waited. Hawkes stood over him, shaking his stinging fist, and then after a few moments, when he realised Cayal wasn't going to get up and fight back, he turned and strode back toward the cottage, cursing.

Once he was gone, Cayal pushed himself up, dabbing at his painful, bloody nose. He smiled. Arkady was lost to him, but he was assured of the power of another Tide Lord to help him die.

That was worth more than a punch in the face. Tides, it was everything he had ever wanted.

Chapter 54

"There, how does that feel?"

The feline, Jojo, sitting on the edge of the scrubbed wooden table, touched her face tentatively, her round eyes full of wonder. "It's all better!"

"Of course it's all better. That's what I do." Smiling, Arryl turned to Arkady. "They beat her, sure enough, with a knotted rope, probably. But it looked a lot worse than it was. All that blood matted in her fur didn't help either."

"It's a remarkable thing to watch someone being healed by magic," Arkady said. She'd been too busy denying the truth when Cayal cut off his fingers trying to prove he was immortal, to pay attention to the process. And when Declan came to her rescue and did the same to her, she was half-dead and delirious. Watching Arryl work had been quite a revelation.

Arryl nodded in agreement and turned back to Jojo. "Why don't you go clean yourself up, dear?" she said, probably aware of how much felines hated to be dirty. "And then come back here when you're done."

"To serve you is the reason I breathe, my lady," Jojo said, hopping off the kitchen table. The little ginger feline bowed and turned for the door with her freshly healed wounds, snarling silently as the door opened before she reached it and Azquil walked into the small kitchen with Tiji close behind. With teeth bared, she pushed past the two chameleons and disappeared into the darkness.

"What was *that* about?" Arkady asked, wondering at the feline's odd behaviour.

"We don't get along with her kind," Azquil explained. "They think we're prey and we think they're murderers."

"It's an age-old prejudice," Arryl said. "Many of the natural instincts of the original animals the Crasii were formed from have followed them into their unique version of humanity." She shrugged. "Cats like to play with lizards."

"They like to *torment* lizards," Azquil corrected, "right before they kill them."

"You don't seriously think Jojo would try to kill one of you, do you?"

"She would if an immortal ordered her to."

Arkady glanced at Arryl. "Well, that's not likely to happen here, is it?"

"That doesn't mean another immortal wouldn't tell her to do it," Tiji said with a frown, obviously referring to Cayal—and possibly Declan. Things were still quite fraught, Arkady gathered, between Declan and his little pet lizard.

"I think you malign the poor creature unnecessarily," Arryl said. "What news of our invaders, Azquil?"

"They were sailing up the channel toward the Delta Settlement, last we saw. Lord Cayal and Lord Declan were waiting on the dock when we left, to ensure they didn't turn back."

Arkady couldn't get used to hearing her childhood friend from the slums of Lebec referred to as "Lord Declan." Neither could Tiji, if the flicker of colour that washed over the chameleon's skin at the mere mention of his name was anything to go by.

"Then we have a few days to prepare before they come back."

"Do you *really* think they'll do what you asked?" Arkady said, still not convinced this plan would work. She was having trouble picturing anyone in Cydne's family allowing themselves to be dictated to by a woman, immortal goddess or not.

"Time will tell." Arryl looked past Arkady and smiled. "Ah, Declan, you're back. Where's Cayal?"

"Outside," he said, in a tone that implied he couldn't have cared less. "Could I have a word, Arkady? In private?"

The only thing that surprised Arkady about Declan's request was that it had taken him this long to make it. She nodded and picked up a candle from the table without looking at the others, afraid to wonder what they thought of her strange, ever-fluctuating relationship with this man. "We can talk in the other room."

Ignoring the others, Declan followed her to the small bedroom with its narrow bed and unpleasant memories, where she had, only a few days previously, smashed all the remaining bottles of Cydne's lethal tonic. The floorboards were still stained with the evidence of her deed, and the room still reeked of wood alcohol. Declan closed the door as she put the candle on the windowsill and turned to face him.

"Are you all right?" he asked.

"I'm fine." She held her arms out. "See! Not a mark."

Declan eyed her speculatively. Self-consciously, she folded her arms across her breasts, which gave her at least the illusion of modesty, even if it did little to conceal her nakedness.

"It was very brave, what you did out there."

Arkady shook her head. "Insulting a child wasn't brave. Neither was defying her brother. Not when I knew I had a couple of Tide Lords poised to rescue me in the nick of time. That was an impressively theatrical entrance by the way. Whose idea was it? Yours?"

"I think it was Cayal's."

"Now, why doesn't *that* surprise me?"

"Are you sure you're not hurt?"

"Positive. Was that all you wanted to ask me?"

Declan hesitated, unable to meet her eye.

"I'll be getting back to the others, then," she said, heading for the door.

"Arkady . . ."

"What?" she asked, turning back to face him.

"I'm sorry."

"I beg your pardon?"

"I said I was sorry."

"Yes, I heard you the first time. I just wanted to see if you were going to choke on the word if you had to say it more than once."

Declan wasn't amused. He sighed and threw his hands up in defeat. "Tides, Arkady, what do you *want* me to say?"

"Oh, I don't know," she said, taking a step toward him. "How about I forgive you, Arkady, for all the terrible things you've had to do recently, just to stay alive? How about, I was wrong to accuse you of being a whore?"

"I never said that!"

"You accused me of trying to sleep with you to discharge a debt, Declan," she reminded him, determined to make him understand exactly how much he'd wounded her. "The only difference between that and actually taking money for sex is the nature of the contract."

"I didn't mean . . ."

"Yes, you did," she accused, the urge to lance this festering wound more than she could resist. "It's exactly what you meant. You think that's what I do. When you found out I was sleeping with Fillion Rybank, you were furious, even though it started when I was fourteen and didn't know any better, and only did it because I thought it would save my father. I even thought you'd forgiven me for it. Until I got married. *Then* you were convinced I was sleeping with Stellan for his money, until you discovered he wasn't that way inclined, which must have confused the Tides out of you. And when I told you what happened with Cydne, you just assumed I was doing it again, didn't you?" She shrugged, her eyes glistening with unshed tears. "I suppose, in hindsight, I shouldn't be surprised. Why *wouldn't* you think I was willing to give my body to the heroic rescuer who saved me from the man-eating ants, with that sort of history?"

Declan stared at her for a long moment without saying a word.

Disappointed that he seemed to have nothing more to say, Arkady shrugged. "Apology accepted, Declan. I hope you have a very nice eternity without me."

She turned for the door, but before she'd taken more than two steps, Declan grabbed her arm and pulled her to him. He didn't say a word; didn't offer any excuses or any more hollow apologies. Instead, he did what he should have done the other day at the Outpost when she shared her deepest hopes and dreams with him. He kissed her. Kissed her the way she'd wanted him to kiss her all her life . . .

Shocked by the unexpectedness of his mouth on hers, Arkady responded without thinking, anger at his presumptuousness fuelling her desire. His strong arms pulled her closer, her naked body pressing against the weave of his shirt as if every fibre was determined to caress her skin.

For a fleeting moment, Arkady let herself drown in the glory of it . . .

And then sanity prevailed and she pushed him away, her heart pounding, perversely determined not to give in to such blatant manipulation.

"Tides, Declan!" Part of Arkady wanted to teach Declan a lesson punish him for doubting her—even as another part of her wanted to throw herself back into his arms and surrender to the safety and strength of his embrace. "Think you can make it all better with a kiss, do you?"

Declan reacted to her accusation the same way he always reacted to anything she'd ever scolded him about when they were children.

He broke into a grin. "Thought it was worth a try."

Arkady punched his chest angrily. "You're incorrigible."

"You've known that since you were eight years old, Arkady. Why do you sound surprised?"

Arkady opened her mouth to say . . . nothing. Declan was right. She knew this man better than she knew herself. She knew what drove him; knew what he was like better than he did. And she knew he loved her.

She'd known *that* since she was eight years old too.

"You make it impossible, sometimes," she accused, fairly certain glaring at him sternly would achieve absolutely nothing at all.

Gently, he drew her closer. "But I *am* sorry, Kady . . ."

"Don't call me that."

"Kady? Why not?"

"That was my slave name."

He took her in his arms and kissed her again, long and lingeringly, and this time Arkady didn't try to fight it. She closed her eyes, yielding to the blissful notion that in Declan's arms, there was probably nothing in the world that could hurt her, ever again.

"I don't care if they branded you; you were never a slave, Kady," he said softly when she lay her head on his chest with a sigh.

She smiled, relishing the feeling of being held by a man she not only loved, but more importantly, one she *trusted*. "That's not what I was thinking when I was on my hands and knees—"

"You don't have to explain, my love."

"I was going to *say*," she said, leaning back in his arms, "scrubbing *floors*. You've got a dirty mind, Declan Hawkes." Reaching up to put her arms around him, she studied him for a moment and wondered, *Tides, why have I spent half my life keeping the only man I've ever really loved, ever really trusted . . . at arm's length?*

"Do you forgive me, Arkady?"

"Do you forgive *me*?" she asked, searching his face for some hint that he was merely pandering to her; saying what she wanted to hear in order to put an awkward argument behind them. She knew him well enough not to put that past him, either.

"There's nothing to forgive."

"Not even Cayal?"

For a brief moment, Arkady thought she saw a flicker of anger, maybe even jealousy, in his eyes, but it was gone almost before she had time to register it was there. She hoped he could get past that because there was no way to explain what she felt for Cayal other than the realisation that in his arms she'd never really felt safe. Living in a constant state of danger, exhilarating as it was in the short term, was not the way she wanted to spend the rest of her life.

"Cayal's not going to be a problem between us, Arkady," he promised, "ever again."

It seemed a very brave statement to make, and Arkady didn't want to ruin this watershed moment in their relationship by pointing that out, but . . .

"Declan . . ."

He placed his finger on her lips and shook his head. "No. Don't say it.

We've got a fresh start. You're free—from slavery, from Stellan, from everything. And so am I. I love you, Arkady. I always have, and I will go to my grave wishing I'd—"

"You'll *what?*"

He smiled. "Bad choice of words."

She reached up to touch his cheek. It felt rough under her hand, darkened by a shadow of stubble that hadn't grown noticeably in the last few days. "It's all right, Declan. I understand."

Drawing her close, he kissed her again, like a lover not a friend, and then held her to him for a long time in silence. She closed her eyes again, listening to the dull, thudding beat of his heart, wishing this moment could be distilled and kept for posterity, so she could drink from it whenever she was in need of a dose of sheer bliss.

"I don't know what's going to happen next, Arkady," he said, his lips buried in her hair. "I don't know why I became immortal. I don't know if it was random chance or there is some grand, yet-to-be-revealed purpose in it. I don't know if I can help the Cabal, or even if I still want to." He took her by the arms then, and pushed her away a little so he could see her face. "The only thing I know for certain is that I'm not going to let you go."

"You won't have to, Declan," she said, kissing him soundly to seal her promise. "Because you're right. We have a chance for a fresh start, and however strange, however unexpected, I'm not going to pass up the opportunity. I'll stay with you for as long as you want me."

"I'll want you until the end of time, Arkady."

"That sounds grand, Declan. But I don't have that option."

"Then let's settle for being happy now," he said, hugging her close. "And let eternity take care of itself."

PART IV

When the tide of misfortune moves over you,
even jelly will break your teeth.

—Persian proverb

Chapter 55

As far as he was able, Stellan avoided taking his meals in the dining room with the rest of the royal family. Were it not for his promise to Nyah to keep her safe, he'd have eaten every meal in his room and had no social contact with the Caelish royal family at all.

Queen Jilna was an attractive woman in her mid-thirties, but her looks were fading fast. She seemed in awe of the handsome young man who'd offered her his hand when everyone feared her daughter was dead and she might be required to produce another heir. Her new husband—the man who'd tried to marry little Nyah before fixing his attention on her mother—Lord Tyrone of Torfail, was a heart-stoppingly beautiful young man who looked to be no older than twenty-five. Jilna, of course, had no idea he was thousands of years older than that.

The Tarot named him Tryan the Devil, according to Declan Hawkes, although at first Stellan thought the Tide Lord sadly maligned by history. It wasn't until he'd been in the palace for a while that he began to understand the man's cruel nature, and discovered how aptly he'd been named.

Jilna appeared besotted with him, which disturbed Stellan greatly. Although only her consort rather than her king, Tryan was all but ruling Caelum in her name. She deferred to his every wish, referred every decision to him. Stellan couldn't decide if it was because she was in love, she'd been drugged or was under some magical compulsion. The few times he'd seen the Caelish spymaster, Ricard Li, and been able to question him about the queen's behaviour, the older man had shrugged helplessly. Jilna's erratic behaviour was part of the reason he'd helped Nyah flee Caelum in the first place.

Of course, the problem with Tryan was more than that he had effectively stolen the Caelish throne. Tryan came with relatives and they were even more worrisome.

Syrolee, who was calling herself the Grand Duchess of Torfail, had taken over the palace. The only resistance she'd encountered was from her son, who clearly resented her trying to usurp the place he'd carved for himself, and from Nyah, whose position as heir to the throne gave her a certain amount of protection. Stellan winced every time he heard Nyah sniping at her, fairly certain that there would come a time when the Tide was high enough that Syrolee no longer felt the need to restrain herself around the Caelish heir. Or worse, she decided they no longer *needed* a Caelish heir.

Engarhod, the so-called Emperor of the Five Realms, appeared to be little more than a bored drunkard. That in itself fascinated Stellan, because it was his understanding that—thanks to their immortal powers of healing—it was very difficult to get an immortal drunk. It was a testament, therefore, to the majestic quantities of alcohol the man consumed that he managed to remain in that state most of the time. Stellan watched him consume fortified wine by the jugful, uninterested in anything else going on around him. As far as Stellan could tell, Syrolee could be angling to rule the world, for all he cared, and he wouldn't have lifted a finger to help her. Or stop her, either.

This, Stellan supposed, was the curse of immortality. Engarhod had come to the same conclusion as Cayal. Only he wasn't trying to kill himself, content to drown his sorrows in wine.

Engarhod's two sons were a rather different matter. Rance and Krydence hadn't been at the palace for as long as the others, and were still enjoying themselves, as far as Stellan could tell. They used their tenuous link to the throne to demand all manner of considerations, which Jilna did nothing to prevent. After meeting them briefly the day he'd arrived, Stellan decided they were thugs, and nothing they had done since then had changed his mind.

The most interesting immortal of them all, Stellan decided, was Elyssa. She was very much as Cayal had described her—a face lacking form or character on a body sculpted to perfection by immortality. She seemed to know people disliked her, just as she knew most people who pretended to like her did so because they sought to use her influence with her brother. There were rumours about young men being invited to her rooms and never being seen again, but Stellan had never witnessed her flirting with any man, so he wasn't sure the rumours could be trusted.

She seemed a bookish young woman, intent on studying . . . something. Stellan didn't know what it was, but she spent a lot of time reading through old texts and arranging meetings with various academics both from Caelum and abroad. A few days after he arrived, he'd even run into Andre Fawk, Arkady's old colleague from the University of Lebec, on his way to meet with Lady Alysa. Virtually destitute since Jaxyn had assumed control of the duchy and decided he wasn't going to support the university any longer, Fawk was apparently working on something for Elyssa, although Stellan had no idea what.

It intrigued him, though, particularly when he realised that after Elyssa had disappeared from the palace for a few days a couple of weeks ago, Warlock had vanished. When he inquired about the canine's whereabouts, he learned Elyssa had left him watching over Fawk at some archaeological dig she'd decided to fund as part of her research into . . . well, whatever it was she was researching.

The news not only fascinated him, but it also reminded him of his promise to help Warlock's family escape. And that raised its own set of problems, because, in the normal course of events, Stellan had no right or reason to go anywhere near the Crasii kennels in the palace.

He needed help, and the only true ally he had in this place was Princess Nyah.

So here he was at breakfast, ignoring the guffawing laughter going between Krydence and Rance—the result of a particularly foul joke the brothers were sharing. He paid no attention to Engarhod either, who'd already consumed a full jug of wine, or Syrolee, who was talking to Tryan, urging him to do something in a low, irritated voice, which her son seemed to be ignoring also.

Stellan filled his plate from the buffet and took a seat beside Nyah at the other end of the long table, as far away as she could get from her immortal stepfather.

"Good morning, your highness."

"Your grace."

"May I join you?"

"*Please*," she said with feeling.

Stellan smiled sympathetically as he shook out his napkin. "Going to be one of those days, is it?"

"It looks that way," the little princess said through a mouthful of toast. "I'm thinking of running away again," she added in a low voice.

"Do you think it will help?" he asked, not certain she was serious.

The princess scowled at her mother who was sitting at the other end of the table, chewing mindlessly, apparently oblivious to everything going on around her. "Staying here doesn't seem to be doing much good."

"Would you like to do me a favour, then?"

Nyah brightened at the prospect. "What do you want me to do?"

"I need to visit someone in the Crasii pens."

She looked at him oddly. "You have friends down there?"

"I owe someone a favour."

"I suppose," she said. "What do you need me to do?"

"Come with me. I've no reason to be in the pens and won't be admitted without one. You, on the other hand, will raise no suspicion at all if you want to take me down and show me the new puppies."

"Tabitha's new puppies?" she asked, her eyes alight.

"That's who I want to visit."

Nyah nodded enthusiastically and jumped to her feet. "Come on, then! Let's go."

"Nyah, dear . . . where are you going?" Jilna asked in a voice that seemed vague and only mildly interested in the answer.

"We have new puppies in the Crasii pens," she told her mother with a bright smile. "I'm taking Stellan down to show him."

Tryan looked up from his conversation with Syrolee. "I'm sure Lord Stellan has better things to do than play with Crasii puppies, Nyah. Let him eat his breakfast."

Stellan smiled at the immortal and shrugged. "It's all right, my lord. I don't mind accompanying her. Nyah really shouldn't be down in a place like that on her own, and she's quite desperate to see the pups."

Syrolee treated him to a suspicious glare. "You're very good with children, aren't you, my lord?"

"I like them a great deal," he agreed with a small bow to the Grand Duchess of Torfail.

"Not as much as he likes young men," Rance added, elbowing his brother and sniggering as he said it. The two men fell about laughing at the joke. Stellan ignored them, and with all the dignity he could muster, he turned, took Nyah's hand and walked from the dining room.

Nyah squeezed his hand encouragingly as soon as they were out of earshot. "I hate those two."

"You can be sure they won't be on the guest list for *my* next ball," Stellan agreed.

"I wish we could kill them."

He smiled down at her. "I believe there's rather a lot of people who are trying to find a way to do that."

"Do you think they'll succeed?"

"I don't know, Nyah," he told her as they turned toward the stairs. "The

only thing I'm certain of is that we can't do anything about them ourselves, so we need to help the people we can, and not lose sleep over the
ones we can't."

Nyah smiled up at him. "Shalimar would have said that's a very philo-
sophical outlook."

"Shalimar was a very wise man."

With Nyah demanding to see the new pups, nobody questioned Stellan's
right to be in the pens. They were led through the dungeon-like kennels
by a female Crasii with a black and white coat, her tail drooping unhappily
as she walked. Stellan had no idea if it was because she didn't like them visiting or was just unhappy in general. Remembering the homely, village-
like setting his own Crasii had enjoyed, Stellan wondered if it was the latter.
He couldn't imagine anybody, Crasii or human, being happy to live down
here in these dark cells.

"Tabitha and the pups are in there," the female told them, pointing to a
cell at the end of the corridor; then she added as an afterthought, "your
highness."

Nyah waited until she'd turned and was headed back up the torchlit corridor before she hurried forward and stepped into the cell. Stellan followed her, squinting a little in the darkness. The pups in question were
sleeping on a pile of furs, just inside the door, watched over by their dam—
and presumably Warlock's mate—Tabitha Belle.

The female looked up as they entered. She ignored Nyah, however, and
jumped to her feet. "Your grace!"

Stellan hadn't expected to be recognised quite so readily by some canine
he'd never met before, but then he looked a little closer and his jaw went
slack with shock. "Boots?"

"Shhh!" she hissed, pushing past him to look outside the cell and make
sure they couldn't be overheard. When she'd satisfied herself they were
truly alone, she turned back to him. "Around here, I'm Tabitha Belle."

Stellan was gob-smacked. "But . . . Tides, are *you* Warlock's mate?"

"Who's Warlock?" Nyah asked, on her knees looking at the sleeping
puppies. "Can I pick one up?"

"I'd prefer you didn't wake them," Boots said, before turning back to
look at him. "How is it you know Warlock?"

Her stance was defensive, her tail high, her teeth almost bared. She was frightened, he realised. "I met him in Lebec," he said. "He asked me to check on you. I'm not here to harm you or your pups, Boots."

Boots seemed to relax a little. "You came to see him at the Watchhouse."

Stellan nodded. "He knew my wife. She spoke very highly of him. An opinion I'm assuming you share, given you're here with him."

Boots shook her head. "I like him, your grace. Sometimes, when I can't help myself, I *really* like him. But I wish I'd never met him."

Stellan glanced down at the pups. Nyah was leaning over them, willing them to wake, but she wasn't touching them. "I'm sure you don't mean that. You'd not have these little treasures, otherwise."

Unaccountably, Boots's eyes filled with tears. "Tides, that's the cruellest twist of all."

"What do you mean," Nyah asked, looking up at her with a frown. "They're gorgeous."

"And they are Crasii, your highness."

"Well, of course they are," Nyah said, rolling her eyes. "How long before they wake, do you think?"

Boots didn't answer the little princess. Her gaze was fixed on Stellan, who at first didn't understand why this Crasii was so upset at having three perfectly healthy Crasii pups. And then it occurred to him. Boots and Warlock weren't just Crasii; they were Scards.

"Tides, Boots, I'm so sorry."

"Can you help us?"

He shrugged. "I don't know . . ."

She was quietly desperate as she said, "I have to get them away from here, your grace. I have to get them somewhere safe. Somewhere there are no suzerain."

"What are their names?" he asked, unable to think of anything more profound to say.

"Despair, Torment and Misery," Boots told him, glancing at her babies. "Elyssa named them."

She turned her tormented gaze on Stellan. The irony of the situation didn't escape him. Once he could have given Boots anything she desired, and she'd run away, only to find herself here, reliant on him once more.

And now, when he was all but helpless to aid her, she needed him the most.

Stellan nodded and gripped her shoulder encouragingly. "I've no notion of how I can, but I will help you, Boots. And your pups. And Warlock too if I'm able. I give you my word."

Impulsively, Boots hugged him. "Thank you, your grace."

He patted her awkwardly and smiled, hoping it made him look confident, wondering when he was going to learn to stop making promises to people that he didn't know how he was going to keep.

Chapter 56

"End it now."

For the third time in the past few days, Declan woke with Arkady in his arms, only this time he didn't question his good fortune. He opened his eyes, blinking in the unexpected sunlight streaming through the window, wondering what had woken him. Arkady was sound asleep, her back to him, snuggled into the hollow of his body as he lay on his side next to her. Her breathing was deep and even, and when he pushed himself up on his elbow, he noticed the faintest hint of a smile playing around her lips.

Blinking, Declan looked toward the door. Cayal was standing there, leaning against the doorframe, arms crossed, watching them sleep. There was no telling how long he'd been there, but Declan was fairly certain now what had woken him.

"What did you say?" he asked softly, gently moving away from Arkady as he spoke to avoid waking her.

"The Fyrennese had a saying once—the old ones, the ones Brynden comes from. *End it now.* It's what you should do at the moment of ultimate ecstasy."

Declan looked around for his trousers, wondering where Arkady had tossed them the night before.

"Why?" he asked, spying them across the room.

"Because once you've reached the peak, it's all downhill from there, old son. So you might as well end it now and save yourself a long and disappointing life." Cayal watched him cross the room to retrieve his clothes, and then added with a sour smile, "Ooops . . . you can't die, can you? Guess you'll need to brace yourself for the long, disappointing part."

"Do you *want* something?" Declan asked, determined not to rise to the provocation. He picked his trousers up off the floor, turned his back to Cayal and pulled them on.

"You."

"For what?"

"Time's a-wasting, Rodent, while you live out your little fantasy with the girl of your dreams. We've only got a few days before the dreaded Merchant Marines come back. We've got work to do."

"What kind of work?"

"You need to learn a few things or I'll have to perform all the heroics."

Declan turned to stare at the Immortal Prince, wondering if he was trying to needle him again, or if Cayal was serious.

Cayal smiled. "Finish getting dressed. I'll meet you outside." Then he glanced at Arkady's sleeping form and sighed. "Tides, but she's gorgeous. Of course, there'll be prettier ones you'll meet in the future. Forever's useful like that. Prettier, smarter, better in bed . . ."

"Who are you trying to convince, Cayal, me or yourself?"

To Declan's surprise, his question seemed to hit a nerve in the immortal. Cayal pushed off the doorframe, the snide smile replaced by genuine irritation. "Don't keep me waiting, Rodent."

The door slamming shut, ever so slightly, made Arkady stir. Pulling on his shirt, Declan squatted down beside the bed and kissed her forehead.

"Shhh . . ." he said. "Go back to sleep."

"I heard voices," she mumbled.

"It's nothing. You should sleep while you can."

She snuggled down in the middle of the narrow bed contentedly. "I love you, Declan."

"Even in your dreams?"

Her eyes still closed, she smiled as he pulled the sheet over her to keep the insects at bay. "Apparently."

"Go back to sleep, Kady."

"I never got to sleep in . . . when I was a slave." Her voice was muffled by the pillow and had a dreamy quality that indicated she was only half awake.

"Then sleep until midday, if you want, sweetheart. You're not a slave anymore."

"Mmmmm . . ." she replied.

Declan kissed her forehead again and stood up. He studied her for a moment longer, wondering at the good fortune that had finally brought Arkady to him, a little disturbed to realise Tiji's suspicions about his reasons for becoming immortal weren't that far off the mark.

Although he'd had no choice in the matter, Declan wasn't entirely certain that, had he been offered one short lifetime with Arkady in return for his mortality, he wouldn't have taken the deal.

———

"How many senses do you have?"

Declan shrugged, fairly certain this was going to be a trick question. "Five."

"Name them."

He rolled his eyes, but answered Cayal's question. Declan was learning, very quickly, that Cayal had his own unique way of teaching, which mostly involved making the student feel like a complete imbecile. "Taste, touch, sight, hearing and smell."

"What about the others?"

"What others?" Declan asked, as he knew Cayal expected him to.

"You can sense the Tide, can't you? You can't feel it. It's not tangible so you can't touch it. You can't see it, or hear it. And you certainly can't smell it."

Declan had to concede he had a point. "So we have *six* senses?"

"Not even close."

"What else is there?"

"What about your understanding of where you are?"

Declan looked around the clearing the Immortal Prince had led him to in order to continue their lessons and then fixed his gaze on Cayal. "I hardly think knowing I'm standing in a jungle clearing, a half-hour walk from some tiny village in the Senestran Wetlands, counts as a sense."

"Are you trying to be an ass, or are you really that stupid?"

"I must be stupid," Declan said. "I have no idea what you mean."

Cayal studied him in silence for a moment, the Tide rippling around him, perhaps debating how to proceed. When he spoke again, it was in a much more conciliatory tone, which drove home to Declan just how much more Cayal needed him than he needed Cayal.

"I was talking of proprioception—your awareness of where you are in relation to everything else around you. Most people don't even spare it a thought, but there's a reason you bump into things when you're drunk that you'd miss if you were sober."

Declan considered the idea for a moment and then nodded. "All right, I'll pay that one."

"You'd better," Cayal warned. "It's far more important for a Tide Lord to be conscious of himself in relation to everything around him when he's wielding the Tide than for some poor sod getting pissed at the local tavern before he goes home each night."

"There are more, I take it?"

"Equilibrioception: the sense of balance."

"Isn't that the same as proprioception?"

"Not at all," Cayal said. "Proprioception is about what's around you. It's external. Equilibrioception is internal. It's what keeps you upright. And like proprioception, it's very easily disrupted by alcohol—among other things—which is why, when a man is drunk, he falls over just as much as he bumps into things."

Despite himself, Declan found himself intrigued by Cayal's lecture. And surprised by the depth of Cayal's knowledge. It was easy to forget this man had been alive for eight thousand years. Clearly, he'd not spent all of them sleeping around, stealing other men's wives or causing cataclysmic natural disasters.

"What are the other senses, then?"

"Nociception," Cayal said, a little less abrasively, now that Declan was paying attention. "The ability to feel pain."

"I never thought of that as a sense."

"It's an amazingly useful sense, actually. Particularly when you're trying to convince someone to do things your way."

"You mean you can torture someone by manipulating his nociception with the Tide?"

Cayal smiled. "You're going to stay true to type in immortality, aren't you?"

"Meaning . . . ?"

"You've just worked out that you can affect a man's perceptions by manipulating his senses with the Tide. I find it fascinating that it took you until the sense that'll allow you to torture a man, before you came to that conclusion. I'll bet you were just the bestest little spymaster ever, weren't you?"

Declan was intrigued enough with the possibilities of this new-found knowledge that Cayal's needling barely registered. "I know what pain does to a man," he said. "And how useless is it. A man will say anything to stop being hurt."

"Not if he believes the consequences of you catching him in a lie are worse than what you're doing to him," Cayal said. "You have to own him first, break him completely, before you can rely on anything a man under torture will tell you."

Declan studied Cayal curiously for a moment. "You say that like you know it for a fact."

Cayal smiled. "I didn't completely waste all those years as a Holy Warrior, you know."

"So how do you affect someone's senses using the Tide?" Declan asked, not sure he wanted to hear the details of how many men Cayal might have tortured over the past few thousand years, and not because he was squeamish. Mostly, it was because the more time he spent with him, the more he discovered how much he had in common with the Immortal Prince, and that realisation was a bit more than he could deal with right now.

"Ah, now that's the tricky part."

"Is it difficult?"

Cayal shrugged. "It's . . . fiddly."

"And that's how you want to deal with the Merchant Marines when they return? By confusing their senses?"

The Immortal Prince nodded. "That's the plan. If you're up to it, by then."

"If it's that *fiddly*, why not just do what we did to the first lot?"

"I explained that to you the other night. Tide's not up far enough to sustain pulling the air out over a wide area for long enough to make it work. And like I said—and you apparently weren't listening—once you start moving the air around, you're messing with the weather. We make a few hundred Senestran marines cough and splutter here to prove our point, and before you know it, Jelidia's melting into the oceans and we've got Lukys hunting us down for ruining his Palace of Impossible Dreams."

"His *what*?"

"Your dear old dad has built himself an ice palace," Cayal explained, looking amused. "Pellys dubbed it the Palace of Impossible Dreams. A poetic, if somewhat ridiculous title that seems to have stuck, mostly because I think Oritha—Tides, that'd be your *stepmother*—likes it. You'll see it when we get to Jelidia. Assuming it's still there."

It was discomforting to hear Cayal refer to Lukys as his "dear old dad," partly because Declan wasn't sure he believed it, and partly because he was afraid it might be true. "All right, so doing anything with the weather is out of the question. What are you suggesting? That we make them all fall over?"

Cayal grinned. "Think about it for a moment, Rodent. Have you any idea how effective that would be?"

Despite himself—and Cayal's insult—Declan smiled. "I suppose it would rather disrupt the invasion if all their marines start falling about like drunkards."

"There you go, Rodent," Cayal said, slapping Declan on the shoulder like a proud father. "Now you're thinking like a Tide Lord. Minimum magic for the maximum disruption, that's my philosophy."

Declan stared at him. "*That's* your philosophy?"

"Sure it is. Why?"

"Weren't you the man who drowned one country and decimated another, just to put out a small flame? Didn't you wipe out your own country in a disagreement with Tryan? Wasn't the last cataclysm caused because you ran off with Kinta . . . ?"

"That was Brynden's work, not mine."

"Still, you have an interesting definition of *minimum*."

The smile faded from Cayal's face. Declan could feel him on the Tide, the angry ripples telling him more about Cayal's mood than his outwardly calm demeanour, forced on the Immortal Prince by his deal and the need to keep Declan onside.

"Come see me when *you're* eight thousand years old, Rodent, and we'll see if you've done any better."

"Won't you be dead by then?" Declan asked, wondering if Cayal had forgotten about his plan to return to Jelidia to die—with Declan's assistance—or if he just didn't really believe it was going to work.

"Not if *you* don't learn something about controlling the Tide," Cayal warned. "So pay attention, Rodent. I'm going to teach you how to manipulate the senses, and you'd better learn good, because if I miss my chance to die when the Tide peaks, thanks to your incompetence, I'll spend my every waking moment until the *next* High Tide, a thousand years from now, making you regret it."

Chapter 57

Azquil volunteered to keep watch for the returning fleet, and Tiji offered to go with him. It was too difficult being around the cottage. Between Declan smelling like a suzerain and mooning about over Arkady, the Immortal Prince, the disturbingly likable Arryl, and that wretched feline, Jojo, with her watchful, unblinking stare, it was the last place she wanted to be.

Fortunately, the best vantage to watch the southern channel was from the large flat rock near the hot springs where Azquil had first shown Tiji the delights of the Genoa moth. They'd spent rather a lot of time since arriving at the springs, trying to catch another one. They'd made love since that first time, of course, but it was never quite the same and Tiji was anxious to try it again, with the aphrodisiac effects of those delicious melting wings tingling on her tongue.

They had the time to indulge in a bit fun. The round trip from the Delta Settlement would take their enemies two days at least, although Arryl's assessment had been that it would be considerably longer. If Ambria and Medwen had been sent to Port Traeker, it would add another day to the trip, and was she fairly certain they wouldn't come back without reinforcements, which meant even longer before the invaders arrived.

And so it had proved. It was nearly five days now since the Tide Lords had confronted Ulag Pardura and the doctor's wife.

And a few hours ago, Azquil had caught another moth.

"What will you do after this?" Azquil asked, when the elation of their moth-enhanced coupling had calmed. Tiji was curled into Azquil's arms, her head resting in his chest, their skin the same shade as the warm rock beneath them.

She stirred sleepily. "Catch another moth."

"Not that, silly," Azquil said. She could hear the smile in his voice. "I mean after Lady Arryl and the Tide Lords secure the wetlands for us. They're leaving, you know."

"Good riddance to them," Tiji murmured, wishing Azquil would find something a little more romantic to discuss after making love to her than the wretched suzerain.

"Lady Arryl has asked me to go with her."

That announcement brought Tiji back to reality with a jarring thud. "She *what*?"

"She wants me to go to Jelidia with her."

"Why?"

"She needs a servant and wants one she can trust."

"Then let her take that horrid cat!" Tiji said, sitting up abruptly. "She can't help but follow a suzerain's orders. That should be enough trust for any immortal."

Azquil pushed himself up on his elbows to stare at her unrelenting back. "A Crasii can be *subverted* by any other immortal. Lady Arryl wants me because I am loyal to her and the Trinity, and I'm a Scard so I can't be ordered otherwise."

"Tides," Tiji grumbled. "Are you sure you're not a proper Crasii?"

"If I was, Lady Arryl would not have bothered to ask. I do have a choice, Tiji."

"Then say no."

"Why?" he asked, sitting up beside her. "This is the chance of a lifetime— a chance to travel, a chance to see things I'd never see otherwise . . ."

Tiji turned to look at him. "You travel plenty," she reminded him. "That's how you found me, remember?"

"And why do you think it was me, and not one of the thousands of other chameleons who live in the wetlands who found you? Because I'm one of the few who wants to leave this place occasionally. That's why I was recruited into the Retrievers. I'm one of the few who wants to see what else this world has to offer."

"Fine," Tiji said. "So travel. See the world. But do you have to do it with a suzerain?"

"Yes," he said with determination. "And I want you to come with me."

She laughed. "Me? Follow a bunch of suzerain to the bottom of the world to watch one kill himself? You're kidding, right?"

"Not at all. I want you to come with me."

"I can't."

"Why not?"

Tiji looked away. "I just can't, that's all."

"Is it because of Lord Declan? Because he has rejected you in favour of a member of his own species?"

Although they didn't know for certain that Declan and Arkady were nothing more than the friends they insisted they were, Tiji figured Azquil had the right of it. Declan and Arkady had vanished into the bedroom to talk the other night, and still hadn't surfaced at dawn the next morning when the two chameleons left to take up their channel watch at the hot springs. She supposed that meant Declan finally had what he wanted. She hoped he was happy, but suspected things had worked out a little too easily for his happiness to be permanent.

In fact, it was guaranteed to be temporary, when she thought on it. Declan might now be immortal, but Arkady wasn't.

Of course, that didn't alter this awkward misconception Azquil seemed to have about her relationship with her former master. Tiji stared at Azquil for a moment and then let out a frustrated sigh. "How many times, you stupid lizard, do I have to explain to you that Declan is . . . was . . . my friend? I never slept with him and never wanted to. And he never once looked at me as anything other than . . ." Tiji hesitated, and then, with the pained realisation it was true, she said, ". . . than a slave. He's a Tide Lord now, and he can take up with any species he wants. I promise you, I'll lose not a wink of sleep over it."

"But his presence makes you so uncomfortable . . ."

"That's because he shows up here, out of the blue, suddenly immortal. That doesn't make me uncomfortable, Azquil. It terrifies me."

"And this is why you don't want to come with me? Because you are terrified of a former master? Tides, it's as if you're still a slave."

"No, I'm not."

"You are if you still act according to the wishes of your master."

That was unfair. And a quite blatant attempt to play on her guilt. "What? You think Declan doesn't want me to go with you?"

"I don't think he cares about you being with me so much," Azquil said. "He may even be happy for you. But I think he is pained by the way you look at him now."

"I can't help it. He smells like a suzerain."

Azquil nodded in understanding. "It's a pity. Jelidia is a very cold place. It would have been much nicer with someone to warm my bed."

"That's why you wanted me to go? As a bed warmer? Thanks a lot."

He leaned forward, running a flickering tongue over her ear and then blew on the damp patch softly, sending shivers down her spine. "I'd keep you warm too."

She pushed him away impatiently. "You can't get your own way just by blowing in my ear, you know."

"We can have a bit of fun while I try, though," he said.

"Tides, that's all you think about!"

"Not true," he said, sitting up with a wounded look. "I think many profound thoughts."

Despite herself, Tiji smiled. "Like what?"

"Um . . . like . . . the best way to catch channel pike, for instance."

"Yes, well, that's a weighty problem."

"I think of . . . countless different ways to cook them . . ."

"Truly, you are the philosopher of your people."

He grinned. "If you loved me, you'd come to Jelidia with me."

"If you loved me, you'd stay here with me, Azquil."

It was flippantly said, but they both fell into an uncomfortable silence. Although they'd been enjoying each other's company for a while now, neither of them had dared suggest there was anything more going on here than a bit of harmless moth-fuelled fun.

Finally, after an awkward silence that stretched for far too long, Azquil moved a little closer and took her hand. "Do you really want me to stay?"

"I want you to follow your heart," Tiji said, which was as close as she was able to come to asking if he loved her.

"Then I will stay here," he said without hesitation. "With you."

"But you want to see Jelidia."

"I want you more."

She wasn't sure how to respond to that, so she didn't even try, figuring that at this point, actions would say more than words. So she kissed him, her skin flickering with desire as he took her into his arms, and tingling as if they were sharing a moth. Maybe that was the true magic of the Genoa moth, she thought, allowing Azquil to push her back down on the warm rock, as his flickering tongue danced over her body. It didn't just enhance feelings, it simulated love.

Tiji moaned with pleasure as his tongue slid down along the crease where her thigh joined her torso . . .

And then suddenly the delicious torment stopped and Azquil was sitting up, staring down the channel, alert and cautious.

"Tides!" he swore, climbing to his feet.

"What's the matter?" she asked, disappointed and more than a little frustrated by how easily distracted he was.

Azquil reached down and pulled her to her feet. "They're here."

"How can you tell?"

"Listen."

She did as he asked and then shook her head. "I hear nothing."

"Exactly. The insects have all gone quiet."

Now he pointed it out to her, Tiji realised he was right. The wetlands, normally filled with the screech of a million insects, were deathly still. They waited, still as only lizards could be, listening . . .

A few moments later they heard them—a soft susurration, the swish of water against moving wood . . . the unmistakable sound of amphibians towing ships toward them.

Azquil hurried to the peak of the sloped rock and dropped to his stomach. Tiji wiggled up beside him and waited, holding her breath.

Even before the ships came into view, Tiji caught a familiar whiff of something foul. "Suzerain," she whispered.

Azquil nodded. He could smell it too. "They have brought Lady Medwen and Lady Ambria with them," he said softly.

"We need to get word to the others," she said, turning to slither back down the rock.

"No," Azquil said, putting a hand on her arm to restrain her. "We need to count the ships first."

Tiji nodded, and slithered back into position. They waited in silence for the enemy to appear, the silence tense, the quiet unnerving.

"So," Tiji said softly, in an attempt to relieve the tension. "If you're really planning to stay here with me, and not go to Jelidia, does that mean you . . . well, you know . . . love me?"

Azquil glanced at her and grinned. "Must do, I suppose."

"Nobody ever loved me before."

"That's because you had to wait until I came along."

Tiji rolled her eyes. *Tides, there wasn't a humble scale anywhere on his skin.* "You are so full of yourself, Azquil."

"But with just cause," he told her. "My mother says I'm a very handsome lizard."

That comment almost caused Tiji to have a panic attack. "You have a *mother?*"

"Most everyone does, Tiji."

"I know, but I never thought . . ." *He has a mother. And a sister. And uncles. And aunts. And cousins . . . Tides, I think I'm going to be sick . . .*

"I've changed my mind. I want to go to Jelidia after all."

"No, you don't," he said, turning to look at her. Despite the determined expression on her face, her wildly flickering skin tones betrayed her. "You're just frightened of meeting my mother."

"A lot more than I am of dealing with the immortals, as it turns out," she said.

"That is so sweet . . ."

"Don't you dare laugh at me, you wretched lizard."

"I wouldn't dare," he promised, but he was grinning from ear to ear. "Would you really rather brave the snows of Jelidia than meet my family? You didn't seem to have a problem with Tenika."

"Tenika is one little sister, Azquil. I'm still getting over finding any others of my kind. I'm not ready to be embraced by the whole clan."

"Are you sure?"

She nodded, amazed at how inviting the idea of following the Tide Lords into peril sounded compared to facing a whole village full of Azquil's family. "Let's go to Jelidia. That gives me a few more months to get used to the idea of relatives."

He leaned across and kissed her. "You are so funny. No wonder I love you."

She smiled. "I love you too." It felt very daring, saying that out loud.

"Then start counting," he replied.

"What?"

Azquil pointed to the channel where the first ship was sailing into view. It was a shallow-draughted craft with two naked women—Ambria and Medwen by the suzerain stench of them—chained to the single mast on the centre of the ship. The ship carried the colours of House Medura, and another flag with the intertwined vine leaves of the Physicians' Guild and there were several men dressed in elaborate robes beside an older man standing on the foredeck next to the distinctive figure of Ulag Pardura.

"Start counting," Azquil repeated. "The fun's about to begin."

Chapter 58

As soon as Andre Fawk's assistant had painstakingly separated the ancient cards of the Lore Tarot, Warlock commandeered them on behalf of his immortal mistress and headed home, prepared to kill anyone who got in his way. He couldn't have cared less about the cards, but he'd been away from Boots and the pups for nearly three weeks. He was going mad, worrying about what might have happened to them in his absence.

Elyssa was delighted when he returned with her treasure, carefully laying out the cards on a large table she'd had moved to her room for just that purpose. She then sat down to stare at them for several hours, trying to decide the correct order. She was looking for something in the cards; Warlock had worked that much out, but he had no idea what it was. Only that it was valuable.

So valuable Elyssa had been prepared to fund Fawk's entire expedition for the sake of one deck of Tarot cards.

Impatient to be gone from her company and find out how Boots and the pups were faring, Warlock was on the verge of risking everything by asking permission to leave when the door to Elyssa's room opened and Tryan walked in.

The stench of the suzerain filled his nostrils. It was all Warlock could do not to gag. He forced himself to bow politely to the Tide Lord. The movement caught Elyssa's eye and she looked up from the table.

"Don't you know how to knock?"

Tryan shrugged. "You would have felt me approaching long before I got around to knocking." He walked toward her as he spoke, until he was near enough to the table to see the cards, which caused him to shake his head in wonder. "Tides, you found them."

"No thanks to you."

"Wasn't my fault they jumped." He leaned a little closer to examine the fragile, faded cards. "You know you're wasting your time, don't you? There's no secret hidden in these cards. I checked them when we searched the prisoners."

"You think it's more likely to be hidden in the sewers of the Herino Palace?" She looked up at him with a nasty smile. "Oh yes, I heard about your little spy who got caught in Glaeba, lurking around the sewers. What exactly were you hoping to achieve by sending him there, by the way?"

Tryan did not look pleased. "There's a chance Jaxyn's already found it."

"Don't be ridiculous. If Jaxyn had found it, we'd all know about it by now. And Maralyce wouldn't be still looking for it."

"You don't know that she is," he pointed out. "For all you know, she's tunnelling her way across Glaeba because she actually likes . . ." Tryan stopped mid-sentence, as if he'd just been struck by another thought.

"Like what?" Elyssa asked.

"Tides . . ."

"*What*, Tryan?"

"Maralyce . . . tunnelling across Glaeba . . ."

"So?" his sister demanded. "She's been at it for centuries."

"Which means she's probably tunnelled all the way to Caelum by now."

Elyssa stopped to consider that possibility for a moment and then she frowned. "That would mean she could come and go in and out of Caelum all she wanted, without us ever knowing about it."

"So could a few other people," Tryan said, "if they had her help." The Tide Lord looked at Warlock then, the first time he'd acknowledged his presence. "Cecil, fetch my stepdaughter for me, would you?"

"My lord?" Warlock asked, realising his mistake as soon as he questioned the order. No proper Crasii would hesitate before hurrying to do an immortal's bidding.

"Princess Nyah, you big dumb mongrel. Fetch Princess Nyah for me. Now."

Warlock bowed and hurried off to do Tryan's bidding, trembling with relief to realise Tryan had taken his question as a lack of understanding, not disobedience. He let himself out into the hall and leaned against the door for a moment to calm his racing heart. Glancing up and down the hall, he was relieved to discover he was alone, which was fortunate, because as soon as he was out of earshot of Elyssa's room, he broke into a run.

"Tryan wants to interrogate Princess Nyah about Maralyce!" Warlock announced, bursting into the Duke of Lebec's rooms and slamming the door behind him.

Startled, Stellan Desean looked up from his desk by the window where he'd been writing something. "What?"

"I've been sent to fetch little Nyah," Warlock explained, panting with the exertion of his mad dash through the palace corridors. "By Tryan. I'm not sure how, but I think he's worked out where Nyah was hiding. If I don't take her to him, they'll know I'm a Scard and they'll kill me and my mate. If I do take her . . ."

, One of the things Warlock liked about Stellan Desean was that he didn't need things explained to him more than once. Before Warlock had finished speaking, he was on his feet, reaching for his coat. "It's all right, Warlock. I'll come with you."

Warlock heaved a great sigh of relief. He had no power to protect the little princess on his own. Desean, however, might have some chance of helping her.

"Do you know where she is?"

"The princess? At this time of day she'd be at her lessons in the library."

Desean nodded. "Then we'll fetch her from there. Now take a deep breath, Warlock. You'll frighten her if she sees you're worried about something."

"He wants to interrogate her, your grace. He's not called The Devil for nothing. If he finds out where she was hiding, he'll learn about you, about the Cabal . . ."

"Then we'll just have to make sure he doesn't find out about anything," the duke said. Then he smiled reassuringly. "It'll be fine, Warlock. Trust me."

Warlock wasn't fond of humans who said that, but in the short time he had before he must return to Tryan with an innocent child for him to interrogate, it would have to do.

They stopped at the threshold of Elyssa's room, Warlock, Princess Nyah and Stellan Desean. The duke had the little girl by the hand and had been talking to her in a low, urgent voice all the way here from the library, exhorting her—much to Warlock's distress—to stick, as far as possible, to the truth.

Warlock thought that was a very bad idea.

"I'll be fine, Stellan," Nyah told him with a tremulous smile, and then she squared her shoulders bravely and stood back as Warlock opened the door.

The immortals had barely moved from where they'd been when War-lock left the room. Elyssa was still sitting at her table trying to sort the Lore Tarot into some semblance of order, while Tryan paced the room impatiently.

They both looked up as the door opened, but didn't get a chance to ut-ter a word before Desean stepped into the room, smiling. "Lord Tyrone! What a pleasant surprise. I was just in the library trying to instruct her highness on the history of the many border disputes between Caelum and Glaeba when Cecil came to fetch her for Lady Alysa. I think we were both glad of the distraction, to be honest . . . Tides!" he exclaimed, seeing the table for the first time. "Is that a Lore Tarot?"

The immortals looked at him in confusion, Nyah all but forgotten. She stood next to Warlock, pressing against him as if that gave her some sort of protection. It was an illusion, however. Warlock could do nothing to protect this child. All he'd been able to do was tell Stellan Desean what was going on. And mention that Elyssa was currently obsessed with an an-cient deck of Tarot cards.

"You know of the Lore Tarot?" Elyssa asked with a puzzled frown.

"I've heard of it," Stellan said, leaning forward for a closer look. "My wife, Arkady, was a historian. She mentioned it."

"What did she say about it?" Tryan asked, interested, Warlock thought, in spite of himself.

"Not much," the duke said with a shrug. "Just that she'd heard it ex-isted. And that it was the Crasii version of the Tarot. Arkady was studying the Crasii, you see. She thought, if such a thing really existed, she'd be able to compare it to the human version." He looked up and smiled. "Of course, I never saw the purpose of it, myself. Never was one for telling fortunes. Which is a pity, when you think about it."

"Why?" Elyssa asked.

"Well, think about it, my lady. If I'd had the ability to foresee the fu-ture, I wouldn't be here now, would I?"

Tryan smiled. "Good point. I didn't realise you were married, your grace. Where is your wife now?"

Stellan shrugged. "I have no idea. I don't even know if she's still alive. She was well enough when I left Ramahn, but anything could have hap-pened to her by now. Lord Aranville ordered her arrested, but I've not heard if he's managed to find her yet."

"Would you like us to find out?" Tryan offered.

Warlock wondered at the motives of the Tide Lord. He couldn't have cared less about Arkady Desean. Maybe he was doing it to convince Desean he wasn't a monster? To ally his fears so the duke would leave him alone with Nyah?

"I'd be most grateful if you could find any news of my wife, Lord Torfail." Desean turned back to the table. "May I touch one, my lady?"

Elyssa nodded. "Just be careful. They're very fragile."

Stellan nodded and gently lifted the nearest card from the table, admiring it. "It's very old, isn't it?" He turned it over in his hand. "What does the map show?"

Tryan and Elyssa both looked at him oddly. "*Map?* What map?"

Stellan pointed to a faded symbol on the back of the card. "That arrow with the eagle wings instead of fletching . . . it's an old compass marker. Ancient mapmakers used it to indicate north, especially those near L'bekken around the time of the last cataclysm. Not that I'm a hundred per cent sure, mind you. Like I said, it's my wife, not me, who's the historian." He studied the table curiously for a moment as Elyssa and Tryan traded a glance that worried Warlock a great deal. Nyah was pressing so hard against him, he had to brace himself to stop taking a step backward. She had, however, all but been forgotten by the immortals.

"Are these cards in order, my lady?"

"Near enough."

"Then it makes sense," he said, placing the card back on the table face down. "This would be the bottom corner of the map. I'll bet, if you turn them over, the other cards will join up."

Elyssa glanced at her brother, who shrugged, as if it could do no harm. So she began turning the cards over. A moment later, Tryan began helping her. Even the duke joined in. It took some time. The cards were dangerously fragile so they had to be gentle, but after a time, all the cards lay face down on the table.

The humans stared at the cards in wonder. Although they were brittle and the map darkened by great age, Stellan Desean was right. Even from where he was standing, Warlock could see the back of the cards formed a map of sorts, although not a very cohesive one. Not all the cards were in the right places, some of the detail had faded beyond recognition, and a few cards had holes in several places, meaning their secrets were lost forever.

He wondered if the Cabal knew about this.

Was that the purpose of the Tarot? Not to tell the story of the Tide Lords, but to hide another secret?

Is that what makes the Lore Tarot different? The Lore Tarot wasn't really a Tarot, it was a map?

Most of the Tarot decks Warlock had seen had decorative, meaningless patterns on the backs of the cards. He'd never seen one like this.

"Look! It really *is* a map!" Nyah said, curiosity winning out over fear. The little princess let go of Warlock's hand, moving forward for a closer look. "What's it a map of, though? There're no place names marked on it."

The duke, who was studying the map almost as intently, shrugged. "Mountains. Or mountainous terrain. Which means it could be anywhere on Amyrantha, I suppose."

"No," Elyssa said, pursing her lips. "I think I've a rough idea where it is." She glanced up at her brother. "It's not the sewers of the Herino Palace, that's for certain."

Tryan ignored the jibe. Stellan just looked at her oddly.

Elyssa, her gaze still fixed on Tryan, said, "This is the countryside in the Shevron Mountains, around Maralyce's Mine."

To his credit, Stellan Desean didn't even flinch. Tryan was silent for a moment and then looked at Nyah. "How did you get to Glaeba, when you say you were kidnapped?"

Without hesitating, Nyah shrugged. "I don't know, my lord. They put a wet cloth over my face that made me fall asleep. By the time I woke up, we were already there."

Elyssa turned her attention back to the map. "Forget the child, Try. She doesn't know anything. Tides, I can't believe it was right here in front of us the whole time."

"You've been looking for this map for some time, my lady?" Stellan asked.

She nodded absently, her attention fixed on the cards. "Like your wife, I also have an interest in history." Nyah moved a little too close, blocking Elyssa's light. The immortal glanced up and frowned. "You may return to your lessons, Nyah."

"But Cecil said you wanted to speak—"

"*Go!*"

Nyah stepped back, her eyes shining with unshed tears. Warlock didn't know if she was acting or genuinely frightened by the Immortal Maiden, but whichever it was, it had the desired effect.

"Oh, Tides, child, there's no need to cry about it. I didn't mean to yell at you."

"I'll escort her back to her lessons," Stellan offered diplomatically. "But I would appreciate you keeping me informed of your progress." He glanced down at the map. "This is truly fascinating."

"Thank you, Lord Stellan," Tryan said, giving Nyah an irritated glare. "If we find anything interesting, you'll be the first to know."

The duke nodded and smiled and took Nyah by the hand. After ordering her to say good morning to her stepfather and her step-aunt, he led her from the room.

It wasn't until he'd closed the door on them that Warlock realised Stellan Desean had not only stopped the immortals from asking any questions of the little princess, but had found a way to distract them from her—and his own Scard-born disobedience—without raising any suspicion at all.

On the down side, in the process he may have given the immortals access to something far worse.

Warlock didn't know what the map was for, but if Tryan the Devil and the Immortal Maiden were anxious to get their hands on whatever treasure the cards were hiding, it was unlikely to be a good thing for anything mortal living on Amyrantha.

Chapter 59

House Medura sent a fleet of fifteen, shallow-draughted, amphibian-towed ships into the wetlands to confront the Tide Lords who'd dared challenge their authority. Cydne's family was not alone in their endeavour. Several ships in the armada carried the colours of the House Pardura and there was even one carrying the colours of the Physicians' Guild. The ship in the lead, however, although it wore the colours of House Medura and the guild, was an entirely different problem because standing on the deck were a dozen clerics wearing dark, flowing robes and the pious expressions of true believers.

"Tides," Arryl muttered when she saw them. "I should have anticipated this."

"Who are they?" Declan asked.

"Clerics. From the Church of the Lord of Temperance."

Tipped off by Azquil and Tiji, they were waiting on the dock when the ships arrived. The three immortals were standing across the end of the wharf as the lead ship threw out lines, which the amphibians hurriedly pulled out of the water to secure to the pylons. The rest of the ships hung back in reserve, waiting to see the outcome of the negotiations before they moved in.

"They're the priests from Jaxyn's cult?" Although Declan knew of the Church of the Lord of Temperance, and could identify some of its members who'd passed though Glaeba, they were a secretive bunch. Almost as secretive as the Cabal. He'd never actually met one of their clerics before.

"They'd be a joke if they weren't so deadly serious," Cayal told him, as they watched the gangway thump down onto the dock. "They've been known to order adulterous women stoned, punish members of the Church for questioning their doctrine. They believe all sex is sinful, except for the purposes of procreation—although apparently the men can take as many slaves to their beds as they want, because they're not actually *people*. Drinking to excess is forbidden; any sort of fun, really."

Declan smiled at the irony. "Clearly, they've never met the Lord of Temperance in person."

"Doubt they want to," Arryl said. "They're entranced by the idea of him, not who he really is." Then she noticed the two naked women tied to the mast and Declan felt the Tide surge angrily around her. "There's Ambria and Medwen. Bastards."

Declan studied the women curiously, a little surprised at how young Medwen looked. Ambria seemed to be in her mid-thirties, but dusky-skinned Medwen seemed little more than a girl. Neither woman looked particularly bothered by their predicament, however. Ambria seemed annoyed, Medwen quite bored.

How many other times had they found themselves in similar situations? he wondered. *How many times in the past had they been run out of towns as witches, tortured for not growing old . . .*

Tides, how many times do you have to be tied naked to a stake and paraded around for all to humiliate you, and ridicule you, to become bored by it?

With the gangway secured, the priests began to disembark in single file and array themselves across the dock facing the immortals. As they did, another two clerics untied the two immortal women and dragged them down the gangway too, forcing them to kneel in front of the clerics. Ulag Pardura and the others on the ship stayed where they were, apparently content to let their clerics deal with these presumptuous immortals. The last man to disembark wore a long black robe, a tall pointed hat and carried a gloriously jewelled staff, which to Declan's mind, didn't seem very temperate at all.

The cleric stepped forward, pointing to the naked immortals. "The spawn of evil is upon us!"

"The spawn of evil is upon us!" the line of clerics behind him repeated in a monotone.

"We curse these evil creatures!"

The clerics echoed his words again, in the same, dead voices.

"Not wasting any time on small talk, I see," Arryl remarked.

"You don't negotiate with evil," Cayal said. "First rule of the religious fanatics' handbook, Arryl. *Engaging a demon in conversation only gives him an opportunity to beguile and tempt you.* You should know that."

"We call upon the power of the almighty, all powerful Jaxyn, Lord of Temperance, to give us strength!" The cleric chanted over them, making a point not to look any of the five immortals before him in the eye.

"We curse these evil creatures!" the chorus line echoed dutifully.

"We call on the power of our deity," the cleric leading the chant cried out, his voice full of passion now he was really getting warmed up. "We call on his power, his wisdom and his wrath, to banish these minions of evil back to the demonic realm from whence they came!"

"We curse these evil creatures!"

"What are they doing?" Declan asked, not sure of the purpose of all this flowery prayer.

Arryl shrugged, a little bemused. "I think we're being exorcised."

Cayal laughed aloud, which obviously infuriated the head cleric, even though he was trying to give the impression he was ignoring the three demons blocking his way into the village. "Exorcised? Tides, does he think we're going to vanish in a puff of smoke when he's finished?"

"I imagine he's hoping we will."

"How would he know?" Declan asked. "I mean, he can't have done this before."

"Which is probably why he hasn't discovered yet that it doesn't work."

"We call on the power of the deity," the cleric repeated, almost yelling now. He raised his staff high. "We call on his power, his wisdom and his wrath, to banish these minions of evil back to the demonic realm from whence they came!"

"We curse these evil creatures and banish them from our realm!" echoed the line of clerics. Unlike their leader, the priests seemed to have fallen into a trance.

"Do you think this is going to take long?" Declan asked.

"No, because I'm putting an end to it." Arryl made to step forward toward her immortal sisters to aid them, but Cayal held her back.

"Now, now," he said. "It probably took these poor fellows years of kneeling on really uncomfortable cold stone floors to learn all this crap, and it would be very unkind of us to stop them now, before they've had a chance to treat us to the full benefit of their suffering."

"I banish you, spawn of evil!" the head cleric called to the heavens, and then he banged his staff on the dock three times. "Once, twice and thrice do I banish thee from this realm!"

Right on cue, the chorus line chimed in. *"We curse these evil creatures and banish them from our realm!"*

Arryl glared at the Immortal Prince in annoyance. "I'm glad you're having fun, Cayal, because Ambria and Medwen are—"

"Just fine," Cayal said. "Let him finish."

"He has a point, my lady," Declan said, realising what Cayal was getting at. Ambria and Medwen, although naked, on their knees and clearly fed up with being prisoners, were not in any immediate danger. The clerics, however, obviously believed they had the power, awarded them by their god, to deal with any other immortal interlopers. "If they don't finish the ceremony and learn for themselves that it doesn't work, they'll just keep coming back to try it again."

Cayal glanced at Declan and nodded approvingly. "Tides, Rodent, you may not be as stupid as you look, after all."

"By the power of the Lord of Temperance, he who commands the Tide, he who led us from the wilderness and into the light of his pure presence, I command thee to flee back to the darkness where thee belong. Begone, foul demons. Begone, whores and drunkards. I command thee in the name of my Lord!"

"Fine. Have it your way. Just so long as you know I think this is ridiculous, and we shouldn't be pandering to these fools." Arryl folded her arms in annoyance, but made no further move to interrupt the cleric.

"*We curse these evil creatures and banish them from our realm.*"

"Is this the first time they've been here, my lady?"

Arryl nodded. "We've gone to a great deal of trouble to keep our presence here secret. That's what was so useful about being known as the Trinity. Nobody but the people living in the wetlands thought we were real."

"Do you think Jaxyn knows about this?" Declan asked, as the cleric ushered a young man with a shaved head forward. He was carrying a small bowl of burning incense. The cleric took the chain from him and started waving it around. The smell, when it reached Declan and the others, was sickly sweet.

"Let the sacred smoke sear your lungs, as the purity of our Lord's essence chokes the evil from your souls."

"*We curse these evil creatures and banish them from our realm.*"

"He knows there's a church where they follow the Lord of Temperance," Cayal said. "Not sure if he knows anything about this nonsense. He really doesn't like being known as the Lord of Temperance, so he's never been that interested in them."

"Let the spirit of the Lord of Temperance imbue thy being! Leave this realm, evil demons, I command thee in the name of our Lord, or risk his righteous wrath!"

"*We curse these evil creatures and banish them from our realm.*"

"Do you think he'd approve?"

"I think he'd fall about laughing at them, actually," Arryl said with a frown. "Jaxyn never was one for ceremony."

"I'm sure if they were offering up virgins as sacrifices, he'd find a way to cope, though," Cayal remarked.

"Begone, wicked whores and drunkards! Begone, men who would lay with their own kind. Begone, women who would seduce righteous men from their wives. Begone, men who would lay with animals. Begone, all who sully our Lord's gift, by using it for pleasure."

The cleric's face had turned quite red and there was a note of desperation in his voice. Declan guessed the poor chap thought they'd be long gone by now.

Wonder what's going to happen when he runs out of chants?

"*We curse these evil creatures and banish them from our realm!*"

"They really don't know our Jaxyn at all, do they?" Cayal said, starting to sound a little cross. "Tides, how long can one exorcism take? That chanting is really starting to grate."

"You were the one who wanted to let them finish," Arryl reminded him.

Cayal sighed heavily, but said nothing further. Declan could feel the Tide around him, though, swirling dangerously. For the clerics' sake, he hoped the ceremony took a little longer, because all hell was going to break loose when they were done and they learned their exorcism ceremony had done nothing but irritate the immortals they foolishly thought they could banish.

Chapter 60

It took the better part of three hours for the head cleric to run through his full repertoire of chants, prayers and curses, designed to banish the immortal spawn of evil from this worldly realm. By the time he was done, the sun was high in the sky, the heat was oppressive and Cayal was fantasising about making the cleric bleed to death through his eyeballs in retaliation for forcing him to suffer through this interminable and utterly futile ceremony.

The cleric banged his staff another three times on the dock and looked around, his expression confused when the immortals failed to vaporise where they stood through the power of prayer.

"Are we done now?" Cayal asked.

The cleric glared at him worriedly for a moment and then turned to his priests and raised his staff. "They are impostors!" he cried. "True demons would have been banished with the power of our Lord's prayers."

Tides, Cayal thought. *This boy thinks on his feet. No wonder he's the head cleric.*

"Medwen! Ambria! Come here."

The two other members of the Trinity, who'd knelt silently, though with increasing irritation, in the hot sun during the entire exorcism, climbed to their feet. The priests who ran forward to restrain them got no more than a couple of steps before they began to gasp and choke, courtesy of the Rodent who was demonstrating a tad more initiative—and control of the Tide—than Cayal felt comfortable with. Medwen turned, kicked the nearest choking cleric in the head, and then walked up the dock with Ambria.

Cayal weakened the metal on their chains with the Tide as they approached, watching the clerics pale as the bindings melted away, with a degree of malicious satisfaction. Arryl hurried to them, embraced both women, and then led them back along the dock toward the village, pausing only to tell him on the way past, "Make sure they don't come back."

The other women followed her, gazing with open curiosity and puzzlement at Hawkes. Arryl would explain their new Tide Lord later, Cayal supposed. Right now, they had the Church of the Lord of Temperance and this wretched invasion fleet to deal with.

He nodded and spared the women no more thought, turning to face the clerics with Hawkes at his side, who, for all his faults and ignorance of being immortal, certainly knew how to intimidate men. Of all the professions one could have trained in before becoming immortal, Cayal supposed spymaster was among the most useful.

Cayal could feel the Tide surging as Hawkes fought to keep it under control.

"You ready for this?"

"No," Hawkes answered honestly.

Cayal smiled. "Let's do it then."

"Do what, exactly?"

"Follow my lead. I created the Lord of Temperance, you know. I can take him down just as easily."

"You're going to pretend to be Jaxyn?"

"In a word . . . yes."

"You don't think they'll notice that you're not?"

Cayal shrugged. "These people don't know Jaxyn from a pile of horse shit."

"How are you going to prove you're him?"

Cayal sighed. He didn't have time to lecture the Rodent on theology. "The trouble with any belief system based on faith is that it's based on, well, faith. You have to believe, with your heart and soul, something you can't prove and quite often something you have solid evidence to the contrary. So, if you *have* faith, you don't *need* proof. Confronted with your god, therefore, to ask for proof is to admit you have no faith . . ."

Hawkes stared at him for a moment and then shook his head. "You're insane."

"Have a bit of faith," Cayal couldn't help responding.

The spymaster looked at him askance and then shook his head. "I'm going to regret doing anything you advise, aren't I?"

"Maybe. One day. But not today," Cayal assured him. "Now . . . front and centre, Rodent. We're on."

Together they turned to confront the head cleric, who was looking quite panicked, as were his followers, who seemed to accept his notion of impostors right up until the chains melted off Ambria and Medwen. On the ships behind them the railings were crowded with silent onlookers. The sailors and marines waiting impatiently to find out how much longer they would have to stand around doing nothing, before they were allowed to disembark and begin wiping Watershed Falls—and any other village in the wetlands they could reach—off the face of the map, for the crime of killing Cydne Medura.

Pity they'd not brought a few ships full of Crasii felines into battle. Then he could really have had some fun.

"How dare you take my name in vain!"

The cleric looked at Cayal in shock. "What?"

"Don't you know who this is?" Hawkes asked, falling in with Cayal's subterfuge without so much as an eye-blink. "On your knees before the Lord of Temperance, you pitiful fool!"

"I . . . er . . ."

Tides, they talk all the time about the will of their gods, but they never spare a thought for what they'd do if confronted by him in person.

"Why do you think your prayers don't work on me?" Cayal asked. "You cannot banish the agents of evil unless they are . . . well, the agents . . . of evil."

"*You* are the Lord of Temperance?" The cleric looked very worried, and not, Cayal suspected, because he'd just called his deity a *minion of evil.* The problem he had now was how to determine if Cayal was telling the truth without appearing to lack faith. Given Cayal had just survived his exorcism and made his prisoners' chains dissolve, this man standing before him might well be his god, so the cleric couldn't really afford to give the impression he was questioning his identity.

On the other hand, he didn't want to look like a fool . . .

"If you are the Lord of Temperance, then you will bless our venture this day."

"It is not your place to tell your god what he will or will not bless," Hawkes said. "I am curious, though, about why you're still on your feet."

It was a little bit worrying, how good the spymaster was at things like this.

The cleric stared at them blankly for a moment and then fell to his knees, motioning behind him to make his priests follow suit.

"Much better."

"My lord . . ."

"I have not given you permission to speak." Cayal looked over the kneeling priests, wondering what would make the most impact on these people. Arryl's insistence he restrict the loss of life to a minimum made the job much more challenging. There must be a thousand men on these gathered ships, waiting to disembark. A thousand corpses washing up against the docks of the Delta Settlement would have sent the message he wanted to get across rather pointedly. "Nor," he added, looking down at the priest, "have I given you permission to annihilate my servants."

The cleric risked an upward glance. "Your *servants*, my lord?"

"The Crasii were made by us . . . me . . ." he corrected, hoping the cleric didn't notice the slip. These people considered everything in creation Jaxyn's work. No true god, after all, needed help whipping up a whole world and every creature on it, into being. "They are not for you to remove on a whim."

"These creatures murdered the scion of House Medura, my lord."

"After you sent him here to murder my servants."

"That was not the work of your believers, my lord," the cleric hurried to assure him. "That was the orders of the Physicians' Guild."

"Then bring me someone from this Physicians' Guild," Cayal ordered loudly "so he may explain to me why I shouldn't destroy every man here for disrespecting my handiwork."

The cleric signalled to one of his priests, who hurried up the gangway of the ship tied to the dock. A few moments later a man emerged from the crowd, wearing an embroidered waistcoat and a very worried expression. Like a pack of dogs, every man here was bowing submissively to the one behaving as if he was born to rule them. That was something Cayal had learned in Tenacia when he was seeding the Crasii farms. There wasn't that much difference, really, between the way the pack animals and humans acted when they got together in large numbers. Victory invariably belonged to the one who was able to intimidate the others into believing he had the upper hand.

The nervous-looking man came down the gangway and stood before Cayal.

"On your knees," Hawkes ordered.

"I do not belong to the Church of the Lord of Temperance," the physician replied. "I'm certainly not going to bow to some fool claiming to be a god. This nonsense has gone on long enough."

Cayal was very relieved to hear it. The cleric had no choice but to believe him, which meant there wasn't anything to prove. But Cayal needed a show of force. In the end, if the wetlands were ever going to be left in peace, they needed to convince every man here it was unwise to return, not just some easily deluded priest.

"You are the one who ordered the poisoning of the wetland Crasii to stop the spread of swamp fever?" Cayal asked. He didn't mind if the man remained standing. The others would be able to see him—and his fate— better that way.

"We value human life over the life of mere animals," the man replied, neatly avoiding taking responsibility for actually issuing the order. "And the creatures who murdered a human in cold blood must be called to account for it."

"The wetlands and every creature in them are under my protection."

"Interesting," the physician remarked. "I thought the Trinity were the goddesses of the wetlands. Does the Church of the Lord of Temperance now claim them as parishioners too?" The man looked thoughtfully at the kneeling cleric, apparently more concerned with the political implications of such an arrangement than he was with the danger he might be in from the self-proclaimed god he was challenging.

"The Trinity are merely my agents," Cayal said, having already thought up an answer to that rather sticky little theological detail. "They protect the wetlands on my behalf. You, on the other hand, send poisoners here to kill my people. Someone must be called to account for that too, don't you think?"

The physician cast his gaze over Cayal's shoulder at the empty village behind them. Only Arryl, Medwen, Ambria, Arkady, the two chameleons that always seemed to be hanging around the Rodent and the feline who'd caused all this trouble were visible.

"*You're* going to call us to account?" the man from the Physicians' Guild asked, with a short, sceptical laugh. "How?"

"Ah, finally," Cayal said, glancing at Hawkes with a grin he couldn't smother.

As the man fell headfirst into the trap, Cayal plunged into the Tide, feeling Hawkes following him a split second later.

"I thought you'd never ask."

Chapter 61

Guessing the prisoners would want something to wear once they were free, Arkady sent Jojo to find them some clothes during the interminable wait forced upon them by the exorcism ceremony. When they were finally released, Arkady was waiting with a wrap for each of the immortals when Arryl hurried them away from the dock. There seemed to be no reason for the women to be undressed, other than the persistent and disturbing tendency of Senestran men to humiliate women they considered beneath them, by removing their clothes.

When Ambria and Medwen reached Arkady and the two immortals realised the woman handing them clothes was the same woman they'd condemned to death, however, they seemed mightily displeased.

"Was I imagining things or did we not tie this murderous little bitch to the Justice Tree a few days ago?" Medwen asked, her dark eyes studying Arkady with open hostility, as she snatched the wrap from her hand.

"Forget her," Ambria said, barely even acknowledging Arkady or Tiji and Azquil who stood beside her as she dressed. "I'm more interested in who that immortal is with Cayal. And for that matter, what in the name of the Tides is *Cayal* doing here?"

"Defending us, no less," Medwen added with a worried frown.

Arryl smiled reassuringly at her immortal sisters. "The who is Declan Hawkes. The *why* is because I made a deal with Cayal to help us. As for Arkady, here . . . well, she's a friend of Hawkes's. He . . . intervened in her execution."

"*Intervened*? Tides, Arryl, where did he come from? Who is he? *What* is he? I can feel his power from here," Ambria said.

Arkady stared toward the dock, more than a little nervous about what would happen next. It was hard to tell what was going on down there. A portly man in an embroidered waistcoat seemed to be pushing through the crowd toward the gangway on the deck of the vessel tied to the wharf. Declan and Cayal were still standing in front of the clerics, much as they had been for the past few hours. The women were too far away to hear what was said, and Arkady had no way of detecting any movement on the Tide.

"What deal did you do with Cayal, Arryl?" Medwen asked unhappily as she tied the wrap around her body. With her hair down and her dark, dusky skin, even grubby and dishevelled, she was gorgeous. It wasn't hard to see why Cayal found her desirable. Arkady imagined this was what she'd looked like in Magreth, when she'd first been made immortal. She seemed little more than an adolescent, which was disconcerting because she had to be at least eight thousand years old.

"He wants me . . . us . . . to go to Jelidia with him. Lukys is down there and has apparently discovered a way for Cayal to die and claims he needs all the immortal help he can find to make it happen. I agreed I'd go with him, if he helped me rescue you two and ensure the Physicians' Guild doesn't come back the moment our backs are turned."

Ambria shook her head. "Lukys is having a lend of him, Arryl. He needs all the immortal help he can get for something, I don't doubt, but I don't believe for a moment that it has anything to do with helping Cayal die."

"Be that as it may, that's the deal I've struck," Arryl said. "I promised I'd go with him. Although I didn't make the same promise on your behalf."

"A good thing too," Ambria said. "I'm not going anywhere with that maniac." She turned to Arkady. "Who is this Declan Hawkes?"

Arkady took a step backward in fear. Ambria was much more abrupt and much less friendly than Arryl. "He's . . . a friend. I've known him since we were children. His grandfather was a Tidewatcher."

"Maralyce's son, if you believe Hawkes's tale," Arryl added.

"Maralyce gave birth?" Medwen said in surprise. "Tides, I would have thought her long past that."

"In the normal course of events, we'd all be long past it," Ambria said. She turned to Arryl. "Do you believe him?"

"I suppose," Arryl replied with a shrug. "It's all been happening a little too quickly to give the matter too much thought, to be honest. I was worried about you two."

Medwen smiled briefly. "You needn't have worried. Besides stripping us naked, beating us a bit and threatening to rape us if we didn't confess to whatever it was they decided we were guilty of, they didn't hurt us much."

"They threatened to *rape* you?" Arkady said, before she could stop herself. For some reason, hearing that infuriated her. Why did men think they could command such power? What gave them the right to use what was, essentially, the weakest part of their body, to inflict the most pain?

Medwen didn't seem nearly as bothered by the notion as Arkady. "Men always threaten that. It's the last—and sometimes the first—resort of the unimaginative interrogator."

"They should have threatened to keep praying to Jaxyn," Ambria grumbled. "That would have had me confessing to anything they wanted to hear, had it gone on much longer." She looked past Arkady and beckoned Azquil forward. "Be a pet and find me some wine, would you, Azquil. I could do with a—" She stopped abruptly and turned to look at the dock. "Hello! We're on."

Arkady guessed she meant that Cayal or Declan (or maybe both of them) was drawing on the Tide.

They all turned to watch the gathered ships as a scream split the relatively quiet morning, followed by a splash as someone fell from the rigging on one of the vessels anchored further out in the channel. A few moments later, another man fell, and then another. Astonished, Arkady looked around, wondering if the Tide Lords were creating a wind to blow the sailors off the masts, but the air was still, even the myriad wetland insects pausing for this momentous confrontation.

"Tides," Ambria said, as another sailor fell, "surely that's not Cayal demonstrating restraint?"

"I made him promise to keep the casualties to a minimum," Arryl said. She flinched as yet another man hit the water with a resounding splash.

Arkady had no idea what they were talking about. From her perspective, for no apparent reason men had started falling from the ships. "What are they doing?"

Medwen turned to Arkady, her expression quite peeved. "Why? Hoping you can use it on the next lot of hapless innocents you want to dispose of?"

"Leave her be, Medwen," Arryl said. "It wasn't Arkady's fault."

"So *she* says . . ."

Arryl ignored the comment and turned to Arkady to explain. "They seem to be using magic to disrupt the senses of the sailors. As discouragements go, it's about as benign as you can get using the Tide."

"Not something Cayal would normally do?"

"Not as a rule," Ambria agreed. She looked at Arryl, her expression sceptical. "Which means he *really* wants our help, or your new immortal is actually a good influence on him." She turned back to watch, frowning at the panic spreading through the armada. There were scores of men lining the rails and quite a few of them appeared to be vomiting into the water. The clerics were chanting again, although it was hard to tell if they were back to trying their exorcism or if they believed the men standing before them on the dock really were gods and they were offering them prayers of worship.

Within a few minutes, even some of the men leaning on the railings began to fall. The amphibians slipped their harnesses and began to drag the victims to safety. Her heart in her throat, Arkady watched this strange scene unfold, trying to make sense of what she was witnessing. The idea of the immortals using magic to terrify mortals into submission seemed only slightly less ludicrous than the idea Declan was one of them. Was he wielding the Tide like Cayal? *With* Cayal? Did he have the same sort of power?

Tides, suppose he has the same potential as someone like Kentravyon? Will he lose his temper some day and destroy civilisation as we know it?

Will he turn into a monster?

Arkady's reconciliation with Declan was too fresh, the realisation they were finally together after so many years apart too fragile to rattle with that sort of doubt. And then a memory flashed to mind, one of those childhood snippets that had an unfortunate habit of clawing its way to the surface when she least expected it. It was a memory from back when they were happy, back when they were free to roam the slums at will.

They'd been watching a parade, Arkady recalled, she and Declan, one that passed through the slums of Lebec on its way to the more salubrious part of town. She didn't remember exactly what it was for, only that the king and queen had been part of it, and the old Duke of Lebec. It must have been spring, around the time of the annual King's Ball, because the king rarely visited Lebec at any other time of the year. They'd watched all those fabulously dressed, wealthy and powerful people ride past for an hour or more, dreaming of a life neither of them ever imagined they would be a part of.

"*You know, Pop says it's not good for any man to be too rich or too powerful,*" Declan remarked after a time.

"*Why not?*" Arkady remembered asking, clinging to Declan for fear of falling from the high wall he'd coaxed her into climbing to afford them a better view of the proceedings.

"*He says power corrupts men. And the more you get, the more it corrupts you.*"

"*So, what happens if you get all the power in the world?*"

Arkady remembered Declan grinning mischievously. "*I dunno. I think it would be fun, though, to find out . . .*"

"The new boy seems to be holding his own on the Tide," Medwen remarked with a frown, dragging Arkady's attention back to the matter at hand. "How did you say he was made?"

Arryl answered Medwen without taking her eyes off the scene on the dock. "He was accidentally immolated in a fire. We think he had more than a Tidewatcher grandfather too. We think he had an immortal father."

"Cayal suggested it might be Lukys," Arkady added.

Medwen and Ambria both turned to look at her briefly. "Lukys found a way to have an immortal son?" The dark immortal smiled sourly at her sister.

Ambria shook her head. "I don't care whose son he is," she said. "I've spent too much time caught up in the schemes and plots of the Emperor and Empress of the Five Realms, thank you very much. I've seen first-hand what immortality does to a family and I want no part of it." She fixed her gaze on Arryl. "Go to Jelidia if you want. Take Medwen with you. Take this mortal assassin and this feline here that you seem to have acquired; take all of them with you, if you must. But this reeks of trouble I want no part of. I'm staying here."

Chapter 62

Declan's blood sang with the Tide. There was nothing comparable in his experience; nothing in his life had prepared him for the exhilaration, the power, the feeling of invincibility that imbued every fibre of his being when he plunged into the Tide.

But the feeling that somehow it was wrong tainted his elation. All his life, Declan had been taught to hate the Tide Lords, to despise their weakness, their venality. *How easily they seemed to succumb to the lure of power*, he'd once arrogantly scoffed. How quickly they scrabbled for dominance over each other.

Now he was here with the Tide surging through him, Declan no longer wondered at how easily men fell victim to its lure.

He wondered how they managed to resist it at all.

They were not swimming very deep in the Tide. Declan knew that. They were merely making waves that disrupted the inner-ear fluids of the men arrayed against them, until barely a man among them was able to stand upright, and that took hardly any power at all. Some of the men reacted badly, the disorientation making them ill. Others fell, either from the rigging or where they were standing. The amphibians remained relatively unaffected. Cayal had shown Declan exactly where to pitch his disruptive wave so it would affect only humans.

He was taking his promise to Arryl about minimum casualties seriously, it seemed.

There was no sense of time, swimming the Tide; just a feeling of exhilaration matched by nothing Declan had ever experienced in the mortal world. *How easy it would be*, he realised, *to swim out deep, to drown in the glory of this*. How easy to call on every drop of magic you could drink and not care about the consequences.

Tides, what must it feel like when the Tide is at its peak?

"Concentrate!" Cayal barked impatiently beside him, as Declan began to drift.

He reeled in his senses, glad of the reminder. It was so easy to slip away. So easy to let the Tide take you whole.

Causing a cataclysm, even accidentally, didn't seem nearly so implausible any longer.

"Stop it!"

Declan opened his eyes at the physician's cry and looked around in amazement. The water was full of men struggling for air; the ships lined with sick, disoriented sailors.

"Enough!" the man from the guild cried again, looking around him in horror. He was on his knees, a pool of vomit on the dock in front of him. "Stop this sickness!"

It was then that Declan realised the physician, even though he'd experienced the same symptoms as the other men, had no notion of what they'd done to him. He thought their magical disruption of his sense of balance an illness, some sort of fast-spreading plague.

And Cayal, apparently, was quite happy to let him keep thinking it.

"I warned you swamp fever would seem mild by comparison," the immortal said, looking down on the man without pity. "So let this be a lesson to you." He turned to address the cleric and his minions. "You have witnessed my power, priest, and now I charge you to take word back to the rest of your people. The power of the Lord of Temperance must not be denied."

"I am your servant, O Great and Fearful Lord," the cleric said, touching his forehead to the dock.

Looking more than a little smug, Cayal observed the chaos that had been, until a short while ago, an orderly and dangerous invasion fleet. He opened his arms wide, speaking loudly enough to be heard by every man present. "You will inform your people that the wetlands enjoy my special protection. No man who does not believe in me, and the power I have vested in the Trinity, shall be permitted to set foot in this region." He stopped for a moment, and then added, "I command you to send clerics here, to enforce my will. They will have no control over the residents of the wetlands, only my permission to destroy any non-believer who dares sully this sacred ground. So sayest I, Jaxyn, Lord of Temperance!"

Cayal was doing a proper job of this, Declan realised. He was making it possible for Arryl and the others to leave Senestra, certain they wouldn't follow him anywhere if they considered the Crasii of the wetlands in any danger of attack once the Trinity was no longer physically present.

"I am your servant, O Great and Fearful Lord," the cleric repeated, pale and awestruck by this demonstration of power that he was too fearful to admit he needed to witness in order to believe this really was his precious deity. "It shall be as you command."

Cayal's expression was suitably thunderous. "Then I free you from the terror of my wrath," he said, as Declan felt him pulling back from the Tide.

With a great deal of reluctance, Declan followed suit.

"Begone from this place! Take word back to your people your Lord walks among you. Tell them of the fever and how I will smite your cities with my wrath if you defy me!"

Sailors and marines were superstitious creatures at the best of times. They didn't need to be told twice. Once the immortals released the Tide, and their equilibrium was no longer being affected, the men recovered quite quickly and began to scrabble aboard their ships. The amphibians, for whom a command from a Tide Lord was irresistible anyway, didn't even need to be ordered to slip back into their harnesses.

The man from the Physicians' Guild struggled to his feet, glared at Cayal and Declan for a moment, and then staggered toward his ship, where he was helped aboard by Ulag Pardura and the man Declan guessed was the one actually in charge of this invasion, who was probably Cydne's father. A short, bitter argument they didn't quite catch ensued, followed by the doctor staggering below and the older man angrily giving the order to cast off.

The invasion of the wetlands, for all intents and purposes, was over.

Pulling back from the Tide left Declan bereft. Cayal must have known it would, because as they waited for the clerics to board their ship, and the fleet get itself organised enough to withdraw, he put a hand on Declan's shoulder. It might have looked like a brotherly gesture from a distance, but his grip was so tight it was almost painful.

"Take a deep breath."

"I'm fine."

"No, you're not. Take a deep breath and let it go. Slowly."

"Get your hands off me."

"Don't make me make you, Rodent. It won't be pleasant."

Despite the threat, Declan forced himself to release the last of the Tide. It drained out of him like a wave running back to the sea. He could have wept for the loss of it.

"Rule one," Cayal said, taking his hand from Declan's shoulder as he felt him letting go. "Never hang on to the Tide a moment longer than you have to."

"Who made that rule up?"

"The second immortal to touch the Tide, I'm guessing."

"Why the second?"

"Because he saw what it did to the first one."

Declan glanced at Cayal, a little surprised to see he wasn't joking.

"You feel like crap now, right?"

Reluctant though he was to admit any weakness to Cayal, Declan nod-ded. "I've felt better."

"And the best you'll ever feel is when you're swimming the Tide," Cayal warned. "Learn to live with the disappointment. And learn to deal with it. You'll find a way eventually, but you're in for a fun time of it un-til you do."

"Why do you care?"

"I told you, Rodent. I need your power and I need you with some idea of what to do with it."

"Ah yes, I forgot about your altruistic motives there for a moment."

They stood watching the ship pull away from the dock, their conversa-tion completely at odds with their surroundings. *Is this what it's always go-ing to be like? Pretending to be normal, while the world recedes into the distance? Fighting the urge to plunge into the Tide and never return? This fidgety, unset-tling absence that can only be filled with the Tide? Tides, my skin's on fire . . .*

Finally, Cayal said, "You'll find out the hard way, Rodent, that in the end there's nobody who cares for you but you. Altruism is for mortals who never have to learn that lesson the hard way."

"Is cynicism a side effect of the Tide too?"

"No, that comes from living too long."

"So I have that to look forward to as well? Eternity sounds like just one fun thing after another. I can't wait."

"You won't have to if Lukys succeeds," Cayal said, an odd emotion in his voice that gave Declan a glimmer of the suicidal desperation driving this man. "Why don't you go back to the others?" he said a moment later, his instant of weakness gone before Declan had barely registered it. "I'm sure explaining everything, all over again, to Medwen and Ambria is going to take a while. Good thing you and Arkady have sorted things out."

"Why?"

"Because if you're anything like me, Rodent, the quickest way to cure what ails you right now is to find a woman—if possible a willing one, which I've always thought preferable to taking them by force—and take your ease in her warm and understanding embrace." Cayal smiled. "I wonder how grateful Medwen's feeling, right about now, about being rescued?"

Declan shook his head, idly wishing bashing Cayal's head into a bloody pulp would actually achieve something useful. "You are crude beyond belief, Cayal."

The Immortal Prince smiled. He didn't seem bothered by Declan's low opinion of him. "But sadly right, Rodent. It's one of the things nobody gets about wielding the Tide. There's a *reason*, you know, why none of us want anything to do with Elyssa after she's been swimming the Tide."

Declan shook his head. "I suspect, if I had any brains, I'd get on that ship and have it take me as far from you and your lunatic kind as I can get."

Cayal looked at him then, his expression bleak. "Only we're *your* lunatic kind, now. And you can't ever escape that. Believe me, I know what I'm talking about. I've tried."

Cayal was right about one thing: Declan was not looking forward to the whole "how is it you're immortal?" conversation again, this time with Medwen and Ambria. Fortunately, he was saved from it—temporarily, at least—by Arkady. As soon as the last of the fleet sailed out of view, he and Cayal turned for the village and Arkady ran down to meet them.

Apparently she wasn't any more enamoured of the company of these new immortals than he was.

"Do you think they'll be back?" she asked as the immortals approached.

Cayal glanced back over his shoulder at the now empty channel and then shrugged. "Not for a while."

Her gaze fixed on Declan. "Were you . . . ?"

"Using Tide magic?" Cayal finished for her. And then he laughed. "Tides, you two must be having a time of it. A year ago you didn't even believe it existed. And look at you now."

"Cayal," Arkady said impatiently. "Just shut up, would you?"

The Immortal Prince smiled, their dilemma a source of endless amusement, it seemed. "I will, I will. We have a deal, after all." He turned to Declan. "Why don't you and Arkady get lost for a while, Rodent? I have to talk to Medwen and Ambria anyway, and it'll be easier if they're not sitting there staring at you, wondering where the hell you came from." With a knowing smile, Cayal left them standing in the street, and headed up the road toward the three immortal women and their Crasii servants.

"Do you want to go back to the others?" Declan asked.

"Tides, no," she said, taking his hand. "Let's get out of here. I've had all the immortals I can handle for a while." She smiled up at him and added apologetically, "Present company excepted, of course."

They walked in the opposite direction from where Cayal had gone, the sky darkening with the clouds that had been building up all morning. Declan realised it would rain again soon, and wondered if the Tide magic he'd been wielding had affected the weather, or if this was normal for this time of year in the wetlands.

Arkady must have guessed the direction of his thoughts. She looked up at the clouds and then squeezed his hand. "It's all right, Declan. I don't think the coming rain is the result of anything you did."

He smiled humourlessly. "How would you know?"

"I don't, I suppose," she said with a shrug. "But I've been in the wetlands for about three weeks now and it's rained like clockwork twice a day, every single day, so I'm guessing there's nothing to worry about."

Declan wished he was as confident. "It's scary, you know, having that sort of power, and then not even being sure you've done anything with it."

She looked at him curiously. "What's the Tide feel like?"

Their walk had taken them beyond the limits of the village. The path narrowed, the vegetation crowding the edge of the well-worn track that led (so Tiji had informed him with a rainbow-coloured blush) to a hot spring. He was still holding Arkady's hand, still acutely aware of her touch, acutely aware of everything around him. It was as if swimming the Tide heightened his awareness a little more every time he touched it. His skin still itched and burned and despite Cayal's crass suggestion about how to calm his raging senses, Declan knew he wasn't far off the mark. Arkady would only have to look at him with the slightest hint of desire, and he'd be on her, right here on the path, a few hundred paces from the village.

"Declan?"

He realised he'd forgotten what she'd asked. He looked at her, and although she was wearing quite a demure shift, all he could see, in his mind's eye, was her statuesque body in that wretched slave skirt.

Arkady stopped walking, letting go of his hand. "Tides, are you even listening to me?"

The loss of contact with her hand was almost painful, his skin was so sensitive. Thunder rattled overhead. The sky was dark now, the heavens set to open any moment. He shrugged apologetically. "I'm sorry. I'm . . . distracted."

She smiled. "No? Really?" And then she looked skyward as the clouds rumbled threateningly. "We're going to get drenched if we don't find shelter. Did you want to go back to the village?"

He shook his head. "Let's keep walking."

She fell in beside him again as the first few raindrops plinked onto the broad leaves of the bushes bordering the path. "What was Cayal talking about, back there?"

"What do you mean?"

"He said something about a deal."

"He wants me to go to Jelidia with him. He seems to think I can help him die."

"And can you?"

"I wouldn't mind trying."

Arkady didn't seem to think that was very funny. She stopped walking again as large raindrops spattered the vegetation around them with a loud plopping noise as each individual drop landed and then skated off the shiny leaves toward the ground. "You shouldn't mess with Cayal, Declan. He's dangerous."

"You're telling *me* that?"

"I know this must be hard for you," she said, reaching up to wipe a stray raindrop from his face. "But you have time, Declan, to work out how to handle this. I don't think you should rush into anything. *Particularly* anything to do with Cayal."

He grabbed her hand, not sure he had the strength to resist if she touched him like that for too much longer. "Who are you really worried about? Me or Cayal?"

She frowned. "I thought we'd agreed to let the past go, Declan?"

He released her hand, taking a deep breath. "I know. I'm sorry. I'm just . . . on edge . . . It's something to do with the aftermath of swimming the Tide. I feel like my skin's on fire. From the inside."

As if to emphasise his point, the clouds rumbled once more and the sky finally opened. The downpour drenched them in seconds. Arkady squealed involuntarily and moved closer to him for shelter. Declan pulled her to him, the noble, conscious part of his mind intending only to shield her from the rain. But there was another part of him now—a part of him that was alive and humming in tune with the remnants of the Tide, a part of him driven by something more primal, far more visceral. Something not easily contained by a veneer of civilisation.

He kissed her, and she responded without hesitation, although a part of Declan feared it wouldn't have made a difference if she had resisted. The rain pelted down on them, but Declan hardly noticed. He pushed her backward off the path until the bole of a slender palm prevented them moving any further, drinking the raindrops from her skin like a man dying of thirst. If she said anything, he wasn't aware of it. She moaned as he pulled the drenched shift from her shoulders but he had no idea if it was from pleasure or pain, and was a little appalled to realise he didn't care. Although he wasn't drawing on the Tide, the magic had left its mark on him. It had scoured him internally, leaving raw flesh behind that could only be soothed by the total immersion of himself in something that required no thought, no conscious effort. Arkady cried out at some point. He wasn't sure why. He might be hurting her or she might be lost in the ecstasy of their coupling.

Declan didn't have the wit to tell the difference.

It wasn't until he was spent, exhausted and finally back in control some time later, that he thought to wonder about it. Time to realise what he'd done.

Full of remorse and self-loathing, Declan let Arkady go and stepped back from the tree. Arkady sagged against the trunk, staring at him with an unreadable expression. Her shift was drenched, her breasts exposed and the skirt pushed up around her waist.

"Tides, Arkady, I'm so sorry . . ."

She smiled weakly and began to straighten her clothes. "For what, exactly, are you apologising, Declan Hawkes?"

Declan was a little surprised to realise she wasn't angry. "I didn't mean . . ."

"Yes you did."

An awkward silence followed her words that seemed half statement of fact and half accusation. He wondered if he'd destroyed everything between them, yet again, but it seemed Arkady was more forgiving than he gave her credit for. Perhaps there were some things, he thought, that old friends could never put into words. And that sometimes you didn't need to.

Perhaps Arkady knew him too well to need an explanation.

He threw his hands up helplessly, not sure what else to say. "Did I hurt you?"

Arkady shook her head. "Not especially." She held her face up to the rain for a moment and then looked at him curiously. "Is that going to happen every time you use the Tide?"

"I don't know. Didn't happen the last time, after I healed you."

"Only because I stormed off in a huff."

He smiled. *Tides, was a man allowed to be this lucky?* "I don't deserve you."

"No, you don't," she agreed, pushing off the tree. "You appear to be stuck with me, however."

Declan glanced up at the sky. There seemed to be little chance the rain was going to stop for a while. "Do you want to go back to the village?"

Arkady shook her head. "Isn't there a hot spring along here somewhere?"

"I think so."

"Then let's go find it." She held her arms out wide and shrugged. "It's not like we can get much wetter."

It seemed too easy. Arkady seemed far too ready to forgive. Perhaps her time on the Justice Tree really had changed her, but Declan wasn't sure he wanted to wager his future with her on that. "Are you *sure* you're all right?"

She nodded. "How do *you* feel?"

"Better."

"Then it's all good," she said, offering him her hand.

Declan took her hand and accepted then that maybe it was. Whatever the future might hold, for now it *was* all good, or at least about as good as it was ever likely to get.

Chapter 63

A week later, when there was still no sign of a returning fleet full of vengeful physicians or slave traders, Arryl cautiously announced they'd probably
made their point and the wetlands were, for the time being, safe.

Cayal, who'd been champing at the bit waiting for the women to declare
themselves ready to leave for Jelidia, could have cried with relief when she
made the announcement. Of course, it didn't solve all of his problems, but
it meant one more thing out of the way, one step closer to the end.

At least, it *should* have meant that. Cayal truly believed it did, right up
until Ambria and Medwen announced they weren't going anywhere.

Cayal wasn't surprised to hear Ambria refuse to leave the wetlands.
From the moment they'd rescued her, she'd made it quite clear that she
wanted nothing to do with Cayal or his plans to die. She was going to stay
in Senestra, partly to ensure the Physicians' Guild or Cydne Medura's family didn't return, partly because the swamp fever epidemic was still far
from over and the Crasii needed her healing skills, and partly, Cayal suspected, out of sheer perversity. Ambria and Cayal had never really been
friends. She considered him—even on a good day—to be almost as dangerous as Kentravyon, and she really didn't care to help him with anything.
Not even to die.

Medwen's refusal surprised him much more.

He'd always considered Medwen a friend, sometimes a great deal more.
She'd come willingly enough back to his bed, even though it took her little
more than a heartbeat to realise it wasn't so much desire for her, as his wish
to demonstrate to Declan Hawkes that he intended to keep his promise regarding Arkady, that was driving his lust for her.

It pained him to see Arkady with the spymaster. It irked him even more
to realise she was happy to be with him. Around Cayal, Arkady was skittish
and uncertain. Hawkes had the opposite effect on her. His presence seemed
to calm her. It was as if their long friendship gave her something to cling
to, something firm and solid to support her in a world gone mad. He was
jealous of Hawkes for that. Cayal could make Arkady want him. Tides, he
could make *any* woman want him if he set his mind to it, but he could
never make her feel safe the way Hawkes could.

"Tell me that's what you want, Arkady, and I'll give you the world . . . Tides,

I'll conquer Glaeba for you, if that's what you want. I'll make you her queen . . . " he'd offered, when he caught up with her at the Tarascan Oasis a few months ago.

"*Listen to yourself, Cayal,*" she'd said. "*You don't want me. You don't even know me. If you did, you'd not define what you think I desire in terms of how much of the world you can conquer on my behalf.*"

"*Then what do you want, Arkady?*" he'd asked.

"*Whatever I want, Cayal, I'm fairly certain it's not being the petty distraction you need to give your life meaning while you wait for the end of time.*"

Cayal knew what she meant now, even if Arkady wasn't sure herself. Arkady didn't want an empire. She wanted to feel safe.

That she felt safe around someone like Hawkes peeved him even more. Hawkes wasn't *safe*. He was an immortal with no idea of the power he had access to, what to do with it when he was holding it in his hands, and likely to make a lot of very powerful enemies in a very short space of time.

Whenever Cayal felt the urge to point this out to Arkady, however, he took a deep breath and reminded himself of the prize. Death awaited him, provided he could gather enough Tide Lords to aid Lukys. Hawkes might be a danger to Arkady, but Cayal needed him more than he needed Arkady.

And in a way, it was fitting. Arkady, after all, was the biggest danger Cayal had faced for quite some time.

"You look pathetic when you're moping."

Cayal looked up to find Medwen standing on the veranda of the Outpost, studying him with interest. He was sitting on a rickety stool; leaning back so far it was balanced on the back two legs, his feet resting on the railing. Down by the dock, Declan Hawkes, Arkady, Jojo and Tiji were apparently learning the finer points of channel fishing, courtesy of Azquil and the chameleon's sister, Tenika. Although he couldn't hear what they were saying, there was much laughter and general frivolity going on, which did nothing but vex him even more.

"I'm not moping."

"Yes, you are," Medwen said, taking a seat on the edge of the railing, effectively blocking his view of the dock. "You're like a little thundercloud, Cayal, all mopey and weepy and feeling sorry for himself."

"I want to die, Medwen. Being mopey and weepy and feeling sorry for myself goes with the territory, don't you think?"

She smiled and looked over her shoulder at the dock before turning back to look at Cayal. "Tides, if you want her so badly, just take her and be done with it," she advised. "Hawkes still hasn't got a clue what he's doing with the Tide. You could probably beat him in an unfair fight, magical or otherwise."

"I could *probably* beat him? Thanks for the resounding vote of confidence." He sighed and let the stool thump down so it rested on all four legs again. "Anyway, I can't."

"Why not?"

"We have a deal. He gets the girl, I get a funeral."

"You *traded* Arkady for his cooperation?"

"More or less."

"Tides, I'm not sure which one of you that makes the most despicable, Cayal—you for suggesting such a bargain, or Hawkes for agreeing to it."

"Why do you assume I'm the one who suggested it?"

"You are, aren't you?"

"Well, yes . . . but you might have considered the possibility it *wasn't* my idea."

She smiled. "It's disrespectful, unfair to Arkady and shows a complete lack of consideration for anybody else's feelings, Cayal. Of course it was your suggestion."

He studied her expression hopefully. "Does that mean you've changed your mind and you're coming to Jelidia with me after all? I mean, if I'm such a despicable bastard, you'll be glad to see the end of me, won't you?"

Medwen wasn't so easily manipulated. She shook her head. "I'm not going to pander to your maudlin self-pity, Cayal. I understand you want to die—even empathise with your pain—but you can't make me feel guilty for not helping your death along. Besides, you don't need me. I suspect you don't need any of us, even though Arryl insists on keeping her promise to you about going to Jelidia. You have Hawkes to help you now. One shiny, brand new, totally unexpected Tide Lord to help push you into oblivion is worth far more than three moderately talented immortals who'd rather you *didn't* find a way to die, because we're actually at peace with ourselves and the idea of living forever."

"Are you really?"

"Yes."

"Aren't you bored?"

"Not at all," she said. "I have a purpose."

"What purpose?" he scoffed. "Making beads? Curing swamp fever? Tides, I'd *rather* die if the only thing I could find to live for was the idea that I can save a few score lizards from puking and shitting themselves to death."

"But you see, that's my point, Cayal," she said, refusing to let his scorn dent her serenity. "It doesn't really matter what it is; you just need something. And I *have* something to live for. The Trinity gives me and Arryl and Ambria a function. It might seem trite and silly to you, but we have a reason to get up every morning. You don't, and that's why you want to die."

"I've changed my mind," he said, leaning back on the stool. "Stay here with Ambria and tend to your flanking lizards. I'd rather not listen to your why-can't-you-be-happy-with-your-lot-in-life lectures all the way to Jelidia, anyway."

Medwen shook her head and smiled at him fondly. "If you succeed in this folly, I will miss you, Cayal."

"You won't miss me. You'll thank me. If I succeed, you'll have a way out."

"Even if I don't want one?"

Cayal shook his head. "You say that now, Medwen. You may keep on saying it for another ten thousand years. But there will come a time when you reach breaking point. I may have reached it sooner than you, but it's there, waiting for us all. And when you get there, you'll have somewhere to go. Thanks to me."

"And if you fail? What then?"

He shrugged. "Then I will have failed *this* time, that's all. It won't stop me from trying again."

Medwen laughed. "Tides, I was wrong. You *do* have a purpose, Cayal. Whether you realise it or not, you're as driven as any of us."

"I'm driven by the desire to be *dead*, Medwen," he said, her laughter doing nothing to improve his mood.

"But the point is, you are *driven*, Cayal, and that makes you just as pathetic as you think we are for trying to help the chameleon Crasii."

There were a few loose ends to tie up before they left the Outpost for Jelidia, and until they were taken care of, Arryl refused to go anywhere. The most pressing issue was the swamp fever that had caused the problem with the Physicians' Guild in the first place. It still needed to be brought under control, something she and her immortal sisters had been struggling to cope with. But Arryl now had two powerful Tide Lords at her disposal and she wasn't going to let them go anywhere until they'd done what she and the others couldn't: cure the fever outright.

When she informed Cayal of this new condition on her cooperation, he refused. He'd done enough, in his mind.

"I saved your wretched swamp from invasion, Arryl," he said, pushing aside the tea she tried to serve him, as if that would somehow lessen the blow. "Now we leave."

"You turned back one incursion fleet," Ambria said, firmly behind her immortal sister in this outrageous demand. "That doesn't get to the root of the problem, which is the swamp fever."

They were gathered in the kitchen, sitting around the large scrubbed table. Cayal didn't know where the Crasii had gone, but the only mortal in the room was Arkady, who sat next to Declan on the other side of the table.

"First sign of an outbreak in Port Traeker, and the guild will be back," Medwen said. "And it won't matter how many priests are standing on the docks praying to Jaxyn. It won't hold them back."

Arryl nodded in agreement but she directed her next comment to Declan, and probably Arkady, who was still guilt-ridden over her part in the death of the infected Crasii of Watershed Falls. "We can cure the fever, but we can't eradicate it. Between you and Cayal, you can." She turned back to Cayal. "Once that's done, you will have fulfilled your part of the deal, and I will leave with you."

"And I suppose *you* can't wait to help them?" Cayal said to Declan. "Not going to turn down a chance to use your sparkly new powers for good, are you?"

Declan turned to Arkady. "What do you think I should do?"

"Tides! Don't ask her! She's still tormented by what she did to these wretched Crasii with her tonic. Let Arkady have a say in this, Hawkes, and you'll have to cure every ill that ails mankind before you're allowed to go anywhere!"

"Cayal, being obnoxious isn't going to endear anybody to your cause," Arryl pointed out calmly. "You have my condition. If you want my help, you will help me first."

"I don't need your help, Arryl. As Medwen so astutely pointed out yesterday, one Tide Lord is worth far more than three moderately talented immortals who'd rather I *didn't* find a way to die."

"But you don't *have* a Tide Lord," Hawkes said. "Because I happen to think Arryl is right. If we don't remove the threat of swamp fever, all the religious fervour in the world isn't going to protect the wetlands from another incursion." He turned to Arryl, smiling. "You'll have to show me what to do, my lady, but if I can help you, I will."

"Thank you, Declan."

"So much for your deal, Cayal," Medwen said with a sour smile.

"What deal?" Arkady asked.

Medwen turned to Arkady. "Ah, that's right; they haven't let you in on their little arrangement, have they, dear? Declan's going to help Cayal die, you see, Arkady, in return for you in *his* bed and not Cayal's."

Hawkes visibly paled. Cayal let out a long sigh and treated Medwen to a look that spoke volumes. She smiled at him unapologetically. "What? You think she *shouldn't* be told? Tides, the poor girl deserves to know, don't you think, that the men she believes saved her from slavery are still treating her as a tradeable commodity?"

Arkady's gaze swivelled between Cayal and Declan, her eyes wide. "Is she serious?"

"It wasn't like that . . ." Declan began.

"Then what *was* it like?"

Hawkes looked to Cayal for help, but he shrugged, figuring there was no delicate way out of this for either of them. "I want to die, he wants to live," Cayal said with a shrug. "It wasn't about you, so much, Arkady, as . . . a matter of practicality."

Arkady's expression grew thunderous. "*Practicality?*" She turned on Declan. "Oh, I think I'm beginning to see what a *practical* arrangement this is. For some people, at least."

Hawkes put his hand out to her, at a complete loss as to what he should say. "Arkady . . ."

"Don't touch me," she said, jumping to her feet, her anger a palpable thing. She turned to Cayal then and added, "Either of you. Ever again."

And with that, Arkady turned and stormed out of the kitchen, leaving the immortals staring after her.

"Thank you, Medwen," Cayal said in the uncomfortable silence that following Arkady's departure. "That was very helpful."

"Don't try to make *me* feel guilty," she said. "You and your new best friend here are the bastards who did the deal."

"I'll speak to her," Hawkes said, rising from his chair.

"Leave her be, Declan," Arryl advised, putting her hand on his arm to restrain him. "She needs to calm down first. Trust me, nothing either of you says to Arkady at the moment is going to help."

Declan seemed to accept that as the bitter truth, and nodded reluctantly.

"In the meantime," Ambria said, "while your little friend is pacing the foreshore, discovering the futility of plotting the demise of any immortal, no matter how immoral or inconsiderate he is, you two can do something useful with your time and eradicate the swamp fever for us."

Cayal shook his head, knowing he was caught. Hawkes would do this now to spite him, which meant he had no choice but to follow suit. Besides, two Tide Lords could work much quicker than one, particularly when the one was as clueless about swimming the Tide as Hawkes was. The sooner it was done, the sooner they could leave.

And once it was done, with a good deed behind them to soothe troubled waters, perhaps Arkady would have calmed down enough to accept Hawkes's apology.

And then, finally, with another Tide Lord to help him die, Cayal could return to Jelidia and find the welcome arms of oblivion.

Chapter 64

"They're gone."

Ambria was sitting at the kitchen table sewing and didn't look up when she spoke. Arkady wasn't sure how Ambria knew she was there, but the immortal seemed neither surprised nor concerned that Arkady was soaking wet. It was raining outside, the raindrops pattering on the thatched roof, thunder rumbling lazily in the distance. Arkady was drenched but the rain was warm and she wasn't particularly cold. If anything, it felt very appropriate. The weather matched her mood perfectly.

It had another advantage too. When you'd been drenched by a downpour, it wasn't possible to tell tears from raindrops.

"I saw them heading off in a boat with Tiji and Azquil just before the rain started," Arkady said, taking a seat opposite the immortal, wondering if Ambria would complain she was dripping on her kitchen floor. "Do you know how long they'll be gone?"

Ambria shook her head. "Not exactly. Could be as long as a month, though, if they want to cover all the coastal villages. Plenty of time for you to make yourself scarce."

Arkady stared at Ambria, wondering how the immortal knew what she was thinking. Telepathy was not a skill she thought the immortals owned. On the other hand, Ambria may not have a clue what Arkady was thinking and was simply kicking her out. The Outpost was her home, after all, and Arkady hadn't really been invited to stay.

"Do *you* think I should leave?" she said, hedging around the question.

Ambria shrugged. "Up to you, I suppose. If it was me . . . well, I know what I'd do, but then I have the advantage of several thousand years of experience dealing with the likes of Cayal and his ilk. You might *like* learning things the hard way."

Arkady smiled thinly. "I think I've seen the error of my ways in that regard, my lady."

Ambria bit off the end of the thread, shoved the needle through the hem of her sleeve to get it out of the way, and smoothed out the seam of the shift she was sewing before she bothered to answer. "Then you have two choices, as far as I can tell. Stay here, get on my nerves for the next month or so, then leave with Cayal and your friend when they get back, go to Jelidia with them and meet up with Lukys. You can console yourself with the thought that when they finally come to blows over you—as they inevitably will—it may or may not end in a Cataclysm that destroys civilisation as we know it provided it happens quickly enough and it's not High Tide when they turn on each other."

"And my *other* option?"

"Get away. Now. While you still can."

"Where would I go?"

"Anywhere you want, I suppose." The immortal studied her for a moment. "You strike me as the resourceful type. There's a whole world out there to get lost in, Arkady. Trust me, I've done it often enough to know."

But were you trying to avoid a lover? Did your heart ache like this? Arkady wondered silently. "You were married to Krydence once, weren't you?"

The change of subject seemed to take Ambria by surprise. She hesitated and then shrugged. "So?"

"Was immortality what drove you apart?"

"Krydence will sleep with anything that walks," Ambria said. "That's what drove us apart." She sighed and shook her head. "Tides, don't look to me for advice about affairs of the heart, girl. I've lived far too long to care for romance. The only thing I can tell you as an absolute is that there is no possible way to be happy if you get involved with an immortal."

"Not even for a short time?"

"Define *short*," Ambria said. "You'll find you and I have a rather different perspective on that."

That was true. And maybe Ambria was the wrong person to ask advice of. She certainly didn't seem bothered about Arkady's fate one way or the other. But Tides, it hurt so much. Arkady needed to talk to someone, even an immortal who couldn't have cared less.

"I can't believe Declan did a deal behind my back like that."

"What? You would have preferred he asked you first?" She smiled as she turned the garment over, looking for another seam that needed stitching. "I can't believe you're getting all wounded about it. Their arrangement struck me as being an eminently workable solution to a potentially awkward situation for everyone involved."

"That's because you aren't the one being traded, my lady."

"True enough," the immortal conceded. "We all look at the world through our own eyes. Yours seem a little more sensitive than most."

Arkady shook her head. "The irony is, Cydne used to accuse me all the time of not acting enough like a slave. Of not thinking like one. And, you know, he was right. I *never* felt like a slave. Not for a moment. Not the whole time I had to walk around half naked, working like a drudge from dawn 'til dusk, at the beck and call of a man who wanted to use my body to relieve his own frustration, mostly because he was scared of his wife. Not for an *instant* . . . until I heard those two had done a deal to decide who got to have me."

"Do you love Declan?"

"I thought I did. Until a few hours ago."

Ambria smiled. "Then that's a *yes*. You don't fall out of love with someone in the space of a few hours. A few centuries will take care of it, though."

"Even if I do, that doesn't ease the hurt much."

"Only because you won't let it."

Arkady looked at her askance. "So . . . what are you saying . . . love conquers everything?"

"Of course it doesn't!" the immortal scoffed, taking the needle from her sleeve to resume her sewing. "Love causes no end of grief. It causes more pain than war, and more wars than religion. We'd all get along much better without it, I'm sure."

"What are you suggesting I do, then?"

Ambria fixed her attention on her sewing. "I'm trying very hard not to suggest anything," she said. "I've no wish to be responsible for you. Or what you do. But I will tell you this. Cayal desperately wants to die and he believes your friend Hawkes can help him. He won't let anything stand in the way of that, particularly not a woman."

"Are you saying he'd harm me?"

Ambria laughed. "Harm you? Tides, woman, he murdered a couple of million people putting out a fire. Have you no concept of what they're capable of?"

She shook her head in denial. "*Declan* would never do anything like that."

"Nor did Cayal set out to drain the Great Inland Sea. This is not about good or evil, Arkady, it's about misguided intentions. If you stay, one of those boys is going to do something stupid. I'm fairly certain you know that. You just want me to tell you that you're wrong."

Ambria wasn't wrong, however. Arkady knew that.

If she stayed, deal or no deal, her presence would become a bone of contention between two immortals capable of breaking the world in half with their rage.

Even if she could forgive Declan, even if she could find it in her heart to understand what had driven him to make such a dreadful bargain with her life, she didn't want to be responsible for that sort of destruction. Worse, she didn't want Declan to be responsible for doing something like that.

Arkady would die eventually. Her remorse would end with her death.

Declan was immortal now. Any regrets he had would follow him into eternity.

"Do you think the amphibians would take me back to Port Traeker?"

"They might," Ambria said, her tone giving nothing away. "If you ask them nicely."

Arkady rose to her feet, wondering how she could get a message to the amphibians. There must be some way to call them, she supposed. They always seemed to know when they were needed. "Then I'll be out from underfoot as soon as I can arrange it."

"As you wish."

"Will you give Declan a message for me?"

"Of course."

"Tell him I said not to follow me."

"Think that'll stop him?"

"I don't know," Arkady said, her way clear for the first time in months. "I only know I can't remain here and be responsible for what might happen between Cayal and Declan if I stay."

Chapter 65

The weather grew increasingly cooler as winter progressed. A bitter chill permeated the air and people remarked on its severity. Snow blanketed the streets of Herino and for the first time in living memory the Lower Oran began to freeze.

Jaxyn watched it happen, cursing the time it was taking. The Tide wasn't up far enough for him to do much more than give winter a helping hand, and he couldn't sustain it for long. Jaxyn knew the peril of holding on to the Tide too long, just as he knew the consequences of messing with the weather too much. He wanted a cold winter, cold enough to freeze the Great Lakes, but not so that it messed everything up. That would mean he'd spend the next High Tide sheltering from the century's worth of violent storms he'd unleashed on Amyrantha with his impatience.

He needed to *coax* winter along, not force it.

It was painstakingly slow work. Every night, when the rest of Herino slept, Jaxyn would stand on the balcony of his room in the palace, looking out over the darkened city and the lake beyond, and plunge into the Tide. With his senses stretched as far as they could go, he would feel out the atmosphere. He would reach up into the clouds, give the air a push, seek out differences in the air pressure somewhere else and carefully nudge them in the right direction.

The result of all this delicate and careful manipulation of the Tide was the coldest winter Glaeba—and Caelum for that matter—had ever experienced.

And a frozen lake. One that should soon be solid enough to march an army across.

He stamped his foot on the ice, pleased to feel the solid, unyielding surface beneath his feet.

"Another few weeks and we'll be able to walk all the way to Cycrane."

"Your grace?"

Jaxyn hadn't realised he'd spoken the thought aloud. He glanced over his shoulder at the feline bodyguard who'd spoken. Her name was Chikita, and although she acted like a loyal Crasii, there was a spark of intelligence in her eyes that made him wonder, sometimes, if there wasn't a bit of Scard in her too. Still, from the moment she'd fought that snow bear in Lebec and been won by Stellan for his kennels, she'd passed every test Jaxyn had set for her, and if she was a Scard, she'd slip up sooner or later. They all did in the end.

"How long do you think it would take to walk an army across the lake?" he asked the little ginger feline. "Assuming it was frozen solid?"

"That would depend on the army's footwear, I suspect, your grace. At the very least, at a walk, it would take the better part of two days, but barefoot, a feline's feet would be frostbitten long before they arrived on the other side."

Jaxyn frowned, concerned at both the point she raised and that she had the wit to raise it. "Can you skate?"

"You mean like human children do? When they're playing on the ice?"

He nodded. The Crasii thought about it for a moment and then shrugged. "I've never tried, your grace, but I suppose it's really just a matter of balance."

Jaxyn turned to study the ice thoughtfully, wishing he had a sizable human army rather than a feline one. Humans, at least, could wear boots for protection against the cold and have some chance at arriving at their destination in a fit state to fight. He would have the Tide's own job getting the felines to wear anything on their feet and still be able to fight effectively, even with his ability to order them to die at his command. And logistically, where was he going to get the cobblers to knock up a few thousand specially designed feline ice boots on short notice, anyway?

Still, the thought gave him a small measure of comfort. If he was having trouble figuring out how to get his army across the frozen lake, they'd be having the same problems in Caelum. Assuming the thought of attacking across the ice had even occurred to those unimaginative fools.

He turned and glanced at Chikita, wondering if her comment about the frostbite had been prompted by the fact that he'd had her standing out here on the ice for the better part of an hour. Her feet must be numb by now.

"If the felines wrapped their feet in rags, would that be sufficient protection, do you think, to get them across?"

"Skin or fur would be better, my lord."

Jaxyn nodded, thinking she had the right of it. He looked around the frozen Lower Oran and smiled, pleased with his work. Although it wasn't yet frozen solid, it wouldn't be long now before one could walk from Glaeba to Caelum in a straight line.

And nobody—not the mortals of this country, nor the immortals trying to seize power across the lake—had any idea it was his doing.

That was the beauty of something so subtle. After a time, it took on a life of its own. The whole continent was now trapped in the coldest weather it had ever experienced, and he hadn't touched the Tide for days.

He smiled, pleased with the way his plans were progressing. "I think, Chikita, there's going to be rather a lot of recrimination and blame shifting in Cycrane a few weeks from now. Right before we storm the palace, I suspect. And not for a minute will those fools in Caelum realise I am the cause of their downfall."

The feline smiled in open admiration. "You mean this ice is your doing, my lord?"

He nodded. It was stupid, bragging about it to a feline, but Chikita was Crasii. Who was she going to tell? Besides, Jaxyn felt he deserved at least a pat on the back for thinking up something so fiendishly clever. Diala was too stupid to appreciate the subtlety of what he'd achieved, even if she'd been the sort to award him any credit for their victory, in the first place.

Chikita dropped to her knees, awestruck by his power. "You truly are a god, my lord."

Jaxyn looked down at her and smiled. "I know."

When he returned to the palace, Jaxyn dismissed Chikita and sent her back to the kennels, a little irritated by her fawning appreciation of his god-like powers. If he had any doubt she was a Crasii, her mindless, blubbering appreciation quashed the last of his suspicions. The feline was visibly limping by then too, her feet frozen and possibly frostbitten. Which was rather useful, actually, because now Jaxyn had a pretty good idea of how long a feline could last on the ice before it began to incapacitate them.

Armed with that useful knowledge, and with his bodyguard disposed of, he headed for the Council Chamber, where at this time of day, with his queen by his side, King Mathu of Glaeba would be taking care of the business of state his wife and his Private Secretary deemed it safe for him to handle.

When Jaxyn arrived, Mathu was dealing with a dispute between the Duke of Blayken and his neighbour, the Duke of Callendale, regarding a border dispute involving access to a well that both men believed was vital to the survival of their duchy. The dukes themselves weren't here, of course, just their advocates, and Mathu wore the pained look of a man desperate to escape a nightmare. He looked up with relief when Jaxyn opened the door, and then jumped to his feet.

"Is there a problem, Lord Aranville?" he asked hopefully as Jaxyn stepped into the chamber. "I can deal with these gentlemen another time, if you need me for something urgent."

"I'm afraid I do require your urgent attention, your majesty," he said, glancing at Diala who was sitting at Mathu's right hand, doing little to help him. She enjoyed seeing him struggle to rule his kingdom and would offer to help only insofar as it suited her to do so. Given how mind-numbingly boring this border dispute between Blayken and Callendale was proving to be, Jaxyn guessed she'd offered her poor husband no help at all.

Mathu smiled apologetically at the two men. "You'll have to excuse me, gentlemen. Perhaps we can take this up again next week?"

The ducal envoys looked displeased, but were in no position to argue about it. They gathered their papers, bowed a little impatiently, and left the room, leaving Jaxyn alone with the King and Queen of Glaeba.

"Tides, you're a sight for sore eyes, Jaxyn," Mathu said, flopping back into his seat. He was wearing gloves and a scarf over his fur coat. "I was about to die of terminal boredom."

Even here inside the palace, with a blazing fire going in the fireplace, the large Council Chamber was freezing. Diala, of course, wasn't bothered by the cold in the least, and wore a very fetching gown that set off her blue eyes and displayed an alarming amount of cleavage.

Jaxyn smiled. "Glad to be of service, your majesty."

"So what do you want, Jaxyn?" Diala asked, leaning back in her throne. "Are the Caelish sailing across the Lower Oran in battle formation?"

Bitch.

"No, your majesty. Nobody is sailing *anything* across the Lower Oran. Nor are they likely to. It's all but frozen solid."

Mathu smiled. "Well, that puts paid to any Caelish invasion to avenge their wretched kidnapped princess, doesn't it?"

"It's also an opportunity we'd be a fool to ignore, your majesty."

Mathu frowned. "What do you mean?"

"I mean, Mat, that we can't *sail* across, but we *can* march."

The king's eyes widened in surprise. "You mean march our army across the *lake* to Caelum? Can we do that?"

Even Diala seemed surprised. "I suppose. How do we know the ice can carry an army's weight?"

"It will," Jaxyn assured her. "Trust me."

Mathu was shaking his head. "But that's . . . it's . . . well, it's inspired! Tides, I can't believe nobody's thought of doing it before now."

"The Lower Oran hasn't frozen in living memory," Jaxyn pointed out. "But I'm assuming I have your permission to make the necessary arrangements?"

Mathu hesitated to give the order. "It means we'll be the aggressors."

"Caelum has all but declared war on us now, Mathu. They've certainly made their intentions known. And they've refused to return Stellan Desean to us, even though they know he's a criminal and a traitor. I think we'll still command the moral high ground, as well as the tactical one, even if we strike pre-emptively."

"Then of course you have my permission. Tides, it's brilliant, when you think of it. Their fleet is ice bound. They'll be sitting across the lake, fretting about the weather, while we're marching across a force twice the size we could manage to sail across. And four times the size of anything they can throw at us."

So you're not a complete tactical moron, Jaxyn concluded silently. "You have the right of it, your majesty." He bowed respectfully. "And with your permission, I'll begin to make the necessary arrangements."

"Do we have the forces to make this work?"

"If I call up the armies of every duchy in Glaeba, we'll be sitting in Cycrane, deciding where best to display Stellan Desean's head, no more than a month from now."

"Provided the Caelish don't get wind of what we're up to," Diala said.

Jaxyn shrugged. "Even if someone sent them a message today, detailing our plans, they don't have the resources to defeat us. They never have."

"I was thinking more about them finding some *other* way to subvert our strategy?"

She was asking if Tryan or Elyssa could do anything with the Tide to thwart them. Jaxyn shook his head. "They won't have time."

Diala frowned, not entirely convinced. "But if there was some sort of freak . . . storm?"

"It would only serve to aid us, not them."

Oblivious to the true meaning of their conversation, Mathu smiled.

"Tides, it's not often one can stage an invasion confident the weather is on their side, is it?"

"Glaeba is truly blessed," Jaxyn agreed.

"Have you found an assassin yet?"

"I'm still working on that, your majesty," he said.

"Let's not," Mathu said with uncharacteristic bitterness. "Let us defeat Caelum and then make Desean face me. On his knees."

Diala smiled. "I like that plan."

You would, you vindictive little bitch.

"It shall be as you command, sire," Jaxyn promised, and then he turned and left the Council Chamber, his thoughts not on Stellan Desean, but on where he was going to get enough skins to protect the feet of his feline army as they crossed the ice into Caelum.

Chapter 66

Dressed as a free woman, Arkady found the streets of Port Traeker a much less daunting affair than they had been when she was dressed as a slave. Men bowed to her and stepped aside to let her pass. Doors were held open for her, lesser beings pushed aside so she could be served first. She wasn't dressed as a duchess, she wore only the simple shift Arryl had loaned her at the Outpost, but she was free and that meant she was a real person again, not a chattel to be bought and sold.

Or traded.

But even a free woman needed to eat. Arkady had no money, no papers, the wrong colour eyes and an accent that immediately branded her as a foreigner. She did, however, have a small sack of polished nacre beads. Ambria had given them to her with a gruff goodbye and the assurance that she would be able to sell them in the gem markets when she reached Port Traeker. It wasn't much, and even Ambria wasn't sure how much a ticket on a ship sailing out of Senestra was worth, but it was better than the only other way a destitute woman had of earning money.

Arkady was done with trading her body for the necessities of life.

The problem she had now, of course, was that it was dark, the gem markets wouldn't open until tomorrow morning, and she needed shelter. She didn't want to try trading one of the beads for a room, for fear it would alert the ever watchful thieves of Port Traeker to the fact that she carried something valuable. So her options were to risk sleeping in the streets or try the only other place she could think of where she might find a sympathetic reception and a bed for the night, dangerous though it was to try.

Arkady had left the Outpost the same day as Arryl and Medwen, Cayal and Declan, Azquil, Tiji and Tenika. Plenty of time for her to reach Port Traeker. Plenty of time for her to find a way out of Senestra. Plenty of time to lose herself somewhere no immortal, even with magical powers, could find her.

Izzy and Lenor, the two amphibians who'd rescued Tenika from the Delta Settlement, offered to take her to Port Traeker. Having made her position quite clear, Ambria made no attempt to stop her leaving, although Arkady did try to convince Jojo to come with her. But the feline Crasii re-fused, preferring to stay at the Outpost and wait for the others to come back. She had found immortals to serve. She wasn't willingly going to leave them, unless one of them commanded her.

Other than their discussion in the kitchen, and her uncomfortable offer of the beads, Ambria said little about her decision to leave. Arkady was fairly sure the immortal would be glad to see the back of such a trouble-maker.

The trip to Port Traeker was uneventful, leaving Arkady the time to won-der if she was doing the right thing. A part of her ached to be with Declan again, but the sense of betrayal she still felt was overwhelming. To dis-cover that immortality had made Declan as venal as the rest of his Tide Lord brethren was heartbreaking. She'd trusted him; thought he wanted her because he loved her, not because he needed a convenient outlet for his lust after working the Tide. His turnabout made sense now. One minute he'd rejected her because he thought she was acting like a whore. The next he'd forgiven her, promising to put the past behind them.

After he worked the Tide. After he discovered what it did to him.

When Arkady acting like a whore was just what he needed.

He was no better than Cayal. No better than Jaxyn.

Actually, he's worse, Arkady decided bitterly. *Jaxyn and Cayal at least know they are bastards. Tides, they're almost proud of it.*

But Declan . . . Declan thinks he's still one of us. Still thinks there's some noble purpose to his actions . . .

"*So, what happens if you get all the power in the world?*" she'd asked him when they were children.

"*I dunno. I think it would be fun, though, to find out . . .*"

The memory burned like acid. And Arkady had her answer.

The clinic where Cydne once worked in Port Traeker was much as Arkady remembered it. She wouldn't have come here had she any other place to go, but the closest thing Arkady had to a friend in Port Traeker was the slave Geriko. He might turn her in the moment he saw her, or he might be able to help her. Geriko knew people. He knew people who might know the best place to sell the beads. He might, if she was really lucky, not im-mediately report her and have her taken back into custody as a runaway slave.

Of course, *that* was assuming Geriko was even still at the clinic. Assuming it hadn't been staffed by another physician from the guild, by now, who'd sent the Medura slaves back to the family compound and staffed it with his own people.

Her fears proved groundless, however, when she knocked on the clinic door a few hours after sunset, and it was opened a few minutes later by a bleary-eyed Geriko.

"Kady?" he exclaimed in surprise when he realised who was standing on the threshold. "What are you doing here? Out of uniform?"

"Can I come in, Geriko?"

"Of course!" He stood back to let her enter, glancing up and down the dark street before closing and locking the door behind her. "Tides, you're a popular woman."

She lifted the shawl from her head with a puzzled look. As a disguise it wasn't very effective, but it gave her the illusion of being hidden. "What do you mean?"

"Are you hungry?"

"Starving. What do you mean, Geriko? Why am I so popular?"

"Come on," he said, lifting the lamp from the side table by the door. "Let's get you some food while we talk. You're even skinnier than you were before you left."

A little concerned, Arkady followed Geriko down the hall and out into the kitchen at the back of the clinic. There was no sign of any patients. The whole place looked as if it had been closed since they first left for the wetlands.

"Thought they would have killed you along with Cydne," he said, opening a large clay pot to pull out a half loaf of bread.

"They nearly did," she said, taking a seat at the table. "You heard about what happened, then?"

"Bits of it. Kinda hoped your old master found you before the troubles started."

"My old master?"

Geriko nodded, handing her the bread. "Glaeban chap, he was. Said his name was Aleki someone . . . I guess he didn't find you." Geriko frowned then. "You know, if they catch you posing as a free woman, they'll hang you."

Arkady nodded, but didn't bother to tell him she *was* a free woman now. The missing slave brand might be a bit hard to explain away.

"You said I was popular," she reminded him. "Was that just because of . . . my Glaeban master?"

"Tides, no, we've had all sorts of people lookin' for you. Last one even left you a letter." He scratched at his beard thoughtfully for a moment and then vanished into the darkened hall toward his quarters. Arkady bit into the bread, wondering who else could have found her here.

And why they hadn't been around when she *wanted* to be rescued.

Geriko reappeared a few moments later with a letter, sealed, Arkady was astounded to discover, with the Glaeban Ambassadorial seal, one identical to the seal Stellan had used in Torlenia.

She tore the letter open, her hands shaking. Who from the Glaeban Embassy knew where to find her?

Tides, Jaxyn has found me . . .

Then she told herself sternly to settle down. If Jaxyn had found her, he wouldn't have left her a letter telling her about it.

My Dearest Arkady, the letter began. *I hope this letter finds you. When we heard you'd been sold into slavery in Elvere, we were devastated. I can't imagine what the experience must have done to you.*

Fortunately, help is at hand. The slave I am leaving this letter with expects you back shortly. As soon as you get it, either come to the embassy or get a message to me. We will get this nonsense about you being a slave cleared up and see you safe and free once more.

The news from Glaeba is not good, as you can well imagine. With Stellan seeking asylum in Caelum, the king is very angry with him. And I can understand if you're afraid to come to the embassy for that reason. I will be honest. My husband has a warrant for your arrest, but he knows nothing of your fate, or even that you are here in Senestra. Nobody knows, I suspect. It is only a happy accident that I found out.

It is safe for you to come here. When you arrive at the main gate, ask for me and tell them your name is Kylia (I'm sure you'll see the irony). I want to help you, cousin. My loyalty is to my family first and there are many of us, as I'm sure you know, who believe in Stellan and would support him as king.

As soon as you get here, I will get a message to Stellan and arrange passage to Caelum for you to join him.

Tide willing you're still safe.

Your cousin,

Loriny Devale

"Well?"

"Well *what*?" she asked blankly, a little overwhelmed.

"Is it good news?"

"Possibly."

"You can't *tell*?"

Arkady studied the letter thoughtfully. "It might be a trap."

"She seemed nice, the lady what brought the letter here."

"What did she look like?" Arkady asked, trying to recall what her husband's cousin looked like. Lady Loriny Devale was a cousin of Stellan's, but Arkady had only met the Devales once, at her wedding to Stellan. Loriny's husband was a career diplomat and spent little time in Glaeba. She didn't think she and Loriny had become such fast friends at that one brief meeting to warrant her taking this sort of risk for her cousin's wife.

The news Stellan was in Caelum and in direct conflict with the king left Arkady feeling ill. *What was he thinking?* Declan had said he was in hiding. *Now he's challenging the king?* Not that they'd spent much time talking of her husband, but he'd certainly not given the impression Stellan was planning to challenge the throne directly.

Arkady was torn with indecision. If this letter was genuine, she had a safe way out of Senestra, with help from people she could trust. She had no trouble believing that Stellan would attract a lot of support if he set himself up in opposition to Mathu. That was the reason Reon Debalkor spent so much time trying to undermine him.

"Dark hair, pretty. I dunno. All Glaebans look the same to me."

"Did she say how she knew I was here?"

Geriko shook his head. "Didn't ask, truth be told, but your old master found you, so you can't have been that hard to track down."

Arkady wished she could believe it was that simple. This offer was exactly what she needed—which was part of the problem.

Perfect solutions rarely were.

"Can I stay the night here, Geriko?" she asked, too tired and too confused to make a decision about this now.

He smiled at her hopefully. "Sure? In my bunk?"

Arkady tossed and turned all night, and decided, in the end, to trust herself rather than an all-too-good-to-be-true missive from some distant cousin of Stellan's. She tucked the letter into her pocket next morning and, as they ate breakfast, asked Geriko where she could sell some nacre beads. Better she

buy her own ticket out of this Tide-forsaken country than rely on the dubious family ties of a man now disgraced and considered a traitor.

"Down at the Gem Street markets, I s'pose," the slave told her. "Why?
You got some treasure to sell?"

"I have some nacre beads . . ."

"Show me." His eyes were a little too eager, but Arkady had no choice,
now she'd admitted to owning something valuable. She reached into her
pocket and scooped up a small handful of the beads, leaving the rest of
them concealed in the pouch.

Geriko's eyes lit up with amazement. "Tides, Kady, these are worth a
fortune!"

"Do you think I can sell them for enough to buy a ticket out of Senestra?"

He nodded. "I'd say so. But . . . Tides, woman, you can't walk around
the street carrying this sort of wealth!"

"I don't really have much choice."

"Let me do it, then."

"Pardon?"

"Let *me* sell 'em for you," he offered. "You don't know the city and don't
know enough Senestran to haggle with those thieves down the markets in
any case. I can sell 'em, and bring you back the money."

Arkady looked at him doubtfully. He had a point. He also had an uncomfortably avaricious gleam in his eye. "I don't know, Geriko . . ."

"Give me only a few of them, then," he offered. "So's I can prove me-
self. I'll bring back the cash once they're sold and then, when you're sure
I can be trusted, I can sell the rest of 'em for you."

Arkady debated the problem for a moment and then nodded. She figured if she only risked a few beads, there wasn't much to worry about. Even
if Geriko stole half the money, which she didn't really begrudge him, she'd
still probably have enough to be gone from Port Traeker by nightfall.

"Very well," she said. "Take a dozen of them. If you bring me back a decent price, you can sell the rest and I'll give you ten per cent as a commission."

The big slave scooped up the beads, nodding eagerly. "Don't worry,
Kady. If there's one thing you can be sure of, it's that nothin' gets between
Geriko and a quick profit."

Geriko's words proved prophetic. Nothing *was* going to be allowed to
get between him and a quick profit. What Arkady had failed to take into
consideration was that the quickest profit he could make wasn't the ten

percent commission she'd offered him on the nacre beads, but the reward the Glaeban Embassy had put on her capture.

They came for her a little over an hour after Geriko left the clinic. She heard the knock on the clinic door, and thinking it was Geriko returning, she'd opened it willingly. Arkady was immediately overpowered, the embassy felines none too gentle in their handling of this former duchess implicated in the death of the King and Queen of Glaeba.

Arkady was put in an embassy waiting room, not a cell, by the felines who'd arrested her. She paced the room fretfully while she waited, wondering who would come for her next. Then the door opened and Arkady sagged with relief when Loriny Devale walked in, unaccompanied by any guards.

"Loriny?"

Stellan's cousin hurried across the room to embrace her. "Tides, you're all in one piece. I couldn't believe it when they told me they'd found you. I thought you were dead."

Arkady clung to Loriny for a moment, more grateful than she could find words to express her relief at such a warm welcome. Perhaps then, the letter from Loriny had been genuine, Geriko's betrayal less devastating than it seemed. Other than the guards who'd brought her to the embassy, there was no sign that she was anything other than a guest.

She let the young woman go and smiled wanly. "On more than one occasion in the past few months, Loriny, I had cause to wish I was."

"You must sit down," Loriny urged. "Have you eaten? You're so thin."

"I wouldn't say no to something other than bread and hard cheese," Arkady admitted as she took a seat on the sofa by the window.

"Then let me organise some real Glaeban food, and you can tell me the rest of it." Loriny quickly moved to the door, called a servant and ordered lunch brought to them immediately, and then hurried back to Arkady, taking a seat beside her. "When we heard the news about what Stellan had done . . ."

"Stellan didn't do anything, Loriny. The charges against him were false."

Loriny nodded. "We never believed he had a hand in the death of the king or queen. But the other rumours—the ones about his . . . choice of lovers. They're much harder to deny."

Poor Stellan, Arkady thought. *How hard you tried to keep your secret. And how futile your efforts ultimately proved to be.*

"Stellan is a good man, Loriny," she said. "I won't hear anyone say otherwise."

She smiled and placed her hand over Arkady's reassuringly. "Of course he is. And you know how we feel about him. But tell me, how did you finish up here in Port Traeker?"

"When the charges were brought against Stellan, I feared what might happen to me," she said, telling Loriny the story she'd practised silently all the way from the Outpost. "So I fled Ramahn and made my way to Elvere. That's where I took ship for Senestra." It was the truth, albeit a heavily edited version of the truth.

"We've been so worried about you," Loriny said, squeezing her hand.

"We?" she asked curiously, wondered who else there was left to care about her fate.

"Didn't you know? Everyone has been searching for you, Arkady. That's why we posted a reward, which, thank the Tides, that slave at the clinic remembered."

"But why? If Stellan is in Caelum agitating for the throne, as you say, I can't imagine anyone would care about my fate, one way or the other."

"Don't be silly, of course people care. In fact, your arrival couldn't have been more perfectly timed."

"Timed for what?" Arkady asked suspiciously.

Loriny never got a chance to answer, because at that moment the door opened and the slaves arrived with lunch. They uncovered the serving cart to reveal a selection of cold meats and fruit, and a plate of pungent cheeses. A moment later the door opened again and another woman entered the room carrying a tray with a bottle of wine and three glasses. Arkady studied her warily. She was tall and dark-haired with dark, exotic eyes and an air of insufferable smugness. This woman was no embassy servant.

"You didn't have to serve the wine yourself, my lady," Loriny scolded pleasantly, as the woman placed the tray on a side table.

"Don't be silly," the newcomer said with a smile. "When I learned of your guest, Lady Loriny, I couldn't wait to be of service. I mean, it's not every day one gets to meet the elusive and notorious Arkady Desean."

Arkady frowned. "You seem to have the better of me, my lady. You know who I am, but I'm afraid I'm unable to return the compliment."

"Oh, I'm sorry, Arkady," Loriny said, looking embarrassed. "I didn't realise you two hadn't met. Arkady Desean, this is . . . Lady Aleena Aranville. She's the new Duke of Lebec's cousin and his fiancée. She came to Senestra looking for you. She's the one who posted the reward."

One look at the future Lady Aranville and Arkady was quite certain she knew where she stood.

And the foolishness of trying to fight it.

Loriny seemed to know it too. She looked down at her hands, unable to meet Arkady's eye. "I'm sorry, Arkady. But my husband is loyal to the king."

"And that means loyal to my fiancé, the King's Private Secretary." Aleena smiled. "My friends call me Lyna, by the way."

Arkady hesitated for barely a moment, beyond being surprised any longer. Lady Aranville, by revealing her true name, had told Arkady all she needed to know about her future. She smiled at the immortal, determined not to give her the satisfaction of seeing her despair. "You *have* friends?"

Loriny gasped. "*Arkady* . . . "

"Oh, don't worry about Arkady's manners, my lady," Lyna said, her eyes fixed on Arkady rather than on her hostess. "Our former duchess has nothing left to fight with but her wit. And I admire a woman who fights back . . . even when she's unarmed."

Bitch. Arkady had no way to fight this immortal, not really—except with the knowledge Cayal had given her about what was happening in Jelidia. "How's your lover, by the way?"

"Lord Aranville is just fine, thank you. He's very much enjoying being Duke of Lebec. And Private Secretary to the king."

"I meant your other lover. Kentravyon."

"Arkady! Please!" Loriny cried in horror.

Lyna didn't flinch, however. She stared at Arkady for a long moment, as she realised the question was a blatant declaration of war. *I know you*, Arkady was telling her. *I know who you are and what you are and what you're after.*

"I beg your pardon?"

"Kentravyon," Arkady repeated. "I believe you thought he'd . . . gone cold on you? Well, my lady, I have it on good authority his brothers, Cayal and Lukys, have been down to visit him. He's . . . *thawed* considerably."

The immortal woman paled. Arkady had no idea if she'd made things better or worse, only that if this woman was now in cahoots with Jaxyn, knowing Kentravyon was back among the living might fracture that alliance.

"I have no idea what you're talking about," Lyna said after a time. Then she turned to Loriny. "Please inform your husband, my lady, that I appreciate his hospitality, but now that I have Lady Desean in custody, we must depart immediately for Glaeba. If he could make the arrangements as soon as possible, King Mathu and Queen Kylia will be very grateful."

Loriny jumped to her feet, spared Arkady a brief, worried look, and then curtseyed to her guest. "Of course, my lady. I'll see to it immediately."

The ambassador's wife hurried from the room, leaving them alone. Lyna's gaze hadn't wavered from Arkady's face the whole time she spoke to Loriny.

"What will you achieve by taking me back to Glaeba, my lady?"

"I'll prove to Jaxyn that he can trust me."

"Why do you even care if he trusts you?"

She shrugged. "I don't fancy spending another High Tide fending for myself. And if you're right about Kentravyon . . . well, all the more reason to find myself a comfortable place to wait it out."

Tides, these creatures are shallow. "And for such a spurious reason you'd hand me over to someone like Jaxyn, knowing what's probably in store for me?"

"I have no interest in what Jaxyn plans to do with you . . . or to you. That's his business." Lyna smiled and it chilled Arkady to the core. "Don't mistake me for someone who cares, my dear. Now, why don't you eat something? You look half-starved and I suspect you'll need your strength in the days to come, so you might as well make the most of Lady Devale's hospitality while you can."

Chapter 67

Boots seemed much happier once she realised Stellan Desean was in the palace and aware of her plight. Warlock supposed it was because she'd been born on his estate and grown up in his kennels. She was used to thinking of him as her master—the human who could make things right for her—even if, in his current predicament, the duke had little or no chance of helping her or her pups.

Still, with the excuse of escorting Nyah down to visit the pups, the former Duke of Lebec was able to check on Boots every few days. It was the only thing keeping her sane, she claimed, when Warlock returned from the dig.

To his credit, even after Warlock returned, the duke kept up his visits. Warlock was more than grateful. There was nothing Stellan Desean could do to free them. Nothing he could do to assuage Boot's fear their pups were Crasii. Nothing he could do at all, really, except offer useless platitudes, but for Boots that seemed to be enough. She was calmer these days, less panicked all the time. More reasonable. More like the Boots Warlock had first met in the slums of Lebec City.

Warlock was thinking as much as he waited in the shadows for the man from the Cabal to show, stamping his feet against the cold to keep his circulation going. Warlock glanced up at the dark, overcast sky, wondering when it would snow again. Hoping that's all it would do. Warlock hated the cold. He wore a blanket over his shoulders, something most of the palace Crasii had taken to wearing, the winter so bitter that even the felines, with their natural fur coats, were feeling it.

Nobody could remember a colder winter, the other Crasii in the palace had told him. Nobody remembered the Great Lakes freezing before, either.

"Psst!"

Warlock turned, a little annoyed at himself for becoming so distracted he'd not heard the man sneaking up behind him. He still didn't know the identity of his contact. Didn't know if he sneaked into the palace for their meetings, or if he was one of the staff here. He didn't really want to know, either.

"Cold enough for you?" the stranger asked from the darkness of the archway leading down toward the Crasii pens. He couldn't see him, but Warlock could see his breath frosting when he spoke.

"Next immortal I spy on is going to live in Torlenia," Warlock said, looking around to ensure they were alone. The snow-covered courtyard was empty, the windows above them dark.

He looked back at the shadowy figure and felt rather than saw him smile. "Tides, a Scard with a sense of humour. Who'd have thought?"

"Is there something you want?"

"I'm more interested in what you have to tell me. You missed our last meeting."

"I was in the mountains. On a job for Elyssa."

"Doing what?" He could hear the man's teeth chattering in the cold.

"She's financing an archaeological dig up there. It's run by a Glaeban human named Andre Fawk. They've found some sort of mass grave at the bottom of a cliff, but that's not what interested Elyssa. She was looking for a Lore Tarot."

The man was silent for a moment.

"Did she find it?"

Warlock nodded. "Turns out it wasn't the Lore she was interested in. The back of the cards form a map when you place them together in the right order."

"A map of what?"

"I don't know."

The figure moved slightly. Warlock guessed he was shrugging. "Well, I'll let the Pentangle know about it. Maybe they have some idea what she's looking for. In the meantime, can you get a message to Desean for me?"

"Probably."

"Then tell him this weather isn't normal."

"It's winter," Warlock pointed out. "What's not normal about that?"

"Jaxyn's been giving it a hand."

Warlock was shocked, not so much because of the Tide Lord's interference in the weather, but that the Cabal knew about it. "How do you know that?"

"We have a Scard close to him."

Warlock suffered a wave of anger at the news. They'd put him in the Herino Palace, got him into this whole flanking mess, on the grounds they didn't have any other Scards capable of getting close to an immortal. Only it was a lie. He'd been gone barely a few months and already they had another Scard close enough to Jaxyn to learn he was interfering in the weather.

"Why is he doing it?" Warlock asked, hoping the man took his hesitation as surprise and not bitter resentment.

"He's planning to attack Caelum across the ice."

"Tides," Warlock swore. "Can he do that?"

"Another few days and you'll be able to walk to Herino from here," the man told him. "Won't take much more effort to get an army across."

"And once I tell the duke your news, what do you expect him to do with it?"

"That's up to him. Our . . . *people* . . . are of the opinion the news might be a mixed blessing."

Warlock nodded, thinking he understood. "If the immortals here find out about it, they might be able to stop him, but in the process, they might do something worse."

"Got it in one, Dog Boy."

"Then why are they leaving the decision up to Desean?" he asked. "Surely something of that magnitude is best left to the people who claim to know what they're doing?"

"I don't ask for explanations, Dog Boy. I just deliver the messages. Maybe they think he's in the best position to judge the reaction of the immortals here in Cycrane to the news? I don't know. Just pass the message on and keep your head down."

"But what if—" Warlock began, but then he stopped when he realised he was talking to himself. As silently as he had come, the Cabal man had melted into the shadows. Warlock was alone.

Elyssa looked up from the table as Warlock returned with the wine she'd sent him to fetch. Fortunately, she had a fire going in the room. The warmth enveloped him and began to seep into his frozen bones. Warlock closed the door gratefully and hurried to the side table to pour the wine.

"Tides, Cecil, did you decide to crush the grapes yourself and wait for them to ferment?"

"Forgive me, my lady," he said, bringing her the freshly filled glass. "The cellarmaster was reluctant to leave the warmth of his room to let me into the cellar."

Elyssa didn't answer him. She was bent over the map, studying it intently, something she had done almost obsessively since Stellan Desean had revealed the map hidden on the back of the cards. She was copying the map out in sections, as she satisfied herself of its veracity, onto a large sheet of paper she had laid out on the table beside it. The map was almost complete, the only blank areas in places where the cards were too faded or damaged to read.

The immortal took the wine and sipped it distractedly, her attention firmly fixed on the map. "What do you think, Cecil?"

He looked at the map and nodded appreciatively. "I think you've just about got it, my lady."

"If only," Elyssa sighed. And then she smiled unpleasantly. "Tides, I bet that crabby old bitch would give her left tit to get her hands on this."

Warlock said nothing, fairly certain a proper Crasii would not respond to such a comment. Besides, he wasn't sure who she meant by *that crabby old bitch*, but guessed, as this was purportedly a map of the mountains around Maralyce's Mine, that she was probably talking about Maralyce.

"Thousands of years scraping around in the dirt, and all the time, there was a map."

"A map of what?" Warlock asked before he could contain himself.

Elyssa looked at him curiously. "Why did you want to know, Cecil?"

"To serve you is the reason I breathe, my lady," he said, realising his error. "If this is a map that leads to something you desire, then it is my only wish to know how to retrieve it for you."

The immortal studied him a little longer and then shrugged, apparently satisfied with his answer.

"Do you remember me asking you some time ago, Cecil, who, according to your lore, are those known as the First?"

He nodded. "Lord Kentravyon. Lord Pellys and Lady Maralyce."

"And you didn't know why they're known as the First, did you?"

"No, my lady."

Elyssa turned to look at the map. "And you've never heard of the Chaos Crystal? Or the Bedlam Stone?"

"No, my lady."

She leaned back in her chair and looked up at him. "We have our own Lore too, you know. Of a sort. According to *our* Lore, Cecil, the First Immortals weren't made by the Eternal Flame, they were made by the Chaos Crystal."

Warlock said nothing. He was afraid to move a muscle for fear she would realise she was telling him the secrets of her kind. Of course, to Elyssa, telling him anything wasn't supposed to matter, because he was Crasii and if she commanded him to say nothing, he'd have no choice but to obey.

"Now, for those of us who've taken the time to look into these things, the only three immortals that we can't pinpoint exactly when they were made are, as you so rightly listed, Kentravyon, Pellys and Maralyce. I know what they say about Pellys being made in that brothel fire, but that's nonsense. He was immortal long before he met Syrolee. I have my suspicions about Lukys too, mind you. He seems to know so much more than the rest of us, but he was with Engarhod when the meteor hit, so I suppose . . ." Her voice trailed off for a moment. Warlock got the feeling she was thinking out loud rather than specifically telling him anything. "Of course, we've always assumed the Eternal Flame made him immortal. But if, like Pellys, he was immortal already . . ." She shrugged and looked up, as if it had just occurred to her that she was rambling. "Anyway, Cecil, the upshot of all this is that the Chaos Crystal was stolen, several thousand years ago, by a very irritating group of mortal humans calling themselves the Cabal of the Tarot. They hid the Crystal in the mountains around the old city-state of L'bekken—which is in Glaeba near the place you now call Lebec—and only a few of them knew where. To keep the information safe from us— and from each other, I don't doubt—they incorporated the location of the Crystal into the Tide Lord tarot. Or at least we thought they did. Turns out we were crediting those larcenous little fools with a great deal more intelligence than they actually possessed."

"*This* is the map of where they hid it?" Warlock asked in awe, thinking any creature, Crasii or Scard, would be surprised by such news.

"This is the map," Elyssa agreed. "So what we have here, Cecil, is the location of the key to ultimate power." She smiled and took another sip of her wine. "And when I find it, it will be mine," she said. "All mine."

Chapter 68

Although he was half expecting it, Declan was still gutted to discover Arkady had left the Outpost for Port Traeker the same day he and the others had headed inland to cure the wetlands of swamp fever.

"Did she say where she was going?" he asked Ambria, when she told him the news over breakfast the morning after they arrived back at the Outpost. The chameleons had gone on ahead to Watershed Falls to speak with the village elders and assure them the swamp fever would not return to cause them problems. In the meantime, the immortals sat down to share a meal and catch up on the news a month in the isolation of the wetlands had kept from them.

It was strange, Declan thought, that even among immortals, they tended to act as if they were normal people and mealtimes were a necessity, rather than a habit.

Ambria shook her head. "She wouldn't say. *Away*, was about as specific as she was prepared to get," the immortal said.

"You can't blame her, Declan," Medwen said unsympathetically, helping herself to a slice of bacon from Cayal's plate. "I'd have done exactly the same thing in her place."

"Except I'd never do a deal with the Rodent for you, Medwen," Cayal said. "Except maybe one guaranteed to keep you out of my hair."

Cayal didn't appear surprised by Arkady's decision to leave. He seemed relieved as much as anything, which irked Declan for no reason he could readily identify.

Medwen pulled a face at the Immortal Prince but didn't seem to take offence at the comment. "Declan, the reality of your situation is that Arkady and you have very different paths to follow. You can't blame her for wanting to move on with her life. She's on a timetable, remember, you're not."

He wished he was as used to seeing people come and go in his life as these immortals were. At the same time, he was horrified to think he might one day be so inured to losing friends and loved ones that he could be just as cavalier about it. "I have to find her."

"Oh, no you don't," Cayal objected. "We're heading south, Rodent. The wetlands are safe, the swamp fever is taken care of, and we've done all the good deeds we're going to do. You have a bargain to keep."

"The bargain we had meant I would be with Arkady."

"And you *had* her, Rodent. It's not my fault you couldn't hold on to her."

Medwen looked at both of them for a moment and shook her head. "Tides, you two are unbelievable."

"I'm not going anywhere without Arkady," Declan insisted.

"Well, you're damned well not staying in my house while you argue about it," Ambria said. "Take your problems elsewhere. I want neither of you in my wetlands for another day if I can avoid it."

"There's gratitude for you," Cayal said, turning to Arryl. "Haven't you got something to say about this?"

Arryl seemed a little more sympathetic than Ambria. Despite himself, Declan was forced to admit that even though he tried not to befriend any of the immortals, it was very hard *not* to like Arryl. She was just that sort of personality.

"I think Cayal's right. You should let Arkady go, Declan," she said. "At least until you've worked out what you want to do."

"What I *want* to do?" He looked around the kitchen, shaking his head. It still seemed surreal that he was even sitting among these creatures, let alone discussing his future with them. "I'd like to roll back time, actually. And not be immortal."

"Do you have a backup plan?" Cayal asked.

"Much as it pains me to admit it," Medwen said, rolling her eyes at the Immortal Prince, "I fear Cayal may be right. Arkady has her own path to tread and you're not likely to be a part of it. You should let her go. You can always find her again later. If you still think it's a good idea."

It was easy for them to say it; easy for them to dismiss Arkady as nothing but a distraction. None of them had any concept of what it felt like to know that through his own stupidity, he might have driven her away.

Nor were they likely to care, he realised. He needed to take another tack. Come up with a reason they *would* understand. "I'm not just saying we need to find her because I'm heartbroken. Jaxyn's probably still looking for her. Even if I concede you have a point about us having different futures, I'll be damned if I'm going to leave her to his tender mercies."

Oddly enough, it was the mention of Jaxyn that seemed to change Arryl's mind. Even Cayal nodded in agreement. "Well, when you put it like that, I suppose there is something to be said for making sure she's out of his reach, at the very least."

"I thought you were desperate to get back to Jelidia?" Medwen said.

"We can do both. We have to find a ship in Port Traeker anyway. It won't take that much longer to track down Arkady. Assuming she's still in Port Traeker and hasn't taken off for parts unknown."

"We have to find her," Declan insisted.

Cayal shook his head. "No, we just have to ascertain that if *we* can't locate her, neither can anybody else. She's spoken with her feet, Rodent. If she wanted to wait for you, if she wanted to *be* with you, she'd be here now."

"The best you can do now is assure yourself she's safe," Arryl agreed.

"And once we've done that, then we're heading back to Jelidia, if I have to truss you up and toss you in the hold of a ship to get you there."

"And you can take that flanking cat with you," Ambria added with a scowl.

"What are you talking about?" Cayal asked.

"That feline who betrayed us. The one Arkady made you heal," she said to Arryl, lifting another plate of fresh bread onto the table for them. "Jojo. She's a Crasii through and through. Not only does her presence here upset the chameleons, but if I hear one more *to serve you is the reason I breathe, my lady*, I'm going to strangle the wretched creature."

"She can come with us, I suppose," Cayal said with a shrug, helping himself to the bread. "It'll make it easier to pose as merchants when we hire a ship, if we have a bodyguard."

"Do you actually have the money to hire a ship to take you to Jelidia, Cayal?" Medwen asked.

"No," he said. "But I don't intend to let that stop me."

"You never mentioned we'd be *stealing* a ship," Declan said.

Cayal looked at him and grinned. "What's the problem, Rodent? Does stealing go against your religion or something?"

Declan shrugged. "I just thought that with thousands of years to work on it, you'd have amassed enough wealth by now to buy a whole fleet of ships, not have to resort to petty theft."

Arryl shook her head, glaring at the men. "I hope you two don't intend to snipe at each other like this all the way to Jelidia. It was getting on my nerves a month ago. If it keeps up for much longer, I'll abandon the both of you and you can live forever, Cayal, and be damned."

"I'm not sniping," Cayal protested. "He is."

"Don't you think it's fascinating," Medwen observed to her immortal sisters, "that one can live to be as old as Cayal without growing up?"

"Tides," Cayal said. "No wonder you three have been hiding out here in the wilderness for so long. There's probably not a civilised place on Amyrantha left that'll have any one of you." He climbed to his feet, pushed his half-eaten breakfast aside and addressed his next words to Declan. "Come on, Rodent. Let's find this feline we seem to have acquired and get back to civilisation. Another day here with these whining women and you'll be wanting to die as much as I do."

Cayal pushed past Arryl and stalked out of the room. It was Medwen who broke the uncomfortable silence, turning to look at Declan. "You will look out for him, won't you?"

Declan gaped at her in amazement. "You want *me* to look after *him*?"

"Cayal can help you, Declan, but I've a feeling you can help him more."

"You people are universally insane, you do know that, don't you?"

"You see," Arryl said, "that's why it's up to you. You haven't been immortal long enough for it to drive you crazy."

They slipped into Port Traeker a few days later, to a city in uproar. There were signs up all over the place about public meetings to discuss the return of the Lord of Temperance, posters stuck on almost every other flat surface advertising prayer services to appeal to their reborn god, and almost as many advocating an end to public professions of faith.

Dressed as merchants, with a feline bodyguard in tow and two chameleon slaves in their entourage, nobody spared Declan, Cayal or Arryl a second glance. The hysterical aftermath of the aborted invasion of the wetlands seemed to be the only topic of conversation in Port Traeker, and everyone had an opinion about it. The only consensus, however, seemed to be that there would not be any further expeditions into the wetlands until somebody made quite certain that the falling disease which had afflicted the sailors of the first invasion fleet had been identified and could be dealt with.

The other interesting by-product of their interference seemed to be the fracturing of the alliance between House Medura and House Pardura. That made a second invasion of the wetlands even more remote. Without the resources and the Merchant Marines of the two most powerful Houses in Senestra, it wasn't likely anybody would be invading anything, anytime soon.

There was, however, no sign of Arkady.

The amphibians who'd taken Arkady to Port Traeker could offer no more help than telling Declan where they'd delivered her, which was a small dock not far from the Medura Palace. He didn't think it likely she'd return there, and the only place in the vicinity which might tempt her was the Glaeban Embassy. Even Cayal laughed at the notion that she might have returned there. With her husband disgraced, and Jaxyn on the lookout for her, he thought it beyond improbable that she would go anywhere near the place.

Declan wasn't so sure, but he couldn't risk approaching the embassy himself, and didn't trust Cayal to do it for him. Besides, neither Cayal nor Arryl was Glaeban, and would be unlikely to get a useful answer out of anybody.

He did, however, have a feline at his command. And she truly was his to command. Declan was used to Crasii following orders, but the blind obedience of the Crasii to their Tide Lord masters was a little frightening.

"You're wasting your time," Cayal said, as he listened to Declan give Jojo her instructions. "Arkady wouldn't be stupid enough to go anywhere near your embassy."

"Do you understand what I want you to do?" Declan asked Jojo, ignoring Cayal.

"To serve you is the reason I breathe," the little ginger feline replied solemnly.

That's not what I asked, Declan thought with a sigh, but he was learning that was as good as he was likely to get.

"Then go. We'll wait for you here."

The feline hurried out of the taproom, leaving Cayal and Declan alone at the table they'd commandeered, which looked out over the wharves. Arryl was out there somewhere, dressed like a Senestran lady with her servants in tow, scoping out a likely ship.

"I tell you, this is a waste of time."

"I heard you the first two dozen times."

"But apparently you're not listening to me. Arkady wouldn't risk going to the embassy."

"The ambassador's wife here is her husband's cousin," Declan told him. "If she was desperate enough, then she might have risked it."

"Which means if the cousin has helped her, she'll say nothing, or she'll get herself in trouble. If she's *not* seen Arkady, she'll have nothing to say and you'll have simply tipped Jaxyn off to her whereabouts. Or Arkady *has* been there, been arrested, and is already on her way to Glaeba, at which point you and I are going to come to blows, Rodent, because the Tide is getting higher every day, and I have no intention of taking another detour to go hunting Arkady."

"Did you ever love her?" Declan asked, wondering if his dismissive attitude to Arkady's fate was genuine or just a show he put on for Declan's benefit.

"Only when she's nearby."

"Tides, but you're a shallow bastard."

"Something for which you should be grateful, Rodent, 'cause the last time my heart got broken, I destroyed a whole damned country. Here's Arryl."

Declan glanced over his shoulder to find Arryl crossing the taproom toward them. Tiji and Azquil, dressed as her slaves, walked a few paces behind her, their eyes suitably downcast. Cayal slid across the bench to make room for her, leaving the Crasii to stand nearby to await their mistress's pleasure.

"Any luck?"

"There's a fishing boat, an ice-breaker, at the far end of the dock." Arryl told them, taking off her gloves. "The captain says he's waiting for the spring melt, but the ship's ready to sail now, if we're offering him enough coin."

"Did you tell him where we wanted to go?"

"I told him my husband and his brother wanted to go ice fishing. He told me you were mad."

"But he didn't refuse?"

Arryl shook her head. "He refused to go much past the southern tip of Senestra at this time of year, but a purse full of nacre tiles convinced him to consider it. He seems to think you'll get all the ice fishing you want, without going too far south."

"Once we're aboard and clear of Port Traeker, it doesn't really matter what he thinks," Cayal said. "When can we leave?"

"On tonight's tide, if we're quick about it." She glanced around with a frown. "Where's Jojo?"

"Rodent sent her to the Glaeban Embassy to check on Arkady."

Arryl looked at Declan sadly. "You can't think she'd go there for aid, surely?"

"It's the last place I'll look, my lady. If there's no sign of her there, then I'll accept she's out of reach. Mine or Jaxyn's."

Arryl put her hand over his and smiled encouragingly. "I'm sure she's fine, Declan. Arkady is a survivor."

Declan appreciated her support, wishing he was as confident. Cayal said nothing further on the subject. Instead, he raised his hand and ordered another round of drinks.

Some three hours later, with the sun almost set, they were about to leave the tavern for the ice-breaker Arryl had found to take them to Jelidia, when Jojo returned.

"Well?" Declan demanded, a part of him hoping Arkady had not only taken shelter at the embassy, but was still there waiting for him. "Has she been there?"

"I spoke to the felines on the gate," Jojo said. "They told me Lady Aranville had been at the embassy, but now she was gone."

"Who is Lady Aranville?" Arryl asked.

Declan frowned. "I don't know. Did they mean Arkady?"

"I don't think so, my lord. When I pressed them, they said the only woman to visit the embassy in the past few months who was out of the ordinary was Lady Aranville. She'd told them to say nothing of her visit or her purpose in Senestra, and they were adamant about adhering to her orders."

"Which means Glaeba has the best trained felines on Amyrantha," Cayal remarked, "or your Lady Aranville was immortal."

"How can that be? The only immortal in Glaeba calling himself an Aranville is Jaxyn. Diala is Queen of Glaeba now."

"The only immortal you *know* about," Cayal said testily. "Now, are we satisfied Arkady's gone, or are you going to stand here agonising over what some Glaeban noblewoman said to a bunch of mindless felines a month ago? The tide won't wait you know. Not the ocean one nor the magical one."

Declan hesitated still, puzzled by the notion of who Lady Aranville might be, wondering why the felines would be so keen to follow her orders . . .

But Cayal was right about one thing: there was no sign of Arkady and if he didn't get on this ship with Cayal and Arryl, he may never find out what the Cabal was so desperate to learn.

Even if he stayed here, he might never find Arkady.

If he went with Cayal, on the other hand, he would learn the secret to killing an immortal.

The decision to abandon the hunt for Arkady tore his soul to shreds, but he didn't see that he had much choice. "We can leave now."

"Finally!" Cayal said, rolling his eyes. He turned to Arryl. "Lead on, Sorceress. You did get some furs for your little pets, I hope? It'd be a pity to have them freeze to death before we get halfway to Lukys's place."

"I'll take care of my Crasii. You just get us there in one piece."

"What about you, Rodent? Ready to meet your maker? Literally?"

In all the fuss with looking for Arkady, Declan had forgotten about meeting Lukys, the man who may or may not be his father. "Just get on the boat, Cayal."

The Immortal Prince grinned; he was in the best mood Declan had ever seen him, which seemed odd until he realised Cayal's sudden euphoria was probably because he believed that he would soon be able to die.

Chapter 69

Tiji had thought she knew what it was to be cold, but every day they drew closer to their destination, she had cause to revise her opinion. Jelidia was beyond cold. It froze the very marrow of her bones.

And it was—the Immortal Prince had informed them cheerfully—still summer here.

"Is something wrong, Tiji?"

She turned her head, copping a mouth full of fur for her trouble. The hooded jacket Arryl had provided for her was a little on the large side. She spat out the fur and moved the hood aside with a mittened hand. "I'm cold."

Declan smiled. "I noticed."

She scowled, partly because he smelled like a suzerain, but mostly because he wore nothing heavier than a light cloak over shirt sleeves and a vest. Like the other immortals in their party, the cold meant nothing to him. And she was certain the only reason he bothered with the cloak was to stop his shirt from freezing.

"Did you want to ride in the sled for a time?"

Tiji glanced at the dog-pulled sled with deep suspicion. Ten harnessed, noisy, hairy and entirely-too-many-teeth-for-comfort dogs strained to drag the sled forward. The man who'd brought it to meet them at the coast when their ship (with its reluctant crew) weighed anchor was yet another immortal. This one was Taryx, and he'd been expecting them. Or at least he'd been expecting Arryl, Medwen and Ambria.

Tiji didn't think he was over the shock of meeting Declan yet.

"Taryx says we'll be there soon."

"So it's not too late to turn back, then?"

"Do you really want to turn back?"

"Funny, I was going to ask you the same question."

Declan turned to look out over the white snowfield stretching before them. "I think we've come too far for that."

"We could go back," she said. "You don't *have* to get involved with these monsters, you know."

He glanced down at her. "Would you have listened to me if I suggested you didn't need to get involved with Azquil?"

She shook her head, but wasn't sure if he saw the movement because it happened mostly inside her hood. "Finding the rest of the chameleon Crasii is a little different to you making nice with the immortals, Declan."

"How?"

"Well, for one thing, my lot don't go about sinking continents into the ocean. Or blowing them up with volcanoes. Or chucking meteors at people . . ."

He smiled. "Point taken."

"So we can turn around, then?"

"No."

"Why not?"

"Because we'd be a fool to turn our backs on this opportunity."

"The opportunity for what? You to learn how to break the world in half the next time you get pissed at Ark—somebody . . ."

If he noted her slip he was too polite—or still hurting too much—to remark on it. "What I mean, Tiji, is that the Cabal has spent thousands of years trying to work out how to destroy an immortal, and here I am, invited along to help kill one of them."

"That's a very convenient excuse, Declan."

"Blame Arkady," he said, unable to hide the bitterness in his voice at the mention of her name. "It was her idea."

Tiji felt for Declan, wishing there was something she could do or say to ease his pain. Nothing she'd said so far had helped. Of course, she wasn't sure what he was suffering over the most—Arkady's disappearance or the thought that he might have driven her away.

"I'm afraid, Declan."

He put his arm around her. "I won't let anything happen to you, Slinky."

She smiled, but didn't reply, mostly because she wasn't sure how to tell Declan the thing that frightened her most was not what the other immortals might do to her; it was what Declan—counting himself as one of them—would do to himself.

It was much later in the day when the ice palace came into view. It should have been sunset by then. Tiji's internal clock was telling her that, but the sun showed no sign of going anywhere. Squinting into the relentlessly blindingly light, Tiji gasped as they topped a small rise to find the palace perched on the glittering white horizon. Their first sight of the crystal palace caused them all to halt in their tracks, with the exception of Taryx who had to bring the dogs and the sled under control to wait for them.

For once, Tiji barely even noticed the dogs or the stench of the suzerain to which she had thought she'd never grow accustomed. She was too entranced by the ice palace to care.

"Tides," Azquil exclaimed, stopping beside her on the rise. "Will you look at that?"

The others stopped beside them, even Jojo. The feline pushed back her hood, her expression as awestruck as Tiji thought her own must be. "It's amazing. Did Lord Lukys really build it?"

"With my help," Taryx said, climbing the slope to stand beside them. The dogs and the sled were still where he left them, the animals sitting patiently on the snow while they waited for their master to resume their journey.

Arryl glanced at Cayal. "Lukys has outdone himself."

"You know he only built it to show off, don't you?"

"Then why build it here, Cayal, where there's nobody to admire his handiwork?"

"Oh, I don't know," Declan said. "He managed to get *you* here to look at it."

"That's Lukys for you." Cayal smiled and looked at Declan. "You look nothing like him, by the way."

"Nice time to decide that."

"Which brings up an interesting point, now I come to think of it," the Immortal Prince continued in a smug tone. "I mean, we don't *know* he's your father for certain, do we? Any one of us could have wandered through Glaeba at the right time. Was your mother pretty?"

"Must have been," Declan said. "I am."

Tiji smiled. The journey to Jelidia had left plenty of time for the spymaster and the Immortal Prince to get on each other's nerves. Cayal goaded Declan constantly, but Declan was getting very good at needling Cayal in return, and the Immortal Prince could do nothing about it. He needed Declan far more than Declan needed him.

"Please," Arryl said with a weary sigh. "Let's not start this again."

"I'm not starting anything," Cayal said. "I was just pointing out that the Rodent is a bastard."

"Tides, you're right," Declan said in a deadpan voice. "That means you could be my father, Cayal. I mean, my mother *was* a whore, and I'm guessing you usually have to pay for it . . ."

Tiji laughed out loud which didn't help matters much at all.

Cayal did not seem amused. He turned on Tiji threateningly. "You think that's funny, do you, reptile?"

Tiji took a step backward, reaching for Azquil's hand. But she needn't have worried. Declan put himself between Cayal and Tiji before she could answer. "Leave her alone."

"Why? You like lizards as well as duchesses, Rodent?"

"Cayal, that's enough," Arryl ordered. "Tiji and Azquil are *my* servants and you'll leave them alone because I command it."

"Who owns the cat?" Taryx asked.

"The Rodent," Cayal said, before anybody else could claim Jojo. "He likes to play a bit of Cat and Mouse, our new immortal."

Taryx glanced at Declan with a frown. He looked confused and more than a little worried about the implications of having an unknown immortal appear out of nowhere unexpectedly. Declan just rolled his eyes.

"Each to his own, I suppose." Taryx turned to the others. "Are we done sightseeing? You'll have plenty of time to admire the palace when we get there."

"Then lead on, Taryx," Cayal said. "We're not getting any younger standing here. Or any older, for that matter."

Arryl sighed again, shaking her head. "The idea that you might soon be dead grows increasingly attractive, Cayal."

"I love you too, Arryl," Cayal replied with an unexpected grin, but he didn't wait for her response, simply headed down the slope toward the sled. Taryx and Arryl followed him, leaving Declan on the crest with the Crasii.

"You know how I can tell he's immortal?" Tiji said to Declan.

"How?"

"Nobody's succeeded in killing him yet."

Declan smiled. "You're going to get yourself in trouble making comments like that around these people, Slinky."

"Lady Arryl will protect us, my lord," Azquil said. "As will you, I suspect."

"Of course he will," Jojo said, staring at Declan with devoted eyes. "The Tide Lords protect us because to serve them is the reason we breathe."

"It might be the reason *you* breathe, kitten," Tiji said. "But some of us aren't so devoted to the cause."

The feline glared at the two chameleons—something she did a lot, Tiji noted with concern—and stepped protectively between them and Declan.

"You are Scards. Abominations who should not be allowed to live. Both of you."

"That's enough, Jojo," Declan informed her, putting his hand on her shoulder to restrain her. "These chameleons are my friends and you will treat them with the same respect you would treat any immortal. Is that clear?"

The feline immediately backed down, dropping to her knees on the snow before her master. "To serve you is the reason I breathe, my lord."

"Harm a single scale on either of those two," he added sternly, "and I'll give you a reason *not* to breathe."

It concerned Tiji a little to see how quickly Declan had learned to use the Crasii compulsion to his advantage, even if he was using it to protect her and Azquil. *Is this what happens when you find you can command anyone to do anything? You find reasons to do it just because you can?*

Jojo didn't seem offended or upset by the order, although it was clear she considered the two reptilian Crasii prey rather than family. She nodded and rose to her feet. "To serve you is the reason I breathe, my lord."

"You may go."

She bowed awkwardly, unaccustomed to the furs, and then turned and hurried down the slope after the sled.

Tiji waited until she was out of earshot and then looked at Declan with a frown. "I think you're starting to like that whole 'To serve you is the reason I breathe, my lord' nonsense."

"Don't be ridiculous."

"To serve you isn't the reason *I* breathe."

"I learned that long ago, Slinky."

She searched his face, hoping he meant it. "Don't let them change you, Declan."

"I won't," he promised. "Now, come on. The Palace of Impossible Dreams awaits us."

Tiji smiled at Declan, forcing an enthusiasm she certainly didn't feel for this venture. And then she let Azquil take her hand and together the three of them headed down the slope to where the other immortals were waiting.

Chapter 70

If Declan had thought Lukys's ice palace was impressive from a distance, it was quite overwhelming close up. About an hour after they'd first spied it, they entered the Palace of Impossible Dreams through an archway that opened into a cavernous chamber from which the rest of the palace seemed to emanate.

A rush of warm air greeted them as they entered, although Declan thought the warmth an illusion. A number of Crasii slaves hurried out to attend them, as if the visitors were expected. Although he was searching for it, Declan couldn't sense another presence on the Tide to indicate Lukys, Kentravyon or Pellys was in the vicinity. The canines brought them hot drinks and warm shawls and eyed the new Crasii warily. Taryx had disappeared with the sled, presumably to release and feed the dogs.

Jojo hissed as a canine got too close, baring her teeth warningly.

"Settle down," Declan ordered the feline he was now apparently the master of, looking around with interest. Although he'd been warned about this place, he wasn't quite prepared for the scale of it. It was beyond huge. It was majestic. And it was pointless. As Arryl had asked when they first spied the palace, *why build it here, where there's nobody to admire your handiwork?*

"Cayal! You're back!"

They all turned at the sound of a female voice. Descending the carved-ice stairs was a young woman, dressed in a long woollen dress and a glorious white fur coat that seemed to be made from the skin of a Jelidian snow bear. Declan wondered why he was surprised. No snow bear was going to harm an immortal. Lukys could have taken the skin off the bear while it was still breathing and complaining about being skinned alive, and wouldn't have come to any lasting harm.

The young woman stopped before their disparate group and curtseyed elegantly. She was Torlenian, of all things—at least Declan assumed she was because she addressed them in that language—but she was smiling in welcome and he figured this must be their hostess, Lukys's young wife, Oritha.

Cayal bowed politely to the woman, turning on his most charming smile. "Oritha, how nice to see you again. Allow me to introduce Lady Arryl and . . . Declan Hawkes." Then he turned to the others, adding, "This is Lukys's wife, Oritha."

She smiled. "You do insist on calling him that, don't you, Cayal? Are the other ladies not with you, Lady Arryl? My husband told me to expect several ladies."

"My sisters declined your husband's generous invitation, my lady," Arryl explained with the glib ease of a practised liar. "They have responsibilities in Senestra not easily abandoned, even for someone as persuasive as your husband."

That was diplomatic, Declan thought, wondering why they were bothering to go through the motions with this woman, even if she was mortal. Given whom she was married to, it seemed a fairly inane charade. Surely, she must know what was going on here.

Oritha turned her welcoming smile on Declan. "And you, my lord? We were not expecting you; however, I'm sure my husband will be delighted to receive you."

"Where is your husband, my lady?" Cayal inquired. "And Lord Pellys? Lord Kentravyon?"

"They've gone hunting snow bears," she explained with a smile and a shrug that spoke of fond tolerance for her husband's quirks. "Lord Kentravyon gets . . . fractious, if he's confined for too long."

"Then I imagine they'll be gone for a while."

"Not too long, I hope. We expected you some time ago, so I know Ryda doesn't like to stray too far from the palace."

"Ryda?" Arryl asked, a little confused.

Declan's heart skipped a beat.

"It's the name of our host," Cayal explained. "Didn't you know? He's a Stevanian gem merchant, by the name of—"

"Ryda Tarek," Declan finished for him, with the sick feeling he had stepped off the edge of a chasm and into an abyss.

Declan woke the following morning to a Tide that felt like the sea during a storm. He had gotten used to the feel of Arryl and Cayal on the Tide. It was easy to tell them apart. Cayal was much stronger than Arryl. Her calming presence was easily distinguishable from the roiling power that was Cayal. But this morning it was different. This was more than the presence of a few Tide Lords, like Cayal, Arryl and Taryx.

This was a maelstrom.

Lukys, Pellys and Kentravyon were here.

Declan wasn't sure what to do. Since learning the identity of Ryda Tarek, he wasn't even sure what to feel. A part of him wasn't even surprised. He'd had his suspicions in the past that the fifth member of the Pentangle was an immortal. Maralyce had told him it was possible, even told him of Lukys and Cayal doing such a thing once before with the Holy Warriors.

But it had never occurred to him, even after he'd met Ryda Tarek in Tilly Ponting's parlour in Herino, that he was dealing with the immortal Lukys.

The immortal who may or may not be my father.

There was a certain inevitability on that point, Declan feared. It all fitted together too well for his existence to be the result of random chance. Although Cayal was right when he said it was possible some other Tide Lord had wandered through Glaeba. That he'd spent the night with a whore who just happened to be a Tidewatcher's daughter and conceived a child with her, was beyond improbable.

And the only Tide Lord who knew Maralyce had even borne a child, was Lukys. He told them as much in Tilly's parlour when he was posing as a member of the Cabal, explaining to them how he thought Cayal had found a way to die and the Cabal should be helping him along, not hindering his progress.

Foremost expert in the world on the Tide Lords, Tilly had called Ryda Tarek. Not hard to understand why, when you discovered the reason.

Declan felt the Tide surging around him and realised there was nowhere he could hide. If he could feel the others, they could feel him.

And one of them was getting closer . . .

Declan turned to face the entrance of his magnificent—albeit icy—chamber. There were no doors here, just lots of ante-rooms and corridors that gave a semblance of privacy, however false.

Privacy was an illusion too, he supposed, when you could feel each other on the Tide.

Jojo was standing at the door on guard. He suspected she'd been there all night.

"You can stand down now, Jojo," he told her. "Go and get something to eat. And rest."

"But there's someone coming, my lord . . ."

"I know. I can feel him. Go. I'll be fine."

She wasn't happy with the order to abandon him, but bowed to his wishes nonetheless. "To serve you is the reason I breathe, my lord."

Jojo left and the approaching turbulence drew nearer. He knew Lukys was there even before he appeared. He had time to brace himself; time to marshal his thoughts and hopefully not give away too much on the Tide. Declan squared his shoulders and took a deep breath, even as the thought occurred to him that it was a pointless and stupid thing to do because he was immortal now. Taking a deep breath wasn't going to make the slightest difference to anything.

"You're angry," Lukys said as he stepped into the chamber.

He was alone, dressed much the same as he had been when Declan met him the last time in Herino. He looked no older than thirty-five, with that strange combination of dark skin and pale, pale eyes. Declan tried to see some common feature between them, but physically they could not be more unalike.

No "*hello, son*" or "*I'm sorry.*" Just "*you're angry.*"

Declan glared at him. "Not without just cause, I would have thought."

Lukys stepped further into the room, eyed Declan up and down critically for a moment and then shrugged. "Would an apology help?"

"Not a lot."

"Then I won't waste your time or mine giving you one."

"You're admitting you're responsible, then?"

Lukys shrugged again and thrust his hands into his pockets. "Responsible? Hmmm . . . let me see . . . am I the reason you're living and breathing? Absolutely. Did I seek out Maralyce's child to find what had become of him? Of course I did. Even if I hadn't discovered he'd very conveniently sired a daughter of loose morals and child-bearing age, I'd have gone looking for him. Your grandfather was a Tidewatcher, Declan. He could feel the Tide returning long before the rest of us could. I've always found it an advantage to know it's on the turn, long before my immortal brethren get wise to the fact. I like to be prepared, you see. But did I make you immortal? Well, no. You managed that all on your own, son."

Lukys's bald-faced admission was bad enough, but there were holes in his story Declan wanted filled. This all seemed a little too glib.

"But that meant you would have met Shalimar as a young man. How come he didn't recognise you when you signed up with the Cabal as Ryda Tarek?"

Lukys walked as he spoke, running his finger over the icy walls as if it intrigued him far more than their conversation. "Ryda Tarek is more than one man. I believe your grandfather thinks of me as the great-grandson of the Ryda Tarek he met when he was younger. You know . . . *I've learned everything from my father . . . my family passed on all the knowledge to me . . .* that sort of thing. Besides, I've only met him a few times and they were decades apart. It wasn't hard to convince him I was a different man each time we met. How is he, by the way? The returning Tide must be paining him greatly."

"He's dead."

Lukys had the decency to look sorry about it. "That's a pity. I liked him."

"He'd have killed *himself,* had he known he'd brought an immortal into the Cabal."

"It wasn't his fault. He was just easily fooled."

"You fooled them all."

"They wanted to be fooled, Declan." He kept walking as he spoke, circling Declan ever so subtly, like a fox honing in on its prey. "Every member of your wretched Cabal likes to believe they'll be the one to find the answer. You can't blame me for offering them a little hope."

Declan had to turn to keep him in view. "Then you *do* know the way to kill an immortal?"

Lukys nodded. "I can effectively put an end to an immortal, yes."

He had a bad feeling *effectively putting an end to an immortal* wasn't quite the same thing as killing one, but at this point, Declan wasn't going to argue semantics. Besides, there was something else he wanted to know.

"Were you planning to make me immortal yourself?"

Much to his surprise, Lukys nodded without hesitation. "I was," he agreed, "right up until I came to Herino the last time and met you. After that, I decided to let you live a long and happy life and die of natural causes in your old age. You have to understand, I never knew for certain if immolating you would make you immortal. I figured being more than half immortal would give you a fighting chance, but it's such a rare thing, there was no way of being certain, until you faced a traumatic death. I just decided not to take the risk."

"And having gone to all that trouble to create a more-than-half-immortal child, what made you change your mind about going the rest of the way and making me immortal?"

"Well, *you*, of course," the immortal said. "Tides, I fathered a bastard on a whore, Declan. You were supposed to grow up in the Lebec slums, learn how to survive, how to lie and cheat and steal, how to keep your head down and your wits about you, that's all. That would have made you the perfect immortal companion. You weren't supposed to have friends in high places who'd find you respectable work. Or get recruited by the Cabal and be sent to work for the King's Spymaster. You certainly weren't supposed to have the wit to wind up in such an exalted position, yourself."

Lukys's reasons for rejecting him struck Declan as being almost comical. "So you decided you'd wipe your hands of me because I made something of my life?"

"I decided to wipe my hands of you because you're dangerous, Declan Hawkes. You managed far too much, in far too short a time, with nothing but your own cunning and intelligence to rely on. I wasn't going to complicate matters—or make things worse—by giving you immortality and access to the Tide."

"And yet here I am," Declan said.

Lukys smiled and held his hands up helplessly. "Which just goes to show you that even the best laid plans can go awry."

"You bastard. Did you never wonder what your little experiment might do to me?"

"What can I say, son? Other than to remind you that sometimes it's easier to beg forgiveness than ask permission?"

"Which might help, if I thought for a minute you *were* begging forgiveness. And would you stop calling me *son*?"

"Does it bother you?"

"It makes me ill."

That seemed to amuse Lukys. "You'll get used to it. Don't suppose you're interested in calling me *father*?"

Declan didn't even bother to dignify that suggestion with an answer. *There will never come a time*, Declan silently swore, *when I will willingly call you father.*

"Well . . . perhaps it's a bit early for that."

"What about the Cabal?"

"What about them?"

"You took them all for a ride, you evil son-of-a-bitch. I'll bet you were laughing at us the whole time you were sitting there listening to us trying to make plans to deal with the immortals."

"On the contrary, Declan, my boy, I have been their salvation. Thanks to me, and you too I might add, they'll achieve what thousands of years of Pentangles have been unable to even get close to. I will give them what they crave—a dead immortal. How exactly does that make me evil?"

"You're using them."

"And giving them what they want in the process. Tell me again how that makes me evil?"

Declan shook his head as he began to realise there was no easy way to argue with this man. "So what happens now?"

"Well, we try to kill Cayal, of course. That's all the poor boy has wanted for the past millennium or so. I'm a little surprised he's been able to rope you into this venture, actually. But glad. You've a lot to learn, but Tides, boy, you've got power to burn. And that's something I wasn't expecting."

"Suppose I change my mind? Suppose I decide to leave?"

"Where will you go?"

When Declan couldn't answer that, Lukys put his hand on his shoulder, smiling. "You're home, Declan. Much as you despise me, much as you think every immortal who ever drew breath is evil incarnate, you're one of us now."

Declan shook him off angrily. "I don't belong here."

"You don't belong anywhere else, son. And you know what the irony is? The more you despise what you are, the more you have to stay."

"How do you figure that?"

"Because I'm the only one who can offer you a way out."

That was painfully true. If Lukys could kill an immortal, if it took a half-dozen other immortals to make it happen, he had no choice but to stay.

"So let's do it, then. Kill Cayal. Kill me."

"Ah . . ." Lukys said, sitting himself down in the large padded chair opposite Declan. "I would, but there's one teensy little problem."

"What problem?"

"Before we can kill anybody, my angry young friend, we have to find the Chaos Crystal."

EPILOGUE

The Warden looked about the icy, triangular cell, nodding with approval. Although it had been cleaned three times now, the faint stench of stale urine still permeated the walls, but nothing short of demolishing Lebec Prison was ever likely to alter that state of affairs. Other than the smell, however, everything seemed in order. There was fresh bedding on the pallet, a clean bucket in the corner and a small stool under the high, barred window that looked out over the exercise yard. The prisoner in the adjoining cell ignored the preparations going on in the rest of the tower, cleaning his fingernails with the end of a stray stalk of straw from his mattress.

There was a brazier in the outer guard room which took the chill off the air in the few feet surrounding it, but did little to heat the rest of the chamber. The Warden thought it might be prudent to arrange another blanket for the cell.

He didn't want to lose his head because he'd allowed his prisoner to freeze to death.

It was a lot of trouble to go to for a single prisoner, the Warden thought, but then Lebec Prison had rarely played host to such an honoured guest—certainly never one so well connected, or with so many powerful enemies.

"Sir?"

The Warden glanced over his shoulder at the feline who had hailed him.

"Yes?"

"They're here, sir. Just coming through the main gate."

The Warden nodded, straightened his jacket and turned for the door. He followed the messenger down the stairs from the west tower, through the main body of the prison to the front entrance. Another guard opened the door as he approached. Stepping onto the landing, the Warden waited as a closed carriage approached, flanked by a full squad of felines wearing the livery of the Lebec. None of the felines seemed bothered by the drizzling sleet falling from the dull, overcast sky.

He waited under the cover of the awning as the carriage rocked to a halt, and the armed, human guard who had been riding with the driver, climbed down to open the carriage door. He lowered the step and stood back as the lone passenger emerged, shackled hand and foot. When it appeared the prisoner was having trouble descending while wearing chains, the guard reached forward to aid her.

The woman spared him a thin, grateful smile and then looked up at the forbidding façade of the prison as if she was bracing herself to enter. She seemed a little thinner than when he'd seen her last. But she was still beautiful, still intimidatingly sure of herself.

But no longer under the protection of the King's Spymaster. Or married to the king's cousin.

Ah, but how the mighty have fallen . . .

The Warden took the steps down to the pavement two at a time, and bowed to the prisoner before he could stop himself. "Lady Desean."

"Warden."

"I'd like to welcome you to Lebec Prison."

"I'd rather you didn't."

"I regret we could not meet again under more . . . convivial circumstances."

"I'm sure you're heartbroken about it," she replied with vast insincerity.

Bitch.

The Warden frowned. "We have your . . . accommodation ready. It's in the west tower. You won't be bothered by the other prisoners."

"And they won't be able to hear my screams?"

He looked away uncomfortably. "My orders are to ensure you are not mistreated, your grace. Lord Aranville was most insistent on that point."

"I believe he's saving that pleasure for himself, Warden. Can I send a message to someone? I believe I have a few friends left who would be happy to arrange representation for me."

"I'm sorry, my lady, Lord Aranville was rather insistent on that point too. You are to have no contact with anyone other than your cellmate and the feline guards who currently accompany you."

She looked around at her guard and seemed resigned more than worried.

"I'm to have company then?"

"So I have been instructed, your grace." He didn't need to call her "your grace." She was the common-born cast-off wife of a traitor. But somehow, it seemed right. She still carried herself as a duchess, even if she wasn't one any longer. He stood back and indicated the maw-like entrance to the prison. "Ladies first . . ."

Arkady Desean negotiated the steps with some difficulty, but the Warden had no intention of releasing her from her shackles and making her progress easier. Let her struggle up the steps and another four flights of stairs. His job was to incarcerate her and keep her whole. Nothing in his mandate from the new Duke of Lebec involved making her comfortable.

It was slow going, making their way to the west tower. To her credit, the former duchess didn't complain once, despite stumbling several times and knocking her shins on the unforgiving stone of the stairs that led to her cell. When they reached the top floor he opened the door for her himself and stood back to let her enter, interested to see her reaction.

Arkady stepped into the tower room and look around. The circular room was divided into three wedges, two of them forming cells and one the anteroom with the brazier outside. The cell allocated to Arkady Desean was on the right, the barred door open and waiting for her. The cell on the left was locked, its occupant standing back against the wall, hidden by the shadows. The Warden had no idea why Lord Aranville had ordered Prisoner Two-Eight-Two moved into the cell beside Arkady's, and knew better than to ask. But he was curious, knowing the connection between the former duchess and the doctor Stellan Desean had ordered incarcerated without trial some seven years ago, about three months before he married his slum-born wife.

Arkady hadn't seen her cellmate yet. She looked around, apparently surprised she wasn't being chained to the wall in a damp, dark, dungeon somewhere underground.

"You'll receive two meals a day," the Warden informed her. "And a jug of water to drink. Once a week, if you behave, you'll be allowed another bowl with which you may wash. You may see no one, speak to no one, write no letters, or have any contact with the other prisoners. Lord Aranville intends to visit when he has the time, but he's not seen fit to indicate when that might be."

"How long will I be here?"

"That is up to Lord Aranville."

Arkady nodded, more accepting of her fate than he thought she would be. She held up her hands and the Warden motioned forward the feline who held the keys to her shackles. She undid the locks and released the duchess, who with very little to-do, stepped into her cell and allowed the feline to close and lock the door on her.

"Your cooperation is appreciated, my lady."

She looked around and shrugged. "Given some of the places I've been lately, Warden, this is quite luxurious. If Lord Aranville was hoping to torment me, then he sadly lacks imagination."

"I'd not be too sure of that, Arkady," her cellmate said, stepping out of the shadows.

The prisoner was dressed in the faded remnants of a once fine suit. His head was shaved—a precaution against lice the Warden insisted upon as a hygiene measure—but hadn't been scraped for a while and was covered with short grey stubble. He was, according to the Warden's records, almost sixty years old. Prison life, little sunlight and a poor diet, made him look far older.

The Warden watched with no small amount of malicious satisfaction as the colour drained from Arkady Desean's face. She stumbled backward, away from the bars of the adjoining cell, all sign of her former composure vanishing in the face of this dishevelled prisoner, whose cultured accent belied his haggard appearance.

"In fact," Prisoner Two-Eight-Two said, stepping up to the bars, looking at the former duchess with tears glistening in his world-weary eyes, "I fear you'll discover the man's a genius."

Arkady Desean turned to the Warden, stricken with horror. "How can this be?"

He frowned, not at all sure what she meant. "Lord Aranville ordered it so, my lady."

Arkady seemed speechless, shaking her head in denial.

The Warden was fascinated. "Ah, but then you know this man, don't you? I suppose you thought him dead." He turned to the other prisoner and added, "That would explain why she's not been to visit you all these years."

The duchess trembled wordlessly, her eyes fixed on the prisoner in the next cell as if he was a demon—or a ghost. The Warden wished he had more time to stay and watch, but his instructions were quite clear. He was to leave them alone as soon as she was confined.

The Warden dismissed the felines, and turned to study the prisoners one last time, wishing he was a fly on the wall in the days to come. But

Lord Aranville's orders had been very precise. Except for the felines permitted to bring them meals, Arkady Desean was to have no contact with anyone except the man in the adjoining cell.

Prisoner Two-Eight-Two. Doctor Bary Morel. Her father.

ML

FALLON   Fallon, Jennifer.

The palace of
  impossible dreams.

DATE			